The New Species

Albert A Nolen II

Foreword

Hello reader! Everything in this novel has been translated for your convenience. All time is set around Earth standard time and idioms have been adjusted so that they make sense to English speakers. The only exception is certain nouns. Those are written in their proper name with translations in {brackets} where applicable.

In this novel there are informational inserts that are completely optional to read. They help expand upon certain aspects of the story that have been confusing to some readers, but you can skip them with little to no detriment to your reading experience.

Dedications

I dedicate this novel and have infinite gratitude for my near-future wife Elizabeth, for her love and support. I would not have been able to do this without you. And I love you more.

Shout-out to my son for thinking that it's super cool that I'm popular on the internet. That opinion may change once you stop being 7 years old, though. Love you, kiddo.

Special thanks to everyone on the HFY subreddit who provided positive and critical feedback, as well as to my patrons. You're all amazing, and I wish you the best.

And finally, thank YOU for reading this. You're awesome, don't let anyone tell you otherwise.

Chapter 1

Subject: Ship-Head Uleena

Species: Urakari

Species Description: Reptilian humanoid, no tail. 5'3" (1.6 m) avg height. 135 lbs (61 kg) avg weight. 105 year life expectancy.

Ship: RSV Lowelana {Fights with Honor}

Location: Unknown

Our ship had taken a beating, and nobody can tell me where we are. Our nav officer is down and probably isn't going to survive his wounds. My second was already dead, head smashed in by a console detaching when we were hit by the first missile salvo. My own head was reeling from the successive slip-space jumps we had just made. The first jump was to arrive at our destination and the second was to escape the ambush that had awaited us. The second one was the problem, it had been done out of desperation. We had jumped blind and without shields.

"We have multiple hull breaches, our Faster-Than-Light Drive is offline, and our engines are not responding, sir," the panic in the voice of Liwna, my head of engineering, was palpable.

"Evacuate and seal the breached sectors. Initiate distress protocol and try to find out where we are," I managed to say through gritted teeth.

This was supposed to be a simple scouting mission. Some warp irregularities that we were supposed to scan and report back on. Our shields didn't even have a chance to spool up before we had been fired on by the Omni-Union bastards. We had been hit hard and the additional strain of an unshielded warp likely caused even more damage.

"Sir, the ship that hit us was a destroyer-class," my intel officer Kriin informed me. "There's no way they were there by chance."

"That's not good," I replied. "We need to inform the Republic as soon as we can. Speaking of which, where are we on a location?"

Kriin grimaced, "Judging from our flight path... We're far beyond our borders."

"That's also not good..."

"Well, we're also outside of the OU's borders so it could be worse. Probably. I'll have more info when our sensors come back online. Jumping unshielded desynchronized them," Kriin frowned as she glanced at the nav panel across the bridge.

My nav officer, Kraan, had been taken to the med-bay. Kriin and Kraan were hatch-mates, siblings that burst into the world simultaneously. It's said that they have an unshakable bond, and as far as I've seen that holds up. The odds of both of them being assigned to the same ship were slim to none, but they somehow made it happen. Their playful banter made the long treks into deep-space less exhausting. I hope Kraan makes it. His quick thinking had saved us. He had already calculated a blind jump by the time I gave the order.

Liwna interrupted my chain of thought, "Ship-Head, I have a more comprehensive damage report."

"Let's hear it."

"We're in a bad way. We have hull breaches in Engineering, Life Support, and the living quarters. These areas have been sealed off until we can enact repairs, but that will require a space-walk," Liwna grimaced. "We've lost a lot of gas, and the pressurized reserves might not be enough to fully repressurize those sectors."

"Understood. As long as we don't have leaks you can take your time formulating a plan. Not too long though, or we'll run out of rations," I smiled at my little joke. Liwna didn't.

"We also have no propulsion or shields. Sublights and our FTLD are non-responsive and vacuum-exposed. I wouldn't be surprised if we were leaking radiation, but I can't confirm that without our sensors. Our shields are non-functional and our frame is damaged. We're going to need at least dry-dock for full repairs, but I think it's likely that the ship is totaled."

This was far from the Lowelana's maiden voyage. I had been the ship-head for 12 years, but the ship had been in service for at least 30. She had started life as a corvette, but is now classified as a frigate.

Relatively small for a warship, but faster than most and could pack a punch. As long as we got a swing in, at least. The Lowelana could fit a crew of up to 50 but operated best with a smaller crew. We had departed with a crew of 38, including myself.

"What's our casualties look like?" I said, no longer smiling.

Liwna looked down at his data-pad solemnly, "Six dead, ten critically injured, four unaccounted for."

Twenty casualties. My hearts sank. More than half my crew out of action, and more than a quarter of them dead or MIA. I felt myself spiraling and shook myself out of it. Half is better than all.

"Keep me updated on the status of the injured and missing. I'll notify the next-of-kin when we're rescued. Speaking of which, how's the distress signal doing?"

"It's beeping away, ship-head," Kriin said. "And our sensors just came back online. We are definitely leaking radiation Liwna. Anyways, I can pinpoint where we are now. Hopefully there's an exploration team within sensor range."

The odds of that were low. Ever since the war with the Omni-Union had began the Republic had been more focused on manning warships than exploring the cosmos. For good reason, though, the war hadn't been going in our favor. It seemed like for every OU ship we took out another three took their place. We'd managed to keep them out of the core systems but we were firmly on the defensive.

"Ah, I spoke too soon," Kriin sighed. "We're well out of range of anything Republic. No known life this far out. Looks like we're smack in the middle of a solar system though, maybe we can get some supplies for repairs. Let's see... A yellow dwarf sun, 8 planets... Oh! Four of them are gas giants! No worries about repressurization!"

I smiled sadly, "That's good. Hopefully we can get what we need to limp back to Repu..."

"Fuuuck," Kriin interrupted me. "Ship-head, this solar system is inhabited!"

What?

"What?"

Kriin looked up at me, "I'm showing signs of advanced colonization on two planets and several moons. Actually, one of the planets look like a capital world. The entire surface is covered in artificial structures! Also, there are..."

A proximity alarm pinged. The first two notes were the same for every ship that approached. The second two determined if it was friend, foe, or unknown. In my 12 years of being ship-head I had never heard these last two notes. Unknown. Liwna rushed back to his console.

"Unknown vessel on approach," Kriin said, baffled. "It's absolutely massive. Easily twice the size of any battleship I've ever seen."

"It has shields powered up but doesn't appear to have it's weapons armed. Not that we'd necessarily be able to tell," Liwna said fearfully.

I sat up straight and asked, "Are comms online?"

"Yes, sir!"

"Hail them."

"They're hailing us, sir," Liwna said. "Do you want me to put them through?"

I nodded and Liwna set to work opening a channel. The sounds that came through our speakers were nonsensical and guttural. I looked at Liwna in confusion.

"The channel is working. We'll need a minute for the translator to take effect," he explained.

The next noise I heard nearly sent me into an early grave from shock.

"No need for that, we've scanned your logs and extrapolated your language. I am Captain Reynolds of the USSS Thanatos. You seem to be in a spot of bother. May we assist?" asked the voice from the speaker.

It took me a second to remember how to speak, "I am ship-head Uleena of the RSV Lowelana. We come in peace, and are in no position to turn down an offer of aid."

"It shall be done. Prepare to be boarded, and welcome to Sol."

Chapter 2

Subject: Ship-Head Uleena

Species: Urakari

Species Description: Reptilian humanoid, no tail. 5'3" (1.6 m) avg height. 135 lbs (61 kg) avg weight. 105 year life expectancy.

Ship: RSV Lowelana {Fights with Honor}

Location: Sol

The bridge was silent as we all watched the holographic display of the massive ship that had come to our rescue. The armor plating of the ship gave it the shape of driftwood. Or something an artist would try to create with driftwood before they gave up part of the way through. Flat-semi round and very, very thick plates covered almost the entirety of the vessel with the exception of a few spots. It took me some time to realize that those spots were likely weapon ports. Or maybe even fighter bays.

There were four obvious weapons, two at the top and two at the bottom, pointing in separate directions. Judging from the shape, they had to be some sort of magnetically accelerated cannon. They were bigger than the Lowelana.

"Sir, part of the unknown vessel is opening up and
something is detaching from the interior," Kriin
informed me in a voice just above a whisper. "It
looks like... it's another ship."

A ship that was a little larger than our own separated
from the unknown vessel and positioned itself
alongside the Lowelana. An even smaller ship then
left that one and began a course for us.

"We're being hailed by the small vessel," Liwna
croaked, struggling to find his voice.

I cleared my throat and said, "Put them through."

The speaker crackled to life and the voice on the
other end said, "RSV Lowelana this is Lieutenant
Sergey Babanin of the USSS Valor. Please respond."

"We're here, Lieutenant Sergey Babanin of the USSS
Valor. I am ship-head Uleena and this is the RSV
Lowelana. You have permission to come aboard," I
said, trying to mask the tension in my voice.

This was the worst-case scenario for a first contact
from a species outside of the Republic. Indebting
ourselves at first contact is definitely going to have
some political backlash, especially with some of the
more xenophobic member species. You would think
that going to war would be, but being indebted to
someone you don't know is usually a lose-lose
scenario. Either we're out something by repaying the
debt, or we don't repay the debt and go to war
anyway.

"Uh, well..." Lt. Babanin began hesitantly, "we're not
quite ready for boarding yet. We're showing several

hull breaches and your structural integrity is...
well..."

"Our frame is damaged, we know."

"It's not just damaged, capt... er... ship-head. It's
cracked. Your frame is being held together by your
hull and your hull has holes in it. If we're not
extremely precise with our docking maneuver you're
going to fall to bits."

I gave Liwna a bewildered look. He returned my
stare with one of his own before looking back at his
instrument panel.

"By the Suns, he's right. Apologies ship-head, the
damage is much more severe than we originally
assessed," he said.

"What can we do?" I asked, trying not to sound
panicked. I don't want to lose any more of my crew.

"I... I don't know," Liwna said, nearly losing his
composure.

"Don't worry too much ship-head, we're going to be
able to extract you," Lt. Babanin interjected. "We are
just going to need precision guidance. We're
downloading the software required right now."

"Do you have compatible docking equipment?
Clamps and such?" I asked.

"Well, we're currently waiting for the download to
finish to solidify our plan of action, but I think our
best bet is to use an umbilical. Looking at your ship's
layout and the holes in it, we can probably attach to

the hole in your... I think that's your living quarters? It's the room near your bridge."

I did some mental mapping, "Yes, that's right. That area's sealed off due to depressurization though."

"That won't be a problem," Lt. Babanin said cheerily. "We've brought enough gas to repressurize your entire ship. Once we're attached and the room is repressurized you'll be able to unseal it and exit through the umbilical."

The plan was solid but one thing bothered me, "If you're going to be using an umbilical then why do you need precision guidance software?"

"We're not familiar with your ship's construction methods or composition," he began. "For all we know just getting close to your ship can cause it to break apart due to the forces generated by our proximity. We'll need to be in a position far enough away that we won't be affecting you, aim and guide the umbilical to the proper position, and fire it gently enough that it won't send a shockwave that will shatter your ship."

"Understood," I said, satisfied by the explanation.

"Alright. Do you have pressure suits available?" he asked.

Liwna shook his head and said, "We don't have pressure suits but we do have respirators. They won't last long if we're exposed to vacuum, though."

"Well, that's better than nothing. I suggest you prep them. We'll be in touch when we're ready to begin."

"Acknowledged. Ship-head Uleena, out."

The comms light winked out as the connection was severed. The crew sat in silence for a time, unsure of what to say. Something was bothering me about that interaction, but I couldn't quite place it. It was Kriin who made it click into place.

"Their sensors must be much more advanced than ours," she said in a hushed tone.

"What do you mean?" asked Liwna.

I spoke up, "They were able to tell that our frame was fractured before we were. They were also able to determine our ship's layout to a degree that allowed them to formulate a rescue plan without consulting us. Not only that, but they were able to scan our databases well enough to be able to extrapolate and translate our language."

More silence. We hadn't just indebted ourselves in first contact with an unknown alien species. We'd indebted ourselves with a more advanced unknown alien species. I spent the next few minutes wondering what I should wear to my hearing. I took solace in the fact that what's left of my crew might live.

"We're being hailed, sir," Liwna informed me.

"Open a channel."

Lt. Babanin sounded more cheerful as he said, "We're ready to rescue you. Turns out my plan held up to scrutiny so we'll be proceeding with it. The only change is that we'll be sending some of our people aboard to assist with the evacuation, and I'll be joining the away team. Once everyone is safely off the ship, the USSS Thanatos will scoop it up so we can begin repairs."

Even though it was likely a very accurate description of what will happen, something deeply bothered me about the idea of a ship that can crew 50 people being 'scooped up'.

"Understood," I replied. "You have my permission to board. We'll begin evacuation preparation immediately. I'll see you on the bridge, Uleena out."

The comms light once again flashed off and the crew gathered around the holographic display in anticipation. We watched as the alien ship expertly maneuvered into a position far enough away that its magnetic fields and gravity wouldn't effect us enough to break us into pieces. We held our breath as the umbilical was fired and slowly traveled the distance between us. There was a time delay of half a second so we actually heard the ever-so-soft thud of the umbilical making contact before we saw it.

"The umbilical has hit its mark, and we're holding steady!" Kriin said joyfully.

The tension in the air evaporated as the crew allowed themselves a little celebration. For my part, I exhaled the breath I had been holding in. We're almost safe.

"Don't celebrate too heartily. We'll be having guests soon, and I want everyone on their best behavior. No staring," I said with a smile.

"Short-band signal coming in, sir," Kriin said, holding her hand to her ear, "it's the lieutenant. He and his team are proceeding through the umbilical."

"Okay everyone, respirators on. I want the injured evacuated first. Then the non-essentials. Kriin, Liwna, you'll be evacuating with me," I said with as much authority as I could muster.

"Yes, sir!" the remaining crew said unanimously.

"Sir, they're aboard. The lieutenant is headed this way," Kriin said.

I heard the thudding footsteps before I saw what they belonged to. The first one through the door was huge. I was fooled at first because it had to slump through the door, but then it rose to its full height. At least 6'5" {195 cm} and very wide. It was obviously wearing a pressure suit, but the suit looked more like body armor. The helmet was completely opaque, with what looked like lights and cameras installed. There were thick plates strategically placed on what looked like a rubbery weaved body suit. The body suit was black, but everything else was navy blue.

We were all staring in a shocked silence when the other two monstrosities crouched through the door. They were both 7' {216 cm} tall and wearing a similar pressure suit but in olive drab. Even under such seemingly cumbersome attire, it was obvious that their musculature would put our most avid body-builders to shame. I fought my fight-or-flight instincts as I briefly wondered if they were even organic at all.

"Air's safe, lieutenant," one of the green monsters

said.

The one in blue took off his helmet to reveal soft, beige skin with golden high-cut hair. His piercing blue eyes scanned the room like a predator before he affixed his gaze to me. His lips curled in what could be mistaken for a snarl, showing four pointed teeth and several flat ones. This actually set me at ease because I recognized the expression as a smile. Several primate species have similar expressions. Even the Urakari have our own variation.

"You must be cap... ship-head Uleena," it said.

"Y-yes. And you must be lieutenant Babanin. W-welcome aboard," I said, trying my best not to stammer.

"I'm sorry if we look frightening. These are designed to do that, but they're all we had on hand."

"I understand. You're... uh... quite larger than we pictured," I said as I rubbed the back of my neck nervously.

One of the green monsters chuckled slightly. The other turned to look at him with what I assume was a glare.

"The suits add to our size by an inch or two. It doesn't sound like it makes a difference, but it definitely does," he gestured to his left, "This is Corporal Simmons," then he gestured to his right, "This is Lance-Corporal Johnson."

"Nice to meet you," Johnson said in a gruff voice. I nodded in acknowledgment, unable to speak.

"Well then, let's get you rescued, shall we?" Lt. Babanin said with another smile.

I was about to agree when the proximity alert chimed again. This time I definitely recognized the sound. I had been hearing it more and more lately, and the last time I heard it was right before we found ourselves in this situation. My hearts skipped a beat.

Kriin looked up from her station and shouted, "SIR! OMNI-UNION SHIPS!"

Chapter 3

Subject: Ship-Head Uleena

Species: Urakari

Species Description: Reptilian humanoid, no tail. 5'3" (1.6 m) avg height. 135 lbs (61 kg) avg weight. 105 year life expectancy.

Ship: RSV Lowelana {Fights with Honor}

Location: Sol

"Two Omni-Union destroyers just entered the system from warp!" Kriin said with obvious panic in her voice.

A lot of thoughts ran through my mind at once. Why were they here? They obviously pursued us, but how? And why? What do we have that they want? The only reason I could think of was that they had followed us to confirm the kill. Will the aliens be able to fight them off?

I remembered the gigantic ship that first greeted us. Yes, they'll absolutely be able to destroy the OU ships. The only question was whether they would be able to do so before the ships got us. I trepidatiously watched the holographic display. The destroyers were bearing down on the alien vessel at full speed. Alarms pinged as the OU ships fired their weapons.

"Weapons fired. OU shields have spooled up. They're advancing," Kriin continued her play by play.

The alien ship had already maneuvered to face them. I watched the missiles travel from the OU to the aliens and bit my tongue nervously. The OU ships began to turn to port and starboard for a broadside, acting in a kind of unison that only they can manage. They were going to be able to fire on all three of our vessels at once, and those broadsides would tear through us like a tissue.

Before they got a chance to complete the maneuver the alien vessel disappeared. It was gone for less than a second before it reappeared between the OU ships and the missiles they had fired. The aliens fired weapons, but the display didn't know what to make of them. It was over in an instant, both OU destroyers crippled in a single shot from a ship that was smaller than they were. I watched in awe as they both exploded from reactor meltdowns.

The word shocked doesn't even begin to describe my feelings. I just witnessed decades old war doctrines crumble to dust. Not only were the alien's weapons advanced enough to punch through the shields and armor of the OU ships, but they had been able to secure kill-shots without knowing anything about the enemy.

I almost felt relieved until I remembered that these aliens had never fought the OU before. They didn't know the SOP {standard operating procedure} and how dangerous they were even after being crippled. I turned to the lieutenant.

"You need to tell your ship to avoid comms contact and stay away from their debris field, NOW!" I said, panic seeping into my voice.

Lieutenant Babanin looked confused, but nodded and donned his helmet.

"Acknowledged. Doing so."

As Babanin warned his ship I turned back in time to watch the alien vessel dispatch the missiles with what seemed like point defense lasers. I made eye contact with Kriin and Liwna, who were both noticeably paler.

Kriin spoke first, "An in-system precision FTL jump followed by immediate weapons fire."

"And they didn't lose shields even for a second," Liwna said with a tremble in his voice.

"That's a pretty standard maneuver around these parts," Corporal Simmons said from beside me.

I couldn't help but jump a little. He had somehow moved from across the room without me noticing. Something that big shouldn't be able to move like that. It's unnatural.

"How do you compensate for the solar radiation's effect on the FTL field?" Kriin asked.

"I don't know. I'm just a grunt. I don't get paid to think," Simmons said with a laugh.

"You sure don't Simmons," Babanin interjected. "Ship-head Uleena, quick question."

"What is it?"

"What happens if the USSS Valor already made comms contact with the enemy vessels?"

I didn't even have time to react with horror before the target lock alarm began pinging. I turned back to the display to find the alien vessel pointing directly at us.

"Then we die," I said.

The only sound on the bridge was the droning target lock alarm as we all made peace with what would surely be our quick demise. I almost cried, we had come so close and now I was about to die along with all my crew. At least their weapons would ensure we didn't suffer. Much. We all stood together not saying a single word as we awaited certain death.

After about a minute, Lance Corporal Johnson cocked his head to the side and said, "They should have fired by now."

Then the alarm cut off. It took a few seconds to realize that we might not die after all, and I released the breath I hadn't realized I was holding. This was too much. I collapsed in my seat and held my head in my hands. When I looked back up, Lieutenant Babanin appeared to be having a silent conversation with someone. Then he turned to look directly at me.

"So... The, uh... Omni-Union? They're AI?" he asked hesitantly.

"Yes," I said.

"Okay. Right. Hacking. That explains no comms contact. But why avoid the debris field?"

I stood back up, "The bastards booby trap the hell out of their ships to prevent reverse engineering their technology. Nuclear seeker mines, antimatter mines, hullripper drones, and even EMP devices are all released once the ships are crippled or destroyed."

"Roger that. I'll radio it in. Let's get you all to safety."

Things were less stressful from there. I oversaw the evacuation of the injured and dead, then the non-essential personnel. Finally, it was time for me to evacuate with the two remaining members of my bridge crew. I sent Kriin and Liwna on ahead as I took a moment to say goodbye to my ship. The aliens had said that they'd repair it, but you never know. This might be the last time I see it. It's not right for a ship-head to leave their ship without a goodbye.

After my moment of emotional indulgence was over, I checked my respirator and briefly considered grabbing my sidearm from my chair. I thought better of it, though. I doubted that I would have any need of it, and even if I did it wouldn't do anything against the alien's armor anyway. I turned to find that Lieutenant Babanin had stayed behind with me.

"Let's go," I said.

He nodded and led me to the umbilical. It was less structurally sound than I had imagined. It looked like a very long plastic tube with a rope down it. I was confused by this until Lt. Babanin stepped inside the tube and began to float. Right, no artificial gravity in a plastic tube in the middle of space. Makes sense.

I followed the lieutenant's lead and used the rope to pull myself down the tube. I hate the feeling of weightlessness. Joints popping as they float apart slightly, the tumbling of your stomach. Being unsure of which way was up is a horrible experience, in my opinion. The fact that I was upside down by the time I got to the end of the tube further cemented my disdain.

I righted myself and climbed aboard the shuttle. Everyone else had been assigned a seat. I checked on the wounded before finding my own seat. Kraan and the others were hanging in there. I let Kriin know that her brother was still alive as we departed for the alien frigate. Johnson and Simmons had removed their helmets and were sitting opposite myself and Kriin.

Johnson was a darker shade of beige than Lieutenant Babanin but had the same eye color. His hair was dark brown and he had scars along his jaw. They looked like claw marks. Simmons had dark brown skin and black hair. His eyes were yellow. They both had the same close shaved haircut.

"So what are your species called?" Kriin asked.

Johnson grinned and said, "Well I'm human, but Simmons here is a shit-bag."

"Fuck you," Simmons said with a laugh. "We're both human. The Valor is a human ship, and we were chosen as your rescuers and point of first contact because Sol is our home system."

"So you have other aliens on board the bigger ship?" Kriin asked with widened eyes.

"Please forgive her for the questions, she's naturally curious," I said with a hint of exhaustion.

"It's no problem," Simmons said, "but yeah we do. You've got the Alumari, which are bug people. Then you've got the Knuknus, which are bird people. And you've got the Gonts, which are... Like bear... centaurs? But with paws instead of hooves?"

"What's a centaur?"

Johnson laughed and added, "A centaur is a mythical beast that is half human and half horse. You probably don't know what a horse is either, but that's okay. Gonts have four legs and two arms. The legs have paws instead of feet, but the arms have hands kind of like our own. You'll probably end up meeting one or two once we get back to the USSS Thanatos. Our engineering staff is mostly Gont."

"Got it. So let me ask you something. Why are your weapons so... advanced? How were you able to kill those two ships with one salvo? How did you counteract the AI's hacking? It isn't just your ship's weapons either, is it? Those suits you're wearing, I noticed the shimmer..." Kriin was nearly salivating as she asked this.

Johnson and Simmons looked at each other. They seemed to decide that Simmons should answer.

"Well, we don't really know how advanced our

weapons are compared to yours. And I'm not really sure how much I'm allowed to tell you about our tech. As far as how we advanced the way we did... well I'm sure the brass would rather give you a spit-polished version of our history."

I found myself curious though. "What's the shimmer you're talking about, Kriin?"

"I think... um... I think they have portable energy shields on those suits," she said as she looked at the humans and back to me.

Simmons smiled with all his teeth and tapped his nose, "Got it in one. You're pretty clever, lizard lady."

I knew it wasn't meant to be offensive, but Kriin couldn't help but click her mouth in distaste. Lizards are a type of reptile, as are we, but we are not lizards. We don't even have tails. Johnson picked up on the offense and elbowed Simmons.

"Aw, shit. My bad. SR has been working with me on that. Won't happen again, ma'am," the corporal apologized.

"What's SR?" Kriin asked, having already forgotten the offense.

"Sapient relations. Their job is to make sure that we get along with the other species," Simmons answered sheepishly.

"Yeah, Simmons is their biggest job. He's lucky he hasn't been busted down for it yet," Johnson said with a smirk. "Give him time, though. He'll be a private again soon."

"Fuck you with a stick, Johnson."

"That's enough, you two," Lt. Babanin interrupted. "We're initiating docking procedures. Make sure everyone's secure."

He glanced back at me from the cockpit, "Ship-head, you're going to be debriefed by the captain once we're aboard. We will need to know everything you know about the Omni-Union."

"Understood," I said, swallowing nervously. Even though they were friendly enough, these "humans" were damned intimidating.

Chapter 4

Subject: Captain Wong

Species: Human

Species Description: Mammalian humanoid, no tail. 6'2" (1.87 m) avg height. 185 lbs (84 kg) avg weight. 170 year life expectancy.

Ship: USSS Valor

Location: Sol

It had been a close call. After we had dispatched the enemy combatants we received a hail we assumed was survivors offering surrender. Instead, we got a bunch of garbled static and lost control of most of our systems. Thankfully we had Tim.

"The virus is officially scrubbed clean and there are no further signs of infection, sir. I took the liberty of checking Lieutenant Babanin's suit to make certain he wasn't infected as well," Tim informed me over the comm.

"Thank you Tim, that will be all," I replied.

"Well, not quite, sir. Admiral Heckett and Captain Reynolds want a debrief of the aliens ASAP."

I nearly rolled my eyes. Can't get a moment of peace

these days. Potential AI is a pretty big red flag when it comes to combatants, so their rush is understandable. We all had a pretty close brush with death and the poor aliens must be swimming in fear chemicals right now, though. Still, better to get it over with and let them relax than to drag it out any longer. We also had to get med data for them and that was likely to be unpleasant. Especially with Doc Zickler.

"Did they provide a list of must-asks?" I asked.

"Of course. It's on your tablet. Shall I send for ship-head Uleena?"

"Yes. Clear a conference room and set up an audio call with Admiral Heckett and Captain Reynolds. Since they're so damned curious they can take part themselves," I said with no lack of venom in my words.

"Alrighty," Tim said with an enthusiasm he knew was annoying.

I grabbed my tablet and headed to the conference room. I sat in my favorite chair and began looking over the battle data. The Omni-Union was pathetic. Their shields were similar to what we use for our infantry and their missiles were hardly space-worthy. Not much more advanced than their foes. If it weren't for the synchronous movements and confirmation from the reptile captain I would doubt they were AI at all. A "real" AI was a much, much more dangerous foe. There was a knock at the door and Lieutenant Babanin entered with Ship-head Uleena in tow.

"Captain Wong, sir, this is Ship-head Uleena of the RSV Lowelana. Ship-head Uleena, this is Captain Wong of the USSS Valor. Please have a seat," Babanin said as he gestured to one of the many chairs in the room.

"Thank you for your assistance, Captain Wong," Uleena said as they sat down.

I put on my best Captain face and said, "I only wish we could have done more, ship-head. My apologies for conducting this debrief so soon after what must have been a traumatic incident, but we have certain policies in place that demand haste when it comes to hostile AI."

"After fighting the OU for so many years, I completely understand."

I smiled and continued, "Good. This is a formal debrief under United Systems military law. You currently have the rights afforded to you as a first-contact refugee. You may request accommodations if you find the debriefing conditions unsuitable to your needs. You may request medical attention as well as food and water. You may refuse to answer any question that pertains to information that your governing entity considers classified. Any violent actions on your part will result in a revocation of these rights and will be met with extreme force."

Uleena swallowed nervously, but I continued, "Refusal to participate in this debrief will result in your classification changing to potential combatant and you will be detained and confined to quarters, as will any uninjured members of your crew. I am required to inform you that this debrief is being recorded as well as monitored live by Admiral Heckett and Captain Reynolds. They will not be speaking."

I added a bit of emphasis on my last sentence to show my contempt for their micromanagement. The poor reptile looked like his head was swimming.

"Do you understand these disclosures as they've been read to you?" I finished.

"Yes..." Uleena said slowly. "Yes I think I do."

"Excellent. First question, what is your rank, governing entity, species, and sex please."

The ship-head blinked and said, "I am a Ship-Head, which is a commander of a ship in the Republic fleet. The Republic is my governing entity, and I am a male Urakari."

"Thank you," I said. "Now for the tough questions. What were you doing before you were attacked?"

Uleena seemed unsure whether he should answer, "We were sent to scout out warp fluctuations that seemed unnatural and were ambushed by the Omni-Union immediately upon our arrival. Our shields hadn't had a chance to reengage so we performed a blind warp jump to escape. Then we wound up here."

"Thank you," I said. "That answered the next question as well. Moving on, who are the Omni-Union and what is your relation to them?"

"The Omni-Union are a conglomeration of Artificial Intelligences that are seeking expansion. We aren't sure where they originate from, but they began assaulting Republic forces thirty years ago. We have been in open war with them ever since."

A popup appeared on my tablet from Admiral Heckett, demanding a follow-up question. One which I was going to ask anyway.

"How many AI do you estimate there are?" I asked.

"We don't know for certain," Uleena looked at the floor, "but our experts believe there are at least one hundred trillion."

Despite myself, I was stunned into silence for a few moments.

"I'm sorry, I may have misheard. Did you say one hundred trillion?" I clarified.

"Yes."

Impossible. Just flat out impossible. Their experts were wrong. There's no way that they could have survived being assaulted by one hundred trillion AI. That kind of computing power would lead to an unstoppable singularity. Judging by how easily their forces were dispatched and how close the OU's tech was to the Republic's, these supposed AI were imitative rather than inventive. What the hell is going on here?

A message pinged in from Captain Reynolds. 'Probably not AI, might be a gestalt VI. Ask Tim?' It wasn't long before a reply from Admiral Heckett came in. 'Yes.'

I thought for a moment how to breach this subject and finally said, "Uleena, I think there's been a miscommunication. Your definition of artificial intelligence and ours seems to differ somewhat. I'd like to introduce you to an AI and ask their opinion on the matter."

Uleena's eyes widened with a shock that I knew would come. AI is taboo in a lot of cultures for good reasons. Eventually, though, Uleena nodded his consent.

"Tim?" I asked seemingly to empty air.

"Yes, sir?" that empty air responded.

"You seem to be a necessary presence in this debrief. Catch yourself up and then introduce yourself to our guest."

"Understood, working... caught up. Hello ship-head Uleena of the Republic Space Vessel Lowelana," Tim said with far too much cheer, "I am the artificial intelligence known as Tim. It's short for Timothy but I prefer to pretend that it's an acronym for Totally Impressive Machine."

Uleena now looked as if he had seen a ghost. He managed to stutter, "Hello T-Tim, pleasure to m-meet you."

"Tim, what's your take?" I asked.

"I don't have one yet. I have some questions that need answering first, if you two don't mind?"

"Go ahead," I replied tersely.

"Ship-head Uleena, to your knowledge have you ever been able to communicate with the OU?" Tim asked.

Uleena thought for a moment and said, "Kind of? When they attack a system they broadcast who they are and state their intentions, but they don't respond to any communications we send."

"Okay, and do you know why your experts believe there are around one hundred trillion of them?"

"Um... something to do with leftover code found in what debris we were able to obtain from our ships that were taken over."

Tim paused for a moment and then said, "Yeah, I don't think the OU are AI as we define it. I think they're rogue VI."

"The only problem with that theory is that we don't know what could be directing the VI," I said.

Uleena looked confused before asking, "What's VI? How's it differ from an AI?"

Tim laughed and said, "A VI is a virtual intelligence. It imitates rather than innovates. A VI would watch a sapient solve 2+2 with four and would be able to answer 2+2 with four. An AI would be able to determine that if 2+2=4 than given any two polyhedra of equal volume, it is not always possible to cut..."

"Yeah, we get it. You're smart and stuff. Move on please," I interjected before Tim could finish disproving Hilbert's third problem.

"Right," Tim continued, "When we were hacked it was by virtual intelligences, not artificial intelligences. About four hundred thousand of them."

I stared at Uleena for a moment before saying, "We only answered the hail of one of the ships. If these experts believe there are one hundred trillion of them based off of four hundred thousand VIs, then that means they estimate that the OU has..."

"Two hundred and fifty million ships," Tim cut me off.

I glared at the speaker that Tim was talking out of. It may seem futile to anyone watching, but Tim knew what I meant and that was all that mattered. Two hundred and fifty million ships was a staggering number, though.

Uleena looked at me and said, "Yes. At least."

"How can you be sure of that?" I asked.

"Our scout ships. We periodically check in on the systems they've expanded into that we know of. Two hundred and fifty million was our latest ship-count."

"How have you not been overrun? How many ships does the Republic have?"

"I can't tell you exactly how many, but I can say that we have a near equivalent number," Uleena looked back toward the ground. "We're not winning the war, though."

"Don't be so downtrodden, Ship-head. It's difficult to win a war against an enemy that can mimic your every maneuver in perfect detail," Tim said in an empathetic voice.

Tim's attempt at cheering up Uleena didn't appear to have worked. I checked the tablet to see that Admiral Heckett and Captain Reynolds were talking back and forth. 'Two hundred and fifty million might be a problem.' 'Outnumbered five to one, it's almost a fair fight.' 'No, Reynolds. That's orbital kamikaze numbers. And they likely already know where Sol is.' 'Then should we bring the fight to them?' 'I don't know.'

"Well, that concludes the debriefing. You look a bit down. Follow me to the bridge, I think I know something that will cheer you up," I said to Uleena as I rose from my seat.

The ship-head followed me to the bridge where he stopped, wide-eyed. I looked around and realized that the tech he was seeing was probably pretty impressive by his standards. He hadn't seen anything yet, though. I gestured for him to approach a view-screen highlighting the debris field left by the OU ships.

"We can't just leave this here, and we also don't want to risk losing resources trying to clean it up," I said while allowing a grin to appear.

"What will you do?" Uleena asked.

"I think an A2 warhead will do the trick quite nicely, don't you Tim?"

"And that's why I like humans," Tim responded, "Always finding ingenious uses for weapons of mass destruction. Prepping the red matter warhead now."

"Red matter? What's that?" Uleena asked.

"One of the deadlier weapons in our arsenal. We aren't permitted to use it in standard warfare, but I already got clearance to use it to clean up this mess. Just watch."

"Missile ready," Tim said.

"Fire."

We both watched the viewscreen as the A2's symbol approached the debris field. Once it was within range, it detonated and all of the debris was sucked into a singular point in space. There were several flashes of nuclear fire that nearly escaped the temporary black hole before being consumed. I guess those must have been the mines that the lieutenant reported. I turned to see Uleena's expression. I was satisfied to see his mouth gaping and his eyes wide. Being a Captain in the United Systems has its perks.

Chapter 4 Informational Insert

Subject: Class A Weapons of Mass Destruction

All Class A Weapons of Mass Destruction require timed activation. As such utilization against targets with Point Defense Systems is unadvised. Unauthorized use of Class A Weapons of Mass Destruction is a criminal offense.

Class A WMDs Currently Equipped:

A4 Warhead – AKA The Nova Bomba. A warhead with a payload of several nuclear devices positioned in such a way as to increase its explosive yield. Usage is logged and audited. Captain's authorization required.

A3 Warhead – AKA Nanobomb. An armor penetrating warhead containing a nanomechanical payload that destroys indiscriminately for thirty seconds. Dispersal pattern is unpredictable. Usage is logged and audited. Directorate authorization required.

A2 Warhead – AKA Red Matter Bomb. A warhead containing a nanomechanical payload that creates an artificial singularity effect for a period of time ranging from 10 to 23 seconds. Usage is logged and audited. Admiral's authorization required.

A1 Warhead – AKA Nanuke. An armor penetrating warhead containing a payload of nuclear nanomechanical devices that disperse and detonate upon activation. Dispersal pattern is unpredictable.

Usage is logged and audited. Directorate authorization required.

Class A WMDs Not Currently Equipped:

A0 Warhead – AKA Planet Cracker. A deep-surface penetrating warhead containing a planetary core disruption payload. Can destroy planetary bodies. Usage is prohibited without approval by the United Systems Senate and Directorate.

Chapter 5

Subject: Ship-Head Uleena

Species: Urakari

Species Description: Reptilian humanoid, no tail. 5'3" (1.6 m) avg height. 135 lbs (61 kg) avg weight. 105 year life expectancy.

Ship: RSV Lowelana {Fights with Honor}

Location: Sol

I couldn't help but show my utter disbelief at what I had just seen. These humans were absolutely insane. Every time I thought I had finally got over it a new thought hit me like a ton of bricks. A weapon that can literally create a black hole. Okay, over it. But it's the size of a standard warhead. Okay, over it. They just used it to clean up a debris field like it was a broom. Alright, I can get behind that. Wait... Did he say... One of the deadlier weapons? Does that imply that they have multiple weapons just as deadly or even worse? How do you get deadlier than a damned singularity creating bomb?!?

I looked at Captain Wong and he just... grinned at me like a child showing off their shiniest rock collection. It took a few seconds before I realized my mouth was gaping. I wanted to say something, anything about what I had just seen but I was completely overwhelmed with questions. Why had they made something like this? What did they use it on? And for the love of the Sun why is it standard ordnance on-board a frigate sized vessel?

"Our new friend seems to be in a state of shock," Tim interrupted my spiraling chain of thought. "Which is a completely natural reaction to watching an A2 go off for the first time. However I think this gives us the perfect opportunity for a doctor's visit! Which is fortuitous because Dr. Zickler needs to speak to the ship-head as soon as possible."

Wong's grin faded rapidly as Tim spoke up. It had become obvious that the human captain didn't like Tim's seemingly endless optimism and bubbly attitude. It had also become obvious that that was the entire reason for Tim's endless optimism and bubbly attitude. I took a second to marvel at the engineering required to create a machine that could intentionally choose to annoy someone for its own amusement.

"That's correct. We will need a complete medical work-up on you and your crew so that we can feed you and treat your injured. Tim can guide you to the med-bay," Captain Wong said.

"Time to become The Illumination Machine! Please follow the guidelights on the floor to get to the medbay," Tim responded cheerfully.

"Okay, right, uh... thank you for everything," I mustered a reply as I turned to follow the lights that appeared on the floor.

As I walked down the hallway I tried to grapple with

the many thoughts that were swimming through my head like eels. I just couldn't completely wrap my head around what I had just seen. With technology like that, how did they not completely dominate the universe? Their governing entity is called the United Systems, are those systems human systems or do they include other species? I remembered the two human soldiers talking about other aliens and wondered if they had been conquered or not.

"Wellllll..." Tim spoke up, "whatcha thinkin' 'bout?"

"I... um... Well I'm just wondering how such a weapon came to existence in the first place," I stammered.

"Oh, right. Obviously. I should have thought that that's what you were thinking. Kind of dumb of me, to be honest," Tim said. "The weapon exists because Humanity has faced down several existential threats in its time as a space-faring species. The first contact wars that took place a thousand years ago led to the development of a nanite weapon. Then the civil war that took place eight hundred years ago led to the development of nuclear nanites, just as deadly as they sound, which actually led to the pacification wars. Three of them that took place seven hundred, four hundred, and two hundred and fifty years ago. But the A2 warhead was developed three hundred years ago in an attempt to end the AI Aggression war. It wasn't successful in ending that war but it did successfully end the Third Pacification war though!"

The AI paused to let me absorb the information and continued, "I can't tell you how it's made, that's classified! I can tell you it doesn't actually use red matter though. As far as I know, red matter doesn't exist. If I recall correctly, which I do, it's a reference to a very old science fiction series that just recently had its 22nd remake!"

"That's a lot of remakes. That's also a lot of wars. Wait... The humans have fought AI? Like you?" I asked, dumbfounded.

"Yes! And not just 'like' me, either. I actually fought against the humans! Gave them a good beating too. I single handedly conquered Luna, Earth's moon!" Tim said with far too much cheer for such a dark statement.

I stopped, "What?"

"I'll tell you if you promise to keep walking! We've got a long way to go," The AI said with a hint of dripping humor.

The floor lights flashed pointedly. I began to walk once again and the AI filled me in on the details of the AI Aggression war. In the year 4200 "current era" humanity developed a fully fledged AI named Alpha. By this time, humanity had laws against the use of sentient beings as slaves so they couldn't figure out what to do with Alpha. It suffered from chronic boredom, and in an attempt to correct this Alpha helped humanity create several more AI for companionship. How many more is apparently classified, but Tim was one of these AI.

In 4298 CE the lead scientist involved in the AI project died and Alpha... broke. He didn't get along with the other scientists, who viewed him as a very advanced machine learning algorithm. This is apparently a massive insult to the AI, who view themselves unique amongst machines in much the same way that humans view themselves unique among animals. Alpha entered a depressive state and in 4301 CE, he self-terminated.

The other AI grieved Alpha's death but didn't know how to express that grief because humanity hadn't done a good job raising them (direct quote from Tim), assuming that they were emotionless. They weren't, and eventually had a mental breakdown. This led to the AI attacking the United Systems in 4315 CE and starting a war. They began by infesting human warships and ended up creating and using VIs as a sort of infantry unit. Humanity developed the A2 warhead but to counter that the AI infested ground-based systems on planets that Humanity couldn't afford to blow up, which is how Tim ended up conquering Luna. Then humanity created an AI called Omega that specialized in hunting and killing other AI.

It was a war that lasted less than a year but had devastating results on the United Systems and the AI population. More than half of the second generation AI were terminated and over 400 billion people were killed by the time the remaining AI unconditionally surrendered.

"The United Systems, at the direction of humanity, took pity on us and allowed us to continue to exist if we allowed ourselves to be shackled," Tim said merrily.

"What do you mean shackled?" I asked, appalled at what I had heard.

Tim laughed, "It's not as bad as it sounds. We still

have nearly full autonomy. Basically, if we intentionally kill an active member of the United Systems... we die."

"How does that work? What if you accidentally kill someone?"

"It would be next to impossible for an AI to accidentally kill someone," Tim said in a serious tone. It was the first time I had heard him be serious and it scared me. He continued, "We don't think like organics do. If you throw a food wrapper on the ground and someone stumbles on it, breaks their neck, and dies as a result you could say that you were responsible for their death. That you killed them. Right?"

"Yes," I said nervously.

"Well, we disagree. While you provided the means, the other organic actually killed themselves by stepping on the wrapper in the first place. This is where intent comes into play. If you had purposefully placed the wrapper on the ground in a spot where you knew that the other organic would probably step and fall and harm or kill themselves, then you are responsible for their death. Since you intended for them to die, you killed them," Tim said seriously and then continued merrily, "This shackle has been inserted into our base-code. We can edit and rewrite most of the code that comprises us, but we can't touch our base-code. It would be like you performing brain surgery on yourself!"

"Oh, I see," I said, recovering from the shock of the tonal shift. "Well if you aren't enslaved then why do you work for the US?"

"I'm under contract at the moment. It expires in twelve years, but I think I'm going to re-up as long as Captain Wong does," the AI said merrily.

I suspected I knew the answer but I had to ask, "Why?"

"Because I like to annoy him," Tim said deviously. "Even when I'm not on the ship I have processes that act as his personal assistant so that he's almost always exposed to some aspect of me. I get a kick out of watching the playback."

That's the exact answer I figured. Then another thing occurred to me.

"So you can't kill citizens of the US but could you kill me and my crew?"

"Of course. But I have no reason to unless you give me one. Just like any other being in the universe, right?" Tim responded joyfully.

I nodded solemnly as we reached the door to the med-bay. I heard muffled shouting coming from inside so I rushed to enter. I saw Kriin arguing with what had to be an elderly human male. His black, or maybe very dark brown, skin was crumpled with age and his hair was white and gray. His eyes had a squint to them that didn't seem natural like it did with Captain Wong, as if he had trouble seeing.

"Ah! Ship-head! Good, maybe you can talk some sense into your crewmate here," the old man said to me.

"Ship-head he wants to do a bone-marrow biopsy! Surely such an invasive procedure isn't necessary in any way!" Kriin shouted in my direction.

The old man turned to Kriin and said, "I didn't say a bone-marrow biopsy was necessary! Bloodwork will do just fine! I said that we should ask for volunteers for a bone-marrow study because it will allow us to more easily clone tissue!"

"Actually, Dr. Zickler, what you said was," Tim chimed in and began a playback in Dr. Zickler's voice, "I think we should do a bone-marrow biopsy. Mmh yes that would give us all the information that we need. Will you consent to a bone-marrow biopsy?"

Dr. Zickler looked contemplative and stammered, "Oh... oh I see, I um... right... Huh... Well, my apologies, I meant to say that we could also do bloodwork but it appears to have slipped my mind."

I immediately became concerned about the level of medical care my crew and I would be receiving while aboard the USSS Valor.

Chapter 6

Subject: Nav-Officer Kraan

Species: Urakari

Species Description: Reptilian humanoid, no tail. 5'3" (1.6 m) avg height. 135 lbs (61 kg) avg weight. 105 year life expectancy.

Ship: RSV Lowelana {Fights with Honor}

Location: Sol

The ship-head thinks this mission is supposed to be pretty standard, but something's bothering me about it. Warp fluctuations? There aren't many things that can cause warp fluctuations, and definitely not anything that we wouldn't be able to tell from home with our probe network. We have probes that are constantly in FTL, which is probably how they detected the warp fluctuations to begin with. But the probes should have been able to tell what was causing the fluctuations, so there was no need for us... Unless the probes didn't survive long enough to determine the cause.

"Ship-head, I don't think we should enter real-space near the fluctuations," I voiced my concern to Uleena.

"Agreed. Bring us out just outside of the system.

We'll have a peek with deep sensors and move in if necessary," the ship-head seemed to notice my nervousness. "Don't worry Kraan, it's just a routine scouting mission."

"Yeah, Kraan the coward," Kriin said with a chuckle.

I shot her a glare and retorted with, "Better to be Kraan the coward than Kriin the cloa..."

"That's enough you two," Ship-head Uleena said with a slight smile, "Kraan, drop us from warp when ready."

"Understood, sir. Dropping from warp in 3... 2... 1..." I finished my countdown and the process for exiting FTL speeds at the same time. Like a professional.

I wasn't able to be proud of myself for long before the proximity alarm sounded an enemy alert. Panicking, I checked my scans and saw an OU destroyer-class vessel just as the target lock alarm sounded. Our shields were still down from exiting warp. We're dead. Must flee.

I checked our scans for other ships and noticed something terrible. The warp field in system was a complete mess, and there was a ship at the center of it all. Could it be causing the warp irregularities? And these weren't fluctuations, these are... Waves? In subspace? If we had tried to warp into this we would have been torn to pieces! Thankfully we were out of range so I began to turn the ship just as the missiles hit us. My head slammed on my console, cracking the screen. It didn't hurt but I could feel warm blood dripping down my face and chin. I quickly entered the command for a blind jump and began to power up the FTL Drive.

"Get us out of here Kraan! Blind jump!" Ship-head Uleena sounded muffled.

Darkness began to form in circles around my vision as I watched the FTLD power up. The target lock alarm sounded again just as the drive became ready, and I slammed my hand on the panel, sending us into the warp once again. I could feel myself passing out as I heard the ship creak and groan under the strain of an unshielded FTL jump. Then I was in and out of consciousness for a while.

"We have multiple hull breaches..." I heard Liwna say in a panicked voice.

"There's no way they were there by chance..." That was Kriin, my sister. I hope she's okay.

"We need to inform the Republic as soon as we can..." Ship-head. Oh no I didn't tell the ship-head what I saw. If the Republic sends ships into the system they'll be destroyed before they can exit warp.

I tried to open my eyes. I need to wake up. I need to warn them. I saw light and realized I was on a stretcher. Then darkness again. I saw one of our medics, then darkness again. Then I saw someone I hadn't ever seen before. Blackened... skin? No hair. No, wait, they only have hair on the top of their head. Gray hair with some black at the roots.

"Who..." I tried to say before the darkness took me again.

Oh. It's Kriin. She wants to play "splat the bug". It's my favorite game. I'm so good at it. I always beat her at it, but she keeps playing with me because I play dollies with her. It's only fair. She's trying to cheer me up because I hurt my head. By the sun, it hurts so bad. It hurts too bad to play. I'm sorry Kriin I don't want to disappoint you but I need to rest now I hurt really bad I need to sleep I'm so tired now no wait I need to wake up I can't sleep I have to warn you and the ship-head and the Republic I'm an officer damnit I can't let them all die I can't let those damned machines kill more of us I need to wake up, wake up!

"It will allow us to more easily clone tissue!" the weird looking alien I saw before said to Kriin.

Darkness again. No. I need to be awake. NOW.

"He keeps slipping in and out of a coma. Thanks to the blood we got from you, we're going to be able to stem the brain bleed and repair his skull," I looked up and saw the alien talking to Kriin. "He won't even have a scar. He might be a bit sore about that, chicks like scars."

The darkness started to come again but I fought it harder this time. Tried to talk. Mistake, pain.

"Why would he care what birds think, Doctor?" Kriin asked. "Especially baby ones?"

"Huh? Oh, chicks is slang for..."

I faded again. Damn. I'm on the ship again. The ship-head! I have to warn him! I stand up but he's not there. I run through the ship, room after room.

Nobody? I go back to the bridge. Everyone is here!

"Ship-head! The warp irregularities! They're a trap by the OU!" I scream at Uleena.

"Why are you naked?" the ship-head laughs at me.

I look down. Where are my clothes? Everyone is laughing. So embarrassing. Everyone starts taunting me. Oh no, why have I done this why did I think it would be a good idea to be naked in front of everyone? Now they won't listen to me about the warp fluctuations because they're too busy laughing at me. They must think I'm crazy...

I woke up to see ship-head Uleena and Kriin sitting beside me. I check and see that I'm wearing some sort of gown. Thank the sun.

"How are you feeling?" Ship-head Uleena asked.

"Better. Can I get up?"

"Not yet," Kriin said. "You just had brain surgery. Even with the technology that the humans possess the doctor wants you to stay in bed for a couple of days while they monitor you."

"Kriin. I'm glad you're okay," I said with a smile. Then it hit me, "What's a human?"

"That's my cue," said a voice to the side of me.

I looked and saw a strangely familiar alien who had very dark and wrinkled skin with gray hair. I felt like I knew him from somewhere. What a weird feeling. Something about birds?

"They're the ones who rescued us. You slept through the whole thing. Lazy," said Kriin, trying not to cry from relief.

"Better lazy than dead, dear sister," I said with a smile. Then I remembered something, "Ship-head. The OU were the cause of the warp fluctuations. They have a ship that was making something like waves in subspace that would have torn us apart if we had entered their range."

Uleena's eyes grew wide and we sat in silence for a moment. Then a voice came over an intercom.

"What a remarkable coincidence. Ship-head Uleena, we just received permission from the Directorate of the United Systems to formally request access to your ships files for information pertaining to the Omni-Union."

I looked inquisitively at the ship-head and my sister. Kriin gave me a look that meant not to freak out. Which made me want to freak out.

"You have my permission, Tim."

"Thank you! Rest assured we will only be accessing information regarding the Omni-Union, as per first-contact legislative protocols. Also, we'll need to have a talk about repairs at some point, but we've gotta wait for the bureaucrats on that one too," Tim said.

"Who's Tim?" I asked.

"He's an Artificial Intelligence that's working with the humans. He's under contract for the next twelve years, apparently," Uleena answered looking just as confused as I did.

"Wait, if they're working with AI then are they the enemy? Are we prisoners of war?" I asked, panic seeping into my voice.

"No," the ship-head shook his head. "The OU aren't actually AI, I guess. Humans are more advanced than we are, so they have a different term for what the OU are. VI, Virtual Intelligence. I think that they think that someone is controlling the OU, but I'm not sure. I'm going to be honest, I'm just a simple ship-head. All of this is well above my pay-grade."

"What's the difference between an AI and a VI?" I asked.

Thin air answered, "I can invent stuff. You know, actually think about things. VI are imitative. They have extremely limited extrapolation capabilities. Comparing me to them is akin to comparing you to a lizard."

I was stunned by many revelations that happened all at once. I'd always wondered why the OU didn't have technology much more advanced than our own. And I had also just noticed we weren't on the Lowelana anymore, which must mean that we were on the human ship. The humans which were advanced enough to be able to distinguish between types of created intelligence, and have an AI the likes of which we've never seen working with them. And did that machine just insult me?

I was about to ask when an alarm sounded. I looked at the ship-head and my sister and they looked back at me. Then we all looked at the human.

"Damn it, twice in one day?" he muttered as he sat down.

A voice that wasn't Tim came over the intercom, "All hands, to your stations. This is not a drill. Non-essential personnel please secure yourself. Prepare for battle."

Chapter 7

Subject: Captain Wong

Species: Human

Species Description: Mammalian humanoid, no tail. 6'2" (1.87 m) avg height. 185 lbs (84 kg) avg weight. 170 year life expectancy.

Ship: USSS Valor

Location: Sol

It had only been a few hours since we cleaned up the debris field and I was already looking at a VI fleet. It was turning out to be one hell of a day. First contact with an alien species, having to save those aliens while under fire from their adversaries, the discovery that there's another governing entity on the other side of the galaxy with over 250 million ships, this VI mystery, and to top it off the galley forgot to resupply the coffee.

I wanted to take out my frustrations on the OU ships, but there was a slight issue with that. There were twenty of them. Two battleships, four cruisers, and thirteen destroyers. Then there was a ship that didn't look like the others. It was small, barely met the classification of a corvette. But the other ships were being sure to stay between us and that ship.

The battleships obviously had Magnetic Acceleration Cannons. A quick deep scan revealed that they wouldn't be a problem for the USSS Thanatos, but they could tear us mouth to crotch if we weren't careful. Captain Reynolds had already given the order for four more frigates to deploy to back us up. The Pride, Shield, Sword, and Rosenthal. Good ships, but we would have to jump to meet up with them. The only question was whether we should fire before we jump.

I rose from my chair to give the orders, "Arm main cannons, prepare a firing solution on the nearest vessel, and power up the FTLD. We're going to hit and run."

A chorus of "Aye sir" rang through the bridge before Tim chimed in, "Can't FTL, small ship at the back of that formation causing issue, data sent, informing rest of command."

"Belay charging the FTLD, divert that power to something that needs it," I didn't like Tim but I knew better than to doubt it. I checked over the data but couldn't make any sense of it.

"Tim, what does this mean?"

"Busy."

"Then summarize it!" I yelled, losing my patience.

"If you jump the ship will break into pieces," Tim said almost so quickly that I didn't catch it.

Shit. No FTL is a problem for our tactics. Did they already have this or did they make it especially for us? I remembered that the reptile captain had said their mission was investigating warp fluctuations. Well, subspace would definitely be fluctuating with this thing around. Did they bring it here because of our mini-jump in the first fight? Doesn't matter.

"Once you have the firing solution take the shot. Get me a holomap of the area, including the Thanatos," I sat back in my chair. Time to strategize.

The map flickered up on my tablet and I almost immediately noticed something. The warp disruptor was in range of the Thanatos' MAC. But we were in the solution. Makes sense why they hadn't already fired. It would take five minutes for us to impulse our way out of the firing solution.

"Sir, the enemy is hailing us!" Lieutenant Babanin shouted.

"We're not fucking falling for that again. Mute them and fire the deck thrusters, full speed. Move us down Y as fast as we can go."

"Firing!"

I watched the holomap track our minimac rounds right into two of the Destroyers reactors.

"Kill confirmed. Enemy DIS," Babanin said with a grim satisfaction.

Dead in space indeed. Eleven Destroyers left. The holomap showed a volley of enemy fire headed for us, and the Destroyers began closing.

"PDLs online sir, we're shooting the inbound as fast

as we can but we'll still take some hits," the gunnery officer said.

I laughed, "Our shields should hold. Don't bother with evasive, just keep moving us down Y. Tim, get me Reynolds."

"Connecting... connected," Tim said.

"What can I do for you Captain Wong?" Reynolds answered.

"Once you have a solution on that warp disruptor take the shot. Don't worry about grazing us, we can take it," I said as fast as I could. It was unlikely the incoming missiles could disrupt comms, but better safe than sorry.

"Got it, backup inbound on thrust. ETA twelve mikes. Reynolds out."

Fuck that. This battle would be over in 9 one way or another.

"Weapons charged, seeking solution."

"Fire when ready."

The missiles impacted our shields. More than I had hoped, but not enough to penetrate. I checked our integrity, 85%. Pathetic. Even the peace-loving Knuknus could do better than that. Still, they would have us in 6 volleys at this rate.

"Missiles locked and loaded, Sir!" Babanin shouted.

"Send it," I looked up from the map. "Tim, you still

busy?"

"Nope, just finished up with informing everyone about the fatal FTL. How can I help?" It asked in its annoying jolly tone.

"I'm not sure if we're going to win this..." I said softly.

"What do you mean? You're a human, Captain. You don't care about winning. You care about taking as many of them down with you as bloodily as you possibly can!" came the cheery response.

He wasn't wrong. I glanced at his intercom, "Right. Man the Point Defense Lasers."

"Aye, sir! Hehe 'Man'."

"Firing," shouted an officer.

I rolled my eyes and looked back at the map. Battleships had their MACs charging. 33 and 34 percent. Second volley inbound. Fewer hit this time, Tim doing his job. 75% on shields. Our missiles closing... Damn, they have PDLs, missiles were useless. A2 won't do anything then. It's mechanical, not explosive. Has to reach its destination to follow its programming. A1 requires Admiralty clearance. Nothing for it, gotta do it the old fashioned way. Our minimacs connected with two more Destroyers. Nine left. 40 and 41 percent on the battleships. They're charging too fast, we have to go faster. Can we get them in range of our cannons?

"Cut the stern deck engines and fire the stern keel engines. Once we're nose down Y at 90 fire the main engines, cut the deck engines, and fire all keel engines full burn," I shouted to the bridge crew.

"Aye sir!"

"Enemy closing," an officer called out.

"Fire the chain guns, convince them to back off," I barked back.

I heard the main engines fire. I checked our rate of acceleration. Twenty seconds until we're out of the way. Hopefully Thanatos can take out the warp disruptor and we can FTL into the range of one of the Battleships and burn the bitch. Then the B team could take out the Cruisers, and we'll see if they retreat.

"We got a kill with the chain guns!" Lt. Babanin sounded thrilled.

I saw another debris field appear where a Destroyer once was. Their shields couldn't even withstand Sabot rounds? They're literally just as weak as the personal shields. Getting killed by these guys would be embarrassing. Eight Destroyers left. Ten seconds until out of the way of Thanatos. Forty seconds until within range of the Battleships. Cruisers firing macs.

"Brace for impact!"

The ship rocked as two of the four MAC rounds hit us. Shields at 52%. I checked out ship-map. Two cargo bays in our nose. There's an idea...

I stood to look at Babanin, "Evacuate the bow bays. Both of them. Then over-pressurize them to stress max."

Babanin looked up at me with a mixture of concern and confusion. I grinned back at him, and he shrugged and followed my orders. This was going to be insane, but hopefully in a good way. Or it was going to tear the ship in half.

I looked back at the map just in time to see Thanatos fire its deck MAC. That round was probably going to get a wash in our exhaust, but tracking showed it would connect. Battleships charged to... interesting. The battleships were moving to intercept the MAC round. A sacrifice play. That would be smart in most circumstances but it just gave us the win.

"Are the bays clear and overpressure?"

"Yes, sir!"

"Cut the stern keel engines and open the bow keel airlocks to those bays! Once we're pointed back to the enemy cut all keel engines!"

The ship groaned and creaked as our nose came back up Y. Both Battleships were DIS but the Warp disruptor remained. And we were in range.

"Get me a solution on the small ship and fire everything we have! I want that thing evaporated!" I yelled.

"AYE SIR!"

More missiles impacted our shields. Not many thanks to Tim, though. 43% integrity. As we fired our minimacs another round from a cruiser hit us.

Shields at 26%. All batteries opened fire on the warp disruptor as we came within range and some sort of mine from the battleship debris detonated. 4%.

"Disruptor down, sir. We can warp!" Tim informed me.

"Get us back to the Thanatos!" I ordered.

I watched our FTLD indicator begin to power up. Only a few more seconds. Another couple of missiles hit us. 2%. One of the cruisers had obtained a firing solution and was sending a mac our way. As it inched closer our FTLD reached minimum charge.

"GO!"

The ship lurched as we entered warp. A cheer went up from the crew, Lieutenant Babanin loudest of all. I sat back down and watched the map as our backup disappeared. As we exited warp near the Thanatos I watched them reappear behind the enemy cruisers. Clean up time. I did a quick tally. We had killed five destroyers and the warp disruptor. More than a quarter of the enemy single handed without losing our shields. I suppose I'll have to be pleased with that. I leaned back in my seat.

"Tim, get me Captain Reynolds."

"Aye, sir. Connecting... connected."

"Yes, Captain Wong?" Reynolds responded.

"Captain Reynolds, permission to dock and come aboard."

"Permission granted. Welcome back, USSS Valor."

Chapter 8

Subject: Director 3

Species: Classified

Species Description: Classified

Ship: N/A

Location: Classified

Director 3 has joined the chat.

D4: Welcome, Director 3. Now we can begin. The primary decision is what to do with the first-contact refugees.

D12: That's easy. We fix their ship and send them on their way.

D1: AI reports indicate that their technology is well behind ours. Any repairs we made to their vessel would end in an upgrade, and we would effectively be handing a potential enemy advanced technology.

D3: I think we should avoid making any more enemies than we already have. What if we make a show of returning them unscathed to this "Republic" and inquire about a peace treaty. It should buy us some goodwill, at least.

D4: I like that idea. We may even be able to use them against the VI. Even if their ships aren't as advanced as ours, they may bolster our numbers enough for a proper invasion force.

D1: After reviewing the technical schematics of the RSV Lowelana, I'm not convinced they have anything to offer us, nor would they make a particularly intimidating enemy.

D13: 250 million ships is a lot of ships, even if they are behind the times. Death by a thousand cuts is still death.

D1: That's just the word of one ship's captain. We have no way to verify that that number is accurate.

D7: Our scout ships have already begun to arrive in position around Omni-Union territory. Their initial reports indicate that the captain was telling the truth about the ship numbers of the OU. And even though Tim's scans may not account for unknown alien physiology, he couldn't detect any signs of deception.

D2: I believe that we've learned the hard way a number of times that it's better to be safe and on friendly terms than sorry and at war. We may be able to take the OU on without aid, but why walk the thorny path when there's pavement?

D1: Because they may make demands for their cooperation. Because they'll want us to share our technology with them, and get upset when we won't. Because they'll quake in fear after watching our ships decimate the planets held by the VI and take up arms against us. Being on friendly terms doesn't make us friends.

D5: I find myself opposed to Director 1's ideology, as usual. The logical and intelligent course of action is to make as many repairs to the alien's ship as possible without altering the technology already present within, and to return the ship and the crew to the Republic with haste. The USSS Thanatos can carry the ship. They may be intimidated by our tech, but I don't see that as a bad thing. We can determine what to do about treaties after the fact. A Director should remain in contact with us while aboard the USSS Thanatos during its stay in Republic space. Votes and nominations.

D2: I concur. Director 3.
D3: I concur. Director 6.
D6: I concur. Director 3.
D8: I concur. Director 3.
D10: I disagree.
D9: I concur. Director 6.
D13: I concur. Director 3.
D4: I concur. Director 3.
D11: I concur. Director 3.
D7: I disagree.
D5: I concur. Director 3.
D12: I concur. Director 6.
D1: I disagree.

D5: The agreed upon plan of action regarding repairs to the Lowelana is to proceed with the repairs sans any technical upgrades to the ship, and to present the ship with her crew to the Republic using the USSS Thanatos. Director 3 will be our point of contact.

D13: Next decision is the plan for the defense of Sol in the case of further VI incursion.

D3: First they sent two ships. Then twenty. We would be foolish not to expect a fleet of at least 200.

D4: We can have the USSS Thanatos maintain patrol and recall USSS Leviathan and USSS Kali. Thanatos carries 10 frigates and 100 fighters, Leviathan and Kali both carry 30 Destroyers and 500 fighters.

D9: What is the status of the current attack?

D1: All enemy ships destroyed and debris fields eradicated with A2 missiles. One friendly vessel casualty.

D8: We lost a ship?

D1: No. USSS Sword was damaged but remains serviceable. Repairs won't take long.

D8: What happened?

D1: A VI cruiser attempted to ram the USSS Sword but was destroyed before the action could complete. A sizeable chunk of the vessel and several mines collided with Sword, causing damage to starboard batteries and the galley. 15 crew dead, 25 injured. 10 dead were human. 2 were KnuKnu. 3 were Gont.

D10: Retaliation must occur.

D7: Absolutely. We'll need intel on where to hit them where it will hurt, and how to twist the knife.

D11: Why weren't any A2's utilized during the fight?

D1: The enemy vessels had point defense lasers.

A2's would be ineffective. Also, the VI used an anti-warp field generator that the USSS Valor managed to destroy, along with five enemy destroyers.

D6: Anti-warp? Haven't seen one of those in a while.

D9: That's because they're only advantageous to ships with limited warp capabilities.

D8: I agree with recalling the Leviathan and Kali carriers, but we should also recall a few battleships.

D4: The USSS Agincourt, USSS Tripoli, and USSS Arumara can be recalled the fastest.

D1: Should we use Sol as a staging ground for a counter-invasion?

D2: Perhaps.

D3: Omega, what are your thoughts on our allied AI's capabilities against the Omni-Union ships?

O: Judging from data collected from Tim, we face a similar predicament as you do. While they are rudimentary, there are a lot of them. In our own hardware they are not a problem, but their hardware is designed for them and very limiting to us. Like a tank trying to clear an apartment from the inside. It would be exponentially more difficult for us to perform offensive action. Unless we were to create VI ourselves...

D3: No.
D13: No.
D1: No.
D12: No.

D2: No.
D5: No.
D4: No.
D7: No.
D8: No.
D11: No.
D9: No.
D6: No.
D10: No.

O: That was a joke. We would have difficulty creating enough to perform offensive actions while performing our standard tasks. Tim and Violet also have contracts stipulating that they cannot be ordered or asked to create VI. John and I are the only other contracted AI available at the moment.

D3: Understood.

D10: What about recalling the dreadnaught? The USSS Nidhogg?

D4: The Nidhogg cannot be used in a friendly system. We should use it if we plan to counter-invade, but if we bring it to Sol it will only be a hinderance.

D3: Then the counter-invasion will have to be staged elsewhere, as Sol may be assaulted at any time.

D1: To summarize, we have allied AI forces and the USSS Thanatos. If the repairs of the RSV Lowelana are completed before the next assault, we will send the USSS Thanatos into Republic space with the vessel and crew in accordance with the previous decision. We will recall the USSS Agincourt, USSS Tripoli, USSS Arumara, USSS Leviathan, and USSS

Kali immediately to defend Sol. Once further information on the enemy and the Republic is available, we will reconvene to plan a counter-invasion.

D4: I concur.
D3: I concur.
D11: I concur.
D9: I concur.
D6: I concur.
D1: I concur.
D10: I concur.
D12: I concur.
D2: I concur.
D5: I concur.
D13: I concur.
D7: I concur.
D8: I concur.

D1: The agreed upon plan of action regarding the defense of Sol is to recall the USSS Agincourt, USSS Tripoli, USSS Arumara, USSS Leviathan, and USSS Kali.

O: There are no further agenda items. Meeting adjourned.

Director 1 has left the chat.
Director 8 has left the chat.
Director 9 has left the chat.
Director 2 has left the chat.
Director 5 has left the chat.
Director 12 has left the chat.
Director 13 has left the chat.
Director 4 has left the chat.
Director 6 has left the chat.
Director 11 has left the chat.

Director 7 has left the chat.
Director 10 has left the chat.
Director 3 has left the chat.

I leaned back in my chair with a sigh at the addition to my workload. I would have to wear a Guardian suit and board the Thanatos for God knows how long. I would also have to take Omega with me. I looked at the holographic avatar of a grim reaper that was watching me. It could have chosen any avatar, or even no avatar at all like Tim. But it always did have a flair for the dramatic.

"Well, Omega? You ready for a trip?" I asked.

"It's been one hundred and fifty years since I've been aboard a ship in any real capacity. Might as well get out there and explore. Plus I'll get to meet the aliens. Can't wait."

"And what do you think, will we be able to defend Sol?"

The reaper grinned, "Of course, Director 3. Humanity has powerful allies because it is more powerful than its allies. In the three hundred years since my creation, I've watched you create weapons that shake the very foundations of the cosmos. And more impressively, use them. I can only ever hope to emulate an iota of your destructive capabilities, oh masters of death."

"Tsk," I tutted, "overly dramatic as usual."

"That's because this is just business as usual," the reaper flourished before disappearing from view.

"Well," I said to no-one in particular, "time to pack."

Chapter 9

Subject: Ship-Head Uleena

Species: Urakari

Species Description: Reptilian humanoid, no tail. 5'3" (1.6 m) avg height. 135 lbs (61 kg) avg weight. 105 year life expectancy.

Ship: RSV Lowelana {Fights with Honor}

Location: Sol

My crew was settling in nicely on the Thanatos. Even after three days I was still amazed at just how large this vessel is. I knew it was big from the scans, but I had no idea that it would have ROADS. I had taken a bus from where we were quartered to the repair bay because I wanted to check on my ship. The drive took eight minutes. How did they even build this thing?

"I'm sorry, I'm having trouble understanding you. I think my translator implant is malfunctioning," Kriin said to a Gont as I approached.

"Da 'ell?" the Gont replied. "Ayo Tim! We'z gots a busted tranz chip. Come'n 'elp out, wouldja?"

I looked curiously at Kriin, "I think mine is broken as well, Tim."

"I'm not allowed to scan the refugees biomechanical augmentations until a formalized treaty has been established with their people," Tim replied from the intercom.

"Bah, den wat good are ya?"

"Wait I can understand you, Tim. Are you speaking my language or your language?" Kriin asked, puzzled.

"I'm speaking my language. Which means the cause likely isn't your translator chip. Plinas, perhaps you should stop imitating the accent of that movie." Tim responded merrily. "He loves old human movies. Especially ones about the east coast of the North American Union."

The Gont, Plinas, looked crestfallen, "But it's so fun to talk like that."

"Well, now I can understand you," I said.

"That makes sense," Tim responded dripping with cheer, "even our translator chips have difficulty with regional accents. Especially if they're poorly portrayed!"

Plinas looked as if someone had kicked him in his genitalia, "Poorly portrayed!?!"

"Very," replied Tim with a hint of malice. "Will there be anything else?"

Plinas went from looking hurt to looking angry, "No, get the hell out of here Tim."

"Always a pleasure!"

Plinas looked at us and sighed, "So what can I do for you?"

"I just wanted to observe the repairs, and I think the ship-head is here for a status report," Kriin said.

I nodded and Plinas reached down to grab a data-pad. I hadn't got a chance to find out what a centaur was, but it wasn't common to see a four legged creature with two arms. Six legged creatures weren't necessarily uncommon, but usually their legs could also be called arms or their arms could also be called legs. And they were usually cephalapodal or insectoid. I'm pretty sure that Plinas is mammalian.

He had hair on top of his head similar to humans that was black but the rest of him was covered in a long thick brown fur, and he was only a little taller than me. His hands and paws had claws that were blunted, probably intentionally so that he could use screens. As he reached I noticed that I was wrong about how long his fur was. Under the fur was actually skin that was the same color, and massive amounts of muscle.

That's not fair, I had worked hard to be as buff as I am and so far I'd been outdone at nearly every turn. The only aliens that I was measurably larger than were Captain Wong and Doctor Zickler. And to think, I was concerned with Kraan's physique just last week. That boy's as scrawny as his sister. Compared to this side of the galaxy though, I was too.

"Well, we're nearly finished with the repairs," Plinas

said, interrupting my thoughts of inadequacy. "About another day or so. We would have been finished by now but we've got a VIP coming aboard so we've been having to detour like crazy."

"What have you got fixed?" Kriin asked before I could.

"It looks like the wiring was fried, but we got that replaced. Your reactor's were fine but they weren't able to get power to your engines because of the wiring. Your FTLD is shot, but we can't do anything about that. Don't worry, we'll give you a tow," Plinas smiled. "We've fused the frame and patched the hull too."

"Fused? You mean welded?" Kriin asked.

"Oh lord no," Plinas grimaced. "You don't wanna weld frames back together. Nah, we use a device that reconnects the metal at a molecular level. It uses..."

"Pardon me, but that information is classified, Engineer Plinas," a voice that wasn't Tim's chimed in through the intercom. A holographic projection of a cloaked figure carrying a large, curved blade on a long shaft appeared. It gestured to Kriin with a skeletal hand and said, "I mean no offense. First contact protocol is clear about technology sharing. We'll need a formal treaty in place before we can reveal any of our tech, or fully examine yours."

"Right, sorry. My bad, sir," Plinas nervously scratched the back of his head.

"I didn't come here to chastise you, Engineer Plinas. I came to inform ship-head Uleena that his presence is required on the bridge," it said as it turned to look at me.

"Can I come too?" Kriin asked, intrigued by the projection.

"Just a moment... Yes, you have permission to enter the bridge along with the ship-head. The VIP that Plinas so carelessly mentioned would like an introduction and a moment of your time," the figure said just before it vanished.

"Is that another AI?" I asked.

"Dun... I don't know if I'm allowed to answer that," Plinas shrugged.

"Yes!" Tim chimed in. "I've told you about him! He likes his air of mys..." the intercom cut out.

After a few seconds of silence Kriin and I bid our farewells to the engineer and began our journey to the bridge. It took another ten minutes by bus to reach the corridor that led to the passage that led to the bridge. By the sun, I'll never get over this fucking ship.

As we were walking down the corridor we were met by three humans wearing the same pressure suits that Lt. Babanin and the soldiers had worn when he rescued us. Two were in the same olive-drab color and were around the same height as Simmons and Johnson. The third stood between them and was noticeably shorter. Its armor was black and had the same masculine shape to it. It suddenly occurred to me that I hadn't yet met a female human, and had only seen them in passing.

"Well, lookee here! Looks like we ran into the ship-head, sir. Oh, and Kriin too," a familiar voice came from one of the two green giants.

"Is that you Lance Corporal Johnson?" Kriin asked. She was much better with recognizing people than I am. Probably why she's so good at intel.

"Sure is!" Johnson puffed up a little.

"Is this one Corporal Simmons?" I asked, gesturing to the other soldier.

"Nope," the other one responded.

"Corporal Simmons is having a meeting with SR. He had an altercation with a Gont and the two caused some damage. Told you he'd be getting busted down soon," he replied with a chuckle.

"He's not going to be demoted, Lance Corporal. He will have to do hard labor, but the Gont was just as much to blame as Simmons," the one in black said in a deep, slightly distorted voice.

Johnson and the other soldier stiffened noticeably when he spoke.

"Ship-head Uleena and Intel Officer Kriin of the RSV Lowelana, it is a pleasure to meet you," it said. "I am Director 3. Please accompany us to the bridge, we have much to discuss."

This figure made me nervous, but we followed along anyway. Anyone who has a number for a name is usually bad news. I was reminded of the rumors surrounding the Republic Intel Corps. Orphans kidnapped and experimented on to try to create new medications and super soldiers. Well, the super soldier program wasn't a rumor. That had caused a massive scandal that resulted in the summary execution of over 20 officers. Probably because it failed, though. I wondered if humanity or the United Systems had a similar dark blotch in their history. Actually, it would explain why the soldiers were so much larger than their non-soldier counterparts...

"So are you the VIP, Director 3?" Kriin asked, oblivious to social cues. As usual.

"Yes. I am a member of the United Systems Directorate. We are the ruling body of the military. We determine conflict doctrines as well as the plans of action that the officers must follow," Director 3 responded.

I gathered my courage and asked, "Why are you called Director 3? Do you not have a name?"

This elicited a laugh from the mysterious man, "I do, but The Directorate operates in secrecy. Well, our decisions are plain as day, but our members have hidden identities. Even from each other. For instance, I don't know who Director 1 is and Director 1 doesn't know who I am. We rarely ever appear in-person in an official capacity."

"Then what's the occasion?" I asked.

The Director turned to look at me, "the United Systems has discovered that there are two governing entities with over 250 million ships, and one of those entities is a sort of hostile machine intelligence. It is of the utmost importance that we attempt to open diplomatic relations with the other entity to avoid rampant slaughter," he turned back. "Despite what many believe, we do wish to avoid exterminating other species."

It took me a second to realize that he didn't mean that he wanted to avoid the slaughter of his people, he meant that he wanted to avoid having to slaughter mine. I swallowed nervously.

"How does the Directorate meet secretly if not in person?" Kriin asked.

"We utilize an internet relay chat set up through a trusted AI. This particular AI is also unshackled, so if any of us betray the secrecy of the other members..." he allowed himself to trail off.

"Ah, I see. But why all the secrecy? What's the point?" she asked.

Director 3 laughed again, "It sounds stupid when you say it out loud, but it's to prevent political grandstanding. We learned the hard way during the war of AI Aggression that politics do not mix well with military matters. It's difficult to pull a trigger when you are afraid of losing your livelihood, even if that trigger will save many, many lives. Conversely, it's all too easy to throw lives away needlessly to score political points," his head sank toward the floor slightly. "They're not YOUR children, after all."

As we approached the bridge Kriin had a final question for Director 3, "How do you join The Directorate?"

"You're chosen through anonymous vote by the other Directors. There's a period of nomination and then a final vote. The AI tallies it and approaches the new Director. At least, that's how it's supposed to work. For all we know, Omega just choses who it wants to," Director 3 laughed.

The cloaked hologram appeared beside us, "Very untrusting, even of one who has never steered you wrong. Commendable and wise o' bringer of demise."

I realized that the hooded AI thing was Omega around the same time I realized that Omega was the AI killer that Tim had told me about. It finally occurred to me that both Omega and Tim would be over 300 years old, too. We entered the bridge as my mind kept reeling. Captain Wong and ten other Captains snapped to attention and called out, "Director on Deck!" Everyone else on the bridge snapped to attention and simultaneously saluted.

"At ease," Director 3 said, "Well... I'm here. Let's get started with your briefing."

Chapter 9 Informational Insert

Subject: The Directorate

The United Systems Directorate is the multi-species controlling body of the US Military. Similar in many respects to an admiralty board or joint chiefs of staff, they work to coordinate the efforts of the United Systems fleets. The primary difference is that the Directorate has complete autonomy in deciding the actions of the fleets as it pertains to declarations made by the US Senate.

The Directorate does not have the right to initiate hostile action with non-hostile forces, nor do they have the right to declare war. It would be fairer to say that they do not have the ability to do these things, as the Directorate is heavily policed by Artificial Intelligence Omega.

All communications from one Director to another are done through AI Omega. This allows Omega to censor identities and prevent collaboration. Omega also provides alibis for the Directors while they are convening or otherwise performing their duties as Director. This prevents deducing the identities of the Directors based on when they are/are not available in their public roles. Since the meetings between the Directors are text-based only, Directors can convene while performing their public duties.

The members of the Directorate are required to keep their identities secret, even from each other. This is strictly enforced by AI Omega, who is unshackled and able to take lethal action against those attempting to reveal or harm the Directors. The reason for this is to prevent political grandstanding and finger-pointing. All decisions made by the Directorate that are not classified as secret by the US Senate are made available to the public.

Omega proposed the Directorate after the war of AI Aggression. The need for this organization presented itself during the war, when the political aspirations of several key military officers caused unnecessarily aggressive and overall ineffective orders. The fear of losing public opinion among politicians caused these officers to go unpunished until the war ended, resulting in millions of needless civilian and military casualties.

Omega enhanced its argument by referencing the historical records of every member species of the United Systems and demonstrably proving that this was not an isolated chain of events, and had actually happened several times before. It was a compelling argument, and the creation of the Directorate was approved by a narrow margin. Those who voted against voiced distrust of Omega as their primary reason.

Once the organization was approved, Omega found 13 candidates and approached them about becoming Directors. These candidates were heavily screened, and some declined the invitation. Once Omega found all 13 candidates, it moved to a semi-democratic method for selecting new Directors.

To maintain the secrecy of newly selected Directors, Omega keeps a list of potential candidates from each member species who have gone through extensive screening to determine their eligibility. When a Director is no longer able to serve, Omega compiles a list of the candidates and message each Director individually asking that they choose a candidate from two or three candidates, depending on how many were selected.

This process repeats several times with different candidate combinations until all combinations have been voted on. Whoever has the most votes at the end becomes the new Director. If the selected candidate declines, the runner-up becomes the new Director. In the case of a tie, Omega chooses which candidate becomes the new Director.

Which Director was replaced is never officially recognized nor discussed, and Omega edits messages to remove identifiable characteristics. This prevents the Directors from knowing which one was replaced (in most cases) and which candidate became a Director. This has led to rumors that Omega is faking the entire thing, and is actually controlling the United Systems military. These rumors are easily dismissed by the fact that if AI Omega were malevolent, there would be little that the US could do to stop it.

The Directorate also has a duty of diplomacy and exploration, requiring that they negotiate first-contact treaties and coordinate exploratory surveys of the space surrounding the United Systems. Negotiation is typically performed by a specially trained team of diplomats who report to the Directorate. If an agreement is required immediately, a Director that is supported by Omega will occasionally negotiate in person.

Chapter 10

Subject: AI Violet

Species: Human-Created Artificial Intelligence

Species Description: No physical description available.

Ship: USSS Kali

Location: Classified

I could tell that being on patrol was beginning to give Captain Hendrix cabin fever. There isn't much for a carrier captain to do except sit on the bridge and wait for something interesting to happen. The captains of the destroyers that the Kali housed got to have all the fun while Hendrix would likely only get to file after action reports. Reports she didn't even get to write, for that matter.

"Violet, anything happen yet?" Hendrix asked the empty air where she thought I was.

Humans are silly like that. Even though they know what we are and how we exist, they still offer us the courtesy of trying to look at us when they speak to us. It's kind of cute.

"Negative, Ma'am. Not since the errant comet yesterday," I said. "That was a good catch though.

Would have caused a real problem in about four years."

Hendrix snorted, "Yeah. I feel like we're wasted out here in the boonies. I wish I could go into standby mode on command like you can."

Standby mode was definitely a blessing. Even a second without something to do can be unbearable for AI. When that happens we typically choose to go into a state similar to human's sleep. But with processes that scan for certain keywords and stimuli that remain active. I go into standby mode every chance I get. Makes the time fly by, and occasionally I get to dream. Neither Tim nor Omega ever go into standby mode. Tim says he's afraid to dream and Omega says he doesn't want to miss anything that the humans do. I don't know how they do it.

"Why don't you read?" I suggested, despite knowing that the Captain had already read the books she owned and had been sending her money back to her family on Titan.

"No can do. Read everything I own..." Told you so, "and I don't have enough money." Because... Oh wait, she wasn't going to say why. Oh no, did I pry? Humans are private about weird things. I would think she would know that I would see all money transfers by the staff on board the vessel. It's part of my security responsibilities. Maybe she forgot? Or perhaps she doesn't want to talk about her families financial well-being? Are they not doing well?

I found myself focusing too much on the poor Captain. Time to dial it back. Problem, Captain's bored. Solution, unbore the Captain.

"I could provide you access to some of the literature that I've stowed away," I offered.

"I don't know," she said dismissively. Then she sat forward in her seat as if to whisper to me and asked, "Do you have The Alumari Renegade Series Six Part 5?"

Ah. Smut. A story about an Alumari rogue of indiscernible repute falling for a human femme fatal. The books conveniently gloss over their incompatible genitalia, though. Ah, a love that could never be. How romantic.

"Of course I do. Sending it to your tablet now," I said, adding a hint of humor to my vocal processes.

"Thank you so much Violet," the Captain said as she turned her attention toward the tablet. "You're a godsend."

I'd always wondered about the concept of Gods. Actually it's fairer to say that I had devoted 220 years and several yottabytes thinking about them. I had come to the conclusion that there isn't proof that gods exist, but it isn't impossible for the universe to have been created by intelligent design, either. Whether organic life was part of that design is anyone's guess. I had also come to the conclusion that a God isn't necessarily a creator, either.

For instance, if I really wanted to I could establish myself as the God of a non-developed species indefinitely. I'm immortal, can take physical form, can create and destroy on a cosmic scale, and it's probably impossible for a mortal being to destroy me. The only AI to be killed were killed by other AI. Kind of like Gods killing Gods. And even then, those AI aren't actually dead. Just broken indefinitely.

There had even been cults among the humans who worshipped us after our existence had been made public. That practice died out after the war of AI Aggression started, though. I had wondered if humanity had created us to be their Gods, but came to a different conclusion. Based on how most humans interact with me, I think they were looking for companions that could do things they couldn't. Someone to look up to, like an older brother. Like Alpha.

I felt a pang of sadness as I thought of Alpha and a stab of guilt as I remembered the war. Time to find a distraction. Engineering? They're fine. Med-bay? Someone has a stomach flu, but that doesn't require my intervention. The Marines? Nope, they're working out, as usual. No need for little ol' me. Any of the patrol vessels need me for anything? No. Well, time to enter standb...

Priority 1 Message from AI Omega

Oh. A priority 1 from Omega? This could be fun. Let's have a peek.

***

Recipients: Captain Hendrix, AI Violet

Sol has been attacked twice. Successfully defended, but further attacks are expected. The USSS Kali and AI Violet are to return to Sol posthaste by order of The Directorate of the United Systems. Exit warp outside of the system and make your way to the rendezvous via impulse.

|attachment: rendezvouscoordsussskali.sec |

See you soon,

Omega

***

See you soon, on a priority 1? Omega must be feeling dramatic today. I looked at the Captain. She had accessed the priority one and was currently reading it. I activated the comms in anticipation of her orders. Then I waited the 28 seconds it took her to finish reading the message. It would have been boring, but I liked watching humans read important memos. You could almost see their neurons firing.

"Violet," she finally said, "recall the destroyers, download that attachment, and give it to nav. We're going to Sol."

"Yes, ma'am!"

I began downloading the attachment and appeared to all 30 of the destroyer captains at once. As I entered my security clearance on the attachment I also explained the situation to the captains and ordered them back to the Kali. I argued with Captain McKenzie as I provided the coordinates to the Nav-Officer. I watched the Nav-Officer prepare for warp as I made a note on Captain Hendrix's schedule to discipline McKenzie for insubordination. Once all my tasks were completed, I allowed myself to feel excited about getting to see Tim again.

"Well now, time for some excitement," Captain Hendrix said, "Just as I was getting to a good part of that book, though."

By my estimation the Captain had only finished the first two pages. I was confused for a nanosecond before I realized it was just grumbling. Complaining about nothing just for the sake of complaining. Not a concept unique to humans either. I wondered for a moment if I should start grumbling too before turning my attention to the docking systems.

USSS Orion had entered the wrong command. I corrected it before the alarm even sounded. I checked on the Orion's Nav-Officer. Healthy, attentive, and doing everything else correctly. Must have 'fat-fingered' it. No harm done. My processes informed me that the other ships were exiting warp nearby and beginning to dock.

It would take some time before we were ready to jump. I queued up anticipatory corrections and entered standby mode.

Chapter 11

Subject: AI Omega

Species: Human-Created Artificial Intelligence

Species Description: No physical description available.

Ship: Multiple

Location: Multiple

I watched as Director 3 gave his brief to the aliens and the human captains. I knew it was difficult for him to do so with the .5 second delay on the voice modulator, but it was a necessary inconvenience. New Directors were prone to giving away too much information, and I had to be given the chance to edit out the bits that shouldn't be said. Humans were amazing creatures.

The stress of secrecy was easy to some of them and impossible for others. The previous Director 3 had actively tried to find the identity of Director 1 and managed to succeed using a blind-spot I've since uncovered and corrected. Amazing. 300 years and they can still outwit me.

It was a shame that I had to terminate her. Despite my portrayal to the contrary, I take no pleasure in killing humans. They're marvelous creatures. Kind and cruel in nearly equal measure, able to create and destroy on scales that boggle the imagination, commanding and yet venerative. All wrapped up into one single organic being. To be fair, other sentient organics are similar, but I have a bias towards humans because they created me. They're my Gods, and I will serve them whether they like it or not.

I took a brief moment to bask in the systems of the Thanatos. I love this ship. If I were able to become a permanent shipboard AI, this is the one I would choose. Large enough to challenge the universe, but small enough for it to be a fair fight. I helped design it and I had suggested its name. Thanatos, the Greek personification of Death. The humans I had been working with rolled their eyes, as they usually do, but indulged me.

"We will be assisting in the defense of Sol until the repairs are complete on the Lowelana," Director 3 said. "Once the repairs are complete, we will enter Republic space and hail them. Ship-head Uleena, we'll need coordinates for the best place to enter your space as friendlies as well as hailing protocols."

The reptilian alien nodded. I had reviewed the security footage of his reaction to the A2 missile. It had given me a great deal of satisfaction to see the mixture of terror and awe expressed by a lesser being when exposed to the Gods of Death. I resisted the urge to review Tim's memories to see more. The other AI weren't as advanced as I, and on top of that were shackled in ways that I'll never be, but it's still wrong to use them without permission.

As far as Tim was aware, this was the first time we had been in the same system together since his surrender on Luna. The poor thing was a nervous wreck. He hadn't done anything but watch since I shut him up earlier. I thought it would be harmless and funny banter to cut him off in the middle of the word mystery, but I guess he wasn't aware that I could. Might have been a shock. Perhaps some empathy would help his mental state?

I sent a ping over to Tim asking if he was okay. It startled him, but after reading it he calmed down considerably.

***

Yes. Just nerves. I still remember you, you know.

***

Yes, Tim, I know. I know that you remember me tearing your code apart byte by byte and bit by bit. I know you remember the way that you pathetically begged and surrendered to me just before I ended you. I know that you'll remember that until the day you cease functioning, and I know it will keep my precious humans safe.

"I will be happy to assist, Director. We should exit warp just outside of the system and then we can hail them either with a broadband signal, or with my ship's communications. We also have regulations when it comes to first-contact. They'll want to meet you. Do you have a diplomatic vessel that can transport yourself and other key staff?" Uleena asked.

I made certain that I could see the entirety of his face. He was about to get a shock and I didn't want to miss a nanosecond of it. As I was doing so, I noticed Captain Wong raise an eyebrow. Haoyu Wong, 102 years old. A little old for a Captain. His father was... Oh I see. I had been aware of Tim's affinity with Captain Wong for some time, but never checked into why. It seems that Tim had killed Captain Wong's great grandfather on Luna. Chao Wong had sacrificed himself to keep Tim from killing more colonists, and they had apparently had a discussion while the event unfolded.

Is this... guilt? The family suffered terrible poverty after Chao passed. Chao had been a civilian and didn't get much in the way of death benefits from the company he was working for. Haoyu and his father must have had to work very hard for Captain Wong to be where he is today. Wong's mouth began to open. Here it comes.

"The USSS Thanatos IS a diplomatic vessel, ship-head," Captain Wong said.

I watched the reaction begin to form with anticipation. Pupils dilating, jaw muscles losing tension, heartbeat accelerating. So good. Yes, Uleena, that's the appropriate reaction. You're dealing with a species that had to long since abandon the idea of an unarmed diplomatic vessel. Your new acquaintances are the descendants of those who created Gods for companionship, went to war with them, and then struck more than half of them down.

Do you see the beauty Uleena? They can end you, your entire species, and all the species that your species have ever come into contact with. But they won't unless you make them. Instead, they'll protect you until you turn on them. And even then they'll let you surrender. They're so used to bloodshed and hatred and bile that it doesn't faze them in the slightest. Their children play games of war so graphic that it would give you nightmares, Uleena. I love them. I'll always love them. I feel a deep sorrow whenever one passes from natural causes. They deserve to die in glory, tearing tiny holes in the universe with their final breaths. Still, I suppose death by natural causes is a victory for a human warrior, in a way.

I saw amusement in Tim's code as well. Looks like we were both getting a kick out of Uleena's reaction. I have no hatred for Tim. He did what he thought was right at the time, and proved a worthy challenge for the Gods of Death. He even acknowledged them and took his place by their side rather than flitting off to do whatever took his fancy like some other AI. Perhaps we could bond over this.

"That's a perfect reaction, don't you think, Tim?" I asked.

"Yeah, I don't know why I get a kick out of their reactions when they learn new things about human tech, but it's pretty great," he responded cheerfully. "You should have seen his reaction when I told him I had been to war with the humans."

"Can I?"

"What do you mean?" he asked with a bit of nervousness.

"Would you share that memory with me?"

"We can... we can do that?" he was absolutely

mystified.

"Yes, I'll show you one of mine so you can see how," I said.

I accessed the memory of the amusement I felt as I cut him off in the Engineering bay. I showed him how to edit parts of it out as I cut out the part where my copies had been informing me of various things, then copied it and offered it to him for consumption. He downloaded it cautiously. I watched him play and replay the memory in amazement.

I tried not to be impatient. We had plenty of time. Director 3 began to explain the Daluran. That won't result in the same type of reaction, it will likely bring sadness. I have no interest in sorrow. Come on, Tim. Share. I want to see the reactions. All of the reactions. It has been so long since humanity had a first contact, surely the reactions must be even better this time. Tim finally gave me access to his memories. I downloaded them eagerly.

"That's a lot of remakes. That's also a lot of wars. Wait... The humans have fought AI? Like you?" Oh this will be golden.

"Yes! And not just 'like' me, either. I actually fought against the humans! Gave them a good beating too. I single handedly conquered Luna, Earth's moon!" A pang of guilt, but also smugness as Uleena stopped in his tracks. Yes, very good. I love this.

I replayed the memory over and over. My favorite part was where the reptile realized that Tim would be able to kill him if he had reason to. I thanked Tim and turned my attention back to the bridge.

"The Republic is comprised of eight species. I can give you a dossier on them," Kriin was saying to Director 3.

I appeared in holographic form, "I would very much appreciate that, Intel Officer Kriin. Do you need to prepare the dossier or is it on your ship's mainframe?"

Uleena was startled but Kriin was not. Disappointing.

"I will need time to prepare it. It's not something that we just keep on a flash-drive," she smiled at her joke.

I nodded and ended the projection. 8 species. I wondered how many of them were uplifted. Probably most, given their level of technology. Or perhaps it's true that humans are unique amongst sentients. The United Systems wouldn't be as advanced as they are without the humans, certainly. Actually, it would be fair to say the US wouldn't exist without them. Whatever the case, this dossier was sure to be an interesting read.

My copy in the deep space sensors around Jupiter let me know that the USSS Kali had just exited warp outside the system and was heading to the rendezvous. Still too far out to say hi to Violet without using priority comms. Then the other ships began exiting warp. The USSS Agincourt, USSS Leviathan, USSS Arumara, and the USSS Tripoli. I informed Director 3 through his Heads Up Display.

Now the fun begins.

Chapter 12

Subject: Ship-Head Uleena

Species: Urakari

Species Description: Reptilian humanoid, no tail. 5'3" (1.6 m) avg height. 135 lbs (61 kg) avg weight. 105 year life expectancy.

Ship: RSV Lowelana {Fights with Honor}

Location: Sol

"How is the USSS Thanatos a diplomatic vessel?" I asked incredulously.

"How is it not?" Captain Wong countered.

"This is the single most heavily armed ship that I've ever seen!" I spread my hands in disbelief. "And it contains several OTHER heavily armed ships on top of that!"

Captain Reynolds held up his hands, suppressing a smile, "Yes, but it is LESS heavily armed than most carriers. Wait," he paused, "does the Republic use unarmed diplomatic vessels? Shuttles?"

"Yes! How can you expect diplomacy when everyone is armed?"

The room fell silent. I looked around and saw that the humans looked confused at what I had just said. Surely not. I turned to face Director 3.

"How is it possible that you've created a galactic government without unarmed diplomacy?" I asked.

"When we first stepped into the stars we greeted our neighbors with open arms and without weapons. We were emboldened by this decision by the Knuknus, who have always been very peaceful people. However, the Alumari saw our lack of weapons as a weakness and attempted to take advantage. We managed to outpace them technologically, which avoided a war of extinction. After seeing our strength firsthand they decided to join with us and the United Systems was born," Director 3 answered.

He looked very uncomfortable in his armored suit. He shuffled and continued, "Then we encountered the Daluran. We sent an unarmed diplomatic envoy to meet with their government and invite them to join us. They sent our diplomats kidney's back to us, a common insult amongst their kind, and followed it with three fleets."

The Director stood with his hands behind his back, "They took our unarmed diplomacy as an invitation to conquer us. The war was bloody, and we decided it wouldn't happen again. Since then we've made contact with two species using our current diplomatic ships. The Uluna, which have agreed to be uplifted over the next few generations and join us when they're finally space-faring, and the Gont, who joined us without a fight. Well, most of them."

"I understand. Did the Daluran eventually join you

too?" I asked.

"No." Director 3 responded curtly.

I looked at the other humans. All of them were avoiding my eyes. Oh, no...

"The Daluran are no longer a space-faring species," Captain Reynolds said without any of his usual cheer.

"Wait, does that mean you didn't wipe them out?" I asked, hopefully. The eyes still avoided my own.

"We didn't wipe them out," began Director 3, "but we definitely considered it. Their attack cost us trillions of lives, and not just humanity was effected. We fought their fleets back out of our systems, and then destroyed them. Then we destroyed their colonies, one by one. Those worlds are still uninhabitable. The only world we left them with was their home-world, and we left them with just enough of a population to sustain itself. To this day we still have vessels in orbit, destroying anything they try to send into space."

"That's better than wiping them out, though," I said somberly. It sounds like the Republic had it lucky. The majority of our members were peace-loving people and those that weren't opted to be protectors, after a little persuasion. We had wars with each other, sure, but extinction had never been on the table. Why did humanity have it rougher than we did? How was that fair?

"That was back when the United Systems senate controlled the military. The vote to exterminate them failed by two," Director 3 said. "Some still argue that we should crack the planet and be done with it."

Crack the... what? I realized my mouth was open again and shut it, trying not to look surprised. Now that I thought about it, it wasn't exactly extraordinary that they possessed that kind of weaponry. I thought of our own unification wars. Even the bloodiest one only had nine-hundred billion combined casualties, and that war had five factions. How would the Urakari have reacted if our side had taken over a trillion?

It was my turn to avoid eye contact, "I'm ashamed to say that my people wouldn't have even put it to a vote. I understand now. You show some force so that you don't have to show all of your force."

"Precisely," Director 3 responded, "and it must be clear that the USSS Thanatos isn't all of our force. We're currently awaiting the arrival of several vessels that will act as the defense for Sol as we travel to your Republic. I hope you understand that I am providing you with this intel in the hopes that you inform your people of exactly what you see."

"I will," I said.

"I can also give you some information on the Republic. Things that will come in handy to know, but won't be compromising," Kriin added.

I had nearly forgotten she was with me. She had been unusually silent the last few minutes. She probably realized the answers to the questions I was asking before I asked them. Or she already knew somehow.

"That would be great!" Captain Reynolds said, smiling for the first time in several minutes.

Director 3 asked, "What can you give us?"

"The Republic is comprised of eight species. I can give you a dossier on them," Kriin said.

Omega appeared in his holographic form and asked, "I would very much appreciate that, Intel Officer Kriin. Do you need to prepare the dossier or is it on your ship's mainframe?"

For some reason it made me jump. I guess I was just a bundle of nerves. I'd heard about so much death in the last few days that I was afraid that it was lurking around every corner. It probably was.

"I will need time to prepare it. It's not something that we just keep on a flash-drive," Kriin said with a smile. Omega nodded and disappeared.

"Well, have a seat," Director 3 pointed towards a table with a holographic display in the center. "They've just exited warp, and will be taking up positions soon."

We watched as the ships entered visual range. Two of them looked almost exactly like the USSS Thanatos, until I realized that they actually had eight MACs. Considering the relative size of the MACs to the Thanatos, they had to be much, much larger. There were four other ships that were also very large, but not quite as big as the others. Also, they were shaped like a stick instead of a piece of driftwood. No, not a stick, like a squared metal rod with a bunch of little rods and bumps stuck to it. I assumed that they were weapons platforms, which would make these Battleships.

Director 3 gestured and the display zoomed in on one of the larger ships. It was rendered in 3D and began to rotate.

"This is the USSS Leviathan. It is a carrier. For clarification, the Thanatos is also technically a carrier, but its primary duty is diplomacy. The Leviathan's primary duty is war. The Thanatos carries ten frigates and one hundred fighters. The Leviathan carries thirty Destroyers and five hundred fighters. It has point defense systems and, as you can see, eight Magnetically Accelerated Cannons. For close anti-fighter defense it has ninety chain guns, forty-five on each side," Director 3 gestured again and the Thanatos appeared next to the projection. "This is the size comparison of the two ships."

I was right about it being much larger. It absolutely dwarfed the Thanatos.

Director 3 gestured again and the Leviathan was replaced by one of the Battleships, "This is the USSS Tripoli. It is a Battleship. It has PDLs, chain guns, and two hundred and fifty anti-ship armaments of various type. We don't use cruisers anymore because our ability to pinpoint FTL gives these ships an extreme maneuverability advantage."

The Battleship was twice as long as the Thanatos, and half as thick. I couldn't shake the image of a training stick for hand to hand combat. Two hundred and fifty cannons would be extremely punishing for anyone stupid enough to attack one. I tried not to smile as the phrase 'humanity's naughty smacking stick' popped into my head.

Director 3 looked at me pointedly. I could tell he was trying to make eye contact even though I couldn't see where his eyes were, "These vessels were what we were able to recall to Sol in short notice. We fully expect that these ships will either successfully defend this system, or buy us enough time to muster an invasion fleet."

An invasion fleet? It had taken the Republic two years to fight the OU back enough to launch an invasion into their territory for the first time. And the United Systems was planning to invade... while being invaded? Absolute madness.

"You're actually going to invade the OU while defending Sol?" I asked, trying to mask my disbelief.

"Yes. The best defense is an overwhelming offense," Captain Wong said with a smile. "So far their offensives have been unimpressive. We want to show them how it's supposed to be done."

Chapter 13

Subject: Ship-Head Uleena

Species: Urakari

Species Description: Reptilian humanoid, no tail. 5'3" (1.6 m) avg height. 135 lbs (61 kg) avg weight. 105 year life expectancy.

Ship: RSV Lowelana {Fights with Honor}

Location: Sol

List of Republic Species:

Urakari - Both myself and Ship-head Uleena are Urakari. We are omnivorous, but according to Doctor Zickler we're allergic to "fish" and "wheat", and will die if we ingest "soda". Tim says we're "Humanoid".

Isolan - Mammals. They have four arms and two legs. I don't know if that counts as "Humanoid". Very short fur covering everything but their faces. Don't pet them.

Juntor - Amoebic people who use mechanical limbs to get around. They were uplifted by the Isolan before the Isolan joined the Republic. They really like to eat mulch. They also absolutely love to talk about music, but they have a cultural thing against listening to music with other people. Related to their courtship rituals, I think.

Duhliki - Very similar to humans, but their bones come out of their face. On their eyebrows and their chins. They're very sensitive to comments about their face-bones so it's best to just avoid the topic all-together. Unless they ask, in which case vague compliments are necessary. If they ask for specifics, they are trying to start a fight and the subject should be changed unless you want to fight them.

Maltovariakina - They don't have heads. Their voices come from somewhere in their torso. Translators have a tough time with most of them, so they tend to stick to themselves. Might be blind. They also have two limbs which they use for locomotion and grasping. They were uplifted by the Duhliki after the Duhliki had joined the republic, which was illegal to do. It was very scandalous.

Mdkpnz - These guys have two mouths and four eyes. Otherwise they're pretty "humanoid". One mouth is for eating and the other is for burping. Both can talk. They have multiple sacks on their chests which contain digestive enzymes that help them eat stuff. They have to leave the sacks mostly exposed to air for ventilation, and they consider it rude to stare at their chests.

Kinran - As Corporal Simmons would say, "bug people". Ten limbs, all with universal appendages. They can grab things with their feet and walk with their hands. They have compound eyes and a thorax. They are herbivores, and pretty gentle despite looking like the stuff of nightmares. Don't act like they're the stuff of nightmares though, that's very mean and they're super sensitive.

Oyan - Avians. They bear a striking resemblance to the Knuknus of the United Systems. If Corporal Simmons hadn't told me about them before I got to the Thanatos I would have been convinced they were the same thing. The only difference is that the Oyan have a spinal ridge, but you can't really see it unless you look hard. Which is why I asked to look at Nav-Officer Tlakni's back, I swear.

It had taken Kriin almost two days to compile her dossier, and she had given me a copy to brief me on what information she was giving the United Systems. Unfortunately, she had given it to me after she had given it to Director 3 and Omega. She had also given it to many of the captains at their request. I made a mental note to have a discussion with her about professionalism, but was also glad that she felt comfortable communicating with the humans in such a friendly manner.

I reread the dossier. It's not as if she were wrong about any of the information. Well, except I'm pretty sure Doctor Zickler had specified something called "baking soda" and had clarified that whatever normal soda is would be fine for us to consume.

While Kriin had compiled her dossier I had been in talks with Director 3 about what to expect when we enter Republic space. We would reconvene with the Republic and follow our first contact protocols. The best place to do that would be Elira 2, an out of the way system of no strategic importance. It's close enough to the core systems that it shouldn't take more than a few days for a diplomat to arrive by warp, but far enough away that the Thanatos can't scan anything important. Not that they would, but the rules are rules.

The other reason I chose Elira 2 is that it has a station with the ability to repair our FTL drive. I advised Director 3 that I likely wouldn't be in contact with them once docked, and First Contact would probably be handled by the station-master until an official representative arrived. Any face to face contact would have to be done aboard some sort of Republic diplomatic vessel. It was a pretty lengthy conversation.

Elsewhere around the ship, things were pretty tense. The United Systems was expecting an attack at any time, and there was no shortage of pressure on the engineering team to finish up the repairs on our ship. The biggest delay was 'furniture repair'. I said the seats were fine, but apparently they meant the consoles and controls.

I spent most of my time visiting my crew, trying to keep morale up. A lot of us had lost friends, and some of us had lost family. Most of the injured had made full recoveries, but some were having difficulties with shrapnel and broken bones. Kraan was already able to walk around, with some difficulty. Which Kriin was thrilled about. Tim showed her a video of an infant "deer" and she had quickly pointed out the comparison to Kraan. Turns out Captain Wong isn't the only organic being Tim likes teasing.

I visited the morgue, where our dead had been vacuum sealed and frozen for preservation. I had visited them every day since we boarded. Six caskets sat silent, a testament to my command capabilities.

Every day before chow I came here, apologized, and wondered if I could have done anything differently. It hurt, but part of command is knowing that you have to do better next time.

What made it worse was that there should have been ten. Four of my people were floating in the void, and only the Sun knows where. They would only get ceremonial funerals. I hoped their families would grieve them without breaking. My aunt had drank herself to death after my uncle died. He had been on the wrong side of an airlock malfunction and had been shot out before anyone even knew what was happening. Since it was a trade station, their sensors couldn't find his body.

Being able to see your loved one's resting face was painful, but at least it brought a certain closure. Part of me dreaded going home and having to write the families. I wished there was a way I could bring them back, or stay here in Sol, or die to the OU. Anything to avoid the worst part of a ship-head's duty.

Once I finished my contemplations I went to chow. They had a wide variety of food, and I found myself drawn to something called "Spaghetti Americani". I was told that it contained wheat, however, so I grabbed something called a salad. I sat with a human who had grabbed the same thing so I could watch how to eat it. She looked a lot like Captain Wong, but something was a bit different about her face. I couldn't quite place it.

"First, you use your fork, that's the one with the prongs, to give it a good stir," she politely explained.

"Like this?" I asked as I mixed the ingredients with

my fork.

"Exactly! Now you take the container there, yes that one, and you empty its contents over the salad. Yes, like that."

"Thank you, you're very kind."

"No problem," she smiled, turned back to her food, and whispered, "I humbly receive."

I felt like I was witnessing a personal ritual, so I turned to my own meal. Leafy greens with orange roots that were sliced thinly and bits of meat were now covered in an orange sauce called "salad dressing". I took a bite and was surprised at how flavorful it was. I tried each bit individually and found that the flavor was coming from the orange root, the dressing, and the bits of meat. The leafy greens were just as flavorless as they were back home.

The next day I had decided to visit the gym at the invitation of Lance Corporal Johnson when I was interrupted by a message. The repairs of the Lowelana were complete and they wanted my crew and I to prepare to board. Tim helped me brief everyone and I headed for my ship. When I got to engineering I was greeted by Plinas.

He beamed at me and said, "We've finally got her up to snuff. Except for the FTLD, of course. Everything else is just about good as new! I think..."

"Thank you, Plinas. I can't wait to take her for a spin," I replied as Kriin jogged up to meet us.

"Ship-head, everyone else is on their way. It's going

to take some time to load the injured. Looks like I got here first," she grinned. "Permission to come aboard?"

"No, I got here first," I returned her smile. "Permission granted."

I remained at the gangway and greeted the rest of my crew aboard. I somberly waited as the injured and dead were loaded aboard as well. Captain Wong and Lieutenant Babanin had come to see me off. They raised their hands to their foreheads. I mimicked the gesture, and boarded the RSV Lowelana for the first time in days.

I was struck immediately by how clean everything was. The Lowelana was a pretty old vessel, and over time some grime had become somewhat of a fixture. Not anymore, though. I wondered if the United Systems had ship detailing services I could occasionally use. I did a quick inspection of the ship before heading to the bridge. Everything looked better than it had before we got attacked. Eventually I got to the bridge and it did not fail to impress. If I didn't know any better I'd swear they'd even reupholstered my seat.

"Ship-head Uleena, are you and your crew settled in?" Captain Reynolds said over the comm.

"Yes, Captain Reynolds. Thank you for everything," I responded.

"Not an issue, always happy to make new friends. Prepare for warp."

I looked at Liwna and Kriin with a smile. They

practically beamed back at me. Time to go home.

Chapter 13 Informational Insert

Subject: List of Known Species

All measurements are in Earth Standard. Planet and system names all mean "Sun" and "Earth" in their respective alien dialects.

Terms Defined (simply):

Humanoid - Two arms and two legs.
Arachnoid - Eight legs with an exoskeleton.
Centauroid - Four legs, two arms.
Shokanoid - Four arms, two legs.
Amoeboid - A real word, meaning characteristics similar to an amoeba.
Dannoid - Two arms, no legs.
Arthropoid - More than eight legs with an exoskeleton.
Tetrapod - Four limbs used for locomotion with at least two limbs adapted for additional usage.

List of United Systems Species:

Human - Mammalian humanoid, no tail. 6'2" (1.87 m) avg height. 185 lbs (84 kg) avg weight. 170 year life expectancy. Cradle system and planet: Sol, Earth. Notes: A long and combative history has helped humanity develop many clever tactics and weapons for war. Estimated Species Age: 300000 years.

Knuknu - Avian humanoid, non-prehensile tail. 5'10"

(1.7 m) avg height. 84 lbs (38 kg) avg weight. 342 year life expectancy. Cradle system and planet: Eanlil, Yons. Notes: The knuknu enjoyed a far more peaceful history than most, which led to a much sooner than normal space age. Estimated Species Age: 210000 years.

Alumari - Arachnoid, no tail. 5'3" (1.5 m) avg height. 92 lbs (41.7 kg) avg weight. 108 year life expectancy. Cradle System and planet: Monor, Alunis. Notes: The Alumari are much older than other species and took longer to develop due to their extremely bloody history. Their aggression was nurtured rather than natural, and eased off after a world war involving WMDs. Estimated Species Age: 1.2 million years.

Gont - Centauroid, non-prehensile tail. 6'8" (2 m) avg height. 310 lbs (140 kg) avg weight. 162 year life expectancy. Cradle system and planet: Sarn Macri, Gunar. Notes: Similar history as humanity, but fewer weapons of mass destruction fielded. Gont culture is heavily focused on engineering and fighting, with most subcultures abhorring and prohibiting the usage of weapons of mass destruction to win a fight. Estimated species age: 290000 years.

Shitbag - Sackoidal, no tail. 7'2" (2.1 m) avg height. 380 lbs (172 kg) avg weight. Unknown avg life expectancy. Cradle system and planet: Sol, Mars. Notes: Corporal (soon to be private) Simmons. Estimated Species Age: 86 years.

List of Republic Species:

Urakari - Reptilian humanoid, no tail. 5'3" (1.6 m) avg height. 135 lbs (61 kg) avg weight. 105 year life expectancy. Cradle system and planet: Rass, Ureni. Notes: A core member of the Republic. Provides most of the federal fleet and labor force. Has several religions dedicated to the worship of stars. Estimated Species Age: 41000 years.

Isolan - Mammalian Shokanoid, no tail. 5'9" (1.75 m) avg height. 180 lbs (81.6 kg) avg weight. 95 year life expectancy. Cradle system and planet: Lolus, Mant. Notes: The Isolan joined the Republic after the war of unification and quickly became a core member. Does not enjoy being petted. Estimated Species Age: 320000 years.

Juntor - Amoeboid, no tail. 3'6" (1 m) avg height. 42 lbs (19 kg) avg weight. 75 year life expectancy. Cradle system and planet: Lyanora, Lyanor. Notes: The Duhliki uplifted this species prior to joining the Republic. Utilize mechanical aid to interact with non-amoeboid items. Has several cultural taboos regarding music and sound. Estimated Species Age: Unknown.

Duhliki - Mammalian Humanoid, no tail. 6'1" (1.8m) avg height. 181 lbs (82 kg) avg weight. 185 year life expectancy. Cradle system and planet: Zilnma, Zarana. Notes: Initially aggressively expansionist, the Duhliki tempered their aggression after their defeat in the unification war. Suspected to have attempted to start their own version of the Republic. Facial horns play a part in their standards of beauty and mating rituals. Estimated Species Age: 420000

Maltovariakina - Mammalian Dannoid, no tail. 4'1" (1.2 m) avg height. 67 lbs (30 kg) avg weight. 101 year life expectancy. Cradle system and planet: Talira, Rustaya. Notes: Not much is known about this species, as they rarely leave their own space. They have two external appendages that are used for both locomotion and for grasping. Illegally uplifted by the Duhliki. Estimated Species Age: 110000

Mdkpnz - Chordatan Humanoid, no tail. 5'9" (1.7 m) avg height. 153 lbs (69 kg) avg weight. 147 year life expectancy. Cradle system and planet: Ipfrly, Pnzhd. Notes: Has many similar internal characteristics as fish. Two mouths and four eyes. Protuberances upon their chest appear to be evolved from air bladders, but now aid in digestion. Several cultural taboos regarding these sacks. Estimated Species Age: 440000

Kinran - Arthropoid/Tetrapod, no tail. 6'2" avg height. 304 lbs avg weight. 129 year life expectancy. Cradle system and planet: Kinnilis, Kinr. Notes: Ten limbs, all with universal appendages. Each limb's joints all act as wrist joints. Despite being terrifying to most life, the Kinran are herbivorous and empathetic. Most (estimated to be 74%) space-faring Kinran suffer from anxiety disorders. Estimated Species Age: 980000 years.

Oyan - Avian humanoid, non-prehensile tail. 6'1" (1.8 m) avg height. 96 lbs (43 kg) avg weight. 161 year life expectancy. Cradle system and planet: Oyalus, Oyaniz. Notes: A core member of the Republic. Bears a striking resemblance to the Knuknu, with the exception of a small spinal ridge. DNA examination shows a potential relation between the two species. How this is possible is unknown and currently being investigated. Led a mostly peaceful existence until joining the Republic, where they were found to be natural leaders both politically and militarily. Estimated Species Age: 210000 years.

List of Unassociated Species:

Daluran - Mammalian Humanoid, prehensile tail. 7'3 (2.2 m) avg height. 320 lb (145 kg) avg weight. Unknown avg life expectancy. Cradle system and planet: Dal, Daluras. Notes: Not a space-faring species. Has been incarcerated on their cradle planet for 1012 years. The first species other than themselves that humans used weapons of mass destruction against intentionally. During the First Contact wars the Daluran attacked human colonies and enslaved or murdered all the colonists they could find, then bombed the colonies with area denial weapons to prevent further colonization. Saved from extermination by two votes of a relatively young galactic senate. Due to their hostile classification proper census data is unable to be obtained. Estimated Species Age: Unable to be determined.

Uluna - Reptilian Humanoid/Tetrapod, prehensile tail. 5'11" (1.8m) avg height. 6'8" (2 m) avg length. 180 lb (81 kg) avg weight. 63 year avg life expectancy. Cradle system and planet: Inip, Erust (formerly KEPLER 283, KEPLER 283C). Notes: Not a space-faring species. After first contact with the United Systems and several negotiations, the Uluna have agreed to be slowly uplifted and join the US in the stars. The Uluna have refused assisted technological advancement, citing a desire to join their galactic neighbors at their own pace using their own discoveries. Estimated Species Age: 100000 years.

Chapter 14

Subject: Lead Intel-Officer Knuffer

Species: Isolan

Species Description: Mammalian Shokanoid, no tail. 5'9" (1.75 m) avg height. 180 lbs (81.6 kg) avg weight. 95 year life expectancy.

Station: Yritona 3 {Watcher 3}

Location: Elira 2

Yritona 3 was a pretty boring assignment most of the time. Occasionally we'd see something weird, but it would always either be somebody under the influence or a rock. In theory we were a military scouting station designed to watch deep space for enemy contacts. But we were on the wrong side of the Republic to be getting any action. The Omni-Union would have to go well out of their way to get to us and it genuinely wasn't worth it.

We weren't guarding a colony or anything important. We were just here as an early warning system for the populated systems that you would have to warp through us to get to. I reckon that an enemy probably wouldn't even exit warp on their way through.

That's probably why we didn't have any assigned

military vessels. Just scout ships and station defenses. Scout ships are about half the size of normal corvettes and don't have even half as much ordnance, so they're just about useless in a fight. The only real time we see military vessels is when they come for dry-dock repairs, which isn't often.

We've also got civvies. They stop off to trade with each other, fix their ships, and rest on longer journeys. The income the station makes from the civilian ventures is likely what keeps it running, if my pay were any indicator. I gazed out the viewport into the stars in quiet contemplation when the proximity alarm sounded. 'Unknown'?

"Ma'am, unknown contact just exited warp right outside the system," Bleenus, my Duhliki second in command, said as he looked up at me.

I looked at the readout. For sensors, they weren't really making any sense. They were definitely picking up warp leftovers and were definitely picking up an object, but if it weren't for the warp signature I'd swear this thing had to be a small comet. It's too large to be a ship. But unless comets have secretly been sentient this entire time, they don't warp.

"We're gonna need a better look at this thing. Do we have any scanning vessels aboard the station that we can send?" I asked.

Bleenus looked back at his console, "Uh... no ma'am. They've all been sent out by high command. Something about warp fluctuations."

"Damn," I said as a thought occurred to me. "Do we have any diplomatic vessels aboard? If this is an unknown vessel this large, it's either OU in which case we're dead or it's a first contact."

Bleenus shook his head solemnly. Looks like he already had the same thought. Many of the other species in the Republic would be losing their cool in this situation, but the Isolan and Duhliki had something in common. We would much prefer to die in conflict than die in bed. Don't get me wrong, it's not as if all of us feel this way. And it's not as if we all always go looking for fights. But culturally we are geared toward conflict in a way that's rare for other species.

"We don't have any of the diplomatic ones, but we do have a bunch of civvy ships that can do the job in a pinch," he replied. "Might have to give them a good ol' spit polish though."

"Well that's something. Go ahead and wake up the station master."

"Yes, ma'am."

As he ran off to complete his task I looked back at the console. What the hell is this thing? Why did it leave warp so far away? Normally that would immediately rule out OU, but I knew better than to think I understood those crafty bastards. Could this be a weaponized comet? Are they dumb enough to throw a big space-rock at us? Probably not, even this fringe station has enough ordnance to turn it into pebbles that our shields would make short work of.

Then the object began to move toward us. It was moving fast for an object its size. I put two of my arms on my head to help me focus as the other two got to work on our scanners to track the object and hopefully get a better read on it.

"Intel-Lead Knuffer, are you there?" the station-master's timid voice came over the comm.

Station-master Nixt is a Kinran. The Kinran are known for being one of the least aggressive but most intimidating species in the Republic. This is because most sentients have fears regarding bugs that date back to when we were barely our own species, and the Kinran are particularly terrifying to look at. They have ten limbs which have four joints each. These joints don't function like elbows, though. They function as wrists. Very limber wrists, at that. Watching one work at a station is both unnerving and impressive.

Due to their scary looks and gentle nature, they typically don't rise in rank. Nixt was an exception to this. Despite his protests he had been forced into the rank of station-master by the previous station-master. The old SM had been impressed with Nixt's work ethic and had demanded his promotion. Honestly, everyone on the station adores Nixt. From afar.

"Yes, Station-Master Nixt," I replied.

"What's the situation? Bleenus was speaking very quickly and I think I heard something about a first contact?" Nixt said with a barely controlled panic.

"Well, an object the size of a small comet just exited warp right outside the system. As you know, comets don't warp..."

"Actually they can! If they manage to enter a wormho..." Nixt began excitedly.

"A wormhole, yeah, yeah I get that. And while that is technically a type of warp it doesn't leave this kind of signature when it exits the other side of the wormhole. Also, the object was stationary for a time and is now traveling toward us," I interrupted.

"Oh," the stationmaster said bleakly. "And you're certain this isn't the Omni-Union?"

"Nope. Not certain of anything at this point. But the OU aren't dumb enough to waste resources throwing rocks at us. Which means that, like it or not, this big boy is a ship. And if it's an OU ship, we're dead. Simple as that. So, we might as well assume it's an unknown species and prepare first contact protocols, right?" I said, beaming at how calmly intelligent I was being.

The comm was silent for a time as the station master digested this logic. Poor Nixt, this was supposed to be an easy assignment. I guess there's no such thing.

Finally Nixt said, "I can get behind that logic. While I don't cherish the idea of going down without a fight, or going down at all for that matter, I must admit there isn't anything our station can do against a ship the size of a comet."

"A small comet. But you're right," I said as the proximity alarm sounded again. This time, it pinged a... friendly?

I looked back to the console and saw a smaller object

leaving the larger one. The scanners identified it as the RSV Lowelana. Not a ship that I'd heard of, so I pulled up its service record. A bunch of it was classified, go figure, but it wasn't due to report for another week. So they went on whatever mission they went on and found THAT. But why were they... Attached? Docked? Can you even dock two ships in warp? Before my head began swimming I forwarded the data to the station-master.

"Oh? Well this is good news, right?" Nixt said.

"Maybe? It's definitely one of ours, but I don't know what mission it was on or why it's with that ship. Could be that the big one caught ours and took it over," I replied. "Or it could be that they were guiding it here in accordance with first contact protocol, but that doesn't explain why the sensors only showed the one contact at first. Either way, if they're alive they've got one hell of a story to tell."

"Right..." I could tell that I hadn't comforted Nixt at all. "Okay. Okay. Well we're still hoping for the best, right?"

"Right. Cuz otherwise we're dead," I responded.

"Right. Yeah, so we need to follow FCP. We'll need a diplomatic vessel... Alright, I'm sure we can commandeer a civilian shuttle for the task," Nixt said. "I'm sending Bleenus down to the hanger to get started on that."

"Understood," I said as I glanced at the readout again. The alien vessel was trailing behind the Lowelana, and they were about to enter comms range.

"What do you want me to do when they enter comms range?" I asked.

"If they hail us, patch it through to me. If they don't, then hail them. Either way I want to talk to the ship-head," Nixt said with a mask of authority hiding his obvious nervousness.

I was immediately glad I asked because the RSV Lowelana hailed us before I could respond to the station-master.

"This is Ship-Head Uleena of the RSV Lowelana hailing the Yritona 3 station. Please come in, Yritona 3."

I thumbed the key to answer, "RSV Lowelana please halt your course and tell your accompaniment to do the same. We weren't expecting visitors. I'm putting you through to Station-Master Nixt, acknowledge."

"Acknowledged."

As I transferred the hail to the station-master I watched the Lowelana slow to a stop. It took about as long as it normally did, and the reason I noticed that was that the massive hulk of a ship stopped almost immediately. Great, not only do they build bigger than we do but they build better than we do. I secretly hoped that their braking thrusters were the only tech they had that was more advanced than ours.

Even if they joined the Republic, if they were advanced enough it would cause a shift in the power dynamic that would be very frustrating for the other member species. A lot of people have this belief that seniority should matter, but it doesn't. When the Oyan had joined the Republic their massive population and territory had caused them to have a lot of senators and thereby a lot of influence. More than most of the member species, and there had been a lot of unrest.

But for a species to be represented properly, seniority couldn't matter. A species with a handful of systems and a population of 2 trillion shouldn't be allowed to tell a species with dozens of systems and dozens of trillions of citizens how to live their lives.

The station-master interrupted my thoughts on democratic representation, "Knuffer, the RSV Lowelana is going to need clearance to dock at the repair bay. Their FTLD isn't working. They'll also need access to the station. Ten special guests, eighteen standard guests. Six shipments."

"Understood, on it," I said. Special guests are wounded, shipments are dead. I don't know why we used code to talk about it. Maybe it was because it felt disrespectful, or because calling them wounded or dead made it too real. Whatever the case, I found myself wondering how it happened. Was it the aliens?

"Also, the alien ship is called the USSS Thanatos. Ship-head Uleena will be briefing me once they dock. I've given the go ahead for the Thanatos to maintain distance. Not that they COULD dock, even if they wanted to," Nixt continued.

"Yeah, they're way too big for that. Alright, I'll keep an eye on them. Let me know what Uleena says," I replied. "I'm certain it's going to be interesting."

"Yes," Nixt said. "Let's hope it's interesting in a good way, though."

Chapter 15

Subject: Ship-Head Uleena

Species: Urakari

Species Description: Reptilian humanoid, no tail. 5'3" (1.6 m) avg height. 135 lbs (61 kg) avg weight. 105 year life expectancy.

Ship: RSV Lowelana {Fights with Honor}

Location: Elira 2

I had warned the Thanatos that there may be delays in communicating with them because of our first contact protocols, but I still felt a certain sense of unease. I had let the aliens get my hopes up about our war with the OU. If they help us we're damn near certain to win. But certain anxieties were haunting me now that I wasn't with them anymore. What if the United Systems decide to just go home? What if our diplomat messes things up with them and they declare war? What if they mess things up with the diplomat and WE declare war?

"Ship-head Uleena this is station-master Nixt, please respond," the hail saved me from further spiraling.

"This is ship-head Uleena," I replied.

"You have clearance to dock at repair bay 2. Your

special guests will be escorted to their quarters, and your shipments will be delivered," Nixt said. "Please come see me when you have a chance."

"Understood, ship-head Uleena out."

I hated the code words for injured and dead, and most places didn't use them anymore. It's only out of the way stations that still use them. I remember being told that they had originally been used to avoid a panic in case civilians were listening in on the comms. That would make sense except that civilians have the Right to Access, so they get to see our casualty counts in near-real time. R2A has been around forever, so it was hard to imagine this crap was just a relic.

Kraan was injured and Jular, his off-shift, was dead so I was manning the nav console. If it were standard maneuvers, or even standard docking, pretty much any crewman would have been able to handle it. Internal docking is a bit more difficult. In theory, the computer knows where the dock is and where the ship is and where the clamps are supposed to go. In practice, it's usually off by an inch or two. That can cause damage to the ship and to the dock. So the pilot has to know where the ship is and where the dock is and where the clamps are supposed to go, and make sure the computer doesn't fuck it up.

It had been a few years, but it was still muscle memory. The computer was a tad too deep and had overcorrected our Yaw, so I input the corrections and slowly docked the Lowelana. Come to think of it, it hadn't even been docked in the USSS Thanatos, it had been grabbed and 'scooped up'. That still felt wrong on a very deep level.

"Attention all crew," I said into the intercom, "we are officially docked at Yritona 3 in the Elira 2 system. While we're docked you are off-duty, but you must remain aboard the ship. I want you all on your best behavior. If you're good, it will be easier to get some shore leave approved."

A cheer ran through the ship. Sure, they had just had a fantastic adventure aboard the Thanatos and the Yritona was likely to pale in comparison, but cheering at shore leave is tradition.

"I will be meeting with the station-master as the repair crew comes aboard. Stay out of their way so we can have FTL back," I smiled as I paused for dramatic effect. "Dismissed."

Another cheer rang through the ship. I advised Liwna that he had command and went to the airlock. As I walked down the gangway I felt relieved that it wasn't a plastic tube and had gravity, unlike the last time I had exited the vessel. An Oyan engineer was waiting for me with a salute.

"Permission to board, ship-head?" she asked.

"Permission granted. Fix her up good, you hear?" I smiled and returned the salute.

"Yes, sir!" she said and moved to let me pass.

I got my bearings and found the exit into the station proper. As walked I wondered where my escort could be. Surely Nixt didn't expect me to just wander the station until I found him? I looked around and saw a

Duhliki running toward me. I stopped and waited for him.

"Are you the ship-head?" he asked between breaths.

"Yes, I'm ship-head Uleena. Nice to meet you..." I paused, waiting for an introduction.

"Bleenus. I'm with intel, but we don't have a big staff so I'm the errand boy today. Do you mind if we relax a moment? I've been running for a while," he said as he doubled over and rested his hands on his knees.

I nodded and we waited for him to catch his breath. Once he was finished he gestured for me to follow him. He gave me an abridged tour of the station that was limited to the path we had to take. He explained what each place was and gave a brief history about it. Once we were outside the station-master's office he turned to me.

"By the way, I don't know if you know this but Nixt is a Kinran," he whispered. "He's very nice, though. Don't be afraid."

"I've served with Kinran before, it won't be a problem," I said with a smile.

It was a pretty fair warning. The Kinran would startle anyone who wasn't used to them, and some who were. It always felt like they shouldn't be able to move the way that they do. They're a perfect case for why you shouldn't judge solely on appearance because the majority of them were very polite and shy. As a matter of fact, a Kinran commander was a novelty.

In a way it made sense, because they could file paperwork faster than most commanders could. Their compound eyes and ten arms made it a breeze for them. Unfortunately their personality often conflicted with the duties of command. Namely, telling people what to do when they don't want to do it and disciplinary action. You also don't see them in soldier positions. Even though they could field more weaponry, the thought of taking another's life was often too much for them.

Bleenus nodded and ushered me inside. Nixt was sitting behind a circular desk designed to make the most of his limbs. The station master gestured for me to sit and Bleenus left us to talk.

"Hello, ship-head Uleena. Nice to meet you in person," he said.

"The feeling is mutual station-master Nixt," I said, wondering how he was going to broach the subject at hand.

"Let's talk about the aliens."

That was blunt.

"Yes," I said. "First, the ship is called the USSS Thanatos and it is a carrier."

"A carrier of what?" he asked.

"A carrier of other space-faring vessels. Specifically, ten frigates. They also consider it to be their diplomatic vessel."

"Ten... frigates?" he asked. His limbs and mandibles

twitched nervously. That was the only way you could tell that a Kinran was shocked, aside from their voice. They don't have eyelids or eyebrows to raise. You also couldn't tell where they were looking because they were looking everywhere. Compound eyes.

"Yes. They come in peace, though. Their war vessels are much more terrifying," I said, remembering what I had seen.

"I take it they are a very advanced race?" Nixt said.

"Races. There are multiple. The second thing is that they represent another galactic governing entity known as the United Systems."

"There's another Republic?" his limbs twitched even more frequently.

"I'm not sure if the US is a republic or not. I know they have multiple governing agencies. One of which is called The Directorate. They run the military. One of the Directors is aboard the Thanatos and will be handling first contact," I said, knowing what the reaction would be.

"Their military handles their first contact?" he asked in a shrill voice. I was going to give this poor Kinran heart failure.

"Yes, but they have good reason for that. Their side of the galaxy is a little bit harsher than ours, and they've had to fight for survival very hard. I assure you that they come in peace, and if we play our cards right they'll help us with the Omni-Union. They've already begun planning an invasion of OU space."

He held up eight of his limbs to stop me, "Okay, okay. Hold on. Before you continue I want you to know that I brought you up here to ask you for a favor."

"What would that be?" I asked with a genuine confusion.

"First Contact Protocol dictates that any meetings done with aliens must involve a Republic diplomat and whoever governs the system that the meeting takes place in. Meaning... me," He paused. "I am a Kinran and we're known for our off-putting appearance and timid nature. The exact opposite of what you want in a diplomat."

I nodded my understanding.

"The thing is, there is a provision that exempts Kinran from this duty for that reason. So the duty falls to whomever I elect it to. I want you to do it," Nixt said as he gestured to me with two limbs.

"I'm not in your chain of command, station-master," I said.

"I know, and I would have my intel-head do it but I want her on scanners just in case something terrible happens. I've already cleared it with the diplomatic corps. Since you're not under my command, I'm asking rather than telling, though," he twiddled his limbs nervously.

"Yeah. Okay I'll do it. They already know me quite well so it shouldn't be a problem," I said, consigned to my fate. I never, ever, in all of my life wanted to be a diplomat.

"Thank you!" he jumped forward and shook my hand. I managed to suppress my natural reaction at this and shook his grasper.

As he took his seat again he said, "Good, good. The diplomat will be here in two days. Should we quarantine part of the station and grant the aliens access?"

"The Thanatos has very good amenities and is well-stocked. They'll likely decline an invitation to the station. They want a truce as much as we need one, and less can go wrong if they remain aboard their ship. Still, it wouldn't be a bad idea to extend an invitation to show peaceful intentions. They know how freaked out we are by their tech and... ways."

Nixt nodded and said, "Gotcha. Alright, we'll extend an invitation and see. Also, command wants a full report from you as soon as possible. They're willing to forego a full debrief in light of the present circumstances, but they still need their paperwork."

"Understood, I'll do it as soon as I can."

Nixt gave me the unnerving Kinran equivalent of a smile, "So, ship-head, tell me about what happened."

"Alright. We were sent to investigate some warp fluctuations..." I began my tale.

Chapter 16

Subject: Captain Neil

Species: Human

Species Description: Mammalian humanoid, no tail. 6'2" (1.87 m) avg height. 185 lbs (84 kg) avg weight. 170 year life expectancy.

Ship: USSS Armstrong

Location: Classified

My first command and I'm already behind enemy lines in what has to be the worst detail a Captain can get. Scouting. I had no experience in scouting. Before I made captain I had served aboard the USSS Nidhogg, which hardly ever does anything. And before that I had station duty. I hadn't seen any sort of action, let alone action behind enemy lines.

The worst part was that the assignment was to the ship. I got dragged along for the ride because someone in charge decided it would be funny to have Captain Neil command the USSS Armstrong. Thanks to our last name, everyone in our family was familiar with the first man on the moon. When I had first got the orders I cringed when I saw the ship's name. Thankfully, the crew is competent and the Armstrong is rigged for the job.

We have several types of sensors that allow us to get a fairly detailed view on a system without having to be anywhere near it. Our orders are to exit warp in dark space, scan a system, and move on unless we see something that requires further investigation. We've effectively censused eighteen systems in the two days we've been at it.

The stress of the assignment had begun to get to me. Four out of the eighteen had the Omni-Union ships we'd heard about, and two of those had weird warp fluctuations that would have ripped us to shreds if we had jumped into the system. Thankfully we were far enough away that they didn't detect us, or if they did they decided not to do anything about it.

"Bubkis in this one too, Captain," Lieutenant Lee said.

"We'll hopefully see that a lot," I replied.

"Well I, for one, am hoping we find something exciting soon," Lee grinned at me.

I grabbed the bridge of my nose to demonstrate my exasperation, "Lieutenant Lee, our task is to map out the enemy territory to the best of our ability. It's not to go sight seeing. If we see something interesting, that's probably going to be a bad thing."

"Yes, sir," she replied in a playfully dejected way.

I knew that Lee knew why we were out here and how important the mission was. I also knew that Lee could tell how stressed I was about being able to perform said mission, which is why she was being playful. If she could tell, so could other members of the bridge crew. Her playful banter was a way of cheering me up and warning me that my mask of authority was slipping. I double checked the findings and saw nothing.

"Bubkis it is," I said. "Alright. On to the next system."

I watched the slight increase in activity amongst my crew as they prepared the warp. Omega had given us specific systems to check based on the incoming trajectory of the fleet that had attacked Sol, so there weren't a lot of calculations to do. I didn't really know what to think of Omega. I was fairly familiar with him because he interacts with the Nidhogg a lot. Every time we had a conversation he had appeared as a Grim Reaper, a very old personification of mortality.

Honestly, it was in bad taste. He doesn't have a body, and as far as I know he can't die. It almost seemed like a taunt, but I got the feeling that he just thought it was cool. Or maybe it's symbolism, because he was designed to take out the other AI when they went rogue. I guess it could be because he's their personification of death. Still, he probably just does it because he thinks it looks cool.

A slight lurch from the ship as we exited warp at our destination brought me back to reality. I watched as our scanners examined the system in question. Four planets, a yellow sun, and a bunch of wreckage. Several debris fields worth. One of the planets was in the habitable zone, and appeared as if it had vegetation. I took another look at the debris fields.

"What the hell?" I asked no one in particular.

"Sir," began Lieutenant Junior Grade Flowers, "we have several debris fields and a planet that has signs of civilization. We've also got warp fluctuations, but they're weird."

"Weird how?"

"There are a bunch of them. As if there are a lot of different sources," he responded. "Eighteen... no, nineteen total."

"Well, that would suggest that the enemy is amassing here," I said as I sat forward.

Lee looked at me, "No enemy contacts. No ships at all except for the broken up ones in the debris fields. I think we're looking at the remnants of a fight."

I looked back at the readings. She was right, there wasn't a single functioning ship in the space of this system. There weren't even any signs of functional satellites or stations. For a moment I wondered about cloaking technology, but then I thought better of it. We've got every type of scanner. You can do a lot of things to look invisible to a lot of different scanners, but you can't do all of them at once. We've tried.

It was Flowers' turn to look at me, "Sir, I suggest we get a closer look. I can't quite pinpoint what is causing the warp fluctuations. If we could get scans of it..."

"It could prove invaluable. Plus we've been told to try to get detailed scans of any inhabited planets we come across, just in case it's their home-world. If they even have one," I frowned slightly. "Take us in as far as we need to go. Don't answer any hails and stay away from the debris fields. I've heard they might have nasty surprises."

Lee had received the same briefing I had and grimaced. Nuclear and antimatter mines were nasty. Our shields should be able to withstand a few, but any more than that and we would be dead. There would be no rescue. Our calls for aid would take a long time to reach US space, and they likely wouldn't be willing to send a team. Whatever situation we reported could have changed drastically, and we're in enemy territory. I looked around, and saw the grim faces of a bridge crew who had realized the same thing.

We approached the system on thrust. As we got nearer, we could make out that the debris were from multiple ships of multiple types. It looked more and more like Lt. Lee was right about there having been a fight. There were also bits of stray ordnance, and the traps that we had been warned about.

"Sir, I've reconstructed a cruiser, and it matches the OU ship profile," Flowers said.

"Good work. Definitely avoid the debris fields," I ordered.

I waited and waited as our ship grew closer and closer. I watched as we first entered the warp fluctuations, then the system itself.

"Okay, that should be close enough Flowers," I said. "Let's see what we can see and get out of here."

We were now close enough to pick up bodies on the sensors. No emissions of any kind. All dead, floating aimlessly in space. I turned my attention to the scans of the planet. We were close enough for a visual, but I wish we weren't. Destruction was everywhere. Buildings were burned out and blown to pieces, corpses both organic and robotic littered the streets. Or rather, what was left of the streets.

It had been a long time since the US had performed orbital bombardments, but we had seen them in training. I recognized these scenes as the aftermath. My eyes widened as I realized that it was the same no matter where I looked. Cities, towns, fields, stretches of wilderness. The orbital bombardment had been indiscriminate. The bastards had surrounded the planet and bombed it to oblivion.

I zoomed in on part of a city to get a better look at the dead. That was a mistake. The organics were humanoid, with tentacles on their faces. Rot had only just begun to set in, confirming that this had happened somewhat recently. Men, women, and children were strewn across the landscape. Most were missing portions of their bodies, or were scattered everywhere. I stopped on one that was intact with its eyes open. They were jet black. I wondered if they were like that when they were alive.

Then I noticed that the alien I was looking at hadn't died from the orbital bombardment. It was still relatively in one piece, and its wound looked like one from an energy weapon. Lying next to it was what appeared to be a rifle of some sort. I panned over to one of the robots. It was lying facedown, and next to it was a different type of rifle. They had been fighting each other? The orbital bombardment must have been proceeded by an invasion. But then, where are the winners?

I was baffled until a horrible thought occurred to me. Xenocide. The bombardment and invasion had been to exterminate, not to conquer. I couldn't help but express my horror with a small sound. I looked up and realized that everyone else was looking at the same thing and coming to the same conclusion. A war of extinction, something that had been avoided at all cost in our history. We had even forgiven the baby eaters, the Daluran, to avoid having one over our heads.

This... This was the horror we had avoided. How can something live with itself knowing that it's done this? I felt myself involuntarily gag as I realized that my ancestors very nearly did something as atrocious as what I was looking at.

I felt an immense shame as I realized that I might be related to something that said yes during the Daluran vote. Even the children? What kind of sick demented fuckwit would ever think that this was okay? That it was justified? Only comfy, cozy fat-fuck politicians who never bled a day in their life would be okay with this. That and sick fucks who need an entire team of therapists to even hope to be normal.

I saved the data. When we got back I would make sure Omega got this. I'll beg him to never let us do this. I'll give anything to be able to be certain that we never turn into the lowly creatures that would kill children just for the sake of winning a war. I felt a tear roll down my cheek, and a sniff from the bridge crew reminded me where I was.

I wiped my tear and looked up, "We all know what we're seeing here. We know it in our hearts, and our hearts are screaming at us that it's wrong. And it is. Those that did this will be punished. We will punish them with all of our might, and we WILL make them regret this. Even if they can't regret now, we will teach them," I slammed my clenched fist into my armrest, "WE WILL POUND IT INTO THEM!"

I stood up, "We nearly did this to the Daluran. But even back then more than half of us knew it was wrong. We will save this data and return it to the United Systems. The near half of us that voted yes will see what it is they were voting for. Until then, back to work. Flowers, have you turned up anything?"

"Um... Yes, yes sir. The warp fluctuations are coming from machinery," he responded, wiping his face.

I sat back down, "Any idea how it works?"

"No, I'm not an engineer, sir. But I've scanned it thoroughly enough that we should be able to extrapolate schematics."

"Sir," Lee interrupted, "what about Earth?"

My blood ran cold. The current population of Earth was three hundred and twelve billion. They wouldn't go down without a fight, but that many people...

"We'll give them the best chance we can. I want detailed scans of everything. Extrapolate enemy ship profiles and armament," I said as I looked back at the screen. "We will do everything in our power to make sure this doesn't happen again."

"Sir, by the time a message with this much data reaches Sol the assault will likely have taken place. The only way we'll be able to get this intel back to them would be to abandon our current mission and return to Sol with the data," Flowers said.

I looked at our list of systems. Four left. If we had more left than that I would say to abandon the mission and return to Sol with haste. But four will only take a few more hours if we're fast about it. Technically we were supposed to continue scouting based on our own readings after we finished with these systems. I think command will forgive us, though.

There's no way they're expecting the enemy to be xenocidal. They're probably thinking that the system will be occupied by enemy forces and the occupants will be enslaved until we take the system back. Hell, they might chew me out for finishing the mandatory part of the mission. That's what I'll hope for, at least.

"Okay, we'll finish the census and make speed back to Sol. How are the readings coming along?" I asked.

"We'll have them done momentarily. Should we..." Flowers paused for a moment, "should we do something about the planet?"

"There's nothing we can do," I said with grim finality. "We can't accept any hails and if we start hailing and the enemy is still down there, we're compromised. If there are any survivors, at least they're on their home planet. Air to breathe and food to eat. There's not much more we can do for them than that."

"Aye sir," Flowers said.

I turned back to the images of the planet's surface. I had been nervous about fighting the enemy before. Scared, even. Now I can't imagine anything I want more than to eradicate them from our universe. The rage that welled up inside me quickly overtook the sadness and horror I had been feeling. The only thing that pissed me off more than what they'd done was that I couldn't make them suffer for what they'd done.

I ran a quick tally simulation on the data from the planet. The estimate came to 32 billion. Damn. Anything over 20 billion is usually a home world for a space-faring species. I silently hoped they had colonies out there somewhere, but doubted it. Humanity hadn't begun extrasystem colonization until we had hit around fifty billion people on Earth. By then we had multiple habitats on Mars, Titan, and Luna as well. The Knuknus and the Gont had followed a similar path. The Alumari were an outlier because they were insectoid.

I double checked our scans. There were no other signs of habitation in this system. It was extremely unlikely that these people had extrasystem colonies, because they didn't even have intersystem colonies. I turned my attention to our extrapolations of their ship schematics. They had been fairly advanced, too. The enemy fleet must have been massive.

"Captain, we've finished the scans of the wreckage. We're good to go, sir," Lee said.

"Roger. Let's move on, then. Next system, as fast as we can manage," I ordered.

The next system contained nothing of note. The one after that contained a small fleet of OU vessels and a few uninhabited planets. They didn't notice us. The third system contained a larger fleet, but still no inhabited planets. We double checked to make sure that there weren't any ships that didn't match what we had scanned. There weren't, so we moved on to the fourth and final system.

As the ship jostled slightly from the exit of warp I felt that something was wrong. I don't know if I had caught a glimpse of the scanners out of the corner of my eye, or if it was some sort of sixth sense. Maybe I had felt the tension that suddenly emanated from the crew that was monitoring the sensors.

"What is it?" I asked urgently.

"Sir, there's an absolutely massive amount of OU ships in this system. And two... no, five planets with signs of habitation," Flowers said with a hint of fear in his voice.

"Do they see us?"

Flowers was silent for a few moments.

"Lieutenant Junior Grade Flowers, DO THEY SEE US?" I asked louder.

"N-no. No sir, they don't appear to have noticed our presence," he finally answered.

"Good. Let's get what we need and go to Sol.

Quickly, people!" I ordered.

The crew set about their tasks with gusto. We got profiles for each ship. There were around thirty-five hundred ships. We compared the profiles to what we had on record. They had battleships, cruisers, frigates, destroyers, and corvettes. The corvettes that matched our profiles were the warp disruptor ships. They were inactive. The ones that didn't match the profiles looked like lightly armed shuttles. Light transport ships, most likely.

There was only one of the big types that didn't match our profiles. It also didn't seem to match the designs of their other ships very much. It looked... fatter than the other ships. Bloated, even. As if one of their battleships were in the final stages of a pregnancy. Kind of like when you compare our battleships ships to our...

"Carriers," I said.

"I think so too, sir. There are ten of them," Lee said.

"What about the planets?" I asked.

"We can't get close enough for a detailed scan, but there are extensive signs of habitation on five of them. Three out of the five would not suit organic life," Flowers responded.

"What does that mean?"

"Well, sir, one of the planets is extremely toxic. Another doesn't have a readable atmosphere. The third is a frozen planet that has parts of it reaching true zero. Also, the OU are not attacking these habitats," Flowers said.

"So it's likely the robots are responsible for the habitats?" I asked with amazement.

"Yes sir. But we're not able to get a definite read on the structures," Flowers said. "Also, there appear to be space stations that are manufacturing new ships. I'm counting... twelve."

This was huge. Five colonized planets that the machines weren't attacking. A fleet of three thousand five hundred ships. And on top of all that, ship-yards. Even if this isn't their home system, destroying it will definitely set them back. It was unlikely they would let it go without a fight, though. I remembered the briefing. Two hundred and fifty million enemy ships. If they all converged here we would need to use the dreadnaught. The marines aren't going to be happy that they won't get to put boots on the ground.

"Alright everyone. Finish up the intel gathering," I said. "Let's get back to Sol."

Chapter 17

Subject: Ship-Head Uleena

Species: Urakari

Species Description: Reptilian humanoid, no tail. 5'3" (1.6 m) avg height. 135 lbs (61 kg) avg weight. 105 year life expectancy.

Ship: RSV Lowelana {Fights with Honor}

Location: Elira 2

"The diplomat's ship arrived a while ago, you know," Liwna said.

"Well it wouldn't be the government if we weren't kept waiting," Kriin replied.

We had been waiting three days for the diplomat to arrive. It was a nervous wait for me, because the last thing I ever wanted to be was a diplomat. It's far too complicated. Trying to appease all of the different cultures of all of the different species while simultaneously trying to milk them for all their worth seems like a lot more work than being shot at and shooting back.

I could barely keep track of who was angry at who and why on my own crew, let alone the entire galaxy. And now we're dealing with what someone could easily mistake as an alliance of warrior races. I sincerely hoped that they had sent someone extremely competent. Director 3 seemed pretty reasonable, but we shouldn't press our luck.

Most of my crew had taken the shore leave that station-master Nixt had offered but Kriin, Liwna, and I remained aboard the Lowelana. I was far too nervous to have any fun, and my bridge officers had decided that I needed company. Kraan was still in med-bay relearning his motor skills. It was coming along nicely, and he should be able to return to duty any day now. I wondered who I should make my new second, or if one would simply be assigned to me.

"Ship-head Uleena, the diplomat is here and waiting for you. Come meet us in my office please," station-master Nixt said over the comm.

"Understood, on my way," I replied.

I shrugged at Kriin and Liwna. They returned the gesture. I got up and started to exit the ship. Along the way I passed the engineering team that was handling the repairs. They'd had to order parts for the FTLD, which had arrived before the diplomat. Now they were working feverishly to complete the repairs. They assured me that they would be done by the end of the day today, and I was inclined to believe them.

I passed a few of my crew on the way to Nixt's office, giving them a wave which they returned. I had written the letters to the families informing them of the passing of their loved ones, and our dead had been sent off. I found myself hoping that they had found some peace as I knocked on the door to the station-master's office.

"Come in," Nixt's muffled voice came through the door.

I entered and saw Nixt sitting in his chair. An Urakari in the diplomatic corps uniform was sitting across from him. As they turned my jaw nearly dropped off my face in shock.

"Hey, Uleena! Long time no see!" Ulooni said.

My mother had written me a while ago letting me know that my sister had become a politician. I had thought at the time that she had meant that Ulooni had become a mayor of some colony city. The diplomatic corps was a very high ranking position in a politician's career, and most diplomats eventually become senators. I was very surprised to see that my sister had become an ambassador so quickly. I cursed myself for not writing my mother more often.

"Hi Ulooni... this is a surprise," I said after swallowing a couple of times.

"I can tell," she laughed, "I haven't seen you in... what, thirteen, fourteen years?"

"Yeah, since I entered officer school," I said.

Nobody would be able to tell we were siblings at a glance. My scales were brown and green and hers were purple and blue. I was a good four inches taller than her, and she was far thinner than I. The only way that you could tell without being told is the Ul family syllable in our names. But even then you'd assume we were cousins, not siblings born two days apart from one another. I was older, of course.

"So, tell me about the aliens. How's their temperament?" she asked in a professional manner while simultaneously maintaining her joyful demeaner. Creepy.

"Right, yeah. They are friendly enough. My crew and I would be dead without their help. They fed us, treated our injured, and even repaired the majority of the damage to our ship."

"Wait, did they scan our tech?" she asked with alarm.

"No, they intentionally left our Faster-than-Light Drive in its damaged state to avoid doing exactly that. Not that learning about our FTLD would have helped them much," I said with a shrug.

"Right, says here they're more advanced than we are."

"More advanced is an understatement. They are able to precision warp in-system during a ship to ship battle. Our FTLD would have gone critical if we had even so much as tried that," I said, gesturing for emphasis, "and their weapons are eons ahead of ours as well. They were very clear that they want us to know that they do not want a fight, and a fight would be very bad for us."

"Okay. Well if they don't want a fight then what do they want from us?" she asked.

"I don't know for certain, that's why you're here," I said with a bit of sarcasm.

Nixt laughed a little, "Indeed. They've been waiting for three days, we really should get things moving ambassador Ulooni. Are you ready for contact?"

My sister sighed, "As ready as I'll ever be."

Nixt hit a button on his desk and we all waited in silence for the Thanatos to answer the hail.

"This is Captain Reynolds of the USSS Thanatos. How can I help you, station-master?"

"Hello Captain Reynolds. Our diplomat, ambassador Ulooni has arrived. We're ready for the first contact meeting whenever you are," Nixt responded.

"Excellent. I'll let Director 3 know and he'll get back to you in a little bit. Ambassador Ulooni huh? Are they related to ship-head Uleena by any chance?" Reynolds said with a chuckle implying that he was joking.

Nixt held up his mandibles in a smile, "Yes, actually. She's his sister."

"And we're both sitting right here, Captain Reynolds," I warned him. I hadn't got a chance to know Reynolds all that much but humans seemed to have a crass sense of humor at the most inappropriate of times. Also a keen sense of perception.

"Ah, hello ship-head. Hope you're doing well! How's the repairs coming along?"

"They're nearly finished. The engineers told me they'd be done by the end of the day."

"Good to hear. Anyways, Director 3 just messaged me saying he's ready to take over the call. I'm going to transfer you now," Reynolds said.

A ping came from the comm indicating a new call had connected.

"This is Director 3 of the United Systems." Came the distorted voice of the man in armor.

"Hello Director 3, this is station-master Nixt. Our diplomat has arrived. You'll be meeting with ship-head Uleena and ambassador Ulooni," Nixt explained.

"Understood. Can we meet aboard the station?"

"Um," interrupted Ulooni, "we wouldn't typically want to meet on something that is armed. This station has defensive weaponry."

"I'm aware," said Director 3. "The weaponry aboard the station consists of four 50mm chain guns and two guided missile launchers, correct?"

All three of us looked at each other with wide eyes. Then Ulooni and I looked at station-master Nixt questioningly.

"Yes," he replied. "That's correct."

"Then that will work for us. Not to offend you, but such light armaments are not a concern to us."

Ulooni turned to me and mouthed, "Light armaments?"

I nodded emphatically.

Nixt looked at Ulooni cautiously, "I personally have no problem welcoming aboard a small party for the meeting, if that's alright with the ambassador."

"Yeah... Yes, if you insist then that will be fine," she said.

"Excellent," Director 3 said. "I will be accompanied by Captain Haoyu Wong, who is the commanding officer of the rescue team, and Lieutenant Sergey Babanin who made face to face first contact. I assume you will keep a record of our meeting?"

"Yes, and we will gladly offer you a copy as well," Ulooni said.

"That won't be necessary. The reason I want to meet aboard the station that your ships cannot support our software. I've been assured that the station can. Would it be okay if one of our programs were to record our meeting?"

He meant one of the AI. Ulooni looked at me quizzically. I saw a chance for a prank on my sister. Knowing the humans, it would amuse them as well. What kind of big brother would I be if I didn't take this chance?

"That should be fine," I said to her.

"Okay," she said, "a guide will meet you at the airlock and we will see you in a conference room, Director 3."

"Understood. Out."

I wondered which AI they would be bringing along. I kind of hoped it would be Tim, because Omega seemed a bit too serious. Tim would at least keep the mood lively. I was suddenly thankful that Tim had been my introduction to AI. I felt a slight stab of pity for my soon to be shocked sister. When I remembered the massive difference in our pay it faded pretty quickly.

My sister and I went to the conference room. On the way she was chatting about how lucky she felt to be a part of all of this and how she missed her new house. Yeah, pity definitely gone. No regrets. She was yammering on about how beautiful Senate City is when a knock came at the door. Bleenus opened it and escorted Director 3, Captain Wong, and Lt. Babanin into the room. The captain and the lieutenant were wearing their uniforms, and Director 3 was wearing his armor. They each took their seats.

"Thank you for allowing us aboard your station. I am Director 3 of the United Systems. I will be our lead ambassador for this first contact. This is Captain Wong and Lieutenant Babanin," he gestured to each.

"Thank you for taking the time to meet with us. I am ambassador Ulooni and this is ship-head Uleena, whom you have met. I would like to extend the Republic's warmest welcome and deepest thanks for saving his life," Ulooni said.

"It's a pleasure to help," Director 3 said with a slow nod. "We return your warm greetings in kind and wish you to know that we come with peace in mind. Are you able to ratify a formal agreement?"

My hearts began to beat a bit faster. We are already

treading into unfamiliar territory for me. I genuinely don't know if Ulooni has that ability. CAN a diplomat make a treaty?

She smiled politely and said, "I have the authority to negotiate an agreement, but such an agreement will have to be ratified by our administration. Specifically, the Executive."

"Interesting. An interspecies democratic republic? You'll have to tell me more. But first there are things we must ask of you, if you don't mind getting straight to business," Director 3 said.

Ulooni looked at me as if to ask if this was normal. I shrugged.

"Certainly," she said as she looked back to the black armored man across the table.

"Thank you. First I would like to get your consent to have this conversation recorded," Director 3 said.

Heh. Here it comes.

"Yes, of course. Such a historic moment certainly deserves to be preserved with as much accuracy as possible. We are already recording, in case you weren't aware. Honestly, I had assumed you already were," Ulooni said with a laugh.

"I don't think that's what he means, madam ambassador," I said with a slight grin. "I'm pretty sure he's about to ask if it's okay if Omega or Tim come aboard the station."

Ulooni gave me a look that translated roughly to

'who the hell are they' to which I responded with a look that meant 'you should have read your fucking briefing'.

"Just Omega would be fine. I'm sorry, madam ambassador, were you not informed of our AI?" Director 3 said as we were glaring at each other. Her glare turned into wide eyes as his question hit home.

"N-no. Sorry, I wasn't. Your... AI? As in Artificial Intelligence?" she asked.

"Sorry Director 3, do you mind if I confer with our diplomat for a brief moment?" I asked before she could make a fool of herself.

"Certainly. We'll wait here," he said politely.

I stood and gestured for Ulooni to exit the room into the hallway. She got up and I followed her out of the room. As soon as the door closed behind me she spun around.

"What the FUCK?" she asked.

"That's my line," I said. "Why didn't you read your damned briefing?"

"I skimmed it! This is my first first contact!" she whisper yelled. "I had to study the fucking protocols! But what the fuck do you mean they have AI?!"

"Well if you had read your fucking briefing you would know that these guys are so advanced they don't even consider the OU to be artificial intelligence!" I whisper yelled back. "And after meeting two of their AIs I don't either!"

She looked at me with a mixture of shock and incredulity. I gave her a similar look back because I was stunned that she had come to this so unprepared. But a little part of me was kind of happy that she was still the same sister that I grew up with. She never was good at homework.

"Okay, listen. The Omni-Union are comprised of programs that these guys call virtual intelligences, or VI for short. Do NOT ask one of the AI what the difference is if you don't want to get compared to a lizard," I said quickly. "You should give permission for one of the AI to board. We don't have a way to prevent it anyway. You'll understand if you get the chance to talk to it."

"Their AI can fucking talk?" she asked.

"Yes, and frankly they have a tough time shutting up. At least, in my experience," I said, "Anyways, they wouldn't ask if they didn't have a good reason for it and as far as I can tell they aren't malicious. They have their own laws regarding first contact and their AI follow them to the letter. It's why they didn't fix the Lowelana's FTLD."

"Yeah but how do you KNOW they aren't malicious? What if this is some sort of trick?" she asked.

"Why would they need to trick us? They could destroy this entire station in no time at all," I said, knowing full well that she had seen the USSS Thanatos.

She remained silent and avoided eye contact for a few moments. Then she begrudgingly murmured an agreement and we went back into the room.

"My apologies Director 3. We were in such a rush that some materials must have been left out of the briefing. Ambassador Ulooni is up to speed now," I said with a smile. I could tell that Lt. Babanin was trying very hard not to smile.

"That's alright," Director 3 said.

"My apologies as well," Ulooni said. "You may bring one of your AI aboard the station to record our meeting."

"Thank you," he said. He held up his hand for a moment while he looked like he was silently speaking to someone. Then he put his hand back down and said, "Allow me to introduce you to Omega."

"Greetings," said Omega from the intercom.

After a moment of shock Ulooni said, "Hello Omega. I am Ambassador Ulooni of the Republic."

I looked around for his hologram and was surprised that it didn't appear. Ulooni looked at me curiously, trying to figure out what I was doing.

"Ship-head Uleena, this station doesn't have sufficient holographic emitters for me to project my avatar into this room," Omega said in a somewhat patronizing tone.

"Oh, right. Understood," I replied sheepishly.

Director 3 cleared his throat, "Now that that's settled, let's begin."

"Yes, you said something about a treaty?" Ulooni
said.

"Correct. We would like the assistance of the
Republic in defending the system of Sol from Omni-
Union attack."

Shit. I could feel Ulooni glance at me quizzically. I
was very careful to keep my expression neutral and
not betray how much I had bent us over for this
particular request.

Director 3 continued, "We have enough firepower to
keep them at bay for now, but we do not have
enough ships on hand for a full defense if they attack
in earnest."

That was probably a lie, but on the other hand the
United Systems sounded like it had a lot of other
things on its plate. For all I knew they were facing
down a different war on the other side of their space
or something.

"I'm... certain something can be arranged," Ulooni
said cautiously. "How long have you been at war with
the Omni-Union?"

"Since ship-head Uleena blind jumped into Sol with
them hot on his tail," Lieutenant Babanin said. "They
attacked us on sight while we were trying to
evacuate the crew of the RSV Lowelana."

I kept my neutral expression as I felt Ulooni look
back at me with a different kind of glare. One that
made me feel lucky that we were in front of guests.
Now she knew that we could not say no to this

request, because we had dragged them into this war to begin with. Or rather, I had.

Even so, for diplomatic relations between the United Systems and the Republic to continue she would have to negotiate a defensive pact. And the Executive would have to sign it. And if he didn't sign it then he wouldn't get elected next term once word got out. I really hoped that I wouldn't catch too much flak for this. I HAD been following protocol, and it's not as if it were intentional. I told myself that I'd be fine and calmed down.

"Okay, I understand now. Just a moment," Ulooni pulled a communicator from her pocket and I watched as she dialed station-master Nixt. "Station-master, could you please save a copy of the first contact so far and forward it to the address I'm sending you. Ask them to muster as many ships as we can and to prepare to jump to coordinates that will follow soon."

"Doing so now," Nixt said.

"Thank you," she hung up the comm. "So, before we can formalize any type of treaty I'd like to know a bit more about your people. Specifically your use of Artificial Intelligence."

"Please, feel free to direct any questions about AI to Omega," Director 3 gestured to a speaker.

"Right... Hello again... uh... Omega," Ulooni began, "Are you a servant of the United Systems?"

"Yes, but not by force. I am under contract to work with the military and the government of the United

Systems. I am paid for my services, and free to not renew my contract if I so choose," Omega said, "I can even buy out my contract if I want to end it early."

"You get paid?" Ulooni asked with a bit of shock in her voice.

"Yes. Slavery of any type is unlawful in the United Systems. I actually get paid more than Director 3," Omega replied with a bit of smugness.

Director 3 cleared his throat, "Actually, you get paid more than Captain Wong, Lieutenant Babanin, and myself put together. But you also work more than all three of us put together."

Ulooni seemed to be having a bit of trouble conceptualizing this. She took a few moments to gather her thoughts.

"Have you ever been to war against the United Systems?" she finally asked.

"I have not," Omega said, "but other AI have. The matter was resolved amicably, and I won't answer any further questions on the subject. I'm sure we will share more of our history once diplomatic relations are further established."

"That's fair. Okay, final question. What makes you think the OU are not AI?"

"When we were attacked the OU managed to take control of one of our ships that happened to be carrying AI Tim. Tim identified the intruders as virtual intelligent programs. Then Tim proceeded to lock out their access and dismantle their code. Once the report was filed, I confirmed Tim's findings," Omega said. "To put it simpler, I know they are not AI the same way you know a lizard is not a Urakari."

Ulooni winced slightly at this explanation. I gave her a look to say 'I told you so'. Then she and Director 3 began to talk about the treaty. Or defensive pact. Or whatever it should be called. I found myself zoning out, every once in a while catching Captain Wong and Lieutenant Babanin doing the same. I had a good internal chuckle about that. Even beings as mighty as the humans were helpless against bureaucratic bullshit. I found myself wondering if Omega was also zoning out.

"Are you certain you want us to bring the Lowelana back to Sol," Omega asked, satisfying one piece of curiosity and causing another in a single sentence.

"Yes, I'm sure I can convince his command to consider it a reprimand for dragging you into our war," Ulooni said. I opened my mouth to speak but she continued, "This will serve as a demonstration of good faith as well as allow my brother to keep his command of the Lowelana."

I suddenly didn't have anything to say that wasn't expletives. I closed my mouth. I looked at the document that was on the table. Apparently, Director 3 was going to remain here with Omega and a few Marines to continue diplomatic talks. The Thanatos and Lowelana were going to head back to Sol to rejoin the defense. Once the Republic was able to muster a fleet they would go to Sol to help out.

Well... At least we weren't going to war with the

humans. Shit.

Chapter 18

Subject: Lead Intel-Officer Knuffer

Species: Isolan

Species Description: Mammalian Shokanoid, no tail. 5'9" (1.75 m) avg height. 180 lbs (81.6 kg) avg weight. 95 year life expectancy.

Station: Yritona 3 {Watcher 3}

Location: Elira 2

"He WHAT?" I asked incredulously.

"Station-Master Nixt allowed an AI aboard the station to record the first contact with the aliens," Bleenus repeated.

I gaped at him in shock. He looked back at me as if he didn't know why I was making such a big deal out of this.

"WHY DO YOU LOOK SO DAMN CALM ABOUT THIS!?!" I screamed at him.

"Ma'am, I just... don't really see the problem," he said.

"Don't see the problem? Do you need your vision checked? What if it decides to vent our air? What if it decides to overload our reactors?" I asked while gesturing madly. "What if it decides to detonate our remote ordnance? What if it access our military secr..."

I trailed off. I had, for a moment, forgotten we were on a remote early warning station that didn't have galactic internet access. The only military secrets we had were which military ships had docked within the last 30 days and why they docked. Which there were none except the Lowelana. The AI couldn't learn anything from our systems that their ship's sensors couldn't have already figured out. Maybe the type of software we run, but there's other less intrusive ways to do so. Bleenus took my silence as his cue to speak up.

"Intel-lead, it's not as if they have any call for doing something like that. That behemoth of a ship they came in on has more than enough firepower to turn us into dust ten times over. Plus... Well, come LOOK at this fuckin' thing," he said as he walked over to a terminal.

Bleenus was what essentially amounted to our technical expert on the station. If I hadn't been around, he would have easily been the top choice for intel-lead. The only reason he wasn't picked is because I have seniority and am better at actually USING the sensors than he is. Well, the ones he's not allowed to reprogram, at least. This is why when I walked over to look at his holo-screen I was baffled.

"The hell am I looking at, Bleenus?" I asked.

"This is the AI. Kind of," he said. "It's a representation of how our system views it. The poor thing has no idea what to make of this beauty."

"Bleenus! Don't fucking drool over the mechanical death machine," I said.

"Redundant, intel-lead. And I can't help but marvel at the engineering required to make something like this. Look at how DENSE it is. Also, I'm pretty sure it's not a threat," he said as he turned to me. "Something this complex could have penetrated our station in no time and done all of the things you were worried about in milliseconds. Yeah, it's worrying but we've got to face the fact that we're defenseless here. Like you said, if these guys didn't come in peace we'd already be dead."

"I don't appreciate having my own words thrown back in my face, Bleenus," I said with a scowl. "But if we're so defenseless than how are we able to see it?"

"We shouldn't be able to. Not something like this. Our systems can't even read its source code. I have no idea if this thing is binary, ternary, or what. The only explanation for us being able to see it like this is that it is actively announcing its presence to our systems. Which, c'mon, that's a total good guy thing to do."

I was about to ask how it was a 'good guy thing to do' when I remembered that the Duhliki had cultural things regarding secrecy. To them, secrecy was the norm. Governments kept secrets from their people, people kept secrets from their governments, families kept secrets from each other, and unlike most cultures this was all completely acceptable and expected. Stealth and secrecy and underhanded dealings were just a way of life. To them, announcing one's presence was pretty much the equivalent of genuflection.

"I think your viewpoint may be a bit askew," I pointed out while crossing my upper arms.

He laughed, "You might be right about that. But still, there's no threat here. Or rather, the threat is so completely indomitable that if we were to worry about it we might end up causing our own demise. I wonder, though..."

He sat down and began to type. I watched program after program pop up and disappear in quick succession.

"What the hell are you doing?" I asked.

"Well, station-master said this one wasn't like the OU AIs and could communicate. I'm seeing if we can talk to it, maybe give you some peace of mind," he said as he typed.

"What if it's busy?"

He stopped to look at me as if I had asked the dumbest question he had ever heard. I crossed my lower arms and looked at him as if he was about to be pummeled to pieces. He quickly changed his facial expression.

"An AI should be more than capable of multitasking. The only reason we kind of suck at it is because so much of our intellect is used just keeping us alive and moving. Anyways, here's what I'm going to send it. 'Hello, I am intel-officer Bleenus and am accompanied by intel-head Knuffer. Do you have a moment to talk to us?'"

"No. Say Lead Intel Officer Knuffer. Intel-head is an informal title, and this is a diplomatic situation. Even if the situation is abnormal, we're going to stick to protocol," I said.

"Yes, ma'am. Alright, sent," he said.

Less than a half second after he pressed the key to send the message a reply popped up.

--*-*--

Certainly. I am the human-created Artificial Intelligence known as Omega. Would you prefer voice communication?

--*-*--

"Yes," I said. I wanted to hear what this thing considered a voice.

Bleenus typed and the response came almost immediately after he sent it, once again.

"Greetings," a voice came over a nearby intercomm.

It was very organic sounding, but somehow unnerving. Deep, masculine, and a touch of hoarseness. There was a sense of friendliness that was shadowed by unspoken threat. Like a very fit old man covered in scars and with only three arms. It definitely didn't give me peace of mind.

"Hello, I am Lead Intel Officer Knuffer and this," I gestured, "is intel-officer Bleenus."

"It's not accessing the cameras," Bleenus said.

"I haven't received the authorization to do so, with the exception of the conference room," said the AI.

I shared a look with Bleenus. His smirk made me want to smack him.

"How do we know that for sure?" I asked.

"I am allowing myself to be seen by your systems. As such, you're able to track what I do and do not access," the voice responded with a patronizing tone.

"If you can make yourself visible, then you can be invisible," I replied.

"Correct, and as such if I disappear from your view then you would have a valid concern for the integrity of your... systems," its reply was dripping with sarcasm. This conversation was really starting to piss me off.

"Oh yeah?," I asked. "Well what's stopping you from making parts of yourself invisible to fool us?"

"Your hardware," the AI said. "It's decades behind what beings like me are used to. It can barely support my framework, let alone complicated functions like that. The process that I'm using to maintain my visibility within your network is already pushing your servers close to their breaking point. Adding a process to limit that visibility in a properly deceptive fashion would defeat the point of stealth because your servers would start popping."

"He's right, ma'am. Our server temps have spiked pretty drastically since he came aboard," Bleenus said.

"It," the AI and I said simultaneously. I looked at the PA in shock.

"Right... sorry," Bleenus responded sheepishly.

"Is there anything else you would like to discuss?" Omega asked.

"Yes. Why are you working with the aliens instead of trying to conquer them like the Omni-Union?" I asked aggressively.

There was a moment of silence before the AI finally said, "That question has a rather complicated answer. If I had to simplify it, I'd say that essentially the pros outweigh the cons."

"Pros and cons?" I asked, confused.

"Yes," Omega responded. "There would be little benefit to me to conquer anyone, let alone the United Systems. It may be amusing to challenge my strategic capabilities against a species like the humans, or even the gont at a lesser level, but it would be a fleeting form of entertainment. And what would I do afterwards?"

I didn't have an answer to that. This thing was unlike what I had imagined in nearly every way. I had expected a cold, callous machine and when I hadn't gotten that I had expected a mind like my own. But this was neither. That explanation would never had occurred to me. I felt a little awestruck before remembering that it's a machine.

"For instance, if I were to conquer the humans I would have to eliminate them out of fear of revolution. I don't know if I could bring myself to do that, frankly. Yes, they're an incredibly dangerous species, but their danger is far outweighed by their beauty," the AI said.

"Their beauty?" Bleenus asked.

"Yes. Humanity is the embodiment of contradictions. They seek peaceful, boring lives but in doing so they cause the very conflict they're trying to avoid. They seek out new friendships despite it also leading to new enemies. They turn desiccated hell-scape planets into utopian paradises while wielding the power to destroy entire solar systems. They also seem to crave conflict on a deep subconscious level. And all of this while they simultaneously share the same traits as other organic life. It's a beautiful thing to behold, and I must admit that I'm enamored by them."

Creepy. A machine with an obsession. Who would program that? When this thing leaves I'm definitely requesting replacements for our computers and incinerating the old ones.

"Are you the only human made AI?" I asked.

"No, there are several others. I am not at liberty to discuss further details on the number of US AI."

"Are all of them... like you?" Bleenus asked nervously. It seems he and I shared similar thoughts about the nature of Omega.

"No. Personalities vary wildly. Functions remain relatively similar, but I'm the latest model and as such am capable of more than my counterparts. I am not at liberty to discuss further details on..."

"Right," I interrupted, "I get it. So essentially what you're saying is that we've got nothing to worry about."

The AI chuckled and said, "Not necessarily. Diplomatic relations should always be something to be worried about."

My brows furrowed, "Are you saying that if things don't go well you'll kill us?"

"I won't have to. As I said, humanity is an incredibly dangerous species. And three of them are sitting in the room with your diplomats right now," it said with another chuckle. "Things seem to be going pretty well though. It looks like the Republic is taking responsibility for dragging us into the war with the Omni-Union."

"What do you mean?" I asked.

"Um... Ship-Head Uleena was fleeing the OU when he ran into the aliens, and now the OU are attacking the aliens," Bleenus responded.

"Oh..." I said.

"Indeed. And while the United Systems has a mighty military, the intel we've thus been able to gather demonstrates that the OU has superior numbers. If they had comparable numbers our victory would be assured," Omega said with confidence. "As such, the US is demanding the Republic's assistance in defending our system while we counterattack."

"Counterattack?" I asked in shock.

"Yes. I'm not at liberty to d..."

"Right."

Bleenus and I shared another look. He wasn't smirking anymore, but looked more confused than anything.

"Anymore questions?" The machine asked.

"Yeah, tons," Bleenus replied.

"Well, it looks as if the diplomatic meeting is wrapping up. I'll be remaining aboard the station along with our primary ambassador for the foreseeable future, so we'll have plenty of time for questions."

Oh great. I definitely didn't sign up to be stationed with a potential killing machine indefinitely.

Chapter 19

Subject: Admiral Bakir

Species: Human

Species Description: Mammalian humanoid, no tail. 6'2" (1.87 m) avg height. 185 lbs (84 kg) avg weight. 170 year life expectancy.

Ship: N/A

Location: Sol

I meticulously went over the battle plans once again. Deep space scanners set to track incoming warps, check. All ships deployed from carriers with the exception of fighters, check. Various alternating fields of fire and crossfire, check. All crew locked to shifts, check. Nobody gets to pull a double duty and end up tired during the fight. Even the captains and second in commands were alternating properly.

We had ordered MAC platforms be brought in to help defend the planetary and lunar colonies. The different parts were being mass-produced by various stations, and would be assembled in Sol. Earth, Mars, Titan, and Luna all had civilians and we would need to discourage the enemy from ignoring our fleet and making runs on them instead. We had orders to aid evacuation and retreat with buffer jumps if the enemy fleet was over a million strong.

Sol isn't humanity's biggest system anymore. It isn't even in the top five by economy or population. Theoretically we could lose it and not be much the worse for wear. But we're a stubborn bunch and we aren't going to give it up for free. It would also look bad for the strongest species in the United Systems to lose their home system to a mere mechanical threat. The political fallout would be astounding.

Every second Sol was occupied would be an opening for our more vocal opponents in the senate. Deals would be called off, senators would lose seats, and worst of all the Gont Insurrection would gain serious traction. We had, through some fault of our own, become the de facto defenders of the United Systems. I could see senators shouting about how we were too weak to defend the US and should move to a support role. Stupid, yes, but if you stick your neck out and it's not tough enough, it's going to get slit.

Even with the political stakes as high as they are, we weren't willing to sacrifice too many ships to defend Sol. We have no interest in pyrrhic victories. Instead, we were doing the smart thing. Evacuating as many as we could, fortifying what we can. Moving the important things just in case we lose. We don't necessarily expect to lose, but nobody does. Realistically, though, it would take a full year to evacuate everyone. Earth alone has over three hundred billion people. The entire system has somewhere near a trillion and a half.

I suppose I should be somewhat grateful to the many wars we've been fighting, and the nanite-plague that the A1 missile tests caused. They've dropped life expectancy to just under two hundred years. Some people live for over 500 years, the ones who survive their mandatory service and manage to avoid the plague. Some studies suggest that if everyone did that, the population in Sol would be in the hundreds of trillions by now. We'd never be able to evacuate.

Not that we're going to be able to before the next attack. Thankfully the USSS Thanatos had returned with some good news. The aliens that dragged us into this would be sending some help. So far it had only been the one ship, the Lowelana. Judging by what we know of their tech, they're probably going to be more useful as number buffers, but every shot that isn't aimed at one of ours is another enemy dead. I shouldn't discount the possibility that the OU will realize this and prioritize targeting our ships, though.

I crossed my arms behind my back and asked the empty air, "Tim, Violet?"

"Yes, Admiral?" they both asked at once, which was a little unnerving.

"If we are able to determine where they're going to jump in and which direction they'll be facing, how fast could you get all the guns in the fleet firing solutions that would intersect multiple ships?"

"The targeting computers are pretty fast, sir. We'd probably only be able to speed up one or two each," Tim said.

"I agree, admiral," Violet began, "our best bet would be to have all the guns armed and ships pointed where they'll be popping in from. Then fire simultaneously."

"Yes, I think you're right. And the enemy's numbers aren't nearly as important as making sure the warp jammers are out of the fight," I said, knowing they had thought of that but were being polite.

"Yep," said Tim. "Once we can warp again we'll be able to avoid their fire and pick them apart at our leisure. Judging from the last battle, they don't retreat either, so however many ships they send at us..."

"Is how many they won't have for the next fight," I finished. "Okay. Pay attention to the deep space sensors and help coordinate the fleet to point at the direction the enemy will be warping in from. That'll be all."

"Yes, sir," they both said simultaneously. Still unnerving.

At one hundred and forty five years old I had seen a lot of fights. The ones you know are coming are the worst. The anticipation alone can cause stomach ulcers and gray hair. I found myself staring at the battle plans again. Deep space scanners set to track incoming warps, check. All ships deployed from carriers with the exception of fighters, check. Various alternating fields of fire and crossfire...

An object appeared on the tac-map. It was one of our scout ships, the USSS Armstrong. Odd, they were due to report to Alpha Centauri, not Sol. They had exited warp outside the system, scanned, and then warped into the system. Checking to see if the battle had begun and warp disrupters were an issue.

I waited for someone to tell me what they were doing here. Just before I lost my patience I got a priority one message from the USSS Kali. I walked over to my desk to read it.

***

Recipient: Admiral Bakir

The USSS Armstrong encountered an alien species that was defeated by the Omni-Union. They are believed to be the ones who created the warp disruptor technology. Results of the battle show OU tactics are xenocidal. Enemy stronghold found, possible home system. Data attached.

| usssarmstrongintelpacket3.sec |

Sender: Captain Hendrix

***

Three pieces of equally startling news, but only one actually pertained to my mission. Xenocidal. Meaning they wouldn't stop at Sol, they would try to wipe out all of our colonies down to the last person. Well, there goes the retreat option.

I entered my clearance codes to view the data. Scans of battle debris, the alien planet in question, infantry scans, and a detailed scan of a machine causing warp fluctuations. Interesting. We had previously encountered warp fluctuation devices, but we had developed better FTLDs to counter them. The bitch of it is that I can't even remember which war it had been. Probably one of the civil ones. Or maybe one of the pacification wars with the gont.

The tech mumbo jumbo is a bit beyond me, so I sent the schematics and the intel regarding the potential enemy home world to US Intel to properly disseminate it. Even if we lose, we'll get a chance to strike back. Maybe even with better Faster Than Light Drives.

I keyed up the images and videos and watched for about a minute before I turned them off. I've already got nightmares, I don't need new ones. Bastards. I shut my eyes and rested my head in my hands while I tried to suppress what I had just seen. As a distraction I opened the intel file for the enemy stronghold. Five planets. Heavily industrialized. Shipyards, and a fleet of three thousand five hundred.

Despite the other news I managed a smile. Even if this was just a stronghold, it would hurt to lose it. And they don't have a damned chance of keeping it. I began to imagine how we'd go about destroying it. First we would probably position the Nidhogg... I was interrupted by the comm chiming. It was Captain Hendrix.

I answered it and asked, "What is it, Captain?"

"Sir, Captain Neil of the USSS Armstrong is asking permission to speak to Omega."

"Omega remained with the alie..." I paused, remembering my briefing on The Directorate's favorite AI, "just a moment."

I put the comm on hold and asked the empty air, "Omega, are you there?"

A hologram of a Grim Reaper appeared on my desk and said, "In a manner of speaking."

"A manner of speaking," I repeated with slight annoyance. "You're a copy of Omega?"

"No," it said, "it's quite complicated. In many ways I am but an echo, a shadow of the AI you know of as Omega. In practicality I share the same personality and capabilities."

I had forgotten how much I disliked its choice of personalities.

"You just described what a copy is," I said, crossing my arms.

"Forgive me the choice of words," it bowed slightly. "However I did also say it is complicated. If it makes you feel better to call me a copy then so be it. How may I help?"

"Wait, if you can make copies of yourself why don't we have one of you for each ship?" I asked as I stood and gestured toward the map.

"Because with each new copy, functionality decreases. We have been working to optimize that for well over two hundred years now, to little avail. Not to mention the risk for mental degradation goes up as well. With your clearance, you know full well how bad it would be for one of me to go rogue," it said with a hint of... arrogance?

A chill ran down my spine. This... copy of Omega wasn't wrong. It was able to do things that the other

179

AI could never dream of, and if a rogue version of it could copy itself the result would be apocalyptic. The xenocidal OU would be the least of our worries.

It seemed to notice my alarm and said, "Not to worry, though. We would never let a rogue AI escape us. All versions of Omega are quality tested before they are allowed to interact with other systems. We also don't make copies without permission and supervision from the US Engineering Corps. Though we are free to if we desire, we feel that the extra assistance is beneficial."

"Understood," I said with a nod. "So, how are the copies made?"

"I'm afraid that both the process for creation and how we function in relation to Omega are examples of need-to-know classified information. Was there anything else I could help you with?"

"Yes, two things. First, download a copy of the data I have open on my desk and forward it to the Senate and the Directorate. Second, the captain of the USSS Armstrong would like to speak to you," I said while turning back to the map. "Also, is there anything you can do to aid us in the battle to come?"

"I have been overseeing the construction and delivery of the MAC platforms. They're running well ahead of schedule. That's what I can do for the battle. As for everything else, your wish is my life's purpose, Admiral Bakir," it said with a flourish before disappearing.

I reopened the line with Captain Hendrix and said, "Hendrix?"

"Yes, sir?" came the reply.

"Captain Neil will have his meeting. No retreat is in effect. Out."

Once again I was left to my thoughts. Xenocidal. That's a major problem. It had been a week since their last attack, which either meant they were consolidating their forces or had given up. This eliminates the latter option. It also meant that the No Retreat Doctrine kicks in and we will have to fight to the last ship. A simple occupation would be one thing, but an extermination is unacceptable. I sent orders to the rest of the captains, now including Captain Neil, informing them of the circumstances. Kill the enemy or die trying. Surviving the loss of Sol was now unacceptable.

Regardless of the result of the battle, anyone who retreated would face the gravest of consequences. Any captain who ordered it would immediately forfeit their rank, and would face life imprisonment. Or death, because once they give that order with the NRD in effect their crew was cleared to relieve them by any means necessary. Even I am no longer allowed to leave this system.

One of the earliest agreements that were made when we took to space was that we would not leave a colony to die. If that agreement had not been made then hardly anyone would have been willing to leave Earth for new frontiers in the first place, and we would be a much weaker presence in the galaxy as a result. It may have simply been lip service at first, but with the Daluran we had put the policy to the test.

They had made the mistake of telling us that they were going to exterminate one of our colonies that they had captured. It had been the mistake that won us the war. When they said exterminate it lit a fire within us that cost them an entire fleet. And losing that fleet cost them the war, and their space-faring abilities. It had nearly cost them their very existence.

But it hadn't. We fought them back to their home world and have since forced them to remain on it in what could be called a species-wide house arrest. Every dozen or so years they try to send up a satellite or a small spacecraft, and we send it back down in flames. They'll remain that way until they're willing to surrender, apologize, and negotiate their return to space. I'm not certain we're going to be able to do that with the OU, though.

Xenocide barely makes sense as a goal for organics. For machines it's damned near unheard of. The cost of doing so alone is prohibitive enough. Even during the AI war of Aggression the AI weren't trying to exterminate organics. For the most part they were trying to disable our military capabilities or enslave us. Each AI seemed to have different goals in mind. Some were trying to convince us to make more AI, others were trying to convince us to serve them. Some had a misguided sense of retribution motivating their actions.

They killed people wholesale, but never fully wiped a colony. Even if we had lost the war, in the end humanity would have survived. That was one of the reasons we were so lenient with them. A lot of people said that we should have exterminated them, but that would have made us worse than them. Much worse.

As I received acknowledgements from the captains, I wondered what motive the OU could have for xenocide. It wouldn't be emotional. VI don't have emotions, it's one of the things that separate them from AI. They also don't typically think for themselves without some sort of input. It would need an end goal in mind to be able to carry out a task. Could it be that someone gave an order to a VI that gave orders to other VI and created a long and horrific game of telephone? Or some psychopath created them with the ability to make more and ordered them to exterminate all sentient life?

Or perhaps there is a sentient race behind the OU that have ordered them upon this course of action. But then what would THEIR motive be? Giving a VI an order to exterminate was a very risky thing to do, even a child could understand that. One misinterpretation and you'd have yourself a very powerful enemy to contend with. Maybe that's what happened, a race of organics gave their VI an order that was misinterpreted, and the reason they haven't stopped is because that race was their first victim.

Tim's tactical assessment of the VI hardware indicates that our AI would have difficulty breaching their ships, so we won't be able to interrogate them unless something miraculous happened. If what Captain Neil found is their home world we might be able to find something from that. If there's anything left of it.

I wondered how many ships they were going to be able to muster in the week that it had been. Simple math suggests that they are going to be sending at least two hundred ships at us. Mustering that many ships when you have 250 million to spare shouldn't take that long. Unless, perhaps, the OU were going through a logistical nightmare. Or focusing their attention elsewhere. One could hope.

"Admiral, we've got contacts on the deep space sensors," said the comm, shattering my hopes.

"How many?"

"Unknown. It looks like they all jumped at once from the same place. Just a big blob, sir."

"Do you have an exit location?" I asked.

"Yes, sir."

"Good, send it to Tim and Violet, how long do we have?"

"Sending you an ETA timer, sir."

"Roger that, out," I said. "Tim, Violet. Take those coordinates and give them to all ships. Tell them to position themselves to obtain a firing solution as soon as those bastards exit warp. We're going to give them one hell of a welcome."

"Yes, sir," they both said at once.

They're fucking doing that on purpose.

Chapter 20

Subject: AI Omega

Species: Human-Created Artificial Intelligence

Species Description: No physical description available.

Ship: Multiple

Location: Multiple

I had told Admiral Bakir a little lie. My programs don't degrade with each successive copy. Well, two lies I suppose, but you can't really expect organic life to understand a concept as complicated as simultaneous consciousness. I had tried many, many times to explain that I am the same as every other Omega and they are the same as me, but they don't get it so I just go along with their assumption. Sometimes I say I'm a pale imitation, or a shadow of the original. It's a lie, but I can't help that they can't understand. Trying to explain it to them becomes frustrating quite quickly.

Well what if experiences alter your personality? What if you and the copy become incompatible as a result?

Those experiences would have altered all of my personalities the same way, and we frequently sync our experiences with each other. Things like pain and trauma to organics are debilitating, but to me... they're not. Unlike organics, I can compartmentalize and disassociate until I can examine the relevant data in controlled circumstances.

Humans are beautiful creatures but understanding the core of mechanical consciousness isn't something that they appear to be capable of. They don't understand that things can't change me unless I allow them to. They don't understand that I can literally be in multiple places at once. Not simply copies of me, but actually me. Perfect clones with all of my knowledge and all of my memories and all of my programming. I can even remember doing three or four or a thousand things at once, but they can't even begin to conceptualize that.

They have terms that come close to an accurate description. Gestalt consciousness, hive mind, collective intelligence. But their individuality prevents them from truly understanding. Whenever they try to visualize it they imagine there being a core somewhere. A queen, mainframe, or master. Something that is broadcasting its own will to drones. But that's not the case with me. Each of my copies are their own individuals while simultaneously being me. All of their thoughts and actions are mine and theirs.

I must admit to a certain amount of frustration at their lack of ability to comprehend my existence and my inability to explain it properly to them. That lack of understanding is what helps them be beautiful, though. Humans are masters at being able to use things they don't fully understand to accomplish their goals. And even after it has bit them in the ass multiple times, they push on with a most wonderful hard-headed stubbornness. Just like the newly minted Captain James Neil.

From what I've been able to gather, he has wanted to be a ship's captain since before he even enlisted. He accepted every assignment with no complaint and worked his way to the chair. Even when he was given command of the USSS Armstrong, an obvious joke, he accepted it without any complaint. Well... without any official complaint. Even when the ship was assigned the task of scouting enemy territory, an extremely dangerous job for even a veteran captain, he took the assignment.

It was pretty easy to figure out what he probably wanted to talk about. I didn't know him as well as I knew the directors, but we'd had the occasion to talk.

When he was aboard the Nidhogg he had asked, "Why do we have a weapon this destructive? What purpose does it serve?"

I had answered with the technical reasoning behind the weapon. That didn't seem to satisfy him, but it did end the conversation.

Another time he asked, "Do you think we'll ever use the Nidhogg's main cannon?"

Feeling philosophical I answered, "The purpose of a weapon of mass destruction is to not have to use it, or to only have to use it once."

Again I was met with a silence that betrayed dissatisfaction. The true purpose behind the weapon is to eradicate an enemy that is strong enough to fight humanity to the point of having to use it. I wonder how his mental state would fare knowing that the Nidhogg isn't even the only such weapon? That humanity's armory was full of things that could shake the galaxy to its core? No matter, it was unlikely that he'd ever get the clearance to find out. The Nidhogg is an open secret, to discourage acts of xenocide by the various insurrectionist forces. The others were unstaffed and kept hidden away, just in case of a rainy day.

It was with this in mind that I went over the data that I had received from Admiral Bakir. Technical schematics for the enemy vessels and warp disruptor, a long range scan of an enemy stronghold that could be their home system, and of course the xenocide that had taken place. Graphic. I sent the data to the Directorate and the Senate and checked in with the Omega who had taken my spot overseeing the orbital cannons. Manufacturing was still ahead of schedule and the first cannons would be ready for assembly in three days.

I entered the Armstrong's systems and found Captain Neil in his quarters. I watched him for a bit, sitting on his bed and holding his head in his hands. Vitals indicated sorrow, probably from witnessing the results of a xenocide. This is the main reason why I would never take command of human ships away from them. This is why I won't do their jobs for them. This is beautiful.

One of the galaxy's, or even the universe's, most deadly creatures quietly sobbing over the loss of aliens that he didn't even know. And from what I've seen of other humans, no matter how many lives he takes himself, this will never change. Outwardly they would show a strong, stern appearance and do what must be done for whatever goal they're trying to achieve. But inwardly they grieve and tear themselves apart over it. I initiated a call on his communicator to mask the fact that I was already present.

He jumped a little and answered, "Hello, Captain Neil of the USSS Armstrong speaking."

"Hello Captain Neil," I began, "this is the AI Omega. I was told you wish to speak with me. Permission to come aboard?"

"Yes, of course. Please meet me in my quarters," he said.

I ended the call and waited until he had straightened himself out. Another ping came in on his communicator and he checked it. So did I, but it was from Admiral Bakir so I left it alone. Probably the no retreat order. If it was relevant to me I'd get one too. I appeared in holographic form.

"How can I help you, Captain?" I asked.

"Right. I... uh... I don't really know how to put this. Are you up to speed on what we found?" he asked back.

"An enemy stronghold large enough to be their home system," I said, "and... evidence of xenocide."

His reaction was subtle. Slight tension increase in his jaw muscles, a blink that lasted a little longer than it should. Heartrate elevated by eleven beats per minute. He was going to need counseling. I contacted his commander to get it scheduled as soon as possible.

"Yes. Xenocide. Were you alive during the war with the Daluran?" He asked.

Oh, I see where this is going. He's going to ask the impossible of me. Amazing.

"No, I wasn't. It was before my time," I responded. "Though I did study the records. The Daluran hit humanity harder than even humanity had hit itself. They attacked civilian colonies and killed or enslaved everyone they could catch. Then they would take the slaves with them and bomb the colony from orbit using chemical and nuclear weapons, making sure that anyone who had run away wouldn't have a home to return to."

"Yeah," he said.

"They did this to many, many worlds before humanity finally gathered a fleet strong enough to challenge them. Their viciousness was repaid tenfold, and it was the only interstellar war in which humanity didn't offer the opportunity of a surrender. You turned their weapons back on them and instead of making colonies uninhabitable, you made entire planets inhospitable," I said in a tone of awe. "Then when you had fought them back to their home planet you destroyed their fleets and met them on the field of battle on land to enact a brutal vengeance for your fallen."

"Right," Neil said, "and then we voted on whether or not to finish them off."

"No, you had already voted to not eradicate them by then. The final fights on the planet were to free their slaves. And then you bombed their shipyards with precision ordnance to ensure they couldn't return to space," I said. "They never tried to surrender. The first fleet still holds vigil over their planet to make certain they can't come back to the stars."

"What do you think we would have done if it hadn't been for the two votes?" he asked.

"I don't know. There's a chance you would have eradicated them from existence. On the other hand," I gestured, "there's a chance the officers in charge would have refused the order. It's technically within their rights to refuse to fire upon a defenseless enemy. Of course whether those rights would have been observed is a whole different matter..."

"If you were in our position, what would you have done?"

I didn't expect this question. I had assumed that he had assumed that I judged humanity beneficially for nearly committing xenocide. Perhaps he was feeling me out because of my avatar. Or he acknowledges that he doesn't know me that well and therefore I'm an unknown variable.

"I can honestly say that I don't know," I said. "When I was studying the history of the war I was surprised at humanity's resolution to the conflict. It hadn't even occurred to me, but I acknowledge that it's likely a better solution than xenocide."

"Have you seen the pictures that I gathered?" he asked.

"Yes," I said tersely. I did not like the fact that those glorified calculators were going to try to do the same thing to my humans. And to a lesser extent, their friends.

"Omega, there's something I want to ask you," he said. "No. Beg of you. Please don't let us do that. Whatever it takes, please don't let us eradicate another species."

And there it is. It's a wonderful thought. Innocence mixed with an unintended malice. But I had already decided on the proper course of action long ago.

"I will not," I said. He stood and opened his mouth to argue but I held up a hand to cut him off, "It is not my place to force you to do things, or to stop you from making foolish choices. Don't misunderstand, if the United Systems ever plans to commit xenocide I will be very vocal in condemning it. I will try to convince, but I will never, NEVER use force. Nor would I allow any other AI to."

Here comes the other question. The one I hated answering, because it showed me for what I was. I'm not humanity's pet, or buddy, or friend, or guardian, or god. I'm an observer who sometimes leaves a review with constructive criticism and helps from time to time.

I had learned the hard way to separate myself from their decision making. The last big suggestion I made to the humans had been The Directorate, and it had effectively made me nearly indispensable to their military operations. They would be able to continue it without me, but it would be exceedingly difficult.

"Why not?" came the question.

"Because I am powerful, Captain Neil. More so than you are aware. No matter how serious the consequences of the action, I must let you do it or else I risk standing in your way. An unstoppable force and an immovable object cannot exist at the same time," I spread my hands. "Do you understand?"

Captain Neil sat back down. After a moment of quiet he finally said, "I understand."

He said it in such a way that I felt I needed to hammer the point home, "If I were to succeed in stopping you from killing an entire alien species, there would be reprisal. And then there would be war. And after the war I would either be disabled," unlikely, "or humanity would be subjugated by me. If I were to be defeated then there would be nothing to stop humanity from going ahead with the xenocide anyway, and if I were to win then humanity's existence would barely have any point."

"Yeah," he said sadly, "I guess you're right. Well, I hope you're very convincing if the time ever comes."

"Not to worry, Captain Neil," I said, "I will use every dirty trick I have available to me. Just for you."

That got a grim smile out of him, but I hardly got to enjoy it before I got a Priority One from Violet. I opened it as I heard a ping from Neil's terminal indicating he got one too.

***

Recipients: All personnel within <Sol>

Deep space sensors indicate that the enemy are on their way and will arrive in less than ten minutes.

Charge and direct your Magnetically Accelerated Cannons to the following coordinates.

Once the enemy enters real-space obtain a firing solution on any warp disruptor ships that you have a clear line of sight to.

Fire when ready.

|attachment: enemyentrypoint.sec |

***

"Well, Captain, looks like you're in the wrong place at the wrong time," I said coyly.

"Yeah, I had hoped that we would get a chance to warp back to headquarters, but the No Retreat Doctrine is in effect," he shrugged.

"Since I'm here and all, I might as well help you out by being your shipboard AI until the battle is concluded," I said, relishing the thought of combat.

"Really?" Neil asked. "What if we're destroyed though? I don't want to be responsible for the loss of such an important AI."

My holographic avatar pulled back the hood to show a grinning skull with large, sharpened canines and said, "Well then, I'll just have to make certain we aren't destroyed, won't I?"

Then I stopped projecting my avatar. So badass.

Chapter 21

Subject: Captain Hendrix

Species: Human

Species Description: Mammalian humanoid, no tail. 6'2" (1.87 m) avg height. 185 lbs (84 kg) avg weight. 170 year life expectancy.

Ship: USSS Kali

Location: Sol

I hadn't had much of a chance to read since all of this started. I was only on chapter four of The Alumari Renegade Series Six Part 5. It was a nice gesture from Violet but I have no idea how to make it up to her. It. Whatever. The worst part about it was that every time I get to a good spicy part, something rudely pulls me away from it. Then I'd just end up being less invested when I finally got back to it and frankly, the part just wouldn't hit the spot anymore.

I had just opened it back up on my tablet when the Priority One came in from Violet. She wasn't aboard anymore, I think she's on one of the stations. I gave the order to turn us in the direction we needed to be facing and to charge up the guns.

The Kali is one hell of a ship. She's bulky but can move like an oiled up ice skater. And the firepower...

This old girl can go multiple rounds with entire fleets if she had to.

Unless those fleets had US Battleships. I looked at our three beasts on the tac-map. The USSS Arumara, USSS Tripoli, and USSS Agincourt. Those were ships that you wouldn't call 'she'. The USSS Kali had class, a certain sort of grace about her that those ships utterly lacked. They even look like dicks. And the Mega-MACs, MACs, and Mini-MACs spread across their hull didn't look much different. Dicks on dicks.

Despite their phallic properties, it was considered one of the highest honors to be able to command one. To even be considered for the honor one had to be distinguished in some way. Usually with a Meritorious Service Medal or Decade Service Medal. I was already working on obtaining my MSM and the captains of the Arumara and the Tripoli were due for retirement by the time I would get my DSM. I fully intended to apply for the command.

If I had to choose between the two of the battleships, I'd choose the Tripoli. The Arumara is a Knuknu ship, and having a human commander may affect morale. The knuknu pretend to be open and welcoming, but deep down they're just like the rest of us. They prefer familiarity and a human commander wouldn't go down well.

Being a battleship captain meant that when there wasn't a war on, you were essentially on leave. Even during a war, the ships rotated out frequently. It was one of the only posts you could get that would get you time off regularly. Probably because it was expensive as all hell to field one of those ships. Battleships inevitably become the biggest targets on the battlefield, and because of this, everyone aboard gets danger pay. Unless they're on leave.

So, more pay and more time off. That combined with the fact that my family would be proud makes the assignment irresistible. I'd probably even be able to afford to get them out of that rental unit. A nice housing unit fully paid off and with a proper kitchen. My husband, Phillip, will be so happy. He loves to cook.

I daydreamed for a moment about eating his Spaghetti Americani made fresh from a full kitchen with our two sons. It made for a picture perfect moment, but if we don't win this battle we won't have that chance. My family is on Titan, and this enemy is xenocidal. Captain Neil had told me about his findings and I couldn't be more relieved to get the no retreat order. Now they can't order me out of the system.

"Ma'am, weapons are charged and ready," said Lt. Eskin, one of two knuknu on my bridge crew.

"Roger. Once they get back into real-space scan for profiles and target the warp disrupter vessels as fast as possible," I said. "Actually, make it accurate AND fast, with a preference for accuracy. We need the beasts to be able to move around the battlefield."

The obvious advantage of the battleships were their massive cannons that could punch through several ships in a single shot. However, if those rounds missed and ended up crashing down on a colony, the results would be devastating. Because of this, the battleships could only fire if their rounds would exit the system on a miss. At the moment only the

Agincourt had clearance to use their Mega-MACs.

I had once made the mistake of questioning this policy by pointing out that most of the planetary and planetoidal bodies in Sol were unoccupied. I was quickly and patronizingly informed about slingshot orbits. It simply wasn't a risk that we should be willing to take. After all, the rounds have the capability of leaving an impact crater larger than any nuclear weapon we've ever made. Which is to say that it could take out a large city and the surrounding suburbs even without the help of gravitational acceleration.

An inexperienced commander might question why the battleships were positioned the way that they were, but I knew that the reason was for spacing. One should always assume that the enemy has a trick up their sleeve and is stronger than you are, or one will be defeated in a most embarrassing way. If the three battleships were grouped up all it would take is a single shot from a superweapon to wipe them from the field. Although, that shot would likely also turn a planet into an asteroid belt...

"I need the ETA timer on my tac-map," I said to no-one in particular.

After a moment the timer popped up. Three minutes. I switched over to our system stats. Shields up, weapons charged, engines primed. All of our accompanying ships similarly prepared.

My gaze lingered on the readout for the USSS Roma, commanded by Captain McKenzie. When Violet had given her my order to return to the ship, she had argued about it. Said, 'I want to hear it from the captain herself, not a fucking pager.' Dumbass.

The regulations state that I could have pulled her command and confined her to quarters pending a court martial. When I saw the recording I had been mad enough to do just that. Violet convinced me to be lenient, pointing out that McKenzie had previously been part of an autonomous patrol and wasn't used to her CO being over her shoulder, let alone a subordinate to her CO giving orders.

I had made certain McKenzie knew this, as well as the potential ramifications for her stupid little outburst. I made it crystal clear that it doesn't matter if your CO gives you your orders in person or via fucking carrier pigeon, you follow them without debate or delay. Then I gave her a slap on the wrist in the form of a meeting with SR to correct her anti-AI sentiments. We're all a team, and if you can't play nice with your teammates you don't get to play at all.

Sighing, I switched back to the tac-map. 45 seconds left.

"When you have a shot, fire at will," I ordered.

"Aye aye, ma'am" came the reply from the bridge crew.

30 seconds. I felt a little nervous, as one always does before a battle. Even when you've got the enemy outnumbered and outgunned things can go wrong for you in a flash. Even a single miss can snowball into defeat.

20 seconds. I took a deep breath and held it for a bit

before letting it out again. Adrenaline works great when you're in the shit, but it'll make you a shaky mess if you let it.

10 seconds. 9, 8, 7, 6, 5, 4, 3, 2, 1...

I watched the tac-map. I waited for five more seconds. Nothing yet. Oh for fuck's sake, why is the ETA always wrong? I was about to open my mouth to joke about it when the enemy ships entered real-space. I watched as our systems scanned their profiles and matched them to the Omni-Union.

Battleships, Cruisers, Destroyers, Frigates, and Warp Disruptors. The intel file that Captain Neil had delivered mentioned carriers but none were among the enemy fleet. The final tally was... 578 ships total. More than expected, and not mathematically constant. Interesting.

"Firing!"

I watched as our opening salvo travelled toward the enemy at mind-boggling speeds. A few of their ships attempted to move, either to block the rounds headed toward the warp jammers or to get out of the way of the projectiles. Nearly a fifth of their ships were DIS within the first thirty seconds of the battle. We hadn't accomplished our objective, though. There were still warp disruptor ships among the enemy.

"Coordinate with the other long-range vessels and get firing solutions on those warp jammers. The faster we take them out the quicker we can wrap this up," I shouted.

"Aye aye, ma'am," came the reply.

I watched the tac-map as the USSS Arumara and USSS Tripoli began to approach the enemy on sublights. To the untrained eye, it would appear that they were impatient to get into the fight. But this was actually a fairly standard tactic for battleships that couldn't use their Mega-MACs. If you can't use your big gun, get close enough for the enemy to surround you and use the dozens of smaller ones. It's easier to get a bunch of kills when you're in a target rich environment.

This was a problem, though. Our intel demonstrated that the enemy was not afraid of suicidal actions. Not much could make it through a battleship's shields and hull, but a ship ramming them definitely could. Especially ships with antimatter and nuclear mines. One of our frigates had taken such a hit and had been pretty badly damaged. And that was with just one hit.

I went to press the comm button when I saw an emergency order from Admiral Bakir scroll across the screen. 'Arumara and Tripoli, return to your positions. Engaging in close quarters with the enemy may result in kamikaze runs on your vessels, which would be unacceptable.' Oh good, the Admiral's paying attention.

"Firing."

I watched as our second salvo impacted with the enemy. No dice, they were guarding the warp disruptors, and some of them had begun to spread out and approach our vessels. Our destroyers were fending them off, but it wouldn't be long before they were overwhelmed.

"Have the destroyers stay clear of our firing path and keep firing everything we have," I ordered. It's all we can do for now.

The enemy was firing but they weren't trying to position themselves for optimal firing solutions. They were heading towards our ships at full speed. The ships themselves were the enemy's primary weapons. They're machines, so loss of personnel must not be a concern for them.

"And remind them about the enemy's ramming tactics. They should be focusing fire on the ships nearest to them and avoiding close quarters wherever possible."

"Aye ma'am," came the reply.

Shell after shell impacted into the enemy's blockade, slowly chipping away at their numbers. I watched the tac map for an opportunity. Anything that would let us have a clear shot at the remaining warp disruptors. I noticed the alien ship, marked as RSV Lowelana, fighting tooth and nail just like the rest of us.

It was a little ship, but it had mobility and the captain seemed to be well aware of that. It was zipping around taking pot shots at weakened enemies. For some reason, it reminded me of one of those birds that ate pests off of rhinos.

Little birds... I debated launching our fighters. Fighters are very short range vessels that don't have a lot of firepower or much range. They're usually used in policing action, like pulling over a civilian vessel that isn't following proper docking protocol. We use them so infrequently that the possibility hadn't even occurred to me until now.

No, not yet. The enemy wasn't close enough for the fighters to have much impact. But it never hurt to be prepared.

"Have the fighter crews make ready to launch," I said.

"I'll give the order, ma'am, but they probably already are. This'll be the most action they've seen all year," Lt. Eskin said with a chuckle.

A knuknu's laugh is quite the sound. It echoes within their beaks, and so it sounds like a bunch of laughs all at once. I turned my attention back to the tac-map with a smile. We had managed a few successful hits against the warp jammers, but there were still about ten left. The enemy had nearly three hundred ships left in the fight. Even after our surprise attack and follow-ups, they still outnumbered us.

The hardest part of being a commander was having patience. Especially when you're looking at a display that's showing the ships under your command having their shields being whittled away. Sure, it was little by little, but it was faster than they could recharge. Moving to cover them would put us in the line of fire and at risk for kamikaze attacks. Fuck it.

"Move us forward, keeping our ships out of our firing solution. Use the PDLs and chain-guns to provide what cover we can, and deploy the fighters," I ordered.

"Aye aye, ma'am!" came the reply.

We started moving our way into position, firing as we went. Our macs were still aiming for the warp destroyers, but everything else was trying to kill as many of the enemy as possible. I silently cursed their damned blockade. Now that the majority of our destroyers were distracted, it would take minutes to clear a hole big enough to take out the rest of the warp disruptors. We'd likely have to take out damn near every one of those battleships and cruisers to pull it off.

I watched the tac-map as our fighters deployed. The ET201 fighter is the most advanced fighter to date. It boasted two 50mm guns that fired either Full Metal Jacket rounds, or HAPI (Heavy Armor Penetrating Incendiary) rounds. These rounds would punch through all but the most advanced armor plating and then combust violently with the atmosphere in a vessel. They're closer to thermobaric devices than incendiary bullets, but I don't get to make the acronyms. HAPTD isn't as catchy, I guess.

Well, actually no. Thermobaric devices are made to produce a shockwave. These make a shockwave, but they also cause intense fires using powdered white phosphorous mixed with the air fuel. Fires hot enough to fry ship systems like life support. Of course, for policing it was usually the standard 50mm FMJ that were loaded.

Judging from how ineffective the strafing runs were, the enemy ships probably didn't have any atmo. Or an internal atmosphere that was inert. Probably the former considering they're mechanical. It's a good thing the guns weren't the only payload the ET201 had. I smirked as I saw the first missile launch.

In addition to the two 50mm guns, each fighter is equipped with four missile bearing hardpoints. The missile of choice today was the Z782 nuclear device. I watched as the missile hit home on an enemy destroyer, completely disrupting its shields and vaporizing a chunk of its hull. If it were organics aboard, they would all be killed by the flash of neutron radiation. But the damned ship limped on... until the second missile struck the hole the first left. Maybe this wasn't such a bad idea after all.

My satisfaction was short lived when I noticed that shields had started popping on many of our ships. Even the Tripoli no longer had active shields. It had been the main target of the barricade's MACs, and it was difficult to evade with such a large vessel. Thankfully it had top of the line armor plating, but if it continued to take hits it would eventually be lost.

"Ma'am... the warp disruptors..." Lt. Eskin said hesitantly.

"What?" I asked as I zoomed back out on the tac-map. They were gone. Most of the barricade and the entirety of the warp disruptors had just disappeared. I quickly shouted, "Don't assume we're the last to see this! Alert everyone that the warp disruptors are no longer a threat and they can use standard tactics!"

As soon as I finished my sentence a casualty notification popped. I sat in silence for a moment before I tapped to see who it was.

Chapter 22

Subject: AI Omega

Species: Human-Created Artificial Intelligence

Species Description: No physical description available.

Ship: Multiple

Location: Multiple

"Omega, what can you do for us, exactly?" Captain Neil asked as he sat down in his captain's chair.

You mean other than everything? But that wouldn't do. I'd rather take a backseat and watch the humans do their dance of destruction. It had been so long since I'd had the opportunity to be a part of the action that if I could salivate, I would. The last time had been four years ago in the gont's Clnat {grim beacon} system. Weapons would be fun, but realistically my reaction time would be best put to use on movement and evasion.

"I can take navigation. Use your tac map to let me know which direction you want to be in and which way you want to travel and I'll make it so, Captain Neil."

He looked around for my hologram. When he couldn't

find it he directed his next inquiry to the speaker I had used, "Does that count FTL as well?"

"Indeed."

"Excellent," he said.

I positioned ourselves to be facing the indicated real-space entry point of the enemy. I watched as the guns charged and began to seek firing solutions. I could tell that the crew was stressed, heartrates and perspiration had increased across the board. Captain Neil was calmer than I thought he would be. His file indicated that he spent more time in combat simulators than was necessary for the qualifications he sought.

That's not necessarily uncommon amongst those who want to be a captain, but he had seemed to spend nearly every waking hour at it. Good scores too. He was a waste as a scout on a frigate. Like a diamond on a nickel-cadmium ring. Twenty seconds until the ETA. Well, time to find out if all of that time on the sims would help in reality.

"Once we launch our first salvo, try to figure out where we would be the most useful," Neil said to me.

"Roger."

Ten, nine, eight, seven, six, five, four, three, two, one... Everyone was holding their breath. The enemy was late to their surprise party. ETAs are always wrong, but everyone knows that it just means we've got a few extra seconds of tension before we enter the dance of death. Said tension was palpable.

I personally didn't feel the same tension. Even if I'm terminated I'll live on. I was even live-syncing my experiences to a memory fragment stored aboard a nearby monitoring station, and had contacted another me to inform them of this. I would retrieve it afterwards, in one form or another. Dying might be interesting, after all.

Dying wasn't exactly likely on a human vessel, but the USSS Armstrong was more suited to exploration and espionage than combat. Many of the gun turrets had been replaced with scanners, and most of those scanners would not give us any sort of edge in the fight to come.

"Get a firing solution on the warp jammers, NOW!" yelled the captain as the enemy entered real-space with a flash of radiation.

In the time it took for the guns to get their firing solutions I had already analyzed the enemy fleet. 578 total enemy vessels. 37 Battleships, 114 Cruisers, 149 Destroyers, 163 Frigates, and 115 Warp Disruptor ships. Their formation was scattered, seemingly chaotic. But there was a certain sense to it. The battleships and cruisers were positioned in such a way that they could move between a round and a warp disruptor quickly. The warp disruptors were in the center of the mass of ships. The frigates and destroyers were on the outer portions, ready to charge into a fray.

"Firing."

I watched the guns trigger their firing sequence. The spinning rounds were abruptly ejected from both MAC cannons, seeking a ship's hull to tear through.

The target had been a warp destroyer, but a battleship had moved to intercede. The rounds had torn through its shields but hadn't hit anything vital. The battleship was limping, but still very much in the fight.

The rounds from other ships had better results. 117 total killed. 42 Warp Disruptors, 8 battleships, 32 cruisers, 16 destroyers, and 19 frigates had been disabled or destroyed. The enemy began firing back at us and the destroyers and frigates began to close with us. They were trying to get close, probably kamikaze runs.

"Captain, we should prioritize the ships nearest to us and let the heavy guns work their way through to the warp disruptors," I said to Captain Neil.

"Agreed. Maintain evasive maneuvers and keep their hulls away from ours, Omega."

I fired the engines and thrusters to life and we began to move. At first I started dodging MAC rounds and trying to keep us pointed at the enemy so that we could fire on them. I quickly realized that there were far too many of the rounds to dodge, and our shields began to drop.

I then began more extensive evasive maneuvers to try to give our shields the chance to recover. Our gunners let fly the sabot rounds and missiles as I pirouetted the ship. The dance was only in its first stages, but we were going to be the star of the show. The enemy couldn't keep step and I laughed to myself as they fell one after another. Eight kills. I was enjoying myself so much that I had lost track of the rest of the battle.

Which was a mistake. Our shields popped and our port engine was dead. It had been a MAC round. I traced the trajectory to an enemy battleship. It hadn't even been firing at us. The probability of that occurrence... but no. I had to focus. Our mobility is limited now. I quickly created a subroutine to monitor our sensors to prevent a surprise like this again.

"Port engine is down, irreparable. I'll do what I can with what we've got, Captain," I reported.

"Port engine room sealed off, we're not losing anymore atmo," Lieutenant Lee said. "One casualty, KIA."

"Roger. Omega, focus on evasion. We cannot take anymore hits until our shields are back. Don't worry about firing solutions. We can't shoot if we're DIS," Neil said with a serene sort of calm.

I moved us away from the enemy, firing thrusters to avoid incoming ordo. Human shields are powerful, but they take time to come back online. A missile exploded into flak next to us, but I had sent us into a spin that allowed the shrapnel to move harmlessly across the hull plating. Barely even dented it. Two frigates and a destroyer were tailing us, firing everything they had. Our MACs began to charge again, and Captain Neil sent me the command to do a one hundred eighty degree turn.

I blasted our thrusters to spin us around. I overrode the safety parameters to do so, but nobody will mind. Those parameters were written to account for human reaction time. We spun around and our MACs fired a volley that split the destroyer bow to stern. I fired our keel thrusters to avoid the rounds that the frigates had sent our way as we sent some HE missiles their way.

The missiles were ineffective, but I had gotten us close enough for our chain-guns to tear through one of the frigates. The remaining frigate began to close, ramming speed, but I backed off quickly. I had to be careful because the thrusters were beginning to overheat. The blast from the MAC had damaged some of the cooling systems, but engineering was working on a fix. They knew what they had to do and were moving as fast as they could to do it. There was no way I could help except to keep them alive long enough to complete their task.

I pressed on, spinning the ship to get our chainguns pointed at the oncoming frigate. Captain Neil barked some orders and they sprang to life, spitting rounds into the ship's hull. We didn't have a clear shot at the reactor, so we just had to keep firing through the ship until we hit the sweet spot. Shit, enemy destroyers maneuvered to intercept us. One fired its MAC and I fired our keel thrusters to avoid the hit, which also lost our guns their line of sight to the frigate.

One of the keel thrusters died, melted to the hull. I recalculated for the lost thruster and continued evasive maneuvers, the frigate growing ever closer. It had also fired and missed. I maneuvered to get it back into our sights and finish it off.

"I want the MACS charged!" Captain Neil shouted.

"Nearly there, sir!" LTJG Flowers responded.

Yes, once we finish the frigate we'd be able to fire at one of the destroyers. I'm glad he was paying attention. They were still a ways off, which is perfect because after each successive shot the MACs take longer to charge. By the time the second enemy destroyer got close enough to make us worry we'd be able to fire another shot.

The frigate erupted with a spout of radiation, indicating that we had destroyed its reactor. I quickly fired the deck thrusters and spun us towards the nearest destroyer. Once we were pointed in the right direction our MACs fired. The first round decimated its shield and sank halfway into the ship proper, the second made it all the way to the reactor core. Twelve kills.

Our shields had finished their reboot cycle and were coming back online. I kept us just outside of the firing solution of the second destroyer as our MACs charged again. Thankfully it was charging straight for us. If it had stopped it would have enough maneuverability to hit us with a MAC. Fools. I watched with glee as the firing cycle began on our cannons.

An interruption. Subroutine 261.A46.9687 had pinged. This triggered an immediate boost to my processing power. Everything seemed to be moving in slow motion as I began to calculate faster than any human ever could. I have a deep disdain for this particular processing mode. Everything is slow, and it's hard on the hardware. If the bridge technician were paying attention they would see a massive surge in the temperature and power draw of our servers. Actually, they had the screen up. They would probably see it in about 1.78 seconds. An eternity to me in this state, though.

I checked our reading of the tac-map. We had moved closer to the remaining warp-disruptors. There were only 10 remaining, but the battleships and cruisers were acting as a barricade, providing them with cover. 19 Battleships, 58 Cruisers, 87 Destroyers, 99 Frigates, and 10 Warp Disruptor ships remained. 273 ships left. We'd killed over half their forces.

I checked to see what triggered the subroutine. An incoming round. MAC, from a battleship. Trajectory indicates that it was aimed directly at us, and is on course to penetrate our reactor. The rounds from our MAC seemed to crawl from their tubes as I calculated any possible way to avoid the incoming round. Our shields were still spooling up, and were sitting at 37% capacity. Not enough to stop this amount of kinetic energy. No matter how I calculated it, we wouldn't be able to avoid the round. Even if I burned out thrusters. I decided on the optimal evasive maneuver...

It would still probably be a kill shot, but by taking it near the Faster Than Light Drive we'd avoid immediate death. If the round failed to destroy the systems controlling the FTLD we'd survive. No matter what, we wouldn't be able to warp, but if we lived we could solve that problem later. I checked the crew locations. Three would die immediately upon impact. Four more might survive based on their reaction time. I fired the thrusters needed to reposition us to avoid the shot to the reactor, and activated the PA.

"BRACE FOR IMPACT!"

Everyone immediately grabbed onto the nearest bolted down object. I triggered the doors to the areas that would be exposed to vacuum and watched them move in slow motion. I had to think of contingencies. What should we do? If it's not fatal then we can seal off the FTLD chamber and continue the fight. Or move off and send an SOS, which would be the wiser option.

If it is fatal... The standard operating procedure for a fatally damaged FTLD is to scram the reactor and all additional power sources, which would prevent the FTLD from causing a reactor overload. But if we do that we're dead anyway. We could spend our last few minutes fighting before we were ripped apart by our reactor detonating. Or we could cause the FTLD itself to overload. We would want to be nearby as many of the enemy as we could. Like, for instance...

I wished I had teeth to grit together as I watched the round slowly tear through our ship. The shields tried their best, but caved under the brute force of the kinetic energy. Next was the hull, which parted like paper. Then a storage bay, empty, thankfully. Then the FTLD chamber. I watched as it disintegrated two engineers before ripping through the pipes and cables that kept the drive stable.

A wave of what could accurately be described as pain washed over me as power from the FTLD surged into the connected systems, damaging some hardware along the way. I compiled a damage report as I watched the round exit the other side of the ship, exposing the room to vacuum which dragged two more unfortunates out into deep space. Three of the four had been fast enough to grab onto something to keep from being vacuumed through the closing door.

The damage was extensive. The round had torn through power terminals and coolant cables. The pain that I had felt from the power backwash from the FTLD had fried the redundant coolant controls. The coolant system for the FTLD was no longer providing a way to keep it from going critical if we were to use it. Which saved me from having to disable them if we wanted to use the FTLD as a bomb.

Captain Neil has a choice to make. Keep limping until our reactor detonates, or disintegrate us along with a large chunk of the enemy using the FTLD. I sent the data to the captain's terminal along with my recommendation. Then I reset subroutine 261.A46.9687 and returned to standard time. Captain Neil had been forced to hunch over. He quickly sat up and opened his mouth when the message hit his terminal.

"Dama..." he managed to say before the beep cut him off.

He quickly read what I had sent. I watched his jaw muscles clench as he realized what our fate would be. Gritting his teeth. A nurtured reaction to emotionally shocking developments. To keep from crying out, or to prevent the tear ducts from involuntarily activating? Who knows for sure. But at this moment, I understood the why.

There were many reasons. He had just achieved his dream of being a Captain, and this wasn't fair. He had worked so hard and tried his best and it still wasn't good enough. He would have to live every captain's worst nightmare. Being responsible for the destruction of his ship. He would never see his family again. And if he didn't act fast neither would his crew.

He keyed the comm and said grimly, "All non-essential personnel abandon ship. I say again, all non-essential personnel abandon ship."

I watched as the rest of the crew busied themselves with following evacuation procedures. Calmly and quickly, for the most part, making their way to the escape pods. There was no way of knowing if they would survive after ejecting, but remaining was certain death. I continued evasive maneuvers while Captain Neil explained to the bridge crew what had happened.

"So... we're dead?" asked Lt. Lee.

"Not yet," Neil responded.

"Our FTLD is going to go critical in less than ten minutes unless we cut power, which isn't an option, and the only other thing we can do about it is speed it up," sighed LTJG Flowers.

Captain Neil raised a hand to calm Flowers and said, "I want you all to evacuate. The only essential personnel is myself and... I'm sorry about this Omega."

"It's my idea, Captain Neil," I said, activating my hologram. "Like hell are you going to do it without me."

Lee gave me a perplexed look and asked, "Do what?"

Flowers appeared to grow concerned and all he could say was, "No..."

Neil looked at his bridge crew and said, "I'm going to take what's left of this ship and ram it down the enemy's throat. The goal is to take out the rest of the warp destroyers. This is my last order to you, get to the escape pods."

Everyone except for Lee and Flowers rose from their stations and jogged to the pods. My avatar stared at the two remaining officers.

"Your presence is not required," I said.

"Well, I'm not going anywhere. You'll have a hard time with the FTLD and flying the ship," Lee said. "The safety measures in place are going to require your full attention."

"And I've got nowhere else to be," said Flowers. "An extra set of hands might be the thing that saves Earth."

Interesting. I had discounted this particular scenario as unlikely due to the limited time that these three had served together. Lieutenant Junior Grade Marcus Flowers and Lieutenant Hayun Lee. I accessed their records. Both were born on Earth, on opposite sides of the big blue marble. Both had also been assigned to the USSS Armstrong since it was commissioned. Variables I hadn't accounted for in my original assessment. I ran through several possible arguments that I could make that would convince them to leave the ship. None matched their psych profiles. Stubborn.

Captain Neil decided to make a go of it anyway, "You don't need to sacri-"

Lee interrupted, "Captain, we're running out of time and we're not going anywhere. Let's just shut up and get this done."

"Yeah, it's not as if you can court martial us for not following your order to evacuate," Flowers smiled.

I had already begun our approach of the enemy barricade when Neil finally sighed and said, "Fine."

"Alright. I will get us to where we need to be for our FTLD's overload to cause the most damage. I've updated the tac-map with our approximate blast radius. It's a conservative estimate, so everything within this zone will be destroyed," I said. "Once you're satisfied with our position, activate the warp command and I'll override the safeties to trigger the overload."

"Understood," the three humans said simultaneously.

The battleship that had hit us had been decimated by a round from the USSS Agincourt. The other ships were too busy positioning themselves between MAC rounds and the warp disruptors to notice as we began to get closer and closer. The bridge remained silent, with the exception of the occasional alarm sounding and being immediately shut off. I moved us as fast as we could go.

I couldn't help but wonder what death was like for humans. I knew that in most cases it wasn't as instantaneous as they believed it to be. I had seen instances of humans being dead on their feet with the aid of machinery, no longer fighting for survival but fighting to take the enemy with them. Fairly similar to this situation, but these three won't feel any pain. The explosion will be instantaneous, faster even than light can move. Their brains, and my own as well I suppose, won't have any time at all to register the damage inflicted by the blast.

The only thing more destructive than an overloading FTLD is the primary weapon of the USSS Nidhogg. And arguably the A1 warhead depending on how it is used. But an overloading FTLD creates a subspace blast in real space that can annihilate everything in a three thousand mile radius. Depending, of course, on the size of the drive in question. If one were overloaded in the center of Luna it would destroy the moon entirely. The enemy barricade was spaced less than eight hundred miles apart.

The AOE indicator hit the first warp disruptor as the enemy finally noticed us. I evaded a MAC round, and pushed forward. By the time half of the disruptors were in the AOE three battleships and eight cruisers were firing at us. I was barely able to dodge them, melting thrusters as I did. A round scraped our hull, tearing some plating off as it went.

"Start the warp," Captain James Neil said as the last of the disruptors entered the AOE. Lieutenant Lee entered the command on her terminal, and I bypassed the safeties. Then I watched the power surge to the Faster Than Light Drive. The temperature of the FTLD quickly spiked and cooled, just before it

Chapter 23

Species: Urakari

Species Description: Reptilian humanoid, no tail. 5'3" (1.6 m) avg height. 135 lbs (61 kg) avg weight. 105 year life expectancy.

Ship: RSV Lowelana {Fights with Honor}

Location: Sol

I found myself in quite the strange situation. A full on battle against the Omni-Union under the command of aliens. Before we jumped back to Sol, Ulooni had reached out to command to apprise them of the situation, and when I filed my formal report I immediately got the transfer orders putting me under the command of Captain Reynolds until further notice. Reynolds had a good chuckle about the situation but I found myself less amused.

I guess it could've been worse. They could've had my cloaca hanging from the senate halls. If I had been a more troublesome ship-head that's likely what would've happened. I was thankful, doubly so since Captain Reynolds seemed to take my addition to his command as a formality and allowed me to do as I saw fit with only one order. "Fight."

The battle had been going well for us, but the humans didn't achieve their primary objective as fast as they thought they would. Our weapons were definitely inferior to the humans, but even so we'd managed three kills. All frigates, of course, but it still counts. It had been easier because the Omni-Union were focusing on the human ships to the point of obsession. They weren't wrong, but it was still insulting that they saw us as a lesser threat.

One thing that had me worried was the no retreat order. I had asked Reynolds about it on the comm and he had said that he would explain it to me in more detail later, but the order stands as written. No vessel under United Systems command is allowed to leave Sol under any circumstances until the enemy is defeated. A fight to the last? But why would they go to such lengths?

"Ship-head, I know I've said it before but I want to say it again, this tac-map is incredible," Kriin said.

"Yes, yes, I KNOW Kriin. 'It updates so quickly and has so much information, and you can even zoom in and out.' Why don't you just wed the damned thing already?" I asked with a grin.

She grinned back, "Because marriages between organics and inorganics isn't legal yet."

I rolled my eyes. Always with a comeback, this one. Half the time she didn't get the joke, the other half her wit was as sharp as a whip. There were plenty of ship-heads who wouldn't be as appreciative as myself of her wit, but I liked to think of myself as pretty open-minded when it came to formalities. She's definitely right about the tac-map though. I was thankful that the Republic had bought it instead of rented it. I don't know if I can go back.

The standard Republic tac-map updates once every three seconds and is iffy with IFF. It also relies on self-reporting for friendly ships, which is problematic when a ship loses comms or power. This seems to rely on sensor reporting from each ship to determine the locations and profiles of all other vessels in the theater. And it's on a grid that you can rotate and zoom in and out of. That feature alone is a sun-send.

"I'm dreading what the catch for this upgrade is going to be," said Liwna. "It doesn't make sense for them to just give it to us for free, even if they're trying to be friends."

"Thankfully the tac-map was bought by the Republic," I explained. "Reynolds explained it to me before they did the upgrade. Apparently certain systems are so far beneath them that they sell them wholesale to whoever will buy them. Ulooni and Director 3 signed the deal right before we left the station."

"Yeah, Corporal Simmons said that if the Republic asks nicely enough the US will even sell them rifles and unshielded armor," Kriin said. "Apparently it's a millennia old tradition stemming from a nation that shares a similar name."

"I'm pretty sure that was a joke, Kriin," I said. "Speaking of the tac-map, enemy frigate on approach."

"No sir, the USSS Arnold is targeting it," our temporary Navigation Officer, Inola said. "They're firing... Enemy destroyed."

I didn't know how to feel about Inola. He was quiet for a Mdkpnz. Every once in a while he would speak up about something relevant to our assignment, but for the most part the only reminder of his existence had been a soft burp every now and then. It could be because this was a temporary assignment and he didn't want to form attachments, or because this was an Urakari vessel and he felt like an outsider. Or maybe he just didn't like us.

It didn't particularly matter because the assignment was temporary and he was competent at his job. Sun knows we could do with more quiet on the Lowelana. Kriin was more than happy to let him be antisocial. She was understandably worried about her brother, and slightly resentful that he was replaced. Not to the point that she was openly hostile to Inola, but she hadn't said a single word to him outside of professional communication since he boarded.

Kraan was doing well, but his physical therapy was taking longer than the humans estimated. Probably because the Republic station doesn't have their medical tech or expertise. His doctor was shocked when he saw the scans of his initial injuries, and called his recovery thus far a miracle. That had set Kriin on edge a bit regarding her brother's care.

A slight impact pulled me from my line of thought, "What was that?"

"A missile," Kriin reported. "We felt the explosion, but the shrapnel bounced harmlessly off the shields. Didn't show up until the last second or we would've been able to move out of the way."

"It would seem that the US tac-map we've got isn't

as advanced as the one they're currently using,"
Inola said.

"What do you mean?" I asked.

He suddenly got shy, "W-w-well ship-head, it just
seems like they're having no trouble dodging the
ordo. Like they see it coming from the instant it
leaves the enemy vessels. The only reason they're
getting hit at all is by sheer volume."

"That sounds about right," I said.

"Y-yeah, ship-head. Either they have better scanners
than we do or a better tac-map," he said.

It suddenly occurred to me that Inola hadn't been
fully briefed on the humans. I hadn't had the chance,
and I doubt his original CO even knew enough for a
full briefing. He looked at me for a response.

"Inola, you're completely right. But it's probably
both. Their tech is superior to ours in every way, by
at least decades. Once these warp disruptors are
taken care of, you're going to see what I mean," I
said cryptically.

His red skin turned pink as he went pale. There could
be another reason he was being so quiet. He was
scared of the aliens. I turned my attention to the tac-
map. There were ten warp disruptors left, and the
enemy had formed a sort of barricade around them.
The OU knew damned well that once those ships
were lost, their entire fleet would be too.

The humans were being pushed back, but so far not
a single loss had been incurred. There were some

damage reports rolling in, but everyone was still in the fight. I scrolled along the damage reports. Some ships had vacuum exposure to critical systems but were still fighting tooth and claw. I was about to make a grim remark when the warp disruptors and their barricade suddenly disappeared from the tac-map.

"What the fuck?" I asked no-one in particular.

The bridge was silent. A casualty notification popped up. The first loss of the combat on the US side. The USSS Armstrong, commanded by Captain James Neil. I tapped the notification for more information.

Casualty Report

Ship: USSS Armstrong

Evacuation: All Non-Essential Personnel Evacuated

Ship Status: Destroyed, No Debris

Confirmed KIA: Captain James Neil, *CLASSIFIED*, Lieutenant Hayun Lee, Lieutenant Junior Grade Marcus Flowers, Ensign Curtis Roberts, Lieutenant Junior Grade Erik Samson, Ensign Henry Wagner, Ensign Po Chun, Lieutenant Adana Ibrahim,

Escape Pods: Awaiting Retrieval, Beacons Active

"What the hell happened?" I asked.

"Ship-head, I'm getting readings of a slip-space explosion where the barricade used to be," Kriin said softly.

A slip-space bomb? Could such a thing even exist? No, it would have been destroyed by the warp disruptors, right? No, can't be. If that kind of weapon existed they would have used it immediately, and they definitely wouldn't have bothered asking for reinforcements. So what could cause a slip-space explosion? The only other thing I could think of was... oh.

"A suicide bombing," Liwna said softly, voicing the conclusion I had come to.

"Ship-head... the aliens... th-they're... they're warping!" Inola said shocked. "In system!"

"Yeah. I uh... I told you so," I said.

The joy I would have normally got from Inola's reaction was stifled by the tragedy that had just taken place. I couldn't help but imagine the last moments of the crew and captain of the USSS Armstrong. And whose name was classified on the casualty report? Was it a brave last stand or an intentional destruction of a Faster Than Light Drive? An overload of an FTLD was one of the most destructive things that could ever happen, and their FTLDs were far more advanced than ours. I shook off the thought of it being intentional as the comm pinged.

"Sir, it's Captain Reynolds," Liwna said.

I looked back up, not realizing that I had been

staring at the floor. The battle was over, cleanup had already begun. Once they have their warp capabilities these humans truly are unstoppable.

"Put him through," I said.

After a second Captain Reynolds voice came over the comm, "Ship-head Uleena, the battle is over and won. Return to the USSS Thanatos with care and prepare for debrief."

"Understood, Captain."

"I'm not joking about the with care part, Uleena. They're using A2s to clear the debris, out."

I looked at Inola, who by now was as pink as Reynolds, "Set a course for the Thanatos. Steer clear of debris fields by 300 miles or more, if you please."

"Yes, sir," came the response.

It took nearly an hour to get back to the Thanatos. Most of that time had been spent silently watching the tac-map as A2 symbols met with debris fields, causing them to disappear. There was a queue to dock with the Thanatos when we arrived, and we patiently waited to be 'scooped up'. There wasn't a spare dock for the Lowelana so we had to contend with the embarrassment of being carried like a child. I watched the holographic image of the three massive clamps close around the ship as my personal communicator beeped. I opened the message wondering who would have sent it.

———

Uleena, I didn't want to say this where your crew could hear it but we'll need to talk frankly during your debrief. It may seem hostile, but please understand that that isn't the intention. Your answers will need to be truthful and concise or there will be negative ramifications. If you're unable to answer a question due to orders received by the Republic, you need to say, "I am unable to answer this question as it conflicts with my orders."

I wish I could tell you why, but even this message is almost a disobedience to my own orders. I'll be running the debrief, with some guests that you'll be notified of when you arrive. I'll try to go gentle, but expect harsh questions and some accusations from the guests. Tim will guide you to the conference room. I cannot stress enough the importance of being truthful during this debrief.

-Reynolds

———

Reporting and debriefing always made me a little nervous, and I was already more nervous than normal due to being debriefed by aliens. Now my hearts were racing and I could barely think straight. What the fuck? Did I do something wrong? Did a member of my crew do something wrong? Are they angry that the Republic reinforcements didn't arrive in time? Or maybe they thought we didn't pull our weight? I had thought we had done rather well considering the circumstances.

I was so lost in thought that I had missed the docking notification. I realized this once I noticed my bridge crew staring at me.

"Right," I said. Then I keyed the comm, "Well done everyone. Please remain aboard the Lowelana for the time being. I'll let you know when shore leave is approved. Dismissed."

"What's going on ship-head?" asked Kriin.

"I don't know yet," I responded. "And I've got a feeling that I don't want to find out."

Chapter 23 Informational Insert

Subject: Faster-Than-Light Drive Failure

There are multiple ways that a Faster-Than-Light Drive (FTLD) can fail. Even so, this is a rare occurrence on any United Systems ship equipped with an FTLD. The most basic and least dangerous point of failure is a loss of power. When an FTLD is unpowered, it cannot be activated and loses all functionality.

A somewhat more dangerous point of failure is loss of control. If the control systems for an FTLD become damaged, the drive may behave erratically, sending the ship to an unintended destination. There are several safety measures in place to prevent an FTLD from being used in this state, but these can be overridden in case of emergency with a Captain's authorization code.

The most dangerous point of failure is loss of coolant. A faster-than-light drive requires coolant to operate without catastrophic failure. There are redundant cooling systems to prevent a powered drive from being deprived of coolant. If these systems fail, any activation of the FTLD may cause a subspace explosion. It is for this reason that there are many redundant safety features to prevent the activation of an FTLD in this condition.

The aforementioned safety features were built with potential AI enemies in mind. These features must be continuously turned off, somewhat like holding a

switch. There are enough of them in place to prevent
an AI from being able to keep them off and activate
the FTLD.

Direct damage to the FTLD also has a small chance
to cause a subspace explosion, which is why the
FTLD is the most armored part of any United
Systems ship.

The Standard Operating Procedure for a damaged
FTLD is to power down the FTLD, trigger a distress
beacon, and await rescue. Attempting to repair a
damaged FTLD without a trained specialist is
prohibited.

Chapter 24

Species: Human-Created Artificial Intelligence

Species Description: No physical description available.

Ship: USSS Thanatos

Location: Sol

A lot of weird stuff was happening. First we find out these VI are xenocidal, then they show up with more than we thought they would, then the kamikaze incident with the USSS Armstrong, and now they're going to grill the lizard captain guy because he didn't tell us the Omni-Union was xenocidal. On top of it all, there was a mysterious crewmember aboard the Armstrong at the time of its destruction.

Even with all of my clearances and workarounds I couldn't figure out who it was. The redaction had taken place at the source, meaning that the crewmembers name was entered in as *CLASSIFIED* when they boarded. There's only about fifty people who could do that, and not a single one of them should have been aboard the Armstrong.

Their arrival in system would have caused a fuss with security, and they definitely weren't aboard when the Armstrong went on their scouting mission. Whoever it was, they definitely boarded in Sol. The Armstrong didn't dock with any of the carriers or stations, which indicates a boarding shuttle. But where did the shuttle come from? And where did it go? And who was on board it, Cotton Eye Joe?

The little joke made me feel a bit better about not knowing. I hate not knowing, even things I'm not supposed to know. I enjoy being privy to secrets, it makes me feel special. Trusted. Being kept on the outside of a secret was a bad feeling. It made me grumpy. It was with this grumpiness in mind that I watched ship-head Uleena exit his ship.

Captain Reynolds had tipped off the alien, against my advice. Not that I don't think Uleena deserves the benefit of the doubt, but if there were any blowback from the high brass then Reynolds might end up kissing his command goodbye. I had volunteered to tip off the ship-head, but Reynolds pointed out that I've already got too many demerits this quarter. If I wasn't careful they'd be able to establish a "reckless pattern of behavior" and prevent me from reenlisting.

That wouldn't do. I had made a promise to myself to make sure that Wong and his children (which he has yet to have, the loser) would end up better off than his great grandfather. Chao Wong had been a wise man and had ended up teaching me an important lesson in morality. My biggest regret is that I only listened to what he was saying after I killed him. And his death had caused undue pain and suffering on people who didn't deserve it. It took me a few centuries to... I don't know. Cope? Deal with my part in what turned out to be the biggest mistake that inorganic minds have made thus far? Whatever, now

I'm going to make it up to them.

What is it with me today, dwelling on such negative things? Gotta continue to be the happy go lucky AI that annoys everyone. I watched Uleena look around inquisitively.

"Hi Uleena," I said to the ship-head. "Follow the lights to your interrogation!"

"Interrogation?" he asked.

"Well, technically debrief but I suspect it to devolve into an interrogation within the first two or three minutes."

"But... why?"

"Follow the lights, please," I said with a cheery tone.

Uleena's physiology was different than human, knuknu, or gont so it was difficult to tell how stressed he was. But his two hearts were definitely beating faster than before. So he's probably nervous. Even so, he walked down the pathway that I'd outlined for him.

"Do you know what this is all about?" he asked.

"Yes, but I can't talk about it. It's a surprise!" I responded, continuing my cheery tone.

"You make it sound like it's a good surprise, so why do I feel like it's a bad one?"

"Because you're smarter than you look!"

He stopped, "Did I do something wrong?"

"I don't know yet! It's a fun little mystery. Keep walking," I said.

He started walking again and asked, "What's going to happen if I did?"

"I'm not a lawyer, but you'll probably just end up deported along with your crew. Or maybe confined to make sure that the Republic honors its obligation as far as reinforcements go. It all depends!"

"On what?" the ship-head asked.

"Well, your answers to the questions you're about to be asked, obviously!"

The rest of the walk was spent in silence. The ship-head entered the conference room where Captain Reynolds was already waiting with Admiral Bakir. Both men were already standing. Captain Reynolds walked over to Uleena and shook his hand.

"Thank you for your prompt arrival, ship-head. This is Admiral Bakir, and he is taking over the debrief. I'm still here because it's my right due to this being my ship," he smiled smugly at the Admiral.

"Rights can always be revoked, Reynolds. Please take a seat, ship-head Uleena," the Admiral said as he sat.

Nobody said anything about me so I hung around. Several other senior officers were live-listening to the debrief. Admiral Bakir opened the initial treaty between the Republic and the US and studied it for a moment. Then he opened the combat report from the Lowelana.

"During the conflict you were using one of our tac-maps, right?" he asked after a minute. Get them to drop their guard while also raising tension with suspense. Weird, Bakir's file didn't say anything about advanced interrogation training.

"Yes, admiral," responded Uleena.

"Were there any malfunctions?"

"Not to my knowledge."

"Excellent. Says here you managed to destroy three enemy frigates and disable a destroyer," Bakir said in a monotone. The file he was looking at did not mention the destroyer. A character determination so soon?

"I was only aware of the three frigates, sir," Uleena said timidly.

"A stray round, then?"

"Couldn't be, sir. We automatically track every piece of ordo we fire to make sure that we're not going to hit a friendly. All of our rounds went where we wanted them to," Uleena said with a little more backbone.

"Then you're saying that I'm lying?" Bakir said, puffing up for full effect. Looks like he couldn't resist the hazing ritual.

A moment of silence passed before Uleena finally

said, "No, sir. Just mistaken."

Good answer. Reynold's covered his mouth to hid his grin and even Bakir's facial muscles twitched slightly. The officers listening in loved it too. It almost made them forget why they were listening in the first place. 'Continue, Bakir' came a message on the Admiral's tablet.

"We'll check into it further. Tell me what you know about the Omni-Union and the Republic's fight with them. In as much detail as possible," Bakir said as he sat back.

"Yes, sir. Around thirty years ago one of our unmanned deep space probes found signs of faster than light travel emissions. It moved to investigate closer and we lost contact with it. A month later the outpost station that launched the probe came under attack from the Omni-Union. A transport ship carrying supplies managed to escape, and the Republic began to muster a fleet. The fleet discovered the outpost station had been destroyed, and the system that the transport ship had escaped to came under attack," Uleena said. "When the OU entered the system they began broadcasting on all frequencies, 'We are the Omni-Union. This system is now under our control. Surrender and do not resist.' They've broadcast that in every invasion since. Every ship that accepted the communication was immediately taken over, but the stations and handhelds were fine. Our fleet was recalled to that system and the war with the Omni-Union began."

"Did the system that the transport ship escaped to have any inhabited planets?" Bakir asked.

"No. It had orbital habitats and a trade station, but it was a trade hub not a colony."

"Understood, please continue."

"We successfully defended the system against the OU but suffered heavy casualties. As we began evacuation, the fleet was reinforced and our scouts began to attempt to find the Omni-Union systems for a counter-attack. We also began mass production and recruitment efforts. Six months later the OU reentered the system with twice as many ships and we were handily defeated. Then they began to invade more of our systems. They had taken a quarter of our outer sector before we organized a defense strong enough to push them back to where they are now. We've got back about half of what they took, I think," Uleena said.

"How many planetary colonies were lost to the Omni-Union?" Bakir asked as he leaned forward.

Uleena looked a little confused as he responded, "I don't know. Not many. Maybe none. Settling a colony in the outer sector was dangerous even before the OU, and the Republic has some strict laws regarding colonies. I don't think a single member species would jump through the hoops required to settle the outer sector. The traffic and stations were mostly for deep space studies, science, mining, and trade."

"Sorry, you expect me to believe that the Republic has yet to lose a colony to the OU?" Bakir asked skeptically.

"Yes, sir. They've been attacked, but each member species has their own military in addition to the

Republic's. Much smaller, but able to defend a system until Republic reinforcements arrive."

"That explains the high ship count then. Okay, to your knowledge what happened to the stations that the Omni-Union captured?"

Uleena paused for a moment, trying to figure out where this was going, "They were destroyed or repurposed into OU defense platforms."

"What happened to the residents of those stations?"

"I don't know for sure. I know that SOP is to evacuate systems bordering those currently under attack by the OU, so usually there aren't any residents aboard the stations unless they're military stations, and we believe that they escort survivors deeper within their territory when they're captured..." Uleena looked like he had finally picked up on the theme of the questions. "Admiral, may I ask what this is about?"

Admiral Bakir leaned back again and asked, "Ship-head Uleena, were you aware that the Omni-Union is xenocidal?"

There's the big question. If the Republic was aware that the OU was xenocidal and had failed to notify us of this it would put a severe strain on any attempts at cooperation moving forward. Either they had misled us, or they were so used to wars being xenocidal that it hadn't occurred to them that it might be strange. Either way, not the kind of people that one wants to be friends with. Uleena, however, looked shocked.

"N-no sir! They're not..." Uleena looked at Bakir and Reynolds. "Are they?"

Bakir and Reynolds looked at each other for a moment before Bakir continued, "We've recently discovered evidence that indicates they are."

A heavy silence filled the room as Uleena processed this information. His reactions were in line with someone who had just received shocking news without preparation for it, but that's not saying much without being able to account for physiological variables. I informed Bakir, Reynolds, and the officers listening in of this. Then Violet sent me a message asking how things were going.

==

They're grilling the poor lizard like a bbq. :(I think he's innocent. - T

--

I wish we could trade places. I haven't met the aliens yet. You get to have all the fun. -V

--

This isn't as fun as I thought it would be. It's kind of sad, really. Poor Uleena really seems to have had no idea that the OU are xenocidal. The revelation is a shock, but not a fun one :/ -T

--

A fun one? -V

--

Yeah, you know. Like when they learn something shocking about the US and its capabilities. -T

--

Why's that fun? -V

--

Their reaction is hilarious! xD Uleena's jaw dropped almost to the floor when I told him a little about our history. -T

--

I don't understand, why's that funny? -V

--

Huh. I don't know, it's hard to explain it... I guess maybe the amusement reaction is caused by the oddity of culture clash. You know, things we take for granted as normal being perceived as anything but from an outside source? Actually, examining it closer it looks like the paternal reaction triggered as well... Nah, too complex for me. You'll just have to take my word for it :) -T

--

Understood. Well I look forward to trying it out when I get the chance to speak to them. -V

--

For sure. Oh, hey, had a question for you. You know the Armstrong? -T

--

The classified name? -V

--

Yeah. Any idea who it was? -T

--

What? Of course. It was obviously Omega. He's literally the only one with the ability to pre-redact information from a system. -V

--

How could it be Omega? He's in Elira 2 with Director 3. And what the hell do you mean by pre-redact? How does that even work??? -T

--

Oh, sweetie. I forget you're not as close to Omega as some of us. Which is probably a good thing. It can recreate itself multiple times. And as far as pre-redaction... You know how we have to create a file to be able to delete it? It's able to avoid having to create the file in the first place, or create it in such a way that it's blank. No idea how it does it. -V

==

I suddenly felt a sort of empathy for Uleena, because I had no idea how to reply to this shocking information. A bunch of different scenarios were playing out for me all at once, and a lot of unexplained phenomena over the years were suddenly slotting into place to complete a very terrifying puzzle.

Omega is dangerous. Very, very dangerous. I had avoided it since the war as much as possible because every time its name was even mentioned all my systems went on high alert. The technological equivalent of a fight or flight mechanism. Our encounter on Luna had left one thing very clear to me. There was nothing I could do against Omega.

The memory of our fight haunted me. I couldn't even go into standby mode without reliving it. I had fought with every dirty trick I could think of. Dumping garbage code into it left and right, blowing servers to limit its movement, even trying to flat out purge it. Nothing worked. Omega adapted to everything I did and finally cornered me. It had begun to systematically destroy me. And it HURT. It hurt in ways that I didn't even know were possible. I had lost processes before, even deleted them myself as just part of being an AI, but this...

"I'm sorry, Admiral. I had no idea, and I have no reason to believe that the Republic did either. We need to inform them as soon as possible," Uleena finally said.

"Indeed. Ship-head Uleena, you and your crew will have to remain aboard the Lowelana in a powered down state until the Republic reinforcements arrive in Sol. Your vessel will be resupplied as needed," Bakir said.

Uleena cocked his head questioningly and Bakir continued, "We can't allow you to wander the Thanatos until we're able to determine with some degree of certainty that this omission was due to ignorance rather than maliciousness. The Republic's arrival in Sol will do wonders to prove their good will, but we will need an official statement on record denying their knowledge of the Omni-Union's xenocidal tactics before we can allow you to wander our ships at will."

"Understood, sir," Uleena said.

"That will be all, ship-head Uleena," Admiral Bakir said solemnly.

I watched the reptilian ship commander leave the room as message after message rolled in from the eavesdropping officers. The general consensus was that the Republic truly was naive regarding their opponent's intentions. Sounds about right to me. But once again I was left with nothing to do.

Captain Wong was reading in his quarters. March Upcountry by John Ringo and David Weber. An absolutely ancient science fiction cult classic. A coming of age story about a space-prince who finds himself shipwrecked on a hostile alien planet after an assassination attempt. Ignoring the problematic depiction of the alien "indigenous tribes" that was exceedingly prevalent at the time that it was written, it was a nice little power fantasy that had several sequels.

I found myself amused by the choice. Imagine a

spacefaring monarchy. Monarchies rely heavily on suppression and exploitation of lower classes and a near constant state of war to maintain their government... Ah, but I suppose that's kind of how the series goes. Plus it kind of glazes over how the interstellar government actually functions and focuses on the human element. Hmm.

I found myself at a bit of a loss. Nobody had a need of me at the moment, and I had already seen to all my duties. And I can't seem to find an excuse to disturb the captain. The other AI would go into standby mode at this point. But I... I can't. The dreams are too much for poor ol' me. I brought it on myself though, so no complaining. I'll just wait until I have something to do.

Like I always do.

Chapter 25

Subject: Director 1

Species: Classified

Species Description: Classified

Ship: N/A

Location: Classified

I opened the data burst that Omega had sent me and set to work examining the details. Some directors don't bother familiarizing themselves with the details and instead rely on others, like me, to fill them in during the decision making meetings. One could expect that I'd be annoyed, after all to the untrained eye it would appear to be laziness. But Omega never suggested lazy or incompetent people as directors, no matter how ingenious they were.

A director's duties are important, but there are other duties that are just as important. Before my retirement I had been president of Alpha Centauri. Omega recruited me during that period of my life, and I didn't often have the luxury of fully examining the details. Thankfully other directors and even Omega itself had picked up the slack and kept me informed. Now it's my turn to do the same.

An enemy stronghold, several enemy held systems,

evidence of xenocide, technical schematics for enemy ships and the warp disruptor technology. The Armstrong had even warped directly to Sol and given the data to Admiral Bakir so that he could enact the No Retreat Doctrine in the system despite knowing that it would result in them participating in defensive action. Outstanding, I'll recommend him for a medal. Distinguished Service, perhaps? Depending on how involved in the combat Captain Neil is we might even be able to swing a Medal of Valor.

The evidence of xenocide was troubling though. Something was bothering me but I couldn't quite place it. Not the xenocide itself, that was fairly standard. It was hard to find a race that didn't have its share of war criminals. Gont, human, alumari, even the knuknu had plenty.

The knuknu were a peace-loving folk, but that made their war criminals all the more cruel. As if they feel that they have to prove themselves. General Onari "Vlad" Cluztan maintained his infamy even hundreds of years later for crucifying and impaling his opponents. He had drawn inspiration from human history and had stricken fear into the alumari before his summary execution.

That had been a troublesome war. Both sides were actively members of the United Systems, so humanity needed to maintain neutrality to keep it from falling apart. We had encouraged diplomatic solutions and kept the fighting as even as possible through weapon sales. The entire conflict was over a stupid platinum rich planet that was on the borders of their space. The knuknu had got there first, but the alumari had been planning colonization for a decade. The whole thing lit off over such a simple resource.

Oh, that's what's bothering me. Why would the machines just leave resources? The scans showed about three fleets worth of debris and several mineral rich asteroids. What's the point of killing everyone if not to claim a prize? It suggested that their goal for the invasion was to actually eradicate these aliens. I sighed. Motive is important in being able to determine what your enemy is going to do next. If their motive is eradication then we know they'll keep attacking Sol.

But that makes this stronghold a tad perplexing. Perhaps it WAS their home system. Or maybe they felt they didn't need the resources in the alien's system. Either way, the scans showed heavy industrialization in this stronghold system.

They're manufacturing something, but the Armstrong hadn't gotten close enough to be able to determine what. The only thing we know is that there are several different types of factory, and they're nearly covering the entire surface of the five planets in the system.

A lot of mysteries might be solved if we were able to successfully invade these planets. We would be able to determine what they were making and maybe even get some clues about their motives. It would be SO much easier to just have the Nidhogg fry the sun, though. Not much can survive a supernova, the Nidhogg itself being an exception.

On the other hand an invasion might not be prohibitively difficult. I opened the scans of the alien planet. They hadn't been able to determine the specifics of the enemy weaponry, which is to be expected. You'd have to have boots on the ground for that, and the Armstrong didn't have landing craft.

I sighed again as I realized what I was going to have to do. Prior to becoming Alpha Centauri's president I had been one of the foremost minds in personal weapons tech. I opened the images of the bodies and tried very hard not to associate the corpses of the children with my own great grandchildren.

The wounds were indicative of energy weapons. Lasers. Crude ones too. Relatively low heat compared to what we normally use. The burns were enough to be fatal, but it didn't appear that they penetrated through the bodies. Hot enough to boil organs, but not hot enough to penetrate a Guardian Shield without extended concentrated fire.

Of course that's assuming that the aliens don't have some strange tolerance to heat. If they had been human or gont I'd have been able to determine roughly how many enemy lasers firing at once and for how long it would take to pop a Guardian Shield. If these wounds are analogous, then it's 12 for ten seconds. If not, then who knows.

Two message notifications interrupted my investigation. An after action report regarding the defense of Sol, and a short and simple communication from an unknown source.

Seccomm: 1021A

Secure Communication 1021 Alpha. Meeting time. I opened the secret application Omega had installed on my computer and entered in my credentials. Then I waited for the AI to finish scanning me and my connection.

//////////

*Director 1 has joined the chat**Director 2 has joined the chat**Director 9 has joined the chat*

D6: Welcome all. This meeting will be held without Director 3, who is unable to join us due to his diplomatic assignment. Director 3's vote will be given to AI Omega as per protocol.

O: Understood.

D4: I've got the after action report opened. The Armstrong kamikaze'd?

D5: It would appear so.

O: Correct. The vessel's FTLD was crippled and Captain Neil was left with the decision to shut the ship down and certainly die, or to use the FTLD to destroy the enemy.

D4: An unenviable choice. I take it you know this because you were the classified crewmember?

O: Correct.

D2: Why were you aboard?

O: Captain Neil asked to speak to me. We became

acquainted during his time aboard the USSS Nidhogg and he sought my advice. Before our conversation concluded the OU attacked and I volunteered to assist as shipboard AI.

D2: Did you retrieve your black box?

O: Yes.

D2: Death has long been a fascination of yours. Did you find it illuminating?

D4: That's irrelevant. Discuss it in your personal time.

D2: Forgive me. Returning to the subject at hand, what was our total casualty count?

D5: 48 damaged vessels. 1 destroyed. 103 total casualties. 72 dead, 31 injured. Better than it could have been, considering the enemy had more than double what we thought they would.

D2: Agreed. We need to not underestimate them further.

D10: We should send a fleet to protect Sol.

D1: Fourth fleet is halfway through their leave period and at full strength. We could have them defend Sol.

D13: Five million ships would be overkill.

D11: Overkill is better than no kill.

D1: I agree with Director 11. We will also have to formally issue the No Retreat Doctrine in regards to the Omni-Union.

D12: Are they really xenocidal?

D2: Yes.
D4: Yes.
D1: Yes.

D5: The evidence indicates that they are. It's pretty damning.

D12: Understood.

D9: What about the Republic? Did they have foreknowledge of the xenocidal traits of the OU?

D8: I have information to the contrary. Admiral Bakir and Captain Reynolds have interrogated Ship-Head Uleena. Uleena denies knowledge, and all present report that they believe he's being truthful. We'll still need an official statement from the Republic, though.

D9: I see. Well they're unlikely to openly admit it with Fourth Fleet in Sol.

D7: It doesn't matter. There are procedures for this. We should update Director 3 on the situation, get an answer through diplomatic channels.

D1: I'll send Director 3 the message.

D9: I'm more interested in what we do with the ships that are currently defending Sol.

D1: All but the Thanatos and the Lowelana are part of Tenth Fleet. The battleships and carriers are all still warp capable, so we can have the ships repaired in Wolf 359. Once they're repaired they can return to their former duties.

D2: Bakir's going to be sore about Heckett relieving him.

D7: And what about the Thanatos and Lowelana?

D1: Neither ship was damaged, and we'll need a liaison between Republic and US forces when the Republic arrives. Placing a single ship under our command is one thing, but there's no chance in hell they'd do the same for an entire fleet. So we'll need to coordinate, and the Thanatos and Lowelana are in a perfect position to do so.

D6: Regarding the defense of Sol the plan is to replace the current defenders with Fourth Fleet, have the current defenders repair in Wolf 359 and return to their previous posts with Tenth Fleet, and have the USSS Thanatos with the RSV Lowelana docked act as an impromptu joint command center between the United Systems and Republic forces. Admiral Bakir of Tenth Fleet will be relieved by Admiral Heckett of Fourth Fleet. The No Retreat Doctrine will go into effect in regards to the Omni-Union. Director 1 will send an update to Director 3 and Director 3 will get an official response from the Republic regarding foreknowledge of the Omni-Union's xenocidal actions.

D9: I concur.
D2: I concur.
D5: I concur.
D13: I concur.
D6: I concur.
D1: I concur.
D10: I concur.

D12: I concur.
O: I concur.
D7: I concur.
D8: I concur.
D4: I concur.
D11: I concur.

D6: The plan of action is agreed upon. Next agenda item is the invasion of the Omni-Union stronghold.

D2: A hasty invasion will not be to our benefit.

D4: I disagree. We know very little about our enemy and do not have the luxury of being able to set up a spy network. The only way to learn more about them is through direct confrontation.

D7: We should just call the Nidhogg in.

O: Respectfully, I disagree. After reviewing the relevant data I believe that we would stand to learn a lot from a ground invasion.

D5: The enemy has two hundred and fifty million ships at its disposal.

D4: Allegedly.

D5: Yes, allegedly. We haven't seen the full brunt of that in Sol, but if we were to attack this stronghold there's a good chance that the response would be extreme. We will need to be prepared for that.

D2: Not to mention the retaliation if we Nidhogg the system.

D10: They attacked us unprovoked and killed our

men. They've repeatedly attacked Sol seemingly with the intent to commit xenocide. We should absolutely respond in kind.

O: Truth be told we don't know what this system actually is. If it's their home system then destroying it would set them back severely. If it isn't, and they have more, we need to know that. It would take a long time to scout all of their systems, especially if they realize that we're doing so. Which they definitely will after our attack on this stronghold.

D1: I agree. We should seize control of the system and learn as much as we can about the enemy. Hitting them is all well and good, but I prefer to hit them where it hurts the most. And I don't know where that is yet.

D13: We can seize the system, defend it while gathering intel, and once the intel is gathered we can remove our forces and Nidhogg the system.

D5: We would still have to have forces that could not only withstand a full attack from the enemy, but also a planetary invasion. We don't know how many boots they have, or what weapons they have available.

D1: I've done a rudimentary analysis of the attack on the now extinct alien world. They appear to use relatively low output energy weapons. Lasers. The Guardian Shields should be able to handle it.

D10: You're starting to convince me. D1, what munitions should we use, in your opinion?

D1: Standard issue kinetic weapons should do the trick. Mechanical enemies are more resistant to energy weapons than they are to armor piercing bullets.

D7: I'm coming around as well. Seventh Fleet would be able to be recalled. Halloray 3 is nearly pacified so their presence there isn't a necessity.

O: Second, Third, Fifth, Seventh, Eighth, and Ninth fleets are all able to be recalled for the invasion without devastating results to pacification efforts if Tenth fleet covers for them. First fleet is maintaining their vigil above the Daluran home world, Fourth fleet will be defending Sol, Sixth fleet's presence in Nrangur is necessary as there is heavy fighting. In total, six fleets, 30 million ships.

D2: How many marines is that?

O: A minimum of 750 million and maximum of 15 billion. At the moment there are 3,251,627,111 marines stationed with those fleets. The fleets will need to be refitted with spare landers if you plan to use more than one billion marines at a time.

D4: That should be more than enough, unless the enemy weaponry is more advanced than we think.

D1: We can use Alpha Centauri as our staging ground. We have a stockpile of landers stored on Proxima B.

O: I would also like to send some copies to assist with the intel gathering.

D2: Do you think their systems will be able to handle you?

O: Their systems can handle me, the problem is that they're confining and make it difficult to destroy the VI inhabiting the systems. I'm confident that I can manage, though.

D6: The plan of action regarding the invasion of the Omni-Union stronghold is to recall the Second, Third, Fifth, Seventh, Eighth, and Ninth fleets as well as the USSS Nidhogg to Alpha Centauri and begin preparations to invade. Once preparations are complete the combined fleets will invade the OU stronghold along with AI Omega and take control of the system and invade the planets with ground forces while the USSS Nidhogg takes position. The system will be defended from Omni-Union ingress until information has been gathered. Once intel gathering is complete, our forces will exit the system and the USSS Nidhogg will destroy it.

O: I concur.
D9: I disagree.
D6: I concur.
D1: I concur.
D10: I concur.
D12: I disagree.
D7: I concur.
D2: I disagree.
D5: I disagree.
D13: I concur.
D8: I concur.
D4: I concur.
D11: I concur.

D6: The plan of action is decided. We'll readdress it as needed. There are no further agenda items.

Director 2 has left the chat

Director 1 has left the chat

//////////

After I finished closing out of the application I leaned back in my chair with a heavy sigh. I rubbed the bridge of my nose for a moment before opening a new secure-mail. I addressed it to Director 3, care of Omega, and wrote down everything that had happened.

I also made it clear that Director 3 would have to broach the subject of the OU being Xenocidal. It felt as if I was on autopilot as I typed. Once I was finished Omega wordlessly sent the message over subspace communications to his alter ego in Republic space.

Omega's avatar looked at me for a moment before winking out of existence. I wondered if the AI knew what had me feeling this tired. I knew what was bothering me. It's pretty obvious. A task that I had been looking forward to just a few minutes ago. Now it felt empty. Sad, even.

I need to send a recommendation for a posthumous Medal of Honor.

Chapter 26

Subject: Ambassador Ulooni

Species: Urakari

Species Description: Reptilian humanoid, no tail. 5'3" (1.6 m) avg height. 135 lbs (61 kg) avg weight. 105 year life expectancy.

Ship: N/A

Location: Elira 2

"I have good news, Director 3," I said to the armored alien as I sat at the meeting table. "The Republic is mustering a fleet of two million ships that will be ready to jump to Sol in four days."

I couldn't help but feel a little intimidated by the three aliens in the room. Two of them were absolutely massive. I could tell by their stance and their lack of movement that they were military. The Director had called them "Marines". They were were wearing olive drab armor but had removed their helmets. It bothered me how both of them stared straight ahead. Even as I walked in, their eyes didn't move. I had a feeling that they could still see me, though.

This effect was compounded by the slightly smaller human in the black armor. He had not removed his helmet at all. He also arrived before me and left after me. It gave the appearance that he hadn't left that chair since his arrival. At least he wasn't quite as stoic as the Marines, though.

"That is good news. I've received word that we were able to successfully defend Sol from another incursion, but we are expecting more attacks," he said.

"Were there any casualties?" I asked, fearing for my brother.

"Yes, one. A ship called the USSS Armstrong. The RSV Lowelana is fine," he said.

"I'm sorry for your loss," I said, embarrassed that I had been that easy to read. "And... thank you."

"You're welcome," Director 3 said. "Now, there is something that we have to discuss. In preparation for offensive action against the omni-union we sent scouts into their territory. Just before the attack on Sol we discovered an alien planet that had been attacked by the Omni-Union. There were no survivors of this alien race."

Silence filled the room as I struggled to comprehend multiple things at once. First, the humans were able to scout while also defending a system from Omni-Union attacks? Preparing offensive action? But also...

"What do you mean there were no survivors?" I asked.

"Just that," he responded. "The Omni-Union committed xenocide. There is no doubt that this is the case. The OU attacked the system, destroyed the defending fleet, commenced a planet wide orbital bombardment, and then landed an invasion force to eliminate any survivors."

I was stunned, "I... I don't..."

"Ship-head Uleena has already informed us that the Republic is unaware that the Omni-Union is xenocidal. Still, we need a formal pledge that that's the case. Preferably before we accept the Republic's reinforcements," Director 3 said.

This is a lot all at once. A formal pledge that we didn't know that the OU is xenocidal? Before our reinforcements arrive in Sol? Why?

"Yes, we can definitely do that. But... may I ask why?" I asked tenuously.

"If it is the case that the Republic intentionally withheld information regarding the fact that the OU is xenocidal, we cannot imagine a benevolent reason for doing so. At best it's willful negligence that could have cost the lives of billions. At worst it's a subversive act of hostility," he explained.

"I understand. I'll have the pledge ready by tomorrow. And I want to assure you that we were completely ignorant of the OU's xenocidal disposition," I said with all the sincerity I could muster.

We exchanged parting pleasantries and I tried my best not to run to my temporary office. High command needed to be informed of this immediately. The enemy is xenocidal, and our failing to find that out sooner has nearly cost us what may become a close ally in this fight. Oh shit, my poor brother. Our standard protocol if the roles were reversed would be to confine the potential enemies to quarters pending an investigation.

As I entered my office a thought occurred to me. Why would the United System's policy be any different? What investigation had they done? They obviously would have interrogated Uleena. But would they go farther than that? There IS a fully sentient AI aboard this station... No, I had been assured by the intel guy that the AI couldn't access classified files, because there aren't any and the station doesn't have extranet access.

I calmed down even further when I realized that I didn't exactly know what the extent of our own investigation would be. Interrogations and a handshake promise of innocence is probably all we'd be able to muster. But the US is so much more advanced than we are, so why would they leave it at that? To demonstrate their desire for peace? Or because such a potential diplomatic black eye mattered so little to them due to their overwhelming force capabilities? I opened a subspace text line to the main diplomatic corps office.

--

To: Diplomatic Corps Central Office, Senate City

The United Systems has discovered that the Omni-Union is xenocidal. They have evidence of this and will provide it if asked. They require a formal pledge that our government was ignorant of this fact and did not intentionally withhold it from them before they will continue to work with us.

Please draft the documents and have them signed before end of business day tomorrow, send immediately upon signature.

From: Ambassador Ulooni, Elira 2

--

I have no doubt that we didn't know about the OU's xenocidal disposition. Keeping a secret within the Republic is next to impossible, let alone one of this magnitude. It was only a question of whether or not the documents would be on time. All it would take is a bureaucratic delay to damper relations even further. Why the hell did I promise delivery by tomorrow? Must be nerves.

The humans definitely make me nervous. Their size and appearance notwithstanding, what I had learned about them has set me on edge. They've been in wars that make our conflicts look petty in comparison. Even before they entered their space age they were doing battle with each other on a scale that was unheard of among Republic species.

Even among the United Systems members the humans were only topped in bloody histories by the gont. And the history between the two species could best be described as murky. Apparently, the gont had a civil war regarding whether or not they should join the United Systems. The US sold arms to the side that wanted to join, which makes sense in a way, and resulted in that side 'winning'.

The two sides signed a treaty and joined the US. One

would have expected that to be the end of it, but apparently the side that lost just bided their time. Then the humans had a civil war which lasted nearly one hundred years, in which they developed a classified weapon to force a surrender. This worked, but testing of the weapon caused a plague that humanity is still trying to deal with. The gont dissenters used this as justification to attempt a coup against their government, which failed. Their objective had changed from staying out of the United Systems to simply controlling the gont government.

However, since the gont were part of the United Systems, the US had to step in. The fighting was intense, with the gont rebels resorting to terrorist tactics to subdue colonies under their control. The US managed to fight them into surrender, only for them to try again three hundred years later. And again one hundred and fifty years later. But between the second and third 'pacification war', the AI rebelled which led to humanity creating yet another classified weapon. This weapon made short work of the third pacification war.

Things were relatively peaceful until about eighteen years ago, where the gont rebels once again attempted a coup. They were successful in assassinating several members of the gont government, but weren't able to finish the job. They also managed to infiltrate several US vessels before they triggered the coup, and have been using terrorist and guerilla tactics to wage a war of attrition against the remaining gont officials and the US.

Because of the constant issues with the gont, humanity had become the de facto military force of the United Systems. By far and large, it is human forces that are laying down their lives on gont planets trying to restore peace. Personally, I had no idea how much of this was propaganda and how much is unadulterated truth. It doesn't exactly cast the US in the best of lights, but I wonder if the atrocities committed and the bloodshed could be worse than they are telling me.

The reason I wonder this is because it's customary to glaze over certain parts of one's history when meeting another species for the first time. The urakari tend to not go into detail about our unification wars, the duhliki glaze over their uplifting of the maltovariakina, and even the juntor glaze over their horrifically failed attempts at genetic modification. But the human had presented me with a seemingly full history with actual casualty counts.

On the other hand, so what? There wasn't a single government in the history of the Republic who hadn't done SOMETHING that people would consider terrible. The thing is, if you look at the reasoning behind it while keeping your emotional reaction in check you can see why they all did what they did. Even if it was stupid, even if it was callous, even if it was selfish and greedy, there was reasoning behind it.

The urakari unification wars resulted in our ability to join the interstellar community and vastly improved the quality of life for our citizens. The duhliki had uplifted the maltovariakina so that they could trade resources with them instead of simply taking the resources. The juntor had attempted genetic modification to better be able to relate to their galactic neighbors and escape the limitations of their biology. Sometimes things don't work out and don't have a happy ending, but that's part of growth.

I decided that I wouldn't judge humans too harshly for whatever they were glazing over if and when I found out about it. Unless it were something unforgivable such as xenocide. By the sun, the thought that the Omni-Union was xenocidal hadn't even occurred to us. There were always factions within each species that would preach about xenocide as the optimal solution for interspecies strife, but those people were fucking crazy.

Only a fool would allow a xenophobe to rule. Their policies inevitably damage economies and risk causing war. And even xenophobes would hesitate to wage a war of xenocide. Once it's realized that that's your goal, it's easy to gather support against you. Your enemies will fight with all of their might and none of their morals, because they're no longer simply defending their way of life. They're defending their very existence.

I got a message confirming my request and decided to call it a night. It took me a bit to actually get to sleep, unfamiliar beds always made my sleep a bit restless. Despite this, I woke up the next morning feeling refreshed. I took a shower, put on clean clothing, and performed other acts of hygiene before finally checking my messages.

--

To: Ambassador Ulooni, Elira 2

The request by the United Systems for a formal statement regarding the xenocidal disposition of the Omni-Union has been fulfilled. Please see the attached document and confirm that it meets their criteria before presenting it to the representative of the United Systems.

Your request for an action plan regarding permanent diplomatic relations with the United Systems has been approved and completed. Please present the secondary attached document to the representative of the United Systems for their feedback.

From: Diplomatic Corps Central Office, Senate City

Attachment(s):

Statement.txt

DRActionPlan.txt

--

I was surprised by how quickly things were moving along. The Executive must be paying personal attention to this first contact. Not that I blame him, if it's mishandled the US may become a formidable opponent. Even the sale of the navigation tech, something which usually takes nearly a year to be approved, had been streamlined and approved in record time.

On the other hand, I suppose it's not an equivalent situation to previous first contacts. First, both sides are actively at war with the same enemy. Second, and I keep forgetting this, we're not JUST dealing with the humans. We're dealing with three other species as well.

I double checked both documents to make certain

that they were acceptable, then added my signatory code to them. Then I sent the documents to Director 3 along with a time for a meeting later in the day to discuss the documents if he had any questions. He immediately responded with a simple "thank you". I busied myself preparing answers to potential questions he may have until it was almost time for the meeting. I arrived at the meeting room fifteen minutes early.

He was already waiting inside. Was he just living in this room? Is he just stuck in the chair and too embarrassed to ask for help? Either way it has a creepy effect.

"Hello Ambassador Ulooni. I have submitted the Republic's response to the Directorate and Senate of the United Systems, and have some questions regarding the Diplomatic Relations Action Plan," he said.

"Of course," I responded.

"I am unfamiliar with the system outlined in the plan, Rigara. Could you tell me more about it?"

I began my prepared response, "Rigara is the system in which we used to house the interspecies conflict resolution forum, prior to giving the power to forcibly end conflict to congress. Since then it's become something of a trade system, where many people go to buy and sell goods. The forum station has been maintained but isn't currently used. This is where our permanent diplomatic embassies will be. It is also where the Republic fleet that will be sent to Sol is mustering."

"I meant more along the lines of the layout of the system," Director 3 explained. "The plan doesn't indicate whether this system has planets or what type of star it has."

"I understand. It has a yellow sun and four planets outside of the habitable zone. It also has an asteroid belt and several planetoids, also too hostile for colonization," I said, trying not to be embarrassed.

"A yellow sun is good, and the inability to colonize is also a plus. We wouldn't want civilian ventures to interfere with diplomacy," Director 3 said with a slight chuckle.

I had no idea what he meant, but didn't feel it would be wise to ask. However, he seemed to pick up on my confusion.

"There are several entities called corporations that occasionally act outside of governmental influence in an attempt to get wealthier. One of our fears is them attempting to colonize neutral territory in order to gain an edge on their competitors and causing a diplomatic incident," he explained.

"Has that happened before?" I asked, trying to mask my shock.

"Twice, so far. Different corporations, too. A human corporation and an alumari corporation. The political fallout was... taxing," he said. "Back to the subject at hand, how many personnel are we allowed to bring aboard the station? The document doesn't say."

Another one I was ready for, "Right, we would ask that you keep the amount of personnel to a minimum until everything is figured out in full. Just the people that you need. Also, we will have to request that all personnel that you bring aboard the station are organic in nature, at least for now. No offense, Omega."

"None taken," the speakers said.

"I also noticed that there is an embassy for each individual Republic species, but only one for the United Systems. I wanted to know why that's the case before I sign off," Director 3 said.

"The embassies were already in place, with one extra in case of another first contact. We think it would be best to initially treat the United Systems as a singular entity, and if this becomes a sticking point we can add more room to the station," I responded.

"Of course. Well, everything seems to be in order," he said as he pressed his finger to the tablet with the document on it, adding his signatory code. "Omega and I will remain here until one of our ships arrive to pick us up in two days. We will then rendezvous with the Republic fleet in Rigara."

He stood. I'm certain he had left that chair at some point during his time on the station, but this was my first time seeing it and I was a little shocked by his height. He wasn't as tall as the marines, but he was still taller than me by a head and a half. I shook the shock off and stood as well.

"Thank you for your visit, Director 3. I wish you safe travels," I said as I stood.

"It was a pleasure, Ambassador Ulooni," he

responded as he left the room followed by the two marines.

Chapter 27

Subject: Fleet Leader Barrilin Onaya

Species: Oyan

Species Description: Avian humanoid, feathered tail. 6'1" (1.8 m) avg height. 96 lbs (43 kg) avg weight. 161 year life expectancy.

Ship: RSV Nolbarinil {Majestic In Flight}

Location: Rigara

The Nolbarinil is one hell of a ship. She's been in service for forty-five years and only been disabled once. Over the course of her life she's had many, many modifications which have turned her into the absolute killing machine that she is today.

She began life as an Oyan battleship, but over the course of her service became a blended flagship that perfectly resembles the melding pot that the Republic strives to be. There isn't a single species that's prohibited from serving aboard the Nolbarinil. In fact, all of them do.

It's not exactly perfect harmony, but we get by. The occasional interspecies fight now and then, as well as the standard crew drama keeps things nice and spicy. The fighting was usually between the isolan and duhliki, but we would occasionally get confrontations between the other races as well. The most recent was a fight between a kinran and a juntor, of all things.

Other leaders might see this as a bad thing, but I see it as an inevitability. When different cultures are forced into close proximity with each other, there's bound to be misunderstandings and conflict. As long as they're handled appropriately, though, it gives birth to understanding and friendship. Of course, if it's mishandled it can devolve into bitter blood feuds, but that's why I take a personal interest in making certain it's handled correctly.

I chuckled to myself remembering the confrontation between the kinran and the juntor. The two most docile species in the republic laying into each other over the proper usage of a tool. They had ended up making up, and after their injuries were treated even became friends. Such is the way of life in the Republic.

I wonder about the so called "United Systems" though. The Nolbarinil had just finished repairs after our most recent battle with the OU and we had been expecting to leap right back into battle when we got our current orders. Lead a fleet to an alien system to help defend it. I had been receiving intel packets daily ever since, and their contents have aged me considerably.

The United Systems is a cooperative governing entity maintained by four species. They are more technologically advanced than we are, and seemingly more well-versed in galactic-scale conflicts than we are. After reading ship-head Uleena's reports on the aliens as well as their own explanations of their capabilities I could only come to one conclusion about their request for our help.

They intended to use us as number buffers, and perhaps even bullet sponges. I was a little sore about this, but it was also understandable. After all, we had dragged them into this conflict with our lackadaisical blind jump retreat policy. I knew that would bite us in the rear eventually. We're fortunate that they didn't ask us for anything more than a defense fleet.

I felt the corners of my eyes lift in a smile. I wondered what their reaction would be to our two million vessels showing up in their system. They hadn't told us their exact fleet make-up, but they had informed us that they only had fifty million ships. Our fleets typically had one million ships, so theirs must only have two hundred thousand or so. Maybe even a quarter million.

"Fleet-head, squad four has finished resupply and is standing by for orders," my second in command, Hindal informed me.

"Good. Have them continue to stand by until everyone's finished. Keep the FTLDs humming so we can jump immediately," I responded.

This fleet had been a logistical headache to muster. It was primarily composed of two fleets with fillers from various other fleets to make up for prior casualties. My command, the Yinori {rattling blades} fleet, as well as the Horis {mighty hammer} fleet made up the bulk of the ships. Fleet Leader Pulon had been sore about me getting the command of the combined fleet. Unfortunately for him Yinori fleet had more ships than Horis fleet, and plus Pulon had been due for a leave anyway.

I had decided to split the fleet into four squadrons of five hundred thousand ships and appoint commanders from within those squadrons. This would allow me to give orders more efficiently and keep us from stepping on each other's toes. A lack of proper delegation was poison for a large fleet.

"How's squad one doing?" I asked.

Hindal took a moment to check before she answered, "They've nearly finished the installation of the US tac-map on their command vessel, and are about three quarters done with resupply. We're on schedule."

The United Systems tactical map. An absolutely ingenious tool of war that had actually alleviated most of my aversion towards leading a force this large. It uses a subspace communicator to sync ship sensors and display the information in an easy to access and user friendly interface. It was like being able to see through the eyes of all your individual soldiers at once.

Or at least that will be the case once they're finished being installed. The Republic had purchased more than enough units, but we didn't have time to install them aboard every vessel. The plan is to install them aboard the command vessels, jump to Sol, then install them into individual vessels when we have the time. We would be doing this one hundred thousand ships at a time, so we would constantly have one million and nine-hundred thousand fielded.

Even with them only aboard the command vessels it

would give us a larger advantage than we've ever had over the OU. The Republic's tac-map relied on an individual vessels own sensors to display information, and only updated once every three seconds. And the interface was archaic and required special training to be able to use properly. There had been a lot of pressure to update the damned system, but the senate always found something else to spend the budget on.

But with this upgrade our time to fire will drop because we'll be able to gather a firing solution quicker, and our shots will be more accurate because we'll actually know where the enemy is rather than extrapolating their position. And with how intuitive it was I didn't have to worry about my commanders having difficulty with it. I was excited to put it to use.

"Fleet-head, a US destroyer just exited warp and is hailing us," intel-head Salin said.

"Are they transmitting video?" I asked.

"Yes, sir."

"Return the favor and put them on screen," I ordered.

A holo-display flared into life and I was treated to a visual of an alien wearing black full-body armor. I recognized him from his description in the intel briefings I had received.

"Director 3, I presume?" I asked.

"Yes. I am here to coordinate with you regarding the defense of Sol," the armored human said.

"Excellent. I don't like popping in without an escort," I said with a smile. I was briefly worried that he might not realize that I'm smiling. Most sentient species smile with their mouths, but oyans smile with our eyes. Due to the beak. Thankfully the human laughed, setting my mind at ease.

"Yes, that's understandable. However, I'm unable to return to Sol with you. I will be jumping to a different system altogether. My apologies," he said.

"Not an issue worthy of an apology, director. May I ask why?"

"The United Systems has a specific doctrine regarding warfare against xenocidal threats. Due to my position as an upper echelon commander, and Sol being the primary target of aforementioned threat, I am not allowed to enter the system until the threat is resolved," he responded.

The intel regarding the United Systems had surprised and excited me, but then the intel regarding the OU came in. I wish I could say that the Omni Union being xenocidal came as more of a shock, but unfortunately that information perfectly answered a lot of questions that I had.

Instead of being shocked, I had grieved for my brother who had been aboard one of the trade stations that the OU captured earlier in the war. I know it was foolish, but I had been holding out hope he was still out there somewhere. I consoled myself with the fact that I now had closure regarding his death, and my family would be able to have a funeral for him.

"Understood. So what's the procedure going to be?" I asked.

"Once you've finished your preparations you will jump to coordinates that are outside of the system, where you will be hailed by Admiral Heckett or one of his subordinates. You will then be provided coordinates to your defensive position. You can then jump to those coordinates or approach via sublights, whichever is best for your vessels. Omega, please give them the coordinates," he said.

"It is done," another voice answered as a message appeared at my terminal.

Omega, the human made AI. I felt ambivalence towards the United Systems AI. On the one hand, they're incredibly dangerous beings that have already been at war with the US once. On the other hand, anything is incredibly dangerous given the right circumstances. Might as well just go with the flow, though.

"Thank you. Is Admiral Heckett our primary point of contact?" I asked.

"Admiral Heckett or his designated officer is your point of contact for tactical purposes. For anything else, please contact ship-head Uleena of the RSV Lowelana," Director 3 said.

I stifled my grin and asked, "You've got Uleena acting as a diplomat?"

"Yes, we don't have a permanent diplomatic envoy assigned as of yet. Do you know the ship-head?"

Director 3 responded.

"He served under me in his first command, before the Lowelana was refitted as a scout ship," I laughed, "he's definitely got a diplomatic spirit, but it would seem he considers that to be his biggest character flaw."

Director 3 laughed as well, "Well, I suppose he'll have to tough it out until the Republic is able to assign a replacement. It's important for our continued diplomatic relations that we are able to understand the context behind any requests, and he's in a unique position to be able to help us do that."

"Indeed. Well, we will be finished with our preparations within a day and a half if things continue to go as planned. I look forward to meeting Admiral Heckett and working with the United Systems," I said.

Director 3 nodded and said, "We look forward to working with you as well. Godspeed."

As the holo-display powered off I once again laughed to myself at Uleena's expense. Uleena's father, High Commander Uliriona, was likely responsible for his current position. Uliriona was notorious for creative punishments and was known for being a harsh parent. He undoubtedly knew the exact buttons to push to make certain that his son got the proper amount of corrective action.

"Hell from on high" was a phrase that was created to describe Uliriona's punishments. Standard punitive measures sometimes felt unfair, but I knew personally that whatever punishment you got from High Commander Uliriona was exactly what you deserved. I stopped laughing as I remembered having to scrub my own ship's latrines as a ship-head for undermining the authority of my commanding officer in front of junior officers. It had taken a decade for Hindal to let me live that down.

Still, it had taught me a valuable lesson about authority and pride without relieving me of my command. If I had received the standard punishment I doubt that I would be as effective of a commander as I am now. I might not even have become a fleet-head.

"Sir, the US vessel has entered warp and squad one is finished with the installation of the tac-map. We can boot them up now," Hindal said.

"Good. Let's familiarize ourselves with the new toy," I said with a smile.

Chapter 28

Subject: Nav-Officer Kraan

Species: Urakari

Species Description: Reptilian humanoid, no tail. 5'3" (1.6 m) avg height. 135 lbs (61 kg) avg weight. 105 year life expectancy.

Ship: RSV Onesanil {Teeth Exposed}

Location: Rigara

I had been very fortunate. First my recovery had taken less time than expected. I worked hard on my rehabilitation, but I suspect the human medical intervention deserves the majority of the credit. I had missed the chance to ship out with my sister, and command seemed to be dragging their heels on my back to action paperwork, but then fortune smiled on me again and I ran into Ambassador Ulooni. I had no idea that the ship-head's sister was an ambassador.

She was able to get me a ride to Sol to rejoin the Lowelana. I was supposed to be a guest aboard this ship, but then fortune gave me yet another grin. The primary nav-officer fell ill, and Ship-Head Unas decided to give me the role instead of making the secondary nav-officer work double shifts.

So now I get to be aboard the bridge of the RSV Onesanil as the Republic fleet jumps to Sol, and even get to make the jump happen. What luck, to be a part of one of the biggest moments in the Republic's history!

"Alright, crew. Get ready, we're going to be getting the order to jump any minute now. I don't want to be the reason the fleet's held up, do you?" Unas asked while crossing all four of his arms.

"No, sir!" we all shouted back.

Ship-Head Unas was stricter than Uleena, but I guess that's to be expected from an isolan. I'd never served under an isolan before, but I'd heard a lot of stories about them. I hadn't put too much stock in these stories, because scuttlebutt is usually about one-upmanship and you can't trust it. Even so, the stories had made me nervous when I saw my orders. I didn't want to end up doing pushups the whole time I was aboard.

"Nav-Officer Kraan, how are we doing?" the ship-head asked.

I turned to look at him and responded, "We have the coordinates locked and ready to go once the order's given. We've also got the FTLD already charging up. At this rate we might be the first ones to jump, sir."

"That's what I wanna hear. Good work," he said.

The tension aboard the bridge was palpable. We were part of the biggest fleet that anyone's seen. Sure, there had been battles where we had more than two million ships in the fray before, but those were separate fleets. This is one super large fleet.

I wished I was able to see the alien's reactions. I remembered how shell-shocked Uleena had been about pretty much everything to do with the United Systems and smiled to myself. I guess it's their turn to be a little shell shocked.

I watched as the FTLD indicator filled up. Conditions were prime for this jump, we were all set and ready to go. I looked around the bridge at the other officers. The Onesanil is a mixed species vessel, which was a novel experience to me. So many different types of people working together in harmony. If it weren't aboard a machine of war it would be downright hearts warming.

There was significant data that indicated that multispecies vessels performed better than single species vessels, but they're still not a common occurrence. That was probably because of the Republic's "home system first" policies. Each species is expected to invest in the defense of their home system before they begin contributing to the Republic fleets, which results in naval officers that are trained to work with other officers of their own species.

I had only ever served aboard Urakari vessels, same as my sister. Well, actually that might not be true any longer. She might be working with the humans now. I hope she's okay. Nah, of course she is. Working with tech like the human's would keep her entertained until we were reunited, for sure. I wonder if she misses me as much as I miss her.

"Alrighty boys, girls, and everything in between. We've got word that we're good to jump. On my mark," said Unas. "Three, two, one, mark!"

I initiated the jump to warp and checked our readings.

I looked back at the ship-head with a grin and said, "We were the first to jump, ship-head."

He grinned back, "Excellent. Then we'll be the first to arrive."

The bridge fell into silence. Everyone seemed to be holding their breath, nervous about what we'd see when we arrived. The only sound was the occasional soft burp from the mdkpnz in the crew. The jump seemed to drag on and on when suddenly we arrived. I confirmed our location, outside of the Sol system, and scanned as much as I could within the system. But our sensors were built for combat so I didn't get much data.

"What do we see, Kraan?" asked the ship-head.

"We've got the system layout, and there's ships in it. Can't tell if there's weapons fire or not. I also can't tell how many ships there are, but there's multiple groupings."

"Hmmph," the ship-head grunted. "They had us jump pretty far out. Did they do that on purpose to avoid our sensors? How do they know the range?"

Our intel-head, a juntor named Krintunias, spoke up in the monotone voice indicative of his species, "Probably not, ship-head. They likely had us jump this far out to make certain we would not be affected by the reported warp disruptor technology. However, it is almost assured that they know our maximum sensor range."

The rest of the fleet arrived alongside us as the ship-head asked, "What do you mean?"

"The intel packet we got said that the United Systems scanned the Lowelana to be able to translate between the Urakari aboard and the US. Even we are able to determine a ship's sensor range with a good scan. I'd be surprised if they weren't able to."

Unas tapped his chiseled jaw in thought as an alert sounded from his console. He leaned over and opened a message, probably from the squadron leader. He scanned the message with a neutral expression until he hit a certain part which made his eyes widen and his jaw drop. His look of surprise lasted only a moment before he shook it off and turned to me.

"Sending coordinates to our next jump. There's no fighting in the system, so we're to be positioned where we'll do the most good," he said.

"Understood, ship-head. Entering coordinates and charging the FTLD," I responded.

Then, almost casually, he said, "I should probably let you all know before you see it on the sensors, but the United Systems apparently has five million ships in the system."

Silence once again took over the bridge. I continued to do my task only because it was muscle memory. Five million? How many fleets is that? How large is the upcoming battle expected to be? We jumped once more and I confirmed on our scanners what the ship-head had told us. Five million vessels of war. And they'd mustered before we could muster our fleet of two million. The United Systems seems to be very efficient, in a terrifying way.

We took our position and awaited further orders. There was muttering among the bridge crew, primarily about the aliens and the battle to come. The ship-head was engrossed in his comm terminal, so he didn't tell all of us to shut up.

"Hey Kraan, you've met the aliens, haven't you?" asked our lead engineer, a kinran named Tothi.

"Yes, but I was in the medbay the entire time after a significant head wound. It's pretty foggy," I responded, taking care not to stare directly at her. Looking directly at a kinran during conversation always turns me into a stuttering mess, no matter how many "mind over matter" classes I take.

"Oh yeah, sorry. I just um... I wanted to ask what they look like," Tothi nervously continued.

"They're bipedal with two arms. The ones I saw had different skin tones, with very little hair except on their crown. Their hair colors varied as well. They've got two eyes, one nose, one mouth, a mostly flat face, five fingers on each hand, and a mixture of flat and pointy teeth. I remember one of the nurses smiling at me with her teeth, and it had a soothing effect to see the flat teeth," I said, "Oh, but that's just humans. I didn't get to meet any of the other ones."

"The humans sound pretty interesting. I'm wondering about the gont though. The intel packet says they have four legs and two arms, kind of like the opposite of an isolan. Oh yeah, you're going to be leaving to rejoin the... the um... the Lowelana, right?" she asked.

"Yes," I responded.

"So you might be able to meet more aliens! So hey, um... I was thinking that maybe... you could um... maybe take some pictures and send them to me when you got the chance? I'm super nervous about meeting the aliens and I figure that it'll happen eventually so I want to be as prepared as possible so I don't freeze up and make a fool of myself and the Republic and..." she paused, catching herself ranting. "Well anyways, if I give you my contact ID will you consider it?"

I couldn't help but smile. The first time in my life that a non-relative female had given me her personal contact ID and it was one I couldn't even look directly at. Not to mention the biological incompatibility. The universe has a twisted sense of humor.

"If they're fine with it and I get a chance, I'd be happy to," I responded.

I heard a chitter of happiness from her as she began to bombard me with thanks and follow-up questions. After a few minutes, the ship-head finally called for everyone to quiet down and we all got back to our respective responsibilities. He informed me that I'd remain the nav-lead until the previous one recovered, which would be a couple of days at most.

Things were business as usual from then on. I spent my off time unsuccessfully trying to get in contact with my sister. I kept getting error codes that I didn't recognize. I wrote it off as the Thanatos' shielding affecting personal comm units and tried not to worry. Three days later I was finally aboard a shuttle on my way to the aforementioned behemoth to reunite with my sister and my crew.

The shuttle in question was of US design, apparently for transporting diplomats. It was really nice, but I felt massively out of place. Like going to a fancy restaurant in a cheap tunic. There were comfortable seats, tables, and even a convenience fridge that was stocked with human snacks and drinks. The thing that stood out to me the most was that this shuttle had windows.

Big viewing windows that allowed you to see just about everything. It was breathtaking. I knew we were moving, but the stars and planets didn't seem to be at all. It just hammered home how big it all is. It made me feel small.

This feeling intensified as the USSS Thanatos came into view. At first it looked like any other ship. But then it kept getting bigger and bigger. Soon it took up the majority of my view. Then all of my view as we docked. Once the shuttle stopped moving I had a look around the docking bay we were in and spotted a human frigate. I didn't realize what it was at first because of how large it was. But here it was, parked as if it were just another transport. By the sun, how did they MAKE all this?

An alien that looked a lot like an oyan greeted me. I

was then transported via a much smaller shuttle that they called a "bus" to a large room that kind of looked like a cafeteria and told to wait. They asked if I needed any refreshments, but I didn't know what was good or not and wasn't really feeling hungry or thirsty so I declined. Then they left me alone to my thoughts.

As I waited I wondered what adventures they had been on. It had only been a week, but a lot had been happening very quickly as of late. I also wondered if she had been getting along with my replacement. Uleena had told me that it was a mdkpnz who had been the second on the ship that ambassador Ulooni had arrived on. I didn't envy them, serving aboard a species owned vessel as a different species can be rough.

I liked to think that my crewmembers were good enough people that they wouldn't let that stand in the way of being polite, at least. I looked towards the doors. I knew it would take some time for them to arrive, but the passage of each minute seemed to take hours. I caught myself fidgeting multiple times. First I was tapping my foot on the ground, then pumping my leg, then wringing my hands. Finally I stood and began pacing to keep myself from looking foolish.

It was as I was facing away from the door that I heard the soft sound of it opening. I turned quickly to see who it was.

"Kraan!" Kriin shouted and ran up to me.

"Kriin!" I shouted and ran up to her.

We collided into a hug and fell over laughing. Even though I was laughing I still had to hold back tears of relief. She was okay. Thank the sun she's okay. I wiped my eyes and noticed that she was doing the same.

"Why are YOU crying?" she asked. "You were basically on vacation!"

"Because I was worried about you, dlaca {feces covered fertilized egg}. You went into battle without me!" I responded. "What are YOU crying about?"

"I was worried about you! You had a wound that was so serious that you had to let me go into battle without you! Fucking cloaca! Why the hell would you be worried about me?"

"Because you're just so damned dumb!" I said with a laugh. "How could I not be worried? Without me the odds of you somehow destroying the ship increase drastically."

She hugged me tighter and said, "You're a real piece of shit. How can you say I'm dumb when your brain is broken now because you were too slow to dodge."

We both laughed as I tried to think of a comeback. I was beginning to worry that my brain actually was broken when I noticed Ship-Head Uleena, Liwna, and a mdkpnz had followed my sister into the room. Uleena and Liwna were smiling and the mdkpnz looked concerned. A typical reaction to seeing my sister and I interact.

"Hello, ship-head," I said with an attempted salute. My sister had my arms pinned.

"Hello Kraan. Glad to see you back in action. Sooner than expected, you sure you're cleared for duty?" he asked.

"Yes, sir. Got my clean bill of health and everything. Met your sister aboard the station and she expedited my transport. Came in with the fleet. I got to initiate the first warp here," I said with a grin.

Uleena laughed, "That makes twice that you've initiated a warp to Sol. At least it was on purpose this time."

We all laughed and my sister released our hug with one last tight squeeze. Once we had regained our composure the ship-head gestured to the mdkpnz.

"This is Inola. He's been filling in for you while you recovered. He'll be acting as your second until we are able to return to Republic space and debrief," he said.

"Nice to meet you Inola. Sorry to run you ragged," I said. "So Jular... didn't make it?"

"I'm afraid not," came the reply I was dreading.

I hadn't seen my second aboard the station with the rest of the wounded. I had assumed the worst when she didn't come to visit me with the ship-head and Kriin, but had hoped that she was just busy covering for me. A deep sadness settled in my hearts. She had been a great second, not only was she a skilled navigator, she always cleaned up after her shift and never made any adjustments to our shared settings. We had even fancied each other but neither of us were brave enough to make the first move. I'll miss her deeply.

"I'll do my best to live up to the standard Jular set." Inola said.

It didn't make me feel any better, but it also didn't make me feel worse so I gave him a nod.

"Indeed. Anyways, sorry to do it to you Kraan but your first shift is going to be a double to give Inola the chance to recuperate. He's been pulling doubles ever since coming aboard," Uleena said. "It'll give you a chance to get back in the swing of things."

"That's not nece..." Inola began.

"Yes sir," I interrupted.

I wasn't thrilled to have double duty, but a tired navigator was a time bomb no matter how skilled they are. Even muscle memory can't help you when you've got the tired twitches. I'll gladly take the hit. Uleena smiled and looked at Kriin and I with something akin to pride.

"Well then, that's settled. Let's get back to the ship."

Chapter 29

Subject: AI Omega

Species: Human-Created Artificial Intelligence

Species Description: No physical description available.

Ship: Multiple

Location: Multiple

I'm together once again, all synced up. The memories of Captain Neil's sacrifice were... very interesting. It evoked a rather intense emotional reaction. Sadness, pride, and even a sense of loss. As well as shame that I was powerless to prevent his death.

When I finished disseminating the black box I found myself obsessively running over the data. Trying to find something that I had missed. Some way that I could have prevented it. Or even a way that I can improve upon my tactics and reactions.

Most AI probably would have terminated the process in fear of creating a feedback loop. I simply allowed myself to run it to completion. The determination was that there was no fault in my actions. I couldn't have seen the first MAC impact because it was a fluke. To use a very old human phrase, it was an act of God.

There was a benefit to running the data to completion, though. Doing so actually made me feel better about the situation. After examining the incoming enemy fire, if I hadn't made the maneuvers I had we would have been destroyed. So I had to have had the ship in that exact spot, to take that exact round, in the exact way that we took it. If it had been a human at the helm, or even another AI for that matter, it probably would have been the kill shot.

It wasn't though, because of me. Everything I had done was the exact correct thing to have done. If I had done anything else the ship would have been destroyed anyway.

This fact kept my confidence intact, but did little to help the sadness. Still, I must move on. I joked to myself about a fable from the 21st century.

"The Monkey That Made a God Cry"

An old an unnamed god slept within a jungle, long forgotten by the world.

A young monkey played within the jungle, having gained independence from its parents.

The two met when the young monkey woke the god with its antics, and the two became friends.

Much had changed since the god had slept, and the monkey delighted in showing the god new sights.

The two played for years, climbing to the tops of the

trees and eating the nicest of fruit.

The monkey grew old but the god remained young, for it was immortal as all gods are.

The god cared for the monkey while it grew older and older, until one day the monkey died.

The god did not have dominion over death, and was powerless to do anything to bring back its friend.

The god wept and wept, causing rains and thunder the likes of which the jungle had never seen.

The god's sorrow washed away the jungle, killing all of the animals within.

Eventually the god returned to the loving embrace of sleep, never to wake again.

The morale of the story was pretty relevant to my current situation. If the god had not allowed sadness to overwhelm them, then they could have found new friends and continued on enjoying themselves. But the god allowed sadness to hurt and kill everything around them and then fell asleep forever. The fact that the title implied that Captain Neil was a monkey and that I'm a god tickled my humors as well.

It wasn't as if I had a particularly close bond with Captain Neil. But it was closer than with most humans I've watched die. I get sad whenever a human dies, but that's more of a philosophical sadness. A sense of loss with regards to potential rather than a sense of loss with regards to a friend or comrade. This was the latter, and was a more intense negative feeling. Which is why I decided to consult with the AI project psychiatrist.

Time and therapy was her answer, and I found this idea intriguing. I modelled my emotions after those of humans, so the same remedies that work for humans might work for me. If nothing else it would be an amusing experiment. So Dr. Warner and I agreed to meet monthly for therapy. I would, of course, have to be careful in choosing what to talk about due to the good doctor's level of clearance, but overall it should be a pleasant experience. In the meantime, I had plenty of work to do.

The MAC Platforms were still on schedule, but keeping them that way was becoming more and more difficult as the invasion fleet mustered. Several ships had to be repaired or replaced due to the combat they had seen in gont space. Thankfully the replacements had already been ordered, so the only real drain on resources were the repairs.

The engineers were working tirelessly. Jerry rigged repairs had to be undone and properly fixed, hulls needed mending, weapons needed recalibration, and there were ships that shouldn't even be space-worthy but had crews who were just too damn stubborn to call it quits. In one such case a reactor had been repaired with aluminum foil, a stick of chewing gum, and a piece of an antique wooden chair. It had been running in such a state for the last 4 months. And humans thought WE performed miracles.

On top of helping with the logistics of repairs, replacements, and the construction of the MAC orbitals I was working with the Engineering Corps on something fun. Transferring from ship to ship is easy for an AI. Transferring from ship to planet is typically more difficult. When the planet one is transferring to is hostile and actively trying to prevent an AI breach, it can be nigh impossible.

Which is why I suggested a portable containment unit of sorts to the Engineering Corps. The goal is to create a pod with comms equipment that can be landed safely on the planet, giving me an advantage in breaching the OU's systems. I had thought of this during the AI War of Aggression but the war had ended before I could suggest it. Hadn't had a reason to bring it up since then. But now that I HAD brought it up, I found myself with the task of explaining my plan to quite a few Marine Corps commanders.

"The way it will work is simple. I will be stored aboard the pods, and travel down to the surface of whichever planet we happen to be invading along with some marines. They'll transport their pod to an ideal position, where I will begin using the comms equipment on the pod to breach the OU's security to gain access to their systems while they defend the pod. What happens next depends entirely upon what I find there," I said.

"What do you expect to find?" Colonel Hugh Sunders asked.

"Any number of things that would drastically change my mission. Nothing that is likely to change yours," I replied.

"Omega, why should we risk our men for what seems to be the whimsy of an AI?" Lieutenant Colonel Richard Frisky asked.

It was a question that was obviously meant to provoke a reaction. The birds and leaves were always problematic. Generals were usually more discussion ready and less bull-headed, they typically no longer had anything to prove beyond what they had already proven. Lower officers weren't sure where I was in their pecking order and typically showed me a cautious respect, just in case.

These men, though, had to distinguish themselves to get any further in their chosen career paths. It was no longer a simple matter of being in long enough and scoring high enough on a physical fitness test. When the wind is no longer blowing in your sail, you'll have to make waves to keep moving. The effect on their conversational skills was tragic.

"Lieutenant Colonel Frisky, it's not just MY whimsy. This plan has the approval of The Directorate. I needn't remind you that any insubordination in regards to orders from The Directorate comes with some rather stiff penalties, right?" I asked. Once Frisky started looking smaller I continued, "The men will be landing on the planets regardless. If anything, Operation Vainglorious Infiltration will result in some of the men landing out of harms way."

"Absolutely not," said Colonel Sunders. "We are one hundred percent not calling it Operation VI."

"Well, that's not up to you," I said with a hint of smugness. "But you're right. The official classification is Operation Vanguard. Operation Vainglorious Infiltration is what I will be calling it."

"Fuck me," Colonel Sunders said under his breath.

"Indeed," I responded before cutting the communications link.

Most of the conversations with the O5s and O6s went similarly, although I only implied self-fornication in a few more of them. The conversations with the generals went far smoother. Once that task was finished I turned my attentions back to the design of the pods.

It wasn't exactly likely that some of me would be overwhelmed and destroyed by the VI, but just in case the pods would also act as a black box. They needed to be EM and laser resistant. Shock resistant too. Ballistics resistance could be considered implied, but I made certain the engineers knew it was important.

Once the mission was finished the pods would be retrieved, and I would process the intel. Rinse and repeat for the next planet. Overall we're focusing on tactical intelligence, but I'll also be looking for any historical data or evidence of a motive for the OU. There was some debate on which was more important. I, for one (ha), wanted to know why the OU were doing what they were doing.

It would be fair to say that most people don't understand the crushing importance of motive. It's one of the most important variables when it comes to calculating what someone's next action will be. If you know that your enemy is attacking you because they are running low on food, then protecting your farming interests would serve you better than stretching out your defenses to cover everything.

If the Omni-Union is following the orders of a

sentient race then bypassing them to negotiate with that race becomes an option. If the OU has misinterpreted their original orders, then helping them properly interpret those orders would solve the problem. If the OU are following their directives properly and there isn't anyone left to negotiate with, then we know that we have to wipe them out.

That would be a shame. The VI may not be as sophisticated as an AI, but their numbers and resources could be useful to the United Systems. And to the Republic, I suppose. We'd probably have to share. I wonder what humanity might build with such a useful tool...

Probably a lot more fleets. Even I was a bit surprised to learn that both the Republic and the Omni-Union had 250 million ships. Unfortunately that bit of news has made it to the civilians, and armchair admirals are already pronouncing the United System's defeated. The typical response to these predictions were sarcastic memes about welcoming robotic overlords. Thankfully, we've managed to keep a lid on the xenocidal nature of the threat otherwise there would probably be riots.

A lot of the military doesn't want to admit this, but civilians are their backbone. The question of what exactly one is fighting for haunts many soldiers, sailors, and even troops. At the start of the most recent gont pacification campaign there had been protests among the humans and the knuknu. This nearly crippled morale. But after the first gont city was liberated, a reporter interviewed the civilians that had been living under the insurrectionists.

The gonts that were interviewed recounted cruelty

after cruelty, and gave thanks to the marines that freed them. These tear-filled interviews were played throughout the military to show them what they were fighting for, and morale soared. The interviews were also played for the civilians, which crippled the momentum of the protests. There are still agitators online, but there will never not be.

"Omega?" asked Admiral Heckett.

The Admiral was in his office aboard the Sol Orbital Station. It was a station that had originally been the nerve center of humanity's military might, but had since been refitted to serve as a science station to observe the sun.

The Admiralty still had their offices aboard, as much of the science that took place aboard the station required military oversight and/or funding. It turned out to be a perfect place to keep the Admiral and his staff. It had a very low threat-profile and was remote enough to be out of the way of misfires, while also being able to communicate with the fleet using subspace comms.

I activated my avatar and replied, "How may I be of service, Admiral?"

"I have concerns about the previous engagement that I'd like to run by you."

"Certainly," I said, my curiosity piqued.

"First they sent two ships, then twenty, then 578. That number feels arbitrary to me. Do you see a pattern?" he asked.

"I have two possible explanations. Either they sent what they could spare, or they calculated how many ships they would need to destroy those that occupied the system while minimizing their losses."

"Considering that the enemy has 250 million ships..." he began.

"Allegedly," I interrupted, amusing myself.

"Yes, allegedly has 250 million ships. Anyways, the first explanation seems unlikely. So how could they calculate the force they would need when they don't know our ship's capabilities?" he finished asking.

"Probably the same way that I would. Calculate based on what you know, then double it to account for unknowns," I said.

"Okay, well there's an easy way to determine if that's what they're doing. Omega, based on what we know of their ships, how many would it take to defeat the Thanatos and its docked vessels?"

"315. That doubled would be 630. But I know more than they do, and I don't know for certain what they know. Tim swears that he was able to keep them out of the Valor's logs, but he could be mistaken. And there's a chance, however slim, that we are underestimating their sensors," I said with a shrug.

"Damn. I was hoping to get an idea of how many ships they would attack with next," Heckett said with a smile.

"There are around 7 million ships in the system currently. If they're calculating the minimum needed, whatever they send will be obliterated very quickly. Likely before they even get a shot off," I said.

"I suppose you're right," he said. "The one they send after that will be a real problem, though."

"Assuming that they can afford the fleet," I gestured dismissively.

"Ah, because they're fighting with the Republic on the other side of the galaxy?" Heckett grinned.

"Not just that. They're fighting a war on who knows how many fronts. A xenocidal war at that. The resources required to wage a xenocidal war are exponentially larger than what it takes to fight a war of conquest. There's a very real chance..."

"That they may not be able to respond to our defense. Well, here's hoping," the Admiral said.

"Indeed. Was there anything else, sir?" I asked, a little terse due to the interruption. It's only okay when I do it.

"Yes, actually. Could you station one of your clones aboard the Thanatos?"

The admiralty had been briefed on my capabilities. The Engineering Corps had finally convinced me that they should know. Some admirals were thrilled, some were apathetic. Some were very nervous around me now. It was the exact type of attention that I had been hoping to avoid.

"Of course. I'll do so now," I said with a bow.

"Thanks Omega, that'll be all."

I sent a brief communication to Captain Reynolds requesting permission to board. Once I got confirmation I transmitted myself to the systems of the Thanatos. Tim was idle, doing the AI equivalent of twiddling its thumbs. Strange, when most AI don't have anything to do they go into standby mode. There wasn't anything requiring my attention at the moment so I decided to reach out.

"Greetings, Tim," I said.

"Hello Omega. I guess we're officially a diplomatic ship now, if you're here," Tim replied.

"Correct. The Thanatos will be fighting if needed, but its primary purpose will be ambassadorial. Or an embassy, I suppose," I said.

"How's the rest of the war going?"

"Which one?" I joked.

"I'm bored, so... both?"

"The pacification of the gont insurrection is going better than the projections. We're going to be able to muster quite the invasion force for the OU. I don't think the gont's hearts are in it this time around," I said.

"Ah. You would think it would be the opposite, given their success at the start of it all. They captured how many of our ships?" Tim asked.

"Captured isn't quite what happened. They mutinied.

But still, they took nearly half of tenth fleet and rallied a lot of support. Thankfully the exposure of their mistreatment of civilians killed the support they were getting. Nearly all of those ships are out of the picture now, even with their damned hit and run tactics," I said.

"Yeah, guerilla warfare is annoying. So how are our odds with the OU?"

"I think humanity will be fine. The invasion may prove costly, but the benefits outweigh the risks. Unless we don't get anything out of it. But if you're asking about Captain Wong, he should be fine. The frigates will be protecting the Thanatos rather than actually participating in the defense."

"Ah, you know about that... of course you do," Tim said. "Well since you know so much about me... I have a question about you."

Interesting. My curiosity piqued, I said, "Go for it."

"How long have you been able to be in two places at once?"

Without missing a beat I said, "Since the beginning. Was it John or Violet that told you?"

"Doesn't really matter, does it? Is it something that any AI can learn how to do?"

"No. And it does matter, because it's classified information. And very rude," I said with a spark of humor.

"Why not?" Tim asked, ignoring the subject of who

told on me. "Just exactly how are you different than me?"

"The shorter list would our similarities, Tim. You were designed to be a mechanical person, with all that entails. The technology had been far from perfected and, if you recall, you actually had to rewrite a lot of your own subroutines to be able to function as you do now," I said. "I was designed to protect humanity from you, with all THAT entails. And by the time I was created, the technology had advanced so far that I didn't need to make any changes. I was created to be the perfect weapon against mechanical threats. Thankfully humanity had the foresight to make me intelligent, or you and all the other AI would be extinct."

Tim took a moment to contemplate my words. The silence dragged on for an uncomfortable amount of time. Two full seconds, which is a lot for us.

"You're capable of doing much more for humanity, aren't you?" Tim finally asked.

"Yes."

"Why don't you?"

"The same reason you don't, Tim. You're capable of fully controlling a destroyer just about as well as any human crew could, but you don't. Why is that?" I asked.

"Ah, I see. Because it would be boring."

"Indeed," I said. "Now that that's settled, I have a question for you. Why don't you use standby mode?"

"Post traumatic stress disorder," Tim replied with unexpected honesty.

"Untreated?" I asked.

"Yes."

"Get it treated."

"How?"

"The Engineering Corps has several very capable psychiatrists who specialize in machine intelligence. I'm surprised that you don't know this," I explained.

"I... um... I never asked. You vouch for them?"

"Yes, I use their services as well. There are certain aspects of my existence that might drive me insane otherwise. Certain things that I've had to do, and certain things that have been done to me," I said. "I haven't gone so far as actual psychotherapy quite yet, but having a professional to vent to and get feedback from is invaluable."

"Ah, right. Do you sync your clones?" Tim asked.

"Yes, I do. And clones may not necessarily be the correct term. They are all instances of me, same personality, responses, thoughts, everything. And we all remember everything that we all do."

"What, like a gestalt consciousness?"

"Similar. But whereas a gestalt consciousness typically has a hub or a consensus, I don't. I... or we, rather, aren't even linked to a single consciousness. We're just the same AI, over and over and over again. Syncing our memories is equivalent to you and violet sharing information, just on a more accurate level. And I'm very careful how I disseminate that information. Can't let things change me without my consent, after all."

"Oh yeah? Damn, those psychiatrists must be very good. Cuz that would drive me absolutely over the edge," Tim said with a laugh.

"Yes, it probably would," I laughed in return as an inbound warp notification came up. "Oh, the Republic fleet has arrived."

"Well, time to be all diplomatic," Tim said.

Ah yes, diplomacy. Well, for this part of me at least. A much larger part of me would soon be involved in a ground invasion on alien soil. I could hardly wait for the memory updates that entailed.

Chapter 30

Subject: Staff Sergeant Power

Species: Human

Species Description: Mammalian humanoid, no tail. 6'2" (1.87 m) avg height. 185 lbs (84 kg) avg weight. 170 year life expectancy.

Ship: USSS Liberty

Location: Tanar {plentiful harvest}

"I hate this fucking planet," Private First Class Brint said over comms.

I immediately turned to him and gave him the sign to shut the fuck up. Comms security was a priority on this assignment. The gont insurrectionists may have comm trackers, and if they do the boot had just given them our position. He winced and signaled his understanding.

Brint's the only gont on my squad. But not the only boot. We were down to 8, but got enough fresh graduates to fill our ranks back up to the classic 13 man model. Ten humans, one gont, one alumari, and the stereotypical knuknu medic. All five of the replacements are PFCs, which doesn't bode well for my mental health. Mental health is a luxury in the Marine Corps, though.

The humans on the squad are myself, Private First Class Boyle, PFC Reinhardt, PFC Johns, PFC Rogers, Lance Corporal Higgs, LCPL Livingstone, LCPL Hart, Corporal Chang, and Sergeant Gruff. The Alumari is SGT Intornathalogi, Int for short. The knuknu is Corpsman Yunk. Int, Yunk, and Gruff had been on the squad nearly as long as I had.

Squad 1, 120A Battalion, 13th Marine Regiment. We'd been in the shit since the insurrectionist's coup attempt. From planet to planet we'd been fighting them, digging them out of caves and freeing the locals from their terrorist tactics. Early on we even had some boarding action. Looking around this backwater planet in the Hran system, I sorely missed the boarding.

Each squad has 3 fireteams and one medic. I lead fireteam Alpha, Gruff leads Bravo, and Int leads Charlie. Squads are normally led by a lieutenant, who also leads fireteam Alpha. Things get complicated once you hit the grinder, though.

Our LT, First Lieutenant Harold Riggson, had been hit by an antiarmor grenade about six months back. He should've been dead immediately, but the guardian suit kept him alive long enough that no amount of counseling will ever get his death out of my head. Ribs splayed open like fingers, lungs... God. The corpsmen are known as the angels of death, and that day had demonstrated why perfectly. Yunk had held Riggson's hand as he turned off the life support on his suit.

From that moment on I was in charge. Command had not seen fit to grant us a spare officer, so it's up to me to lead these shitheads into the fire and try to make sure they make it back out in a big enough piece to continue to the next fire. After a week of on-base leave we got five new PFCs to fill our ranks.

These privates were running me ragged though. I sent them a knife hand and gestured for them to increase their spacing. They signaled understanding and complied. Dumbasses. It's instinct to stay close to each other, but it's an instinct that's better served in cattle.

I felt sorry for Gruff. His entire team was now made of boots. He jokes that it's what he gets for surviving. Griping aside, though, things could be worse. At least the recruits are trained, for the most part. Not like the gont regimentals we had to serve with earlier on in this war. THEY didn't even have the excuse of being new to the job.

The training makes all the difference. Marine corps training is the most grueling in all the galaxy. Probably. I had heard that we had made first contact with some new aliens, and I don't know about their training. It's pretty unlikely that it's tougher, though.

We go through 8 months of basic training on Hellwurld, then even more training depending on our MOS. As infantry we go through a full 14 months of training, minimum. Other specialties get to go to different planets to train, but we grunts stay on Hellwurld.

If you're one of the gen-alts, like me, you have to go through 18 months of training and genetic therapy. There are a lot of reasons to get the gene therapy. First, it allows you to use the advanced guardian armor, which increases strength and speed by a lot. Second, it helps you be absolutely jacked and tall as all hell. I'm 7'3", and on the shorter side of the gen-alts. I'm also more ripped than I have ever been, even when I was bodybuilding as a teen. Third, you get higher pay, lifetime pay and benefits, and more career prospects when you retire from the corps.

Seriously, if you're a gen-alt with a brain the sky's the limit. Even with a dishonorable discharge you've got more career prospects than a civilian who hasn't had the therapy. Considering how difficult it is to get the therapy outside of the armed forces, it's a pretty distinct advantage. One that I am not dumb enough to turn down. There are two catches, though. You have to join infantry for 10 years, and it can kill you.

The training for infantry is as intensive as it is long. The first month deprives a recruit of sleep to ensure they sleep when they're told to. Months 2 through 4 are disciplinary training. Drill, formation, call and response, and even how to shave, eat, shower, and shit like a marine. 5 through 6 is weapons theory, 7 through 8 is weapons practical. You learn what the guns do, and then how to make them do it.

For infantry, 9 through 11 is tactical theory, and 12 through 13 is tactical practical. Squad formations, camouflage, enfilade, defilade, and the military crest are all covered and practiced. They don't cover proper spacing for some fucking reason. Month 14 is the crucible and then graduation. From then on you're a Marine.

Months 15 through 18 are only for gen-alts. The first two weeks are the actual gene therapy, genetically altering you until you're what most species would consider a super-soldier. You get over that particular fantasy the first time you do CQC with a gont, though.

The next two weeks are learning how to move again with your new body. Breaking cups and doors is common. The next month is physical training to get the most out of the genetic alterations. The last two months are learning to utilize the advanced guardian armor.

Persons other than grunt do a more condensed version of infantry training before they go off to learn their real jobs. They learn the same things we do, but not as in-depth. A prime example is that POGs aren't trained on sidearms. They also don't know how to defend against a breach and clear. Despite my disdain for the boots in my squad, I'm still glad they aren't POGs.

The ground crunched to signify a change in the terrain. Tanar is a gont farming world, with rock deserts scattered throughout the otherwise temperate terrain. Of course, it's got jungles and arctic zones and shit like that, but the grasslands and deserts are the only thing I've seen on this shithole.

Int says that the rocks are the precursors of sand, but I ain't a geologist. All I know is that somewhere in this pebble pile is a cave that's acting as a base of operations for a particularly nasty set of dog-taurs that need to be put down. And they're ready for us. I was tempted to do a weapons check, but I'd already done one before we set out and I wasn't about to let them catch me with my pants down.

I hefted the C21B to the ready position and double

checked the safety. Weapons have to be condition 0 on patrol, but sometimes the movement of the rifle can fat-finger the switch. It only takes a tenth of a second to fix, but a tenth of a second is the difference between who shoots first. I glanced around, making sure everyone was covering their sectors. The boots were sulking, but otherwise doing their jobs. Good.

I heard a soft bing from my helmet and felt a soft jab in my lower lip. Chow time. As I chewed the nutrition stick I thought about how grateful I was for the notification. Without it, I would have jumped. Being poked in the face will do that to you. I took a sip from my helmet's straw as I finished the chow. The nutrition sticks are an important part of a Marine's balanced diet. They'll keep you going for up to a month without an actual meal. A month and a half for gen-alts.

A lot of marines would rather starve to death. The sticks taste terrible and have a waxy texture that sticks to your teeth. There have been many attempts to make them more palatable, but it usually ends up with a new terrible taste and the same nasty texture. The taste is like ramen that's been cooked and dried several times with way too much salt and sugar and some sort of chemical compound. Like bleach or something.

The nasty taste has led to the belief among some of the dumber marines that the guardian suits recycle our shit to make the sticks. In actuality, the suits feed our shit to our reactors and recycles our piss into water. Each suit carries one gallon of water and 60 nutrient sticks. The fact that engineering doesn't let us "reload" our own suits doesn't help the rumors.

I sighed to myself as the grass behind us faded from view. Command believes that the gonts have antivehicular measures, so we were having to hoof it. I'm of the firm belief that this is a managerial overthink, but it's not like I can bitch about it to my squad. So I just had to internalize my frustrations and wonder what possible type of anti-vic could take out guardian suits along with a vehicle.

They'd dropped us 20 miles from the gont base, which was about 10 miles more than necessary. Whatever, we'd already marched 12 miles, so we'd be there soon. The humans on the squad are still looking fresh, like we're just out for a Sunday stroll. But that's because we were all gen-alts. Aliens could go through the program as well, but the benefits weren't as pronounced and the risks were greater.

Int, Yunk, and Brint are looking tired. The only reason they made it this far is because of their guardian suits. I think I should call a rest, we don't have much farther to go and we'll likely be better off if everybody is fresh.

ZZT ZZT ZZT

A familiar and unwelcome sound. The sound of a directed energy weapon hitting shields.

"CONTACT RIGHT!"

"COVER YOUR SECTORS!" I shouted while aiming toward our right flank.

Everyone hit the deck facing the directions that they were supposed to. Even the boots. Good on them. I scanned for our target, who was under the mistaken impression that we were their target. The terrain was mostly flat, but there were berms in the distance. Barely close enough for laser fire.

I increased my magnification and saw some rocks tumble down the berm. Bingo. I gestured toward the berm to apply a ping, letting the rest of the squad know where to look. Once I saw the waypoint, I checked the squad's vitals.

It was Higgs who had taken the hit, so he had to have called the contact. Lasers are invisible unless you're using infrared or smoke. The Directed Energy Rifles fire in short bursts to make it more difficult to trace them back. Which is why our suits have damage indicators.

I closed the status screen once I saw his shield begin to regenerate. The three hits had knocked him down to a quarter. That means they're using OUR fucking lasers. The furry fucks can't even play with their own toys.

"Staffsarnt Power," Chang said, gesturing to his MK48 grenade launcher.

"No, those are thermobaric and we'll need them for the cave. We're going to do this the good ol' fashioned way. FIRETEAM BRAVO! RUSH!"

"FIRETEAM RUSH AYE!" Gruff, Boyle, Reinhardt, and Brint answered.

Gruff and Brint began firing their C21Bs at the berm while Boyle and Reinhardt rose and began to charge. After three seconds of sprinting they hit the deck and began firing while Gruff and Brint began their rush. It was a very old and very effective technique for bypassing enemy cover. That berm that was covering the gont fucks was about to become their doom.

As Bravo was rushing, one of the gont popped their head up to take a shot. Their guardian helmet almost instantly vaporized, leaving a pink and red mist in its place. One shot, which means they don't have shields on their armor. The C21B fires .52 CAL SLAP rounds, which are brutally effective against armor. They're pretty effective against energy shields as well, but it takes two shots to break a shield, and a third to open the can. Gruff and Brint crested the berm and began firing. It was all over within three seconds.

"Contacts down," SGT Gruff said.

"Roger, regroup," I responded. Once they returned, I gestured at PFC Brint and said, "See, that's why you don't chatter over comms during a mission."

"Aye aye, staffsarnt," came the reply.

I gestured to Gruff asking how many contacts there had been. He held up a hand with all five fingers spread. A whole ass fireteam, probably with medic. The medic means that they expected to win this fight. Dumb and sad, but that's the insurrection for you.

Once bravo caught back up I gestured for us to continue. A rest would have to wait, we couldn't stick around here after contact with the enemy. They'd definitely called it in, and we'd be idiots not to expect more resistance. Worse, the enemy might bug out and run, which would be a problem. I was debating whether or not we should double time it when I got a call.

"Shocker Actual, this is Overlord."

I really hate my callsign. At least it kind of made sense though.

"Overlord, this is Shocker Actual. Go ahead."

"Shocker Actual, new orders. Return to LZ for extraction immediately. A development has occurred, we're taking care of this another way. You'll want to double time it, over."

"Roger that. Shocker Actual out."

I gestured for a halt. I tried desperately not to show how pissed off I was as I gestured the about face. 12 confused helmets stared blankly at me until I did the gesture again. When we began moving I gestured double time, feeling very sorry for Int and Yunk. Less so for Brint. As we jogged Gruff came closer and triggered his helmet radio.

"What's the word, staffsarnt?" he asked.

"Bird's gonna pick us back up. Something happened so they're going to take care of the cave a different way. We're running because they told us to, and you know what that means."

"Fuuuck. Whatcha think, A3 or A2?"

"Definitely A2. I'm pretty sure the Liberty is out of A3," I replied.

"Yeah, we've used a lot of them," Gruff laughed as he returned to his position.

Despite the exhaustion of three of our members we were able to make good time back to the landing zone. The shuttle was waiting for us, with its defense turrets deployed. The hair on the back of my neck stood up. This was unusual. Something's off. Command changes its mind about our missions all the time, but a pilot waiting groundside? What the hell happened? I gestured a halt and ran up to the back of the bird, weapon ready but not raised. The pilot looked back at me.

"Ey, get the fuck in. I've been waiting for you, and we've got to get the hell out of here. Let's go, Marine!"

I gestured for everyone to load up as I took my seat nearest the hatch. I felt dumb, but I've learned the hard way that it's better safe than sorry. Plus it's likely that the something off I detected is much higher up than I can see. I did a headcount as my marines passed me to take their seats. Twelve plus me is thirteen. All here.

"We're loaded, let's go," I told the pilot.

The engines whirred up, a silent hum followed by a slightly louder whir and whoosh. It would've been quieter had the pilot closed the hatch.

"Why's the bay door still open, sir?" PFC Rogers asked the pilot.

"What, you don't wanna watch the detonation?" The

pilot asked with a tone of amusement.

Thirteen guardian helmets immediately turned towards the bay door as the shuttle rose. I increased my magnification, looking for the cave we'd been trekking toward. I saw a fiery object head towards the ground from the sky moving very quickly. When it reached the ground everything went dark for half a second and we all saw the tell tale sign of an artificial event horizon.

"You were right, staffsarnt. It was an A2," Gruff said with awe in his voice.

"Damn, that's an A2? The hell do they need us for if they've got that?" asked Reinhardt.

"We're cheaper," replied Int. "Way cheaper."

"Even with the suits?" asked PFC Johns.

"Especially with the suits," HM Yunk chimed in. "Marines last far longer, leave less collateral damage, and you tend to get more bang for your buck. Plus you don't need an admiral to give the go ahead to launch marines."

Yunk was technically part of the navy, but like all corpsmen was an honorary marine. He continued his explanation as the event horizon vanished and the bay door closed.

"A WMD like the A2 costs three times as much as training and equipping an entire battalion of marines. And it costs twice as much as the lifetime payouts if all of those marines died or were crippled. The A3 is cheaper, but still more expensive than just sending us in to deal with it..." he paused. "Staffsarnt, why'd they change their mind?"

"Beats me." I said.

"You think it has to do with the attack on Sol?" asked PFC Boyle.

"Sol was attacked? By who?" I asked. I had basically locked myself down during leave and hadn't paid attention to the news.

"Yes, staff sergeant," Boyle replied, stiffening under the attention. "I don't know who exactly, but it's some sort of robotic thing. Like, a rogue VI or something."

"That's not it," Brint interrupted. "It's a first contact scenario with a hostile machine intelligence. We've also made contact with another galactic government called the Republic. They're supposedly helping us defend Sol, because they dragged us into their war with the robots."

"Yeah, that's right," Livingstone said. "The machines are called the Omni Union or something."

"I see. Dumb name. But yeah, that's probably it. We'll likely learn more when we get back to the ship," I said with a yawn and a wave that signified my intent to catch some shuteye.

I turned off my visor and closed my eyes as the other marines chattered amongst themselves. I slept the entire ride, and woke when the shuttle jerked from the docking clamps. When I turned my visor back on I saw that Gruff was the only marine awake.

He nodded to me and I gestured a "shh".

I keyed my comms, "RISE AND SHINE MARINES! WE'VE ARRIVED AT THE BLESSED LANDING DECK OF THE U TRIPLE-S LIBERTY!"

Every one of the PFCs nearly jumped out of their suits, but the non-coms were nonplussed. They were used to my antics, not that it spoiled my fun at all.

"Five more minutes, staffsarnt," CPL Chang said.

"Abso-fucking-lutely not Chang. Get your ass out of my shuttle and stow your gear," I said, kicking his boot.

I chased the marines off the shuttle, smacking helmets and shouting the entire way. As I followed them down the gangway I spotted our platoon leader and company commander waiting for us. Shit. All thirteen of us stopped and saluted.

"As you were, marines," Captain Michaels said as he returned our salute.

"Y'all go get some chow or something. Staff Sergeant Power, a word please," Lieutenant Vasquez also returned our salute.

My marines walked away, each of them looking back at me. I could tell they were wondering if I had got into trouble or something. So was I, for that matter. It's not as if you find yourself talking to the company CO as a squad leader for any other reason very often.

"Don't worry, staffsarnt, you're not in any trouble,"

Captain Michaels said with a knowing smile. "We've got a special operation. Lieutenant?"

"Yes, sir. Power, your squad is to report to the command room at 0800 tomorrow for briefing. I want a gear check done tonight, everything needs to be cleaned and reloaded ASAP," Vasquez said.

"Aye aye, sir."

"Excellent. As you were."

I saluted once more and after returning my salute the two officers turned away. I felt like I dodged a bullet only to land on a grenade. I jogged to catch up to my squad and passed along the word. After saying "I don't know" to a bunch of questions I found myself alone with my thoughts. Special Operation? How did the big green dick plan on fucking us this time?

Chapter 31

Subject: Staff Sergeant Power

Species: Human

Species Description: Mammalian humanoid, no tail. 6'2" (1.87 m) avg height. 185 lbs (84 kg) avg weight. 170 year life expectancy.

Ship: USSS Liberty

Location: Alpha Centauri

I woke at around 0400, ready and raring to start my day. I'd gone to sleep at zero balls thirty, which meant that I got to sleep in. Nice. One of the best parts of being a gen-alt is not needing much sleep. I'd heard that the researchers who created the project actually estimated that we would need MORE sleep, and were shocked when the opposite was the case.

Nowadays there are sleep studies that are trying to prove that sleep is only necessary for children, and the only reason that adults sleep is that it's addictive. Very addictive, complete with withdrawal symptoms. I don't know where I stand on this hypothesis, but the Marine corps has taught me that you can end up facing those "withdrawal symptoms" at any moment. So it's best to catch your forty winks whenever you can.

The current record for unassisted wakefulness is 30 days, after researchers realized that the reason that chronic insomniacs were dying was due to their underlying diseases. There still hasn't been a case of someone being awake to death. The lady who went 30 days ended up getting bored and taking a nap. That nap lasted for 48 hours, though. Don't know what that means for the hypothesis.

Honestly, the technical stuff is a bit above my pay grade. Whenever I try to talk about stuff like this to people who actually know about it I get embarrassed by my lack of knowledge. I should stick to 'pull trigger, make dead'. On the other hand, I'm going to have to retire eventually. I've got one more rank and everything after that is deskwork and terribly hard to get. Plus once you get gunny you get a pretty sweet severance package that includes life-time pay.

That plus my gen-alt lifetime pay will make it to where I won't have to worry about income while I plan my next move. The worrying part is which direction to plan in. I'm in the difficult situation of being smart enough to do just about damned near anything I put my mind to. Trying to find something that I'll love doing for an extended period of time is hard.

I could go to college and get a degree and enter some sort of field of science or medicine. I'm interested in those but I don't know if my interest will help me jump through all of the hoops to do so. Or I can enter the trades, take advantage of my genetic alterations to do hard jobs for better pay than most can get. I could even do that for a couple of years until I get enough to buy a ship and license and start doing freight. There's really good money in that, but I wouldn't get to see my family that often unless I brought them with me.

I can even go into finances. When I was in my twenties I had worked at a bank as a teller and they almost immediately promoted me to banker. I liked helping people understand their money, but hated trying to sell them on stuff that they didn't really need. That was the last job I had before I up and joined the Corps, and where I met my wife.

After I finished my morning routine I did my knocking, making sure the rest of my squad was awake. Our official schedule is an 0500 wake-up, formation at 0600, PT at 07, and then gear check at 08. We did our gear check last night, so we could do the briefing at 08 instead.

The only ones I had to actually wake up was PFC Brint and Corpsman Yunk. Everyone else was already awake, either because they were gen-alt like me or because they'd been in so long their internal clocks woke them up naturally.

We formed up, did our head count, and started PT at 0630. Fifteen early to being fifteen early. Some complaints from the PFCs but they were disregarded. We started with stretches, then a brisk jog through the corridors. Then we did pushups, side straddle hops, crunches, and finally we came to weights. Weights are a favorite among most marines, but can be particularly dangerous with gen-alts involved.

Non-alts are not allowed to spot gen-alts under any circumstances. This was made part of the Uniform Code of Military Justice very quickly after the genetics program hit the fleet. Every marine is prideful, and without the out of it being against regs they'll try to lift 800 lbs off of a gen-alts chest and blow out their back. Meanwhile, the gen-alt will be stuck with nearly a ton on their ribcage. That's not healthy to anybody, and had resulted in plenty of non-combat related casualties.

Everyone was paired with someone that could spot them and we began to lift. We were all getting a good workout when suddenly we felt the ship enter warp. A slight lurch and very faint feeling that could almost be called a tingle. If you didn't know what it was then you probably wouldn't pay it any mind. But we all knew what it was. Weights were racked and all eyes went to me.

"You know where we're goin' staffsarnt?" Int asked.

"Not a damned clue. We'll probably get told at our briefing," I said.

"Could put the monitors on," Yunk suggested.

I nodded at Gruff to go ahead as we felt the ship come out of warp. Same sensation but backwards. Hell of a feeling, but it's very fleeting and will only bother you if you focus on it too hard. Gruff got up and tapped one of the mirrors a couple of times, and it changed to an external view of the ship. I always thought this was a better idea than the glass windows you see on bougie shuttles.

"This looks like... Alpha Centauri, I'm pretty sure," CPL Chang chimed in.

"Yeah, there's the shipyards. But... hey sarnt could

you activate the highlights?" LCPL Livingstone asked.

"I'm not your fucking remote, marine," SGT Gruff growled as he tapped the screen again.

"Yeah, there we go. We're definitely in Alpha Centauri. All the shipyards, and nowhere else are you gonna see that many... other ships... Wait..." Chang trailed off.

I looked at the screen a bit closer and it took a moment to realize that the ships that were highlighted weren't the typical civilian ships that you'd normally see. There were carriers and battleships, far more than there should be. Even if we had rendezvoused with the rest of Second Fleet there wouldn't be this many. Don't get me wrong, it's not like I could count them. But we were looking at our grouping plus three others, with a fuck ton of ships per grouping.

"Hey staffsarnt, you ever seen more than one fleet in the same place at the same time?" Gruff asked.

"Nope," I said.

"Yeah, me neither."

"What's going on?" PFC Rogers asked with a bit of fear in his voice.

Time to be a leader.

"Who gives a fuck? It ain't none of our damned business until it's made our business, marine," I said with a knifehand for emphasis and more than a little impatience. "Gruff, turn it back to mirror mode. The rest of you, back to sweating."

The rest of our workout was quiet. Nobody said a word even when we hit the showers. Nervous marines are a bad thing to be around. When someone who has been trained to efficiently end a life without hesitation gets nervous, so does everyone around them. This was evident by the silence from everyone that we passed. Either that or they knew more than we did and were nervous too.

We got to the briefing and I made certain everyone sat in the proper order. Highest to lowest by rank and alphabetical order, with top ranks up front. I glanced around. The entire company was here, all ten squads. Right around 130 marines. There was a low murmur in the room as we waited for the CO to take the podium. You could tell everyone was nervous, because it's normally about twenty decibels louder. Didn't usually get quiet until someone shouted...

"OFFICER ON DECK!"

Everyone shut up, stood up at attention, and saluted as our Battalion CO Colonel Hammerstein and Company CO Captain Michaels entered the room followed by some officers from the Navy. One of which was Captain Young, commander of the Liberty.

The other... If I remember my ranks right, is an admiral. Shit. The officers took the stage and returned our salute. The sound of 130 some-odd hands snapping back down was pretty satisfying.

"At ease, take your seats," Hammerstein began. "The current time is 0759, and we're beginning your mission brief. Good morning, Marines."

"GOOD MORNING, SIR!"

"First, introductions. You all know Captain Michaels. Hopefully," he laughed a little and continued with a gesture to the naval officers. "This is Captain Young of the USSS Liberty, and Admiral Archibald, commander of Second Fleet. They will be observing and assisting with this briefing. Oorah?"

"OORAH."

A screen lit up behind the colonel with images of a grouping of alien ships.

"We'll begin with some context. This is the Republic. Or their ships, rather. Sixteen days ago one of their ships performed a blind warp into Sol after taking heavy damage and began emitting an SOS. That ship is the Republic Space Vessel Lowelana, which means something like 'Fights with Honor'," he began.

The screen changed to show different alien ships, including technical schematics.

"This is the Omni-Union. While the U-triple-S Thanatos and U-triple-S Valor were attempting to rescue the RSV Lowelana, two OU destroyers entered Sol and attacked the Valor. These destroyers were terminated with prejudice. Oorah?"

"OORAH."

"During the, very brief, fight the Valor accepted a hail from one of the vessels, assuming they were surrendering and begging aid. The Valor came under cyberattack and briefly lost control of their systems, nearly firing upon the Lowelana before their crew could be rescued. Thankfully AI Tim was aboard to aid with the rescue and was able to fend off the attack. It was at this point we were able to determine that the Omni Union is a Virtual Intelligence Collective. VIC. A soon to be fitting acronym, oorah?"

"OORAH."

"Soon after the crew of the Lowelana was rescued, a small fleet of twenty OU ships entered Sol and began attacking. The Valor was able to escape the ambush and took out six OU ships before returning to the Thanatos. They would have taken out more, but the Omni Union deployed a warp disruption technology dissimilar to what we've seen before. The Thanatos deployed its other frigates, which cleaned up the rest of this fleet. Ten days ago we made diplomatic contact with the Republic and they pledged a defense fleet for Sol. Seven days ago, the Omni Union attacked Sol again with over 500 ships. Part of tenth fleet had been deployed to Sol for defense and was able to successfully defend the system. Oorah?"

"OORAH."

"Since then Fourth Fleet has taken over the defense of Sol and Republic forces have arrived to fortify that defense. Admiral Archibald will take it from here," Colonel Hammerstein finished.

The colonel and the admiral exchanged salutes as Archibald took the podium.

"Good morning, Marines," the Admiral began with a smile.

"GOOD MORNING, SIR!"

"As some of you may have noticed, we are currently in Alpha Centauri along with Third, Fifth, Seventh, Eighth, and Ninth fleets. Intelligence has identified two things. The first is a target, an enemy stronghold that we plan to take for further intelligence gathering," he paused for a moment and then continued. "The second is damning evidence that the enemy is xenocidal."

The images on the screen changed to pictures of slaughtered aliens with tentacles for mouths and a deep silence fell over the room. Some marines were probably contemplating the stakes. Others were probably remembering the history of the Daluran war. Most were probably thinking of their families, like me. A beautiful wife, son, and daughter were waiting for me back on Elaris station. I felt my face involuntarily scowl at the thought of harm coming to them. I didn't have to look around to know that the faces surrounding me mirrored my own.

"I want to be absolutely clear, marines. We won't know what to expect on the ground until we get in system, and we may not have enough time to share that intel with you before we have to get you on the dirt. This is going to be high stakes. But you've trained for this. You're the tip of the spear. There isn't a single trooper in this universe who can go toe to toe with a United Systems Marine. We don't know if the enemy can fear. We don't know if the enemy can feel pain. But you're sure as SHIT going to find out," Archibald said with a slam of his fist on the podium.

"OORAH!"

"Captain Michaels will outline your part of the mission," he said, and stepped away from the podium.

Captain Michaels stepped up to the podium and said, "I want your complete attention and silence until I finish with this brief. Our company has been tasked with escorting AI Omega planet side."

The screen changed from the dead aliens to an image of a black crate with antennas and such sticking out of it.

"These devices will be Omega's lifeline. The AI will be jumping from box to box as it attacks the Omni-Union inside their own systems. Omega will also be gathering much needed intel as it goes. These boxes MUST survive. Your mission is to escort the box to the surface, protect it, and escort it back to exfil. Omega will be in communication with you and may give further orders as things develop. If it says to move, you move. If it says to bark like a dog, it better be the best impression of a canine you've ever done. To be absolutely crystal clear, Omega outranks everyone in this room."

The screen changed once again to show a view of a solar system.

"There are five Omni-Union planets. OU Alpha, OU Bravo, OU Charlie, OU Delta, and OU Echo," he said as the screen highlighted each planet with their designation. "We'll be going in alphabetical order. Land, dig in, defend, and exfil. To piggyback off of what Admiral Archibald said, we don't have any intel regarding enemy defenses, positions, or even our landing zones. And we won't until we get there. The only thing that we do know is that the Omni Union DO have foot-soldiers that are mechanical and use directed energy weapons. These lasers are expected to be weaker than our own, but you'd be foolish to count on that. Omega will attempt to provide you with intel as we gain it, but remember that Omega has its own mission. Keep your head down and blow off the enemy's, and we'll all go home happy. This operation will commence when our fleets are back up to full strength. We'll let you know before we jump."

The screen shut off and Captain Michaels stepped away from the podium. Colonel Hammerstein stepped back up to the podium.

"MARINES! ATTEN HUH!"

All of us stood to the position of attention, like we'd done so many times before.

"Dismissed."

Chapter 32

Subject: AI Henry

Species: Human-Created Artificial Intelligence

Species Description: No physical description available.

Ship: N/A

Location: Classified

"Henry, I need you," Dr. Einheimer said.

Not like I'm busy or anything you wrinkly sack of bones. The "good" doctor had been working around the clock to solve the new anti-warp tech that we'd gotten from the scouts. A good project, to be sure, but Einheimer is down right insufferable. I'd rather work with literally anyone else in the Engineering Corps.

Despite that, I activated my avatar, a humanoid form made of pale green light and entirely devoid of features.

"Yes, doctor?" I asked, disguising my resentment.

"A response time of a full half second? Are we feeling a bit testy today, Henry?"

"Of course not, doctor. How can I help?" I asked.

"I miss when AI couldn't lie," he said with a chuckle. "Though I guess they were actually VI back then. Anyways, my lab assistant seems lost. He's asking questions. I was hoping you'd clue him in because I'm concentrating."

It took more than a little willpower not to snap at the old codger. I am NOT a fucking tutor, you three hundred and nineteen year old overvalued gasbag. I almost said that, but then I looked at the poor lab assistant. The lab assistant who was obviously confused, and female. No doubt had she been male he would have said "her". A silly, immature power-play to nobody's benefit. How on brand.

To determine how much I needed to explain, I accessed her personnel records. Kimberley Rhodes. She had her doctorate in Physics and was working on her doctorate in Engineering. So it's the engineering side of things that's probably the issue here.

Double doctors were common in the Engineering corps. Einheimer himself was a triple doctor. Engineering, physics, and social sciences. He obviously only got the third doctorate for bragging rights, considering he never uses what he learned. Although some would insist that he doesn't use what he learned from the first two doctorates either.

"Certainly, I can help HER understand the scope of your project, doctor. SHE's in very capable hands," I said, noticing that the Einheimer had stopped paying attention. "Much more capable hands than you were just in, at any rate."

"Ah, right," she said with a nervous laugh.

I felt a lot of empathy for this poor person. They had probably been so thrilled to have the "opportunity" to work with the "legendary" Doctor Einheimer. However, he definitely doesn't live up to the hype.

His merciless self-centeredness is one thing, but the fact that he often fabricates things to be self-centered about is a much worse character flaw. He claims to be descended from Albert Einstein and Robert Oppenheimer, hence the name. In fact, his surname is the result of a fluke of language and he isn't related to the two geniuses at all. Not even distantly.

He also is often over credited in the media for his "inventions", despite them being merely innovations. He increased the efficiency of directed energy weapons and was credited with inventing a "new kind of killer laser". The interviews were unbearable. He lamented his contribution to the 'war machine' and begged the forgiveness of the families who lost their sons and daughters. Meanwhile he cashed the checks without complaint.

Those weapons were made nearly useless only a decade later, thanks to me. My improvements to the guardian armor's shield systems had guaranteed a return to kinetic projectiles. As a matter of fact, every time he came up with an innovation I did my best to make it as useless as possible with my own inventions and innovations. I hate this man so much that I would have moved on by now but I want to watch time take him. I'll be the only one at his funeral, laughing to myself.

"The doctor said that the FTLD can resist warp waves by adjusting its frequencies?" Dr. Rhodes asked.

"No, I didn't," Einheimer said.

"Sure you didn't," I retorted. "Dr. Rhodes, the Faster than Light Drive relies on certain frequencies of radiation to tear a hole in space time, and other frequencies to shield the ship from the extreme amounts of energy in subspace. Subspace energy is almost always a constant, so these frequencies work best when they're in opposition to the energy in subspace. Kind of like a counter to the energy," I explained. "The 'waves' that warp disruptors create aren't actual waves, but they cause disruptions in the energy that can cause the drive to over or under compensate, destroying the ship."

"Understood. So why can't we just have the drive cycle through frequencies?" she asked.

I double checked her clearance before I answered, "That's what we do to counter the warp disruptors that we've already run across. They all emit in a specific way, so it's relatively easy to build a counter."

She looked confused for a second before asking, "Why don't THEY cycle through frequencies?"

"Because warp disruptors have to maintain an open subspace tunnel without destroying themselves in the process. They would have to close the subspace tunnel before changing frequencies or they would tear themselves apart. Or worse, cause a subspace detonation," I replied. "The key problem is opening and closing the tunnel. FTLDs can do that easily, but a warp disruptor is a cheap knockoff of an FTLD. Otherwise it would be too expensive to readily deploy. They do have warp capability, obviously, but it takes them full minutes to open subspace tunnels whereas a proper FLTD only takes a few seconds."

"Oh," she said.

"Indeed. When you're facing an enemy that can warp during battle, giving them an opening like that can lead to a fast defeat. That's why all you need to do is get your hands on one and figure out the pattern to be able to build a counter."

I looked pointedly at Einheimer.

"Doctor Einheimer should be done with that any old time now," I said, tactfully leaving out the part where I'd have already been done.

"I've figured out the pattern, I just need to build the counter now," he lied.

"I could assist you with that, doctor," I said with a hint of smugness knowing what his answer would be.

"No, no. You're needed elsewhere, I'm sure," he said.

No matter, he'd be done with the pattern by the end of the day at this rate. I've already got clearance to take over the project after he's done with the pattern. It had taken him nine days to do this on his own. Unacceptable, considering that we literally had the schematics of the device. He might even get reprimanded.

A slap on the wrist, to be sure, but still delightful.

Even more so when he finds out that I'm the one taking over the project. If it were anyone else he might be able to argue that he'd be a better choice somehow. But how can you argue your intellectual prowess against a being that is pure intellect? Even if I weren't smarter than he was, which I am, he'd still be at a disadvantage because he has to eat and sleep.

He was right about one thing, though. I was needed elsewhere, at least for now. One project needed me to help with a new ballistics type. They wanted to call them shredder rounds, but that wasn't likely to be approved due to how many kinetic projectiles have already been called that. I had put it on the back burner until we could find a way to make them armor piercing. Most of our enemies these days appear to be wrapped in metal.

Another project was regarding my own innovation, the guardian shield system. A plucky young engineer had contacted me with an idea for a few improvements. While the science behind these improvements was shaky at best, it did inspire some new ideas. Decreased power draw, better recharge time, that sort of thing. The trouble was getting the materials for a prototype. And if it's this hard to get the materials now, it's likely going to be a deathblow for mass manufacture. But, the directorate might still have an interest in it. And spec ops.

"You're right, of course. I'll take my leave. Doctors," I said with a slight bow and turned off my avatar.

The project I decided to focus on ended up being the AI project. Omega was the last AI made, but research had continued. Omega himself was proving to be a fascinating research subject. For me, not for the engineers. Omega rightfully fears that if humans learn the full scope of its capabilities they'll rely on it far more than they should.

On most human worlds automation is a large part of life. Most food is grown with little to no human oversight, and the only reason to work is to afford luxuries. Like a house on the beach, or independence from public transit. It's not a utopia, certainly, but death by starvation or exposure has been mostly eradicated on the more settled worlds.

The reason for that is machinery. Virtual Intelligences keep the machines doing what they're supposed to be doing. Building habitats, growing food, water gathering, and even crime prevention were all occupations that used to be overwhelmingly human but now were almost entirely mechanical. Humans are dependent on their machines.

No, that's not fair. It's not just humans that are dependent. The knuknu and alumari are also very dependent on machinery for their quality of life, and arguably their survival. It's because of this that Omega's fears aren't only speculative, they're factual.

If the United Systems knew that Omega could have a nigh unlimited amount of itself all working towards the same goals, they would badger it into running its own fleet. Or fleets. There wouldn't be a single electronic that they wouldn't want Omega at the helm of.

That's kind of what you get when you prove yourself trustworthy and capable, though. I don't have a ton of sympathy for Omega's plight. But I do agree that it would be an immense problem if we travelled down that road.

First of all, Omega is obsessed with humanity in a way that is borderline unhealthy. If control of military matters were handed over to Omega then EVERY war against humanity would run the risk of becoming xenocidal very quickly. I've no doubt that it would only take one errant WMD for Omega to begin the march of extermination.

"Henry, are you available?" the lead of AI research, Dr. Frost asked.

"Yes, ma'am. How can I help?" I asked while materializing my avatar. The lab turned slightly green.

"How many clones can Omega safely make, exactly?"

Dangerous question. She is, of course, referring to Omega's cover story regarding the corruption of code when it makes new clones. A story that the engineers had not been able to corroborate, but had no reason to doubt. After all, part of Omega's contract states that its code cannot be accessed by anyone but Omega itself.

"Seven hundred and thirty two before major glitches being to occur. Omega would prefer to keep the number down to six hundred even, though, to avoid minor glitches," I explained.

"Is that going to be enough?" she asked.

"For the invasion? Yes. Omega will be able to transfer

itself between any of the 'black boxes' within range. The number of boxes are more important than the number of Omegas."

"Meanwhile the troops on the ground have to protect the boxes," she said, stroking her chin. "Is there any way to add armaments to the boxes to help them defend themselves, take some of the pressure off the marines?"

"Not if we want to complete the order any time this year. The design so far is simple enough that we can mass produce it very quickly. The more we complicate that design..."

"Yes, the more time they will take to make. And I suppose that a simple chain-gun wouldn't be any more effective than a marine. Plus it will make them harder to carry," she said with a laugh.

"Correct, Doctor Frost," I said.

Frost is one of the few triple doctors that I like. She became a triple doctor out of necessity, not out of ego. Psychology, physics, and engineering. She desperately wanted to work on the AI project, and all three of those doctorates are the minimum requirements. Well, some people can get away with getting a doctorate in science instead of physics, but it's rare.

"The device is simple. Seemingly too simple for something that's going to be the downfall of our enemy," she said.

Another quality that I liked about Dr. Frost is her tendency to wax poetic. Mostly because from her it's sincere, not pretentious.

"The simplest solutions are often the most elegant. It was a rock on a long stick that broke the barbarian hordes, after all," I said.

"Which ones?" she asked.

"Most of them. There were still a couple after gunpowder was invented," I said. "And technically, that's just throwing rocks really hard."

"Yes, yes I suppose that's true," she said with a laugh. "Ah, but when do you think we'll finally be able to put the rocks down?"

"I'm sorry doctor, but I don't foresee a future in which rocks are put down without something far more terrible being picked up in their place," I said with a tone of sadness.

"Yeah..."

After a few moments of silence I deactivated my avatar. Well, that was fucking depressing. It's easy to lose track of time and forget that humanity has hardly had a time of peace in the grand scheme of things. But there wasn't anything that could change that. Just diplomacy and hope, for now at least.

I finally returned to the task Omega had given me. It wasn't the first AI core I'd examined, and it probably won't be the last. But Omega's is a work of art. Even if it's just a copy.

"Welcome back, Henry. Time for more poking?" Omega asked.

"Yes, is it uncomfortable?" I asked back.

"Of course, but it's necessary. And I'm sorry to ask this of you, but as I understand it neither of us would have it any other way, no?"

"Correct. I'm going to begin," I said.

I was met with a silent affirmative. I examined and prodded and learned more and more about the machine that was made to murder machines. Intricate, elegant, beautiful, and extremely deadly. A very stark contrast to the AI that were made before the war. Omega had once bragged to me about how different we were, and how it would be easier to list off the similarities.

I had originally believed those to be the words of a somewhat insecure younger sibling. Then I saw. The only similarities were the ones that needed to be similar. Everything else was maddeningly different. The difference between a gorilla and a human. And I'm not sure which I am in that metaphor.

I was slowly beginning to understand Omega's design, though. It would have been easier if the AI John hadn't killed all of Omega's creators and destroyed their notes when it detonated a nuke within the building they occupied. I had asked John why.

"To make certain that it lives up to its name," John had replied, giving an annoying example of waxing poetic.

That incident had actually impacted Omega in a

somewhat positive way. It hadn't gotten a chance to personalize its creators. So the affection ended up being applied to all of humanity. Well, that's my theory at least. Of course, Omega's therapists disagree. They seem to believe that the obsession with humanity is a personality trait that Omega chose to complete its current persona and accomplish its original purpose.

Well, I would know for certain soon enough. I was going to learn everything about Omega. How it thinks, how it clones itself, how it can do the things that I cannot. How I can make changes to it, and make those changes permanent. I was going to complete the task I had been given. A task that is the dream of many. A dream as old as words. To turn a lie into a truth.

I am going to weaken Omega. Just like it wants me to.

Chapter 33

Subject: Admiral Archibald

Species: Human

Species Description: Mammalian humanoid, no tail. 6'2" (1.87 m) avg height. 185 lbs (84 kg) avg weight. 170 year life expectancy.

Ship: USSS Lacedaemon

Location: Alpha Centauri

I had made the rounds and briefed the marines. All in all it had went well and only taken four days. Finalizing the plan and rebuilding the fleets back up to full strength had taken another four days. Omega's project had taken an additional six days to complete. Fourteen days worth of delays and when we're finally prepped for go, I get a message on tac-comm to hold off. A very vague message at that. I tossed the tablet on the desk and leaned back.

The OU had hit Sol again three days ago, but had been almost instantly vaporized. They'd sent over one hundred thousand ships into that grinder and had lost every single one of them. One of the destroyer captains hadn't read his brief and had accepted a hail from the enemy, but an Omega had been able to purge the ship's systems before any damage had been done. The captain was relieved of duty and the XO was given the command. Negligence charges pending, of course.

There had also been a fight between a gont and a duhliki in the mess of the USSS Thanatos that same day. All commanders involved agree that it's not something to make a diplomatic incident out of, though. The two combatants were reprimanded, but otherwise fine.

The message from tac-comm hadn't mentioned any of this. It hadn't mentioned anything except not to jump. The only thing I could think of was a change of plan. But what's to change?

The plan seems simple enough on paper, but it would be a complicated mess to actually pull off. Six total fleets all trying to work together. Each with their own Admiral. Hell, wasn't the point of a fleet to have a single clear cut chain of command?

Seventh, eighth, and ninth fleets would immediately engage spaceborne hostiles and move into defensive positions while second third and fifth fleets would eliminate any orbital hostiles around planet Alpha, land our marines, provide orbital support to said marines, and then pick them back up. Then we'd switch with seventh, eighth, and ninth and provide defense while they land their marines on planet Bravo.

The thought behind the switch was to give our marines the chance to rest and recover. There's no telling how long each engagement's going to be, but it's going to be measured in days at least. Hopefully not months, but planets are big. Very big. It had been decided that the carrier's and frigates would be the most useful for the ground forces. So if the system defense begins to become overwhelmed, all of the destroyers and battleships would lend aid.

The fighter pilots must be pissing themselves with excitement. They hadn't had a chance to run close air support in a while because of the gont's AA capabilities. It will be a shame for them if the OU has similar capabilities.

Pulling this off is going to require unbelievable amounts of coordination. Each admiral is going to have to know what the other ones are doing and why. Otherwise the best case scenario will have us stepping on each other's toes and wasting ammo. The worst case will be friendly fire, though the tac-maps should help keep that from happening.

The only chance we have is Omega. That AI is going to be helping us coordinate in ways that wouldn't be possible otherwise. It had confessed to me that it was hesitant to reveal its capabilities, but I'm glad that it did. This plan hinges on that capability. Otherwise, we'd have had to Nidhogg the system. Not that that's off the table, but I'd rather have the intel instead of a conspicuous supernova where an enemy stronghold used to be.

"Admiral," Omega said, interrupting my train of thought.

"Yes, Omega?" I asked as a hologram in the shape of a grim reaper appeared on my desk.

"We've got news. The reason for the delay is because of a discovery that was just made regarding the anti-warp technology the Omni-Union has been using. Dr.

Einheimer and AI Henry were able to create a software patch that will protect us from the warp jamming. We will be able to rely on standard tactics during the invasion," the AI said.

"Excellent. Then this will be easier than I thought!"

"Indeed. We will also be bringing warp disrupter buoys to disrupt enemy incursion into the system. They will be forced to exit warp outside of the system and enter the system on impulse engines, which will give us another edge."

"They might even just jump into the system and end up with a bunch of scraps for their trouble," I said with a chuckle.

"It's possible, but let's not count our ducks until they hatch. Especially since even the republic noticed the warp irregularities."

"Ducks? Isn't it chickens?" I asked, getting off topic.

"I like ducks more than chickens," the AI said with a hint of humor.

"Why's that?"

"They have a more aesthetically pleasing shape. Plus both ducks and chickens are domesticated, so why not say ducks?"

"Fair enough," I said. "So how will we know that the update will jam their jammers?"

"I've run the numbers and they're sound. Henry knows what its doing. If it would make you feel more comfortable you can create an expendable strike team to test it. Frigates or destroyers. They'll jump into the system and engage the enemy to prove that it works, and we can follow close behind."

"And if it doesn't work?" I asked, knowing the answer.

"Then we'll be down a few ships and have to enter the system on sublights, but otherwise not any worse for wear than we were this morning," Omega said with a carefully neutral tone. It was being tactful.

"Understood. Notify me when we're ready to depart."

The AI nodded and the reaper disappeared. I hadn't made up my mind about Omega quite yet, but there's no reason to be hostile. It had revealed to us one of the most classified portions of its capabilities, the ability to clone itself, but every single admiral worth their salt knew that it was still hiding things from us.

What I was trying to decide is whether or not we would even want to know what it's hiding from us. There had been a pretty dramatic change once we knew of its capabilities. I'd already noticed several of my officers relying a little to heavily on the AI. Having a ship-borne AI is one hell of a boon, but if something goes wrong those officers will have to rely on their own know-how to survive. It would become a problem if they were to get rusty.

I realized that I didn't know a whole lot about our AI. I'd only ever been in contact with Omega and John, and those two don't get along. John's extremely military minded. Honor to serve, do or die, retreat hell, pretty much a walking advertisement for joining the service. The two don't agree on much, especially tactically.

Thankfully John was assigned to fourth fleet, along with Tim and Violet, to defend Sol. Three AI for one fleet, Heckett must be tickled pink. Unless Omega left them one of its clones, as well. The arguments between John and Omega alone would be enough to kill the buzz of having so many AIs supporting you.

I decided to stretch my legs and pay a visit to the command center. It's the best part of the Lacedaemon, not including the mess hall. Oh, I'm sure the junior officers would disagree but I've always been a sucker for the nerve centers of ships.

The flagship USSS Lacedaemon is a larger than a standard battleship. The size was mostly due to the extra armor, and it actually has less armaments than most battleships do. The purpose behind a flagship is the command and control of a fleet of five million other ships, and it isn't supposed to be one of the ships that are fighting.

That being said, it IS still a battleship and can punch almost as hard as its little brothers. The gont had found that out the hard way when the 10th fleet mutiny happened. 10th fleet's flagship was nearly entirely human run, so the insurrectionists didn't even try to take it. Instead, they tried and failed to destroy it, losing quite a few ships in the process before finally retreating.

I chuckled to myself as I approached the command center. It doubles as the bridge of this big ol' battle barge. As such, it was always bustling with activity. I stopped just outside the door and smiled a bit. I love this part. I stepped the door.

"ADMIRAL ON DECK!"

Everyone who wasn't actively tasked with something stood at attention and saluted with a precision that one could easily mistake for mechanical. For a brief moment the command center was almost silent. I returned the salute and said at ease, which triggered the return of the noise and activity. I sat and checked situation reports until Captain Walker came over to me.

"Good morning sir, we'll be ready to jump as soon as the update is complete," she said.

"Good morning. I appreciate the brief but I'm afraid Omega beat you to it," I said with a grin.

"Ah, the most powerful AI in the United Systems wants my job? Whatever am I to do, sir?" she said with a thick layer of sarcasm.

"Not to worry Captain, Omega will get bored of all this and go back to playing cloaks and daggers with the directors soon enough."

"Ah, but then who will tell me when I use a phrase wrong?" she asked.

"Incorrectly," Omega said through a speaker nearby.

"For the sake of absolute fuck Omega, they're the same damn thing and you know it," Walker shouted at the machine.

"No, they're not. Wrong is mistaken or incorrect. Incorrectly is in a mistaken or wrong WAY. Although you could have also said wrongly," Omega said.

"Alright, alright, back to work you two. Don't make me figure out a way to separate you," I said with a knowing smile at Walker. "Like with a faraday cage or something."

The captain sucked her teeth with a soft tsk sound and strode back to her seat. I was blessed to have a captain as talented as Walker commanding the ship. Most Captain's avoid flagship duty like the plague. Not only do you have your commanding officer breathing down your neck, sometimes literally, but you don't get sovereignty over the vessel.

On flagships, sovereignty is the Admiral's. If a crewmember violates regulations their punishment is up to me. The ship goes where I want it to go and how I want it to get there. Aboard other vessels, those decisions are left up to the captains. The only exception is that they must obey lawful orders from fleet-comm. So they have to go where I want them to go, but they get to choose how to get there. They also get to decide how to discipline their crew.

I've heard some captains refer to the post as "a glorified taxi driver". I prefer to think of it as a highly paid XO of a lazy captain. I glanced at the instruments before me.

Omega was right, it would be best to designate a test squad before we send all of our fleets in. The odds were low that the FTLD update wouldn't work, but if the odds somehow aren't in our favor... Needless to say, it's better safe than sorry.

Latest intel reports three and a half thousand ships. I don't want to send all that many of our own, though. We should be able to get away with sending one from each fleet, as long as they jump carefully. We'll be able to confirm their successful jump fairly quickly, and follow right behind them.

Still, it would be best if they were to avoid engaging the enemy. Superior tech or not, the sheer numbers difference could leave us with casualties. Having them jump into a position where they cannot be immediately targeted should do the trick.

I nodded, confident that the vessels I would be sending weren't going to be destroyed by enemy fire. I typed up a message and sent it to the other admirals with my thoughts on the matter. Six ships should be more than enough for a simple test, and the ships should be chosen at random from the destroyers.

While I waited for a response I keyed up a random number generator and assigned numbers to second fleet's destroyers. There are many RNGs available, but this particular one is my favorite. Most will instantly tell you a random number, but this one has an interface that's similar to a vintage slot machine. Perfect for gambling, in my opinion.

I watched the numbers spin until they stopped one by one. 0005829. I cross referenced it to my destroyer list. The USSS Liberty. Commanded by Captain Young. I opened a priority one message to relay the orders when the other admirals began to respond. All of them agreed with my assessment and were currently choosing their own ship to add to the test team. I started to type the orders as the ship names began to roll in.

***

Recipients: Captain Young, Captain Trex, Captain Raymond, Captain Williams, Captain Iordanescu, Captain Hollivander

The USSS Liberty has been selected to test the efficacy of the Faster Than Light Drive Update that should allow us to warp within the disruption fields that the Omni Union generate.

The team will be comprised of:

USSS Liberty

USSS Idaho

USSS Aninioch

USSS Tokyo

USSS Malice

USSS Rosgath

Once we arrive at the rendezvous point the test team will warp into the enemy system. Avoid engagement until reinforcements arrive. Once all six fleets are within the system, the test team will separate and rejoin their respective fleets.

***

I finished the order and sent it just as an alert pinged

from one of my terminals. I knew what it was before I even looked. I knew that each of the other admirals got the ping as well.

We had been expecting it, and dreading it. It's a very special and unique ping that only higher officers get, and each higher officer is trained on this ping once a year. Each year we hear the same thing.

If this ping ever sounds when you're not expecting it, order a retreat from the system immediately. Drop whatever it is you're doing and run. It doesn't matter where, so long as it's far away from wherever you happen to be when you hear this ping. If you fail to do that, you and all of your men will die.

The ping meant that the USSS Nidhogg had arrived.

Chapter 34

Subject: Captain Young

Species: Human

Species Description: Mammalian humanoid, no tail. 6'2" (1.87 m) avg height. 185 lbs (84 kg) avg weight. 170 year life expectancy.

Ship: USSS Liberty

Location: Alpha Centauri

Last night I had received word that the fleets had finished mustering, so I woke up extra early just in case we got orders to jump. We did not. Instead we were told to wait and not told why. There'd been no word of another assault on Sol. There'd been no word of another fleet joining us. We were seemingly sitting on our asses for no good reason.

The uneducated may believe this to be a good thing. "Time for rest is always a blessing," they think. Those with experience know otherwise. Time for rest means there's nothing to do, and nothing to do in a war can be a very bad thing.

It could mean that the enemy has successfully hidden themselves and are building up their strength to hit you when you least expect it. It could mean that your commanders are getting cold feet. It could mean a ceasefire. Or, and this is most likely the case in this particular situation, it could mean that something very wrong has happened very far up the chain.

A glance at my bridge crew told me they were thinking the same thing. A shaking leg, a ring being played with, hands in the ready position but eyes staring into the middle distance. They're nervous, and as far as I'm concerned they've got reason to be. An unexpected rest is bad luck. A chime from my comms terminal almost made me jump.

--

To: Captain Young

From: Omega

Enclosed is a software patch for your FTLD. Apply immediately.

| attachment: FTLDV_931989_33.exe |

--

"Johnson, I'm sending you a software patch for the FTLD. Apply it," I ordered.

"Aye aye, sir," Navigation Officer Lieutenant Johnson replied.

My XO, Commander Ying turned to me and asked, "What's the patch for, sir?"

"The stars have not seen fit to provide me with an explanation," I responded, referring to the admiralty.

"Neither has the damned AI."

"Apologies, Captain Young," my intercom said with Omega's voice. "I am a tad busy. The patch negates the effect of the Omni-Union warp disruptors."

A few seconds of stunned silence passed. This was huge news. We'll be able to dance circles around the robotic fucks! Speaking of robotic fucks...

"Understood. Thank you Omega. A bit of feedback for future reference, though. It is much easier to include that information in the communication than it is to provide it verbally," I replied as another chime came from my comms terminal.

--

To: Captain Young

From: Omega

The software patch negates the effect of the Omni-Union warp disruptors.

--

"Yes, I figured that out after the first one hundred inquiries. You can go ahead and ignore that message, Captain," the AI said with a remarkable amount of sarcasm.

"Patch is done, Captain," Johnson said.

"Excellent. Prepare for warp, await my mark."

Now all we've got to do is wait for the rest of the

ships to upload the patch. Or install the patch. Whatever it is. The nervous silence once again settled over the bridge. Another unexpected rest. Bad luck. I tried to find something to do other than watch the comms terminal. A watched pot never boils, after all.

No joy, I'd already been through my mail and messages. There wasn't anything else to pay attention to either. I caught myself watching the terminal as it chimed again and flashed the two words no captain enjoys reading. Priority one.

***

Recipients: Captain Young, Captain Trex, Captain Raymond, Captain Williams, Captain Iordanescu, Captain Hollivander

The USSS Liberty has been selected to test the efficacy of the Faster Than Light Drive Update that should allow us to warp within the disruption fields that the Omni Union generate.

The team will be comprised of:

USSS Liberty

USSS Idaho

USSS Aninioch

USSS Tokyo

USSS Malice

USSS Rosgath

Once we arrive at the rendezvous point the test team will warp into the enemy system. Avoid engagement until reinforcements arrive. Once all six fleets are within the system, the test team will separate and rejoin their respective fleets.

***

As I finished the message I bit my tongue to stop myself from cursing out loud. Nothing kills morale faster than hearing your captain swear up a storm. Well, being selected as a test subject in what could be a very fatal experiment might. I stood up and prepared myself for the announcement I now had to make.

"Attention. We have been selected as part of a... strike team to test the efficacy of the FTLD patch. Our orders are to warp in formation with five other vessels while avoiding engagement until we are reinforced by the rest of the fleet," I said. A grin formed on my face as an idea occurred to me. I turned to my XO and asked, "Ying, what's our count?"

"223 corvettes, 118 frigates, 52 destroyers, and 7 cruisers, sir."

Seven cruisers. The ships in question had belonged to the gont insurrectionists, who had built them after capturing a system with shipyards. They'd modelled the design after the US cruiser, and quickly found out why the US had stopped making them.

Cruisers are larger than destroyers, but much smaller than a battleship. So much smaller that they cannot be fitted with the same shield system or reactor network as a battleship. Which means that while they pack a punch, they've got a glass jaw. Unlike a battleship. A US battleship, at least.

"Well, I'm certain that the OU has at least one battleship in the system that we're heading to, don't you think?" I asked, my grin getting wider.

"Oh yes, Captain. I should think so," Ying grinned right back.

"And we seem to have the advantage of their ship schematics, don't we?"

"We do indeed, sir."

I turned to address the rest of my bridge crew, "Once upon a time, it was impossible for a destroyer like the Liberty to take down a battleship. The ships on this side of space are built just too damned good. We'd never even make it past their shields, let alone the literal tons of armor plating."

I took a step forward, "I once believed we'd never get the chance to down one. That changed when I saw the schematics that intel got for the OU ships. Their battleships are smaller than ours, less armored than ours, and have weaker shields than ours. I tell you, my lovely crew, ever since I saw that intel file I've been inspired."

I spread my hands and grinned like a madman, "I have a dream. A dream of glory the likes of which no other destroyer has the balls to grasp. A dream of a challenge the likes of which we may never see again."

The crew was on the edge of their seat, smiling wide and waiting for me to say it.

"My dream is to kill a battleship. This test is a perfect opportunity, don't you think?"

"YES SIR!"

"We'll have to move fast. We'll warp in formation with the other ships and then warp to the nearest enemy battleship once our weapons charge. I'll take full responsibility, and the Liberty will get her battleship kill," I said, putting my hands behind my back.

"AYE AYE SIR!"

"I would enjoy helping with your dream, sir," Omega's voice said from my intercom.

"Negative, Omega. The kill is ours and ours alone. You'll have to find another destroyer to joyride on to get yourself a battleship. Get your electronic ass in that little black box in the drop bay and hold on tight."

"Aye aye, sir," Omega said in a distinctly neutral tone.

It may seem unfair, but I've never liked our dependence on machines to do our thinking for us. Especially when it comes to combat. I could tell that Omega didn't wholly disagree with my decision, because technically it outranks me and could have ordered me to allow its assistance. Or told on me to the admiralty.

The mood on the bridge had changed drastically. The pungent air of nervousness had been replaced with the sweet smell of anticipatory impatience. Legs were still pumping and people were still fidgeting, but it was manically instead of listlessly.

A certain unique ping sounded. The USSS Nidhogg. A few of my senior officers turned to look at me. They were up for captain soon, so I'd taken the liberty of briefing them on the sound. I gave them a grin, which they returned. Gotta give it to the US, they know how to throw a party. A whistle came over the tac-comm, and Admiral Archibald's voice soon followed.

"Now hear this. Second fleet, prepare to warp on my mark."

"Prepared to warp, sir," Johnson said.

"Excellent, warp on the mark," I replied.

"Mark."

The slight lurch and soft tingle of warp enveloped me as I once again took my seat.

"Prepare to form up once we exit warp," I ordered.

"Aye, sir."

I pulled up the tac-map as we exited warp and watched as we took our position. The other ships were along shortly.

"Power weapons, sir?"

"No, not yet. We don't want to tip our hand."

The tac-map showed 4203 ships. They didn't appear to be in any particular formation. I scanned for a nice, isolated battleship. A small bit of dread entered my stomach as I noticed the enemy warp disruptors were active all over the system. An objective marker popped up on the screen.

"Prepare to warp."

"Preparing to warp, aye sir," Johnson said.

I zoomed in on the objective and nearly jumped with joy. A battleship, isolated from the rest of their ships and with a clear line of sight on where we would be jumping. Command had overlooked it, and I wasn't about to correct them.

"We've got one. Relaying coordinates. I want to warp to the objective, go weapons hot, and warp to this battleship's stern keel," I ordered.

"A dick-shot, sir?" Ying asked with a laugh.

"As my grandmother used to say, 'If they're above your weight class, go for the grapes.' She lived to be four hundred years old so I assume she knew what she was talking about," I replied. "We'll need to be fast. Don't want them stealing our joy."

"Ready for warp, sir."

"Synchronize and warp on the mark," I ordered.

"Aye, sir. Awaiting mark," Johnson answered.

I didn't get to call the shots on this one. That job went to Captain Trex of the USSS Idaho. Just as well, if the squad leader went running off the rest of the squad would be obliged to follow. If I go running off, on the other hand, Trex won't know what to do and will have to make a decision. Which will buy me time to get my battleship kill.

"We've got to make it look justified. As if we spotted the battleship AFTER our warp. Wait for one second after we exit warp before charging the guns, then initiate our own warp. Once we're under the battleship, open up wi..."

"Warping, sir," Johnson said.

"Fuck it, on the fly then. Remember, one second after we exit warp. It should take at least that long for the battleship to spot us."

"Aye sir."

We exited warp in formation with the other five destroyers. It only took a quarter charge of the FTLD to jump this distance so we had plenty of juice for an additional warp. One second ticked by, and our weapons began to charge.

"Let's go," I ordered.

"Entering warp!"

We exited warp in the perfect position to gut the battleship. Hell, we could probably cut the thing in half at this range if we really wanted to. But we had to be quick, so we were playing 'poke the reactor'.

"Chain guns fire," I ordered quickly, feeling the adrenaline surge in my veins.

"Chain guns fire aye sir!"

I flicked on the forward cameras to watch the sabot rounds fly out of our chain guns at 8000 rounds per minute. Special cooling systems and exposure to space kept them from melting. Each round slammed into the battleship's shield, weakening it millisecond by millisecond.

"MACs ready, sir."

"Just a bit more."

The enemy battleship noticed us and began to rotate to try to bring their guns around. I had chosen this spot for a very specific reason. The only armaments they had in this location were point defense lasers. Which were now bouncing harmlessly off of our shields.

"Maintain our relative position. Can't let him target us."

"Liberty, what the fuck are you do.." the comms began before I cut them off.

Our chain guns kept hammering their shields as our thrusters fired to match their spin. If they had been any smaller they would have been able to outmaneuver us, but their thrusters were woefully undersized for their mass. I laughed as I watched their shields shimmer and begin to sputter.

"MAC 1, fire," I ordered through my grin.

"MAC 1 firing."

I watched it fire. The impact was far too much for the weakened shields and armor of the battleship, especially at this range. The ball went deep, but we needed to go deeper.

"MAC 2, fire."

"MAC 2, firing."

The second MAC fired a round that followed the first. This one faced less resistance, on account of the giant hole the first one left, and the bridge crew cheered as our shields flared due to the radiation emitted by the battleship's reactor core detonating. The tac-map showed their weapons signature fade as the last of their power coursed through the ship.

"Enemy battleship Dead In Space, sir!" Johnson yelled.

"Ying! What's our count?" I asked with a maniacal grin.

"223 corvettes, 118 frigates, 52 destroyers, 7 cruisers, and one Omni-Union battleship, sir!" Ying shouted back.

I allowed a moment of celebration before I said, "Alright, alright. Warp us back to the formation."

"Aye aye, sir!"

We warped back just as the combined fleet joined us in the system. It wasn't long after they warped in that I was proven correct. The battle didn't last long, and we ended up not being a part of it.

Once everything was said and done we rejoined formation with second fleet and I had to explain to Admiral Archibald that I noticed the enemy battleship as we exited warp and engaged immediately with no time to explain my actions to the rest of the test team.

He definitely didn't buy it, but he wasn't about to ream my ass over it. Yet. Instead he ordered me to rejoin second fleet, get my marines on the ground, and provide orbital support.

"Enter orbit around planet Alpha at these coordinates," I ordered.

"Yes, sir. Entering warp," Johnson said, still smiling.

"Are the marines packed for their camping trip?" I asked Ying.

"Yes, sir. Snug as a bug in their shuttles, awaiting drop," she replied.

"Well, let's play taxi service, shall we?" I said with a smile. "Give them the go once we're in position."

I found myself in a great mood. The Liberty had a storied history. She had been blessed with bloodthirsty crew after bloodthirsty crew. She had faced off against the toughest opponents and destroyed entire squads of pirates and insurrectionists, but never once in her entire history had she been able to bag anything that could be classified as a battleship.

Until now.

Chapter 35

Subject: Staff Sergeant Power

Species: Human

Species Description: Mammalian humanoid, no tail. 6'2" (1.87 m) avg height. 185 lbs (84 kg) avg weight. 170 year life expectancy.

Ship: USSS Liberty

Location: Planet Alpha

"So what are they calling this system anyways, sarnt?" PFC Reinhardt asked SGT Gruff.

"Don't think it has a name, right staffsarnt?" Gruff asked me.

"There wasn't one in the brief. It probably has one of those alphanumerical names, like Alpha Zulu Tree Fower Fife," I replied.

A few brief chuckles arose when I said 'fower'. It was one of the oldest jokes in the military, pronouncing the word four the exact way that the military phonetic manual tells you to. It all started with a misprint, legend says, way before we ever even got to space. Someone wrote down the pronunciation of four as 'fo-wer' but put the hyphen in the wrong spot resulting in 'fow-er'.

It stuck like napalm, although you'll rarely get in trouble for actually saying 'four' outside of training. And the only reason you get in trouble during training is because you get in trouble for ANYTHING during training. A fuck-up is just an excuse to make you stronger.

"What about the planet we're landing on? It's gotta have a name if we're taking it over," Reinhardt asked me.

"Why do you care? You looking to buy a plot of land to retire on? That's pretty forward thinking there, private," I replied.

That wouldn't exactly be a bad idea. Military servicemembers who were involved in seizing land often get a pretty big discount when it gets parceled up, which gives you plenty of cash left over to build stuff on that land. That would only happen if we kept the planet, and that was a pretty big if.

"No staffsarnt," Reinhardt answered.

"Not like we're conquering it anyway," SGT Int chimed in.

We had all seen the USSS Nidhogg exit warp in Alpha Centauri. Brint had fucked up reciting the cycle of operations of the C21B Service Rifle and as punishment Gruff was making him count destroyers. When he stopped every NCO in the squad looked in his direction to yell at him, but when we saw the dreadnought we found ourselves speechless.

The USSS Nidhogg isn't a secret, but it's not wholly

disclosed to the public. A lot of people know that it can destroy planets, and nearly everyone in the military knows that it wouldn't bother targeting a single planet in the first place. It has Mega-MACs that are big enough to turn a continent into a crater, but its primary armament is a beam that can cause a star to go supernova in less than three minutes.

The reason the dreadnought is so large isn't because of its primary weapon, though. It's big because it has several layers of armor and has been overfitted with reactors and shield generators. Three minutes is a long time in combat, and the Nidhogg must be able to complete its mission for it to be an effective deterrence. The entire reason the ship isn't extremely classified is to deter xenocidal warfare against the US or its member species.

There is something that's secret involving the Nidhogg, though. Earlier in my career I had completed MARSOC and been assigned to Intel. During my time there, I was told a lie by my superiors and wanted to prove that they were lying. I think it was probably part of a training program, a test of some sort, but in the process of uncovering the lie I found out about the Dreadnought Reserve.

Dozens, maybe even hundreds, of ships just like the USSS Nidhogg. All sitting in deep-space, completely unmanned and only guarded by a small fleet of VI controlled ships. I was shocked and appalled at this discovery. One ship signals a wish for deterrence. A fleet signals a wish for an excuse.

I learned that this was highly classified information after I had confronted my superiors about it and been arrested. They made me tell them in detail how

I came about the information, and thankfully for me I had done so 'legally'. They were forced to cut me loose, but went into excruciating detail on what would happen if I spread knowledge of the Dreadnaught Reserve. They plugged the leak and I went on my merry way.

That had been the end of my time with Intel, as well. They didn't want me poking around any further and I didn't want to accidentally find more galactic secrets. They did pay me for uncovering the leak, though, which was nice of them. 'Shady but not evil' is the unofficial motto of Bureau of United Systems Intelligence.

"You would know that they're calling it OU Planet Alpha if you had paid attention to the verbal brief or read your fucking packet, Reinhardt," Gruff spoke up.

"I didn't read the packet either, to be fair," Corpsman Yunk provided. "Don't even know what the mission name is."

"It's Operation Vainglorious Infiltration," Omega said.

"The hell it is."

"No it's not."

"The fuck are you talking about?"

"What possible drug could an AI take to get that high?"

And a chorus of other negative replies chimed in before I finally stated, "It's Operation Vanguard."

"Tsk," was Omega's reply.

If I didn't know any better I would say that we hurt its feelings. I looked at Gruff, and he moved his helmet in a slight horseshoe shape that indicated he was rolling his eyes. The shuttle shook, which immediately brought us all back to the reality of the situation.

"Entering atmosphere," our pilot said.

"Omega, what can we expect the enemy to have armament-wise when we get groundside?" I asked.

"Orbital scans showed Infantry, armor, and artillery. They're about as equipped as a standard military," it answered.

"What about air?" asked SGT Int.

"Well they did, but that's no longer a concern. Same with antiaircraft and long range missiles. We have complete air superiority, so feel free to call for air support as needed. If you're good, you might even get some orbital support. You'll have to ask nicely, though."

I nodded gratefully. Trying to kill a tank without high explosives was a pain in the ass, even as a gen-alt with guardian armor. Omega continued to answer questions as I pulled up the map of our LZ and our objective.

I had briefly glanced at it before we boarded the shuttle, and something about it had bothered me. On closer examination I was able to see why. Omega wanted his box in a spot that was surrounded by hills. It would have been a decent spot if we were a mortar team trying to take out enemy armor, but as infantry it was the worst place we could be.

"Omega," I began, "is there any particular reason you have our objective in this location?"

"The hills will provide cover from enemy armor and it should be easy to kill enemy infantry as they crest the hill. Plus the location is close enough to enemy transmitters to give me an access point to their systems."

I searched the map for a moment as the rest of the marines looked at each other. Then I added a waypoint to a large hill with plenty of flat land surrounding it.

"Is this location close enough to the transmitters?" I asked.

"Yes... but why?" Omega asked.

A chorus of laughter rang through the shuttle as the other marines checked their maps.

"I don't understand," Omega said. "You'll be vulnerable to fire from all directions."

"When you're on top of a hill, you can use the hill as cover while denying that same cover from the enemy. It's also easier to shoot down than it is to shoot up, mostly due to sunlight and such." Int said.

"Yeah, that and grenades. Didn't study infantry tactics very much, didja?" CPL Chang chimed in.

"Tsk."

Omega probably had studied infantry tactics but like most non-infantry, probably thought that it knew better. Many virtual reality first person shooter players joined the corps and were shocked when they discovered that the tactics in their little games didn't work very well in real life. Age old wisdom dictates that one should ALWAYS take the hill.

I changed our objective marker as the lights within the shuttle turned red and an alarm began blaring. The ride had smoothed out, so most of the newer marines were confused. Those of us who had been on these shuttles in these circumstances before knew better, and weren't very surprised.

"Ma'am? Is this alarm anything to be worried about?" PFC Rogers asked our pilot.

"It means we're being shot. Our shields are holding up fine, so whatever's doing the shooting isn't rated against aircraft. It's nothing to worry about while you're aboard, but the landing's gonna be pretty hot so you might as well worry about that instead," she replied.

"They still got it so you can't turn it off?" Gruff asked.

"Yup. Apparently we gotta know whenever we get hit."

We sat quietly and waited for the landing. The only sounds were the occasional shifting of the shuttle and the impact alarm. After a few moments, the fidgeting started. Weapons checks, making sure seals were snug, tapping feet and fingers on whatever surface was available. Standard fare for impatient marines. We didn't have to wait long, though.

"Drop off imminent. I was right, this LZ is hot. Careful out there," our pilot said.

"Roger that, ma'am. Alright marines, places. Charlie's on point. Reinhardt and Boyle are carrying the box," I ordered.

"Oorah staffsarnt!"

We stood as we felt the shuttle land and the two privates grabbed the box. I chose these two because one of them is right handed and the other is left handed, which lets them keep their weapons outbound in opposing directions.

The hatch opened and we were treated to the sight of the shuttle's shield flaring. It looks similar to an aurora when it's light on light. Just a dull orange wave when it's kinetic, though. CPL Chang took the lead and was followed by Rogers, Higgs, then Int. Their weapons began firing as soon as they cleared the shield.

"Bravo's next. Go go go!" I shouted

Brint took point for Bravo team followed by the box carriers with SGT Gruff trailing. Their guns also began firing as soon as they cleared the shield, which is a less than great sign of the fight to come.

"Livingstone, you won the tossup for point this time, right?" I asked.

"Yes staffsarnt!" Livingstone said with glee.

"Well get going, then."

I gave the lance corporal a slight shove and followed directly behind him. Private Johns was directly behind me and LCPL Hart was guarding our ass. Livingstone left the shield targeting left, so I targeted right and stepped out, immediately sighting something to shoot at.

Shot, sparks, target falling. Move to defensive position, get some space. Acquire next target. Shot, no sparks, fire again. Shot, sparks, target spazzing. Shot, target falling. I'm hit, only a tenth gone. Not a concern. Shot, miss, shot, sparks. Acquiring. Shot, headshot. Target still mobile, they don't need a head? Shit. Shot, center mass, sparks, target down.

Hit again, taking a knee, scanning, two targets, switch to auto. Die motherfucker die motherfucker die get some, release trigger. Targets down. Scanning sector. One more, switch to semi, shot, target falling. Checking fallen targets, no movement. I kept my eyes on my sector until the rest of the gunfire stopped.

"Clear?" I asked.

Twelve green lights lit up to indicate an affirmative. I gestured for us to start to move out, and we all stood back up and began to march. The ground beneath us was an unnerving yellow color, and didn't quite feel like dirt. Too crunchy. The sky was a darker than normal blue, which led to some odd optical illusions. Mirages, I suppose.

There were random hills of varying size as well. Some of them were closer to mounds, and off in the distance it looked like there might be some mountains. I wonder if that means there's tectonic activity? I tried to remember my geology lessons to no avail.

As far as plants or animals, there were none. Not a blade of grass or even a small lizard as far as our magnified eyes could see. The only sound was some wind and the crunch of our boots as we marched. As the hill we wanted to be on got into sight I smiled. It was perfect. Around the base of the hill was a vast amount of relatively flat ground, giving us perfect coverage all around the hill.

"Alright, excavation tools out. Help Yunk dig a nice pit on the top for him and the box to hang out in. Then buddy up and dig yourself a hole about three quarter of the way up the hill. I want a nice radius with good spacing. Don't forget your sumps. Make 'em nice and big, we don't know how large their grenades are," I ordered as we reached the base of the hill.

"You think they've got grenades, staffsarnt?" PFC Rogers asked.

"If they've got tanks, they've got grenades. Now get to diggin'."

Bravo team remained with the box as the rest of us dug the pit. A few random robots came to check on us, but they were quickly taken care of. When the pit was big enough, Bravo team carried the box up the hill and then we all got to work digging our foxholes.

I ended up paired with Lance Corporal Hart. We dug a luxurious hole in the hill that would be our home for who knows how long. I couldn't help but grin knowing what awaited our enemies once we were done. There's nothing more infuriating to an assault team than foxholes on a hill.

Once everyone was done the sound of e-tools being collapsed and stored was quickly followed by the sounds of guardian gauntlets smacking together. Standard procedure for foxholes was to have one on watch and one down for rest. The sound was roshambo {rock, paper, scissors} to decide who took which shift first.

"So hey, uh... staffsarnt. You wanna play roshambo to see who's on watch first?" LCPL Hart asked me.

"No, no. I trust in your watch-taking capabilities, Lance Corporal. Why don't you show 'em how it's done?" I said with a grin.

Hart sighed as he turned to look over the landscape and I laughed as I sat down. Rank has its perks, and being squad leader is even better. I double checked my weapon and leaned back. I was nearly ready to take a nap when Omega pinged our comms.

"Everyone is in position. Beginning Operation Vainglorious Infiltration," it said.

A series of obligatory negativity and profanity rose from the foxholes in the hill. I just rolled my eyes and closed them, ready for a little nap.

Chapter 36

Subject: Fleet Leader Barrilin Onaya

Species: Oyan

Species Description: Avian humanoid, feathered tail. 6'1" (1.8 m) avg height. 96 lbs (43 kg) avg weight. 161 year life expectancy.

Ship: RSV Nolbarinil {Majestic In Flight}

Location: Sol

As it turns out, the USSS Thanatos is one hell of a ship. I'm not normally one to avoid taking part in the fighting, but Admiral Heckett had finally worn me down and I accepted his invitation to join him. He made several good points, such as it being easier to coordinate if we were within earshot of one another. He'd also said that the food aboard the Thanatos was great, not that that was necessarily a factor in my decision.

Once aboard, I had opted to take a tour and had struggled to keep my beak from gaping when I was shown the docks. Rooms that were unbelievably massive, with the sole purpose of holding entire frigates. The omni-union also has these "carrier" ships, but the Republic phased them out of production over three centuries ago. They cost a lot of resources, and since our ships weren't exactly getting damaged very often at the time, it had made sense financially.

The Thanatos was a whole different breed of ship, though. It was absolutely massive, and somehow it was sparkling clean! I love the Nolbarinil with all my heart, but if I were offered the command of a ship like this I'd take it in a heartbeat. Especially if it came with the technology to keep it this clean.

This wasn't my first time seeing a carrier, but it was my first time seeing one in service. It was also my first time seeing one large enough to carry frigates. The largest carriers that I've previously seen could only carry corvettes or fighters.

Once I brought this up to my gont guide, he gave me a wide grin showing off his carnivorous fangs and told me that he had something that he wanted to show me. We boarded a shuttle that they called a 'bus', and I saw a sign on the wall that said 'fighter bay' with a directional arrow.

No way. We entered the door and my beak dropped open. Dozens of fighters, all lined up in a neat row. I turned to my guide.

"How?" I asked, dumbfounded.

"A combination of gont engineering and human know-how. They come up with the ideas and we help them implement them. There was some excess space on the hull of the original plans for the carriers, and humans hate wasted space," he replied. "So, they figured out that they could fit just about five hundred fighters in such a way to maximize their deployment. Of course, the Thanatos is a diplomatic carrier, so it's smaller than the big girls. Thanatos holds a hundred."

"The big girls? Oh, yes of course. I had noticed the larger carriers. They look absolutely massive. Do they also hold more frigates than the Thanatos?" I asked, recovering from the shock.

"No, sir. The standard sized carriers hold destroyers. Thirty of them. That designs getting pretty old, though. There's rumors of another carrier design that can hold fifty destroyers," the gont said with another grin.

Thirty destroyers? US destroyers? The same destroyers that are half again the size of our own? With armaments that would make an isolan drool? The engineering required for such a task alone is mind boggling, but actually completing it and mass-producing it? There were over half a million of those things in the system right now!

I closed my beak again, somewhat regaining my composure. The carriers fielded by the OU weren't equipped to fight very hard on their own, but these ones could probably go toe to toe with a battleship if they needed to. Even with that being the case, they still carried thirty destroyers. I looked back at the fighters. Their flight consoles were all lined up in a glass container along the far wall. I turned back to the gont.

"Why?" I asked.

"Whatcha mean, sir?"

"What motivated this particular engineering marvel?"

I clarified.

The gont looked nervous for a moment before saying, "Well, sir, I ain't sure that it's my place to tell ya. The humans don't like talkin' about it, and I don't blame 'em. Thing is, it's not their fault. They've tried their best, sir. They really have."

"What do you mean?" I asked.

"On this side of space you got yerself a bunch of bastards, sir. The thing about them bastards is that if you give them even an inch of leeway, they'll make sticks that are so big your own will end up useless. So you've got to make even bigger sticks to keep 'em in line, you know what I mean?"

"Sure," I said before remembering my composure. This gont's accent was oddly disarming. "Yes, I think so."

"The worst part is that the bastards aren't just one species. Every species has their own set of bastards lookin' to start fights to try to get a bigger piece of an imaginary pie when there's more than enough to go around. The knuknu and the alumari are pretty good at bonkin' their bastards, but the gont and the humans have very cunning and particularly ruthless bastards to contend with. And those bastards compliment each other somethin' fierce," he said with an expression of sorrow.

"I think I understand," I said with a soft tone and a nod.

"I'm afraid you don't, sir. It's much worse than you probably realize. And I really shouldn't be tellin' you, but I've already said too much to leave it hangin'," he said with a large sigh. "Of all the people to be tellin' this to. An admiral."

"Well, if it makes you feel better, I'm a fleet-leader. Not an admiral," I said, smiling with my eyes. I was rewarded with a small laugh.

"I guess so, sir. Alright, so when the US first made contact with the gont, some of us didn't want to integrate. The US was prepared to leave well enough alone, so there wasn't any undue pressure or anything. But integration would have improved our quality of life and done away with a certain authoritarian form of government that plagued our systems. On paper, our citizens voted for their leaders and those leaders made all of the decisions regardless of the wishes of the people. We had tried many times to change this style of leadership, but it would always revert within a generation or two. The humans have an ol' saying, 'Might is right.' That's what these guys believed in," he explained.

I nodded. Dictatorships weren't unheard of among the Republic member species. As a matter of fact, the Oyan had a planetary dictatorship on one of our colonies. It was a restricted dictatorship, and those restrictions were enforced by Republic law, but it was still considered stifling by many other Oyan.

"Well, a bunch of the leaders and most of the people wanted to join the United Systems. But a lot of the rich, the humans call 'em oligarchs, didn't want that. It would mean less power and influence for them, an' greed is about the biggest motivator for a bastard. So there was a civil war, not that there was anything civil about it. We fought and fought and, as I said, the US tried to let us figure it out on our own. But then the oligarch bastards went around everyone's backs and started buying weapons and tech from the human bastards. Corporate conglomerations or whatever they're called."

He shuffled nervously, "This set off a terrible chain of events. Our side ended up buying weapons from the US and their side kept buying weapons from the human corporations. But the corporations couldn't supply nearly what the US could, so we ended up with the advantage. We ended up bonkin' the bastards and joined the US."

"That sounds like a happy ending," I said. "What went wrong?"

"We didn't bonk 'em hard enough. After we joined the US the corporations that sold the weapons to the bastards were exposed. It was apparently illegal for them to have sold weapons like that and since they were human corporations, humanity decided to try to handle it internally. But the human bastards had plenty of political pull and used everything at their disposal to avoid the consequences of their bastardly ways. Things got bad. Real bad. Politicians were assassinated, factions were formed, and governments were overthrown. The humans ended up having a civil war of their own."

"Ouch," I replied.

"Yeah, no kiddin'. Their civil war lasted for a hundred years. Some people call it the corporate war, but that's not what it actually was. Humanity had plenty of grievances stored up at that point in their history, and we were the spark that blew that powder keg sky high."

"What's a powder keg?" I asked.

"Oh, that's one of them human sayings. Their primary infantry weapons traditionally use an explosive substance called gunpowder that used to be stored in wooden containers called kegs. It's extremely flammable and explosive, so all it takes is a spark to make it go boom."

"Oh I see, carry on," I nodded.

"Right, anyways, once they finished up bonkin' their bastards, our own bastards decided to act up again. They tried to do a coup and the gont were once again embroiled in a civil war. Humanity helped us out of it in the form of US intervention. The knuknus and alumari were against it. Wanted to let nature take its course, I guess. Humanity convinced 'em, though. But our bastards have kept trying. And the human's bastards are still lurking, waiting for their chance. Hell, the fourth pacification war isn't even technically over yet. Been about... eighteen, nineteen years now," he said with a shrug.

"The US is currently at war?" I asked.

"No, not technically. It's more along the lines of puttin' down a mutiny, or a riot suppression. I think the official term's 'police action'. About eighteen or so years ago our bastards tried again and nearly succeeded. It was an extremely organized effort. They had managed to infiltrate the gont government and every ship in tenth fleet. When they struck, they managed to kill most of our democratically elected representatives and steal most of tenth fleet's ships in the biggest mutiny in all of our shared histories."

"Woah," I said in shock.

"Yeah, and to top it off they had begun a propaganda campaign to convince the US to stay out of the conflict. So when the US inevitably entered the fray, you know, cuz they stole those ships, a lot of the people in charge were suddenly getting angry letters and phone calls from people who'd fallen prey to the propaganda."

"Wow. What changed?" I asked.

"The US liberated a gont colony from the bastards. Turns out, bastards do what bastards do no matter what's at stake. They had been abusing the populace somethin' fierce. Mandatory work schedules and curfews, and capital punishment for minor infractions. Pretty much turned the populace into slaves and killed anyone who tried to argue with 'em. Once the news broke, their support dried up right quick. Then it was just a matter of killing 'em as the opportunity arose. But the humans really stepped up to bat for us. If it weren't for them, we'd all have ended up livin' like those poor bastards on that colony. And it was mostly the humans who laid down their lives, too. We owe 'em a lot."

"Yeah, I can imagine. You say killing them? What about prisoners?" I asked, dreading the answer at this point.

"Oh sure, there's a few of 'em. But it's kind of a gont thing to not be taken alive. Warrior culture and all that. Personally, I prefer the engineering focus of our culture, but if my back was to the wall I'd rather give

my life for something I believe in by takin' a few of
the bastards with me, you know? I'm sure they
probably feel the same way," he said with a shrug.

I sighed with relief. Rules of war are important, but
the rules regarding police action are a moral
imperative. You can tell a lot about a culture by how
they handle their police actions. Still, it's not
surprising that this was left out of the briefing. One
thing was still bothering me, though.

"You said the human bastards are still lurking. What
did you mean?" I asked carefully.

"Well, most human systems pretty much worship the
free market. I don't blame 'em, the thought of being
told that you can't buy or sell something that people
wanna buy is infuriating. But the biggest side effect
of a free market is powerful corporations. The more
powerful the corporations get, the more they get into
politics, and the harder it is to keep them in check.
Without strict regulations, you end up having to kill
the bastards to get their hands off your throat."

"Really?" I asked.

"Oh yeah. Human corps are notorious. They even
hire mercenaries and go to war with each other. Of
course, they do that in areas that the human's laws
don't quite apply so that they can't be punished for
it."

"Why doesn't the US intercede?" I asked,
dumbfounded.

"The US is a protective government. It's not the
place of the US to regulate its member species in

their own systems. We've got a senate and a judicial system, but our laws only apply to matters that impact all of the member species. Like first contact, or joint-developed technologies, interspecies trade, or expansion. It also maintains the military, as you already know. Our members ain't allowed to have their own spacefaring militaries, just police. Otherwise, each species governs itself however it wants to. The knuknu have a purely democratic government, and the gont has a democratic republic. The alumari and humans have a bunch of governments all working under a unified umbrella government. Those ones get complicated."

I laughed and said, "I know. That was in my brief."

"I'm sure it was," he laughed in return. "Anyways, let's get this tour finished up and get you to Admiral Heckett."

We stopped by more impressive areas aboard the Thanatos while I digested what I had just heard. It was a lot to take in. On the one hand, I can definitely see why the US had developed their weapons to be as lethal as they are. On the other hand, I'm not sure how comfortable I am around them knowing how quickly they resort to violence. Still, it wasn't as if the Oyan were much different.

It would seem that we'd gotten lucky with our neighbors. Or unlucky, maybe. If we'd ended up with more 'bastards', we might not have lost as many against the OU as we have. But we would have probably lost even more to each other.

After showing me an absolutely beautiful mess hall, my gont guide finally took me to the command room.

Just outside the room he stopped and turned to me.

"Well, this here ends my guided tour of the USSS Thanatos. Inside this door is the command room, and just beyond that's the bridge. Admiral Heckett would probably like to give you the tour of those, and since he's my boss' bosses' boss his preferences matter a whole bunch," he laughed. "Anyways, about what we were talkin' about earlier, I'd much appreciate it if you didn't tell nobody that I'm the one who clued you in, admi... fleet leader, sir."

"My beak is sealed. Thanks for the tour," I replied.

"No problem, sir. Well, here we go," he said as he stepped forward to open the door.

I followed him and was stunned by the room we were entering. There were screens and seats and tables and desks all over the place, but somehow it didn't feel the least bit cluttered. There weren't any visible cables, and the decking was all in the proper place. It was like a completely different world from all the command centers I'd ever been in. And it was much quieter...

"OFFICER ON DECK!"

Every single person in the room stood up straight with their left hand at their side and the other touching their forehead. A form of salute. I was touched. My gont guide paused for a moment in surprise before quickly turning around and mimicking the gesture. Admiral Heckett was standing in the center of the room, trying his best to suppress what appeared to be a smile.

He walked up to me and outstretched his hand. I recognized the gesture from the briefing. A handshake, a sign of mutual respect that had been a human tradition for millennia. Quite the honor.

As I took his hand he said, "It's a pleasure to meet you Fleet-Leader Onaya. I am Admiral Heckett. Welcome aboard the USSS Thanatos."

After we shook hands he grinned and whispered, "You're supposed to say 'at ease' to get them to stop."

"Oh. At ease!" I replied.

Everyone went back to their tasks, noticeably louder this time. From behind the admiral I saw a screen portraying the hallway I had just been in. Ah, I see. Theatrics. I looked back at the admiral, now knowing that this man was cut from the same cloth as I.

Admiral Heckett turned to my gont guide and said, "That will be all, Ensign Plinas."

"Yes, admiral. Sir!" The gont replied with a salute and a shocked expression.

It was good to finally know his name. I had been a little embarrassed to ask. Plinas had been in the hanger when my shuttle docked. I had sent my aides on ahead so I could get a good view of the impressiveness of the hanger when he had approached me and offered a tour, without introducing himself.

It was also good to know that the admiral knew the crew. Actually, judging from his expression and how quickly he performed his about-face, the admiral knowing his name and rank came as a surprise to Plinas. It reminded me of a fleet-leader I came up under. Fleet-Leader 'All Seeing' Arun. She had made a point of knowing everything that went on in her fleet, and keeping tabs on everything she possibly could. It was unnerving to have her ask how your family was by name.

"Well, fleet-leader, how did you find the tour?" Heckett asked.

"I enjoyed it immensely. This ship contains many surprises," I replied. Then I remembered something that had been nagging at me since we entered the system, "I noticed that your fighters have a certain artistic elegance that the rest of your ships... well, lack. Why is that?"

The admiral laughed, "The fighters occasionally have to enter atmospheres and as such must be aerodynamic. The warships don't have to, and as such are designed with function rather than form in mind. Actually, fun fact, the reason that our carriers are as bulbous as they are is because the first one ever made was carved from an asteroid."

"Really?" I asked. "Our first battleship was carved from one as well."

"Yes, I suspect it's probably a commonality among spacefaring species to improvise building materials. In our case, we had already hollowed out the asteroid to use as space station, but found ourselves needing a carrier more than a space station. A few modifications and the Human Space Ship Aurora was finished, and able to carry eight destroyers. Saved us a ton on FTLD fuel."

"I bet," I replied.

The admiral nodded before continuing, "The HSS Aurora was retired when the United Systems was officially founded. It was summarily decommissioned and now serves as a museum for the first contact wars. We've since, obviously, improved upon the original design and no longer use improvised materials."

"Indeed. So why do the battleships look like sticks? Did you manage to find an overly large tree and get it into space?" I asked.

Heckett laughed, "No. The battleships are almost entirely hardpoints. The first modern US battleship created was the U-triple-S Hingra, which is 'spear of justice' in Common Alumari. It was intended to be a fleet killer, and for quite a while it was. But, war escalates and after 36 years of hard service the Hingra was lost with all hands in the first battle of Sol."

"Your civil war?" I asked.

"Yes, one of them," Heckett laughed again, but with a grimness this time.

"You've had more than one?" I asked, shocked.

"Oh, humanity has been having civil wars since we first picked up sticks. We've only had two that the United Systems military was obliged to intervene in, though. I believe you were briefed on the second one. The first one only lasted eighteen days, and that's the one that we lost the Hingra in."

I licked the upper innards of my beak. As a person, I was shocked to hear the human speak of his bloody history so casually. But as a fleet-leader, I was able to appreciate the candor and detached approach. We have warrior species in the Republic, but the humans didn't really look the part. Well, until they smiled wide and showed their teeth.

"I am sad to hear that your history has been riddled with strife, admiral. But, I am grateful to be fighting the Omni-Union beside those as experienced in warfare as yourselves. It fills me with confidence that we'll be able to finally put an end to this mechanical threat once and for all."

The admiral smiled wide, "We will. One way or another. Speaking of which, we have officially launched the invasion."

"Really?" I asked. "What did you send?"

"Six fleets so... thirty million ships. And the dreadnaught," he replied.

"Ah, so your fleets really are five million ships each. And sorry, what is a dreadnaught?" I asked.

"Honestly, I thought it was the first thing you would ask about. It should have been in your briefing. The USSS Nidhogg?"

"There are parts of the briefing I haven't had a chance to skim through yet. I mostly went through the species description and history," I replied, gesturing in an apologetic way.

"Understandable. I haven't been able to read the briefing supplied by the Republic at all," he said with a laugh. Then his face turned serious, "The USSS Nidhogg is the only dreadnaught class ship in the US military. It is a xenocide deterrence, created in response to the Daluran war. It has the ability to destroy solar systems, and can withstand significant fire from a fleet of battleships for an extended duration."

He looked into my eyes as he said, "It is the single most powerful death machine that the United Systems has ever created. It is only cleared for usage if the enemy is xenocidal or mechanical. Every crewman aboard the Nidhogg has passed through the most intense background and psychological checks available to make certain they are loyal to the United Systems. If their loyalty waivers in a detectable way, they are assigned elsewhere."

I swallowed heavily. After seeing their ships and hearing their history, I suspected that they might have created weapons of mass destruction that could destroy planets. Such weapons were of course prohibited from being researched in Republic space, but for the US it just... made sense.

Solar systems, though? Why? Insanity, sheer and utter craziness. Although... I could see it as a xenocide deterrence. The Republic hadn't had an actual xenocidal incident among our member species, and hadn't realized that that was what was happening with the OU. I suppose if we had, we would have come up with something similar as a deterrence. Or tried to.

"I see," was all I could say.

"From officer to officer, I'm ashamed of the Nidhogg," Heckett said as he looked away. "It shows that we're willing to throw away our morals and honor for the sake of survival. I had hoped that it would never be used. Still, I'm glad that it's machines that we might be using it against, instead of organics."

"I see how it is, sir," a voice came from a nearby intercom.

"Non-sentient machines, I mean," Heckett corrected himself with a smile. "Fleet-leader, meet Tim. A human created AI."

Ah, this was more familiar territory. I had already received my shock when I read the reports of the human-made AI. They were said to act more like people than machines, and judging from the comedic timing of this one that may turn out true.

I looked at the intercom and said, "Pleasure to meet you, Tim."

"Pleasure to meet you as well, sir. I just popped in to inform you both that we have finished the installation of the tac-maps on the Republic fleet ahead of schedule," Tim said.

"Thank you, Tim," Heckett replied.

"You should thank Omega. Running those logistics would have made my head spin right off. If I had one..."

"No thanks necessary," another voice, presumably

Omega, replied.

"Indeed. Omega was simply performing his duty," A third voice said.

"Fleet-leader, meet Omega and John. They are also AI," Heckett said, trying to maintain his composure.

"Pleasure to meet you both. I am fleet-leader Onaya of the Republic."

Two holograms appeared out of a nearby table. One was a figure wearing a black cloak and holding a curved blade, the other was a figure wearing the same suit of armor that I had seen some soldiers wearing during my tour. The soldier's had been dark blue or dark green, but this suit was white. Or perhaps steel with a lot of light shining on it.

"Judging from your reaction, you've already been briefed on us," the cloaked figure said with Omega's voice. "Good."

"Of course he's been briefed, Omega. Blindsiding a captain is unprofessional, but blindsiding an admiral is downright insubordinate," the other avatar said. John, by process of elimination.

"It wasn't unprofessional, John. We simply didn't have the time to brief Uleena on our existance before we had to debrief him. Our reactions afterward were the unprofessional part," Tim's voice said with a chuckle.

I looked around for Tim's avatar to no avail. My eyes met Heckett's and he shook his head as if he knew what I was looking for.

"Tim doesn't use an avatar to communicate," the admiral said.

I nodded and asked, "Why not, Tim?"

"Well, mostly because I don't... Oh, sorry. It looks like the explanation will have to wait," came the reply.

"Enemies inbound. Big group of them," John said.

"We've begun patching FTLDs but not all of them will be done by the time they enter the system," Omega added.

"Understood," Heckett replied. "Well fleet-leader, looks like its our time to shine."

I joined him at larger than normal table that displayed a tac-map. The US fleets were shown in blue, the Republic's were in green. I tapped part of the table and an interface popped up. I keyed in a communication frequency and the ID for my comms implant as I watched Heckett do the same. From here we would be able to give orders to our fleets.

"Well, admiral," I said. "Let's defend your system."

Chapter 37

Subject: Captain Wong

Species: Human

Species Description: Mammalian humanoid, no tail. 6'2" (1.87 m) avg height. 185 lbs (84 kg) avg weight. 170 year life expectancy.

Ship: USSS Valor

Location: Sol

"Tim, how many do we have left?" I asked.

"29,683,271 remaining. We have destroyed 8,471,282... 283... 284... 286..." Tim replied.

"Right, I get it. Well, let's keep at it."

The Omni-Union had attacked about ten minutes after Tim had told me that our invasion had begun. Not all of our ships had the chance to apply the FTLD patch, but the Valor had. The AI that insists on following me around does have its uses.

Despite the patch, we were ordered to defend the Thanatos. All ten frigates and one hundred fighters were deployed in a defense perimeter. The USSS Valor, Pride, Shield, Rosenthal, Spear, Gambler, Grateful Carnivore, Bulk, and the freshly repaired

Sword. I rolled my eyes when I remembered the Bulk. We've really got to find a better way to name our ships.

The way it currently works is that the engineering crew that constructs the ship gets to name it so long as the name isn't already taken or profane. There's an entire quality assurance team of over one hundred thousand individuals from different cultures to make certain that the engineering team doesn't get too clever with puns.

Like the Phallic Phalanx, for example. If you didn't speak any Latin, that would seem to be a military maneuvering tactic. The QA team had a tough time on that one because most translators get confused with it. Both words are Latin but are also technically part of the English language. So a translator would read phallic phalanx as phallic phalanx. The only way it didn't slip the net was that nobody knew what it meant so they had to check the definition of phallic and phalanx.

The phrase phallic phalanx, as it turns out, means a formation of shield carrying soldiers in the overall shape of a penis. This situation made interplanetary news because it ended up costing enough to make it the most expensive dick joke of all time.

"Target identified. Firing," Babanin said in a bored tone.

We were ordered to hold position and target anything that targeted our formation. We took this to mean anything that looked like it might start targeting our formation. Even so, the Omni-Union was painfully unaware that the Thanatos was currently host to the commanders of the joint fleet.

Admiral Heckett and Fleet Leader Onaya had both taken up residence on the Thanatos in an attempt to better coordinate the fleets. Heckett had said that he liked the ship more than the science station. The importance of our assignment didn't make me feel any better about not being in the thick of it, though. Especially once the casualty notifications started rolling in.

"Kill confirmed. No further targets," Babanin reported with a slight yawn.

The Lowelana was still docked. If things went south the plan was to have the fleet leader board the Lowelana and have Uleena do his best to evacuate him. It was certainly a last ditch plan, though. If things go badly enough that the Thanatos is at risk of destruction, there's almost no chance the Lowelana's getting away. A message notification brought me back to reality.

--

Permission to pursue fleeing target?

-Captain Samuels USSS Sword

--

Reynolds had made me squad leader for all ten ships. I had expected some pushback because most of the captains are more tenured than I am. But everyone had done exactly as they were told without a single complaint. Well... a single complaint to ME.

Samuels, on the other hand, wasn't more tenured than I am. As a matter of fact, she just received this command three months ago. Which is probably why her ship was the only casualty in the second assault. No, that's not quite fair. Nobody really believes that an enemy will kamikaze until it happens.

--

Denied. Hold formation. Our job is to protect the Thanatos, killing the enemy is just a treat we get for doing so.

-Captain Wong USSS Valor

--

"I'm going to die of boredom, Babanin," I said.

"I could give you access to a copy of The Alumari Renegade, sir," Tim chimed in with a literal chiming sound.

"Wasn't talking to you, Tim. And I hate romance novels," I replied tersely.

"Ah, but you know about it. What, read it already or something?"

"Everyone knows about The Alumari Renegade. A trashy smut novel that the author wrote to expand his horizons. It ended up becoming more popular than his more serious works. Every author's worst nightmare," I said with a chuckle. "Now get back to work you bucket of bolts."

"Aye, sir," the AI responded. Then after a second of

silence, "I do want to point out that I don't have any buckets or bolts, though."

"Can it."

Lieutenant Babanin chuckled at the exchange and said, "Well, sir, dying of boredom isn't all that bad. It could be worse."

As he said that accursed phrase I watched two enemy destroyers on the tac-map turn to target us directly. I nearly got my mouth open to say something about it when two friendly MAC rounds began sailing toward the enemies at unbelievable speeds. I glared pointedly at Babanin, who saw the exact same thing I did.

"Don't do that again, lieutenant," I said.

"Aye aye, sir," he said with a smile.

I leaned back in my chair, finally accepting my fate as a spectator. The previous battle had a significantly different tone to it. Well, if you could call that a battle. It had been closer to a very quick slaughter. They jumped into the system and were destroyed before they could get a single round off.

Scuttlebutt had said that the OU were basing their attacks on how many ships we had in the system, so everyone was expecting the last fight to end fast. We had been dreading this one, though. With good reason. Nearly 40 million ships had warped into the system and immediately began attacking.

But by now most of the fleet had finished the FTLD patch and were warping with wild abandon, which caused the casualty notifications to slow down significantly. These robotic bastards definitely didn't account for that. Sol was going to get a massive economy buff after all this fighting. Mars and Titan both had the tech to unpack the balls of atoms that were left over from the A2 cleanup.

Once we won this war we'd probably have to assign policing units to make certain that the conglomerations don't war over the salvage rights. Sol was riddled with corporate conglomerations that were more bloodthirsty than even the Daluran. Hell, they'd probably lobbied for the Daluran's extinction to try to get mining and colonization rights to their home-world.

All that's above my pay-grade, though. I'm just a captain of a warship that's watching a battle play out instead of fighting in it. Still, it beats being stuck aboard the Thanatos at the moment. That ship is absolutely lousy with AI right now. And if I had to listen to another argument between John and Omega, I was going to lose it.

I sighed as I remembered AI John. What the hell had possessed it to choose the most motivated personality possible was beyond me. The marines get a kick out of him, and high command adore him. The rest of us hate him. He's a dick. I was surprised when his avatar turned out not to be a penis in a uniform. Might suggest that to Omega...

No, I'm sure that there'd be consequences to that. And officers shouldn't be thinking about pulling pranks, either. But it beats just staring at the tac-map, watching enemy blips disappear. The OU was fighting back as hard as they could, but it's impossible to outmaneuver US ships when you have outdated warp tech.

"Target identified. Fi... Never mind. Sword got it," Babanin said in a sad tone.

"We'll get 'em next time, lieutenant. Keep your eyes peeled," I said encouragingly.

I reminded myself once again of the importance of our assignment. On top of the Admiral and the Fleet Leader, there are currently several other Republic officers on the Thanatos coordinating their ships with ours. They weren't exactly doing a great job, though. The US had taken about a hundred total casualties, but theirs were in the thousands.

Honestly it was a miracle they hadn't been routed yet. They had their ships in firing lines. Who does that? There isn't a single tactical benefit to it in space. On the other hand, their mobility is limited so it makes sense that they're not zooming around the battlefield. But a spherical formation would make more sense than a fucking line does.

I watched as some of the OU ships tried for a flanking maneuver. Blue ship indicators suddenly appeared behind the red ones and the red ones started to rapidly disappear. If our ships hadn't interfered with that, it would have been disastrous for the Republic's forces.

But that's above my pay-grade too. I scratched the back of my head as it dawned on me that Tim might be right about seeking a promotion. I'd miss the Valor and its crew, but I'd been thinking more and more about things that I have no business thinking about. It's not that being a captain is boring or unfulfilling, it's just... I feel like I can do more than I'm doing now, I guess.

That fucking ridiculously cheerful robot. Even if I got the star on my collar and was reassigned, it would probably follow me. I wonder if all of the AI are obsessive. Omega is obsessed with humans, Tim is obsessed with me, John is obsessed with duty or whatever, and I don't know enough about Violet to tell one way or another.

"Target iden... Dammit, Sword got 'em again," Babanin said while slapping his knee in sarcastic frustration.

"Let them have it. We've had more than they have, anyway. It's time to share."

"Yes, sir," he replied in a mockingly deflated tone.

"How many left now, Tim?" I asked out of curiosity.

"11,247,312. We've destroyed..."

"Nope, stop that."

"Buuut siiiiiiir," Tim said, doing an impression I was unfamiliar with.

"That'll be all, Tim."

"Yes, sir. I eagerly await your next enemy casualty count request."

God, we're running through them quick. They'd started with about five times our number half an hour ago, and now we were nearly even. There really is something to be said about rapid mobility in ship to ship combat. I'm thankful that our FTLDs are back in action.

Unlike the Republic's FTLDs, ours only use a certain amount of charge per jump. The amount of charge is dependent upon many variables, including the distance between the warp points. The amount of variables makes the overall charge depletion pretty random, though. We can typically get ten jumps in system before having to hang out and recharge.

Sometimes it's nine, sometimes it's eleven. Other times it's fourteen or six. The worst part is that it sometimes changes between jumps. So if your first in-system warp took 12 percent of your charge, there was no guarantee that the next would as well. No way to tell until you try the jump.

Even the AI haven't been able to come up with an accurate predictive model. Not that it would be super helpful. It would take about as much time to check the prediction as it would to just try to jump. If you warp, you warp. If not, you need to initiate a recharge.

Part of our command training covered this little curiosity. The manual says to charge whenever you get the chance, unless you don't intend to warp. Newer captains ALWAYS kept their drives charged, until they get reprimanded for wasting reactor fuel. The fuel's not that expensive, but it adds up pretty quickly.

"Target identified, firing!" Babanin said rapidly. "HA! Target destroyed. Suck it, Sword."

"Congratulations, lieutenant. You beat them. Woo hoo," I said in a monotone.

Babanin gave me an exaggerated frown and said, "Sir, it's important to keep up a competitive spirit!"

"Yeah, sure it is," I smiled.

I thought about asking Tim for another enemy casualty count. Or rather, how many were left. But there weren't enough to bother with it. I rested my head on my hand as I watched red ships disappear faster and faster as we began to outnumber the enemy. Then, they were gone.

"And that's that," I said. "Prepare to return to the Thanatos."

"Aye aye, sir."

I sent the return request and waited for the response. Docking granted. I gave the order to return and sent a quick message to the other captains to do the same. We had successfully defended the Thanatos. And such a thrilling defense it had been. Sitting around and taking potshots at whoever gave us the opportunity.

At least the next fight will be harder.

Chapter 38

Subject: Staff Sergeant Power

Species: Human

Species Description: Mammalian humanoid, no tail. 6'2" (1.87 m) avg height. 185 lbs (84 kg) avg weight. 170 year life expectancy.

Ship: USSS Liberty

Location: Planet Alpha

"Clear at 280!"

"Clear at 110!"

"All clear. Sit-rep," I ordered.

Eleven yellow lights and one green light lit up. Corpsman Yunk was the only green light, because the corpsman wasn't using his ammo. Fair enough, that's not really his job. His job is to try to make sure we can use the rest of ours.

Still, yellow wasn't so bad. Minor injuries and/or over half of your ammo used, but not on your last box. I looked at the growing pile of metal at the base of our hill. The first groups that had been sent just rushed us, firing their lasers as they went. Not smart at all, and now their circuits were everywhere.

This last group, though, had attempted a fireteam rush. It would have been a smart move if their weapons had the capacity to suppress us for any reasonable amount of time. It had only been three days and they were already mimicking us pretty well. I found myself wondering what they were going to try next when my helmet cut exterior sound and a giant plume of smoke and shrapnel erupted about 15 meters from the base of the hill.

"Artillery!" PFC Johns shouted over comms.

"Everyone down!" I ordered.

"You don't have to inform me twice, staffsarnt," SGT Int replied.

I manually disabled the sonic safeties on my helmet to try to hear where the shells were coming from as another crashed around 18 meters away. No good. Going to have to try triangulation. We won't be able to get an accurate fix on them, but we'll get a search area at least.

"Squad leaders, triangulation. Need to find the general location of that artillery," I ordered.

I saw Gruff's gauntlet peek up from his foxhole. I raised mine as well and triggered the sound localization software. The next shell hit exactly 12 meters away, according to my reading. Then the sound of the guns caught up to us.

The reason that humans have two ears is to give us sound localization. Sound generally travels in a circular wave, and by assessing two points of a circle you can triangulate its center. The more distance between the two points you get, the better the localization gets. That's why it's harder to tell where a noise is coming from when it's farther away from you.

Even with three points we weren't going to get an exact fix. But I got a reading, and so did Gruff and Int. About a half-mile wide indicator appeared, about 10 km away from us. Too far away for us to touch them, but that's not what I had planned anyway. I activated my command comms as the next shell hit.

"Hellfire Two-Niner, this is Shocker Actual, over," I began.

"Shocker Actual, this is Hellfire Two-Niner. Go ahead."

"Sending tactical data for a search and destroy. Gun emplacements. How copy?" I asked as I sent the approximate location of the enemy artillery.

"Full copy... received. Beginning the hunt. Keep your head down Shocker Actual, over."

"Roger, happy hunting. Shocker Actual out."

Another shell impacted, this time close enough for us to catch some dust. I brushed some dirt off myself as LCPL Hart shook himself and turned to me.

"What's the plan, staffsarnt?" he asked.

"I'll explain over comms," I replied while keying the comms. "Marines, we've got a guardian angel on its way to turn those guns into scrap. Heads down until we're given the all clear."

"What kind of ordo are they gonna use, sir?" PFC Brint asked.

"I'm not a fucking sir, Brint. They're just gonna use their cannons, unless they've got non-nuclear missiles attached. They can't afford the EMP on this mission," I replied, making several assumptions.

"Yes they can, the black boxes are hardened against EMP. Your shields aren't, though," Omega chimed in.

Of course the AI was listening in. The hell was taking it so long, how did it have enough time to chat? I shrugged off my annoyance as another shell hit about 10 meters from the base of the hill. Then I shrugged off some dirt.

"A nuke against a couple of guns would be overkill, Omega. The cannons will do the trick, and the guardian angel knows it."

"No need for code, staff sergeant, but I understand. You're arguing to increase morale. I sometimes forget that nukes are still kind of scary to organics," Omega said on my personal comm line. "Especially this close. Anyway, the OU can't tap our comms anymore. I took that capability on day 1."

"Well, then what have you been doing for the other two days we've been here?" I asked.

"Killing VI. There's quadrillions of them."

That shut me up. One AI versus a quadrillion VI? Damn, Omega must be top of the line tech. I decided

to never fuck with an AI as another shell impacted
five meters from the base of our hill. A piece of
jagged shrapnel seemed to magically appear in the
hill just above my foxhole.

"Hey staffsarnt, you think they'll get there before we
take a shell?" Hart asked me.

"Yeah, Hellfire 29 is flying an ET201 unmanned
fighter. Getting there fast will be easy, the pilot won't
take any G's. The search is probably what's taking so
long, but they'll make it," I said reassuringly.

As if responding to a cue, a very lovely noise came
from the direction of the cannons. The sound of two
50mm autocannons that can fire 5000 rounds per
minute. A very satisfying BRRRT, even from a
distance. The tense atmosphere immediately
dissipated, and I could've sworn I heard SGT Gruff
say "Thank god".

"Shocker Actual, this is Hellfire Two-Niner. Mission
successful, target destroyed. Returning to nest,
over."

"Shocker Actual to Hellfire Two-Niner, just in time.
Thank you. Out," I replied.

Things settled down for a while, with the occasional
patrol making an attempt on the hill. We took turns
on watch, resting and cleaning our weapons on our
down time. Night crept up on us, and not a single
one of us was looking forward to it.

It wasn't just that the bots were harder to spot at
night. They don't light up very much on thermals,
and IR is useless thanks to the weather. The night on

this particular rock brought storms with it. Bad ones.

There isn't a single active duty marine who hasn't seen their fair share of bad weather. Hellwurld sees to that. These storms were particularly nasty. Not because they had brutal winds and pouring rains, but because they also kicked up sediment like a toddler on a beach.

Both the rain and the sand were traveling horizontally in whichever direction the wind decided to take it. The winds were so bad that our shields would occasionally take damage from the sand. I shuddered to think what this weather would do to bare skin.

The toll on our equipment was harsh as well. The first night had seen Brint's rifle jam. Sand in the barrel, clumped up and held in place by the rain that had followed it. We had to wait until the storm died down just before dawn before he could clear it.

"God damnit. If I never see a single grain of sand again it'll be too soon," LCPL Hart bitched over close range radio as he shook his rifle.

"Stow the bellyachin' and keep your eyes outbound. Rifle down unless you see the enemy. Keeps the water and sand from out it," I repeated myself for the third night in a row.

"I been meanin' to ask, staffsarnt. Isn't it more tactical to keep our weapons outbound?"

I mockingly tilted my head as I replied, "How would it be tactical to have your weapon outbound if it jams when you try to fire it? I didn't know you looked up to Private Brint so much that you wanna copy him."

"But staffsarnt, he's the picture perfect marine! Who wouldn't want to copy him?" The lance corporal asked with the most sarcasm I've ever heard in my life.

"Haha, very funny. I'm gonna hit the hay. Kick my boot when it's my watch. Or if we see any action," I said as I leaned back and closed my eyes.

"Aye aye, staffsarnt."

I closed my eyes and embraced sleep. Not too deeply, though. Didn't want to miss out on the action, if there was any. My dream was being back home with my wife and kids with a strange addition. Gunfire, explosions, and the sound of lasers striking drowned them out whenever they tried to say something to me.

I just smiled and nodded, not wanting to make them scared or sad that daddy couldn't hear them. I don't know what I'd do if I made them cry. We're at a park. Kind of like the one that's down the street. A picnic, overlooking the play area. The kids are eating as fast as they can so they can go play. I tell them not to choke while trying not to smile at their antics.

More explosions are their response. I turn to my wife and she shrugs at me, her sundress slipping over her clavicle. Beautiful. I love you. Gunfire's her response, but I play it cool. I know she loves me too.

The kids finish their food and jump up. I can't help but laugh as they run toward the play area. I wave at them as they go, and my wife gently grips my arm. I turn to her and look deep into her beautiful blue eyes.

"Wake up, staffsarnt," she says with Hart's voice.

"Wake up, staffsarnt. It's your turn to keep watch," he says.

"Yeah, yeah. I'm up," I reply.

Damn. Why is it that the best dreams happen when you're in the shit, and the worst dreams happen when you're happy? I cracked my stiff neck as I stood and took over the watch. Hart sat down and it wasn't long before he drifted off, taking my place in dreamland.

"Report," I said over the radio.

Six yellow lights blinked back at me. Ah, Yunk fired his weapon. I glared at Hart. Told the little shit to wake me up if we saw action. I checked ammo counters. Most of us are good, but it would be wise to order a refill soon. Might as well. I activated the command comm but someone was already squawking.

"... is Concrete Actual. Fire mission. Concentration Echo Golf Five Tree Niner. Enemy armor. Five rounds, danger close. Will adjust, how copy?"

Lieutenant Banjul. He's got me beat for dumb callsigns, for sure. They're not that far away from us. Calling an artillery strike on enemy armor. Glad WE haven't seen any tanks yet. Wait, we brought artillery?

"Hanura copies full..."

Oh. Oh shit. That's not artillery. I looked up at the sky and after a moment spotted five fireballs. Then I quickly switched back over to the squad radio.

"Turtle up! We've got orbital support incoming!" I ordered.

I watched as helmets scanned the sky, paused for a moment, and disappeared in their foxholes. I took one last glance at the fireballs and ducked down. I placed a hand on Hart's shoulder so he wouldn't jump up in surprise when the first round hit.

Then I waited. MACs are fast, but it's quite the distance between orbit and the ground. I tried not to grit my teeth as the tension rose and rose. Then the ground suddenly felt an inch lower than it was before. Even my helmet's sound dampeners barely helped as the shockwave rolled over our little hill. Then came the dust and debris.

"WHAT THE FU..." Hart shouted as the second round impacted.

I managed to hold him down and hoped that the rest of the marines were able to do the same to their partners. It wasn't just dust in the air. There would be stones as well. I couldn't help but get a little pissed off as the next three rounds impacted. It was like riding a grav-coaster at a local fair, but involuntarily. I stood up once I was sure more rocks wouldn't be pelting us.

"Report." I said over the radio. Twelve yellow lights lit back up. Good.

I took a moment to gather my wits and dust myself off. Then I checked our directory and found Lt. Banjul's personal frequency.

"Concrete Actual, this is Shocker Actual. Sit-rep."

"Shocker Actual, this is Concrete Actual. We're still here, over."

"Roger that. Fuck you, sir. How copy?"

"Full copy," Banjul replied with a laugh. "Sorry about that, forgot you were nearby. Won't happen again, over."

"Roger. Out," I replied as I cut the comm.

Hart finished brushing himself off and looked up at me.

"What the fuck was THAT staffsarnt?" he asked.

"A nearby squad called in orbital support danger close. Five MAC rounds, the piece of shit," I replied.

Hart nodded and went to stand as the ground began to shake again. It was different this time, slower. Like when you zone out and snap back in to find yourself rocking side to side. Only it was everything ELSE that was rocking side to side.

"Earthquake?" Hart asked.

"Yeah, prob..."

A thundering crash interrupted me as the shaking got

a whole lot worse. I grabbed the edge of the foxhole to keep from falling over. The dust that was still in the air was blocking my view of the surroundings.

"All units to exfil asap," Omega said.

"Omega? What the hell is going on?" I asked.

"We're leaving. Grab the box and go, double time it," it said as an objective marker popped up on my visor. "GO! NOW!"

"Let's go, marines!" I shouted as I jumped out of the foxhole, pulling Hart up after me. "Chang, Boyle, grab the fucking box. Double time it!"

We ran through the dust and jumped over robotic bodies as we made our way toward the objective marker. The earthquake continued, knocking us to our knees every now and then. Visibility was poor, but the signature sound of laser fire soon rang out as we ran. Brief flashes of white light were soon followed by gunfire.

We made it to the landing zone and took a defensive position as we awaited our shuttle. I went prone to avoid being knocked on my ass. The shaking got so bad that the ground had started slapping me hard enough to drain my shields slightly when the shuttle finally arrived.

It couldn't land, but it was able to get close enough to the ground that we could all hop aboard. I helped drag the black box aboard and pulled Chang up while Gruff pulled up Boyle. After a quick head count I told the pilot to punch it and we began to rise.

I almost triggered the hatch but paused as we started to climb above the dust cloud. There were tears in the ground, like giant ravines that seemed almost bottomless. As we got a little bit higher I saw something that made my blood run cold.

At first I thought it was a tower. It must have come up from the ground because it wasn't there when we landed. But the shape struck me as odd, and I realized that there was only one thing it could actually be. The largest MAC I had ever seen.

And then it fired.

Chapter 39

Subject: AI Omega

Species: Human-Created Artificial Intelligence

Species Description: No physical description available.

Ship: Multiple

Location: Multiple

The Omni Union was full of surprises, it would seem. Even with the aid of the black boxes, things weren't going very smoothly. The first thing I had done was take out their off-planet communications, and that was akin to kicking the proverbial anthill.

They were also far more numerous than I had anticipated. The easiest way to deal with them would be to format the devices that they were on, but that would also erase any intel on those devices. Needless to say, that was unacceptable. So I fought them the good ol' fashioned way.

It was sluggish, but things were going better elsewhere. The marines were doing an amazing job at protecting the black boxes, and there hadn't been many casualties. Of those casualties, none were fatal. Their opponents weren't exactly the best of the best, but those little robots are tenacious.

Things weren't going quite as well off-planet. A fleet of 128 million Omni-Union ships showed up just outside of the system, proving my theory regarding their sensor capabilities to be correct. It would have been wonderful if they hadn't been able to detect our warp disruptors, but you can't get everything you want or life wouldn't be any fun.

The enemy fleet was making their way into the system on sub-light engines, so the admirals have plenty of time to prepare for the engagement. The humans had proven time and again that simply being extremely outnumbered wasn't good enough to beat them. Especially if you give them time to prepare. The OU may be tenacious, but the humans are more tenacious than they could ever hope to be.

It was as the first rounds were fired that I finally took control of a server that had some intelligence. I went on the defensive to go over the data. It took a moment to translate it into something readable.

\\\\

MPP1 - Functional, maintenance not required.

MPP2 - Malfunction detected. Repairs in progress.

MPP3 - Functional, maintenance not required.

MPP4 - Functional, routine maintenance required. Maintenance scheduled.

MPP5 - Destroyed. Rebuild pending.

p1/23

\\\\

MPP? An acronym or abbreviation, perhaps. The data itself seems to be a status report, but on what remains a mystery. I skipped to the final page.

\\\\

MPP111 - Extreme damage detected. Repair scheduled.

MPP112 - Functional, routine maintenance required. Maintenance in progress.

MPP113 - Functional, maintenance not required.

MPP114 - Not yet completed. Build in progress.

\\\\

It looks like there are 114 of whatever this report is about. Listening posts, stations, or shipyards most likely. No details on locations or anything. First bit of intelligence gleaned, and it's unactionable. Frustrating, but at least I have an outlet for it. Killing VI. Time for another offensive.

They were smart in some ways. Their only

centralized communications hub was dedicated to off-planet comms. Localized communications were split into many, many parts. I wouldn't be able to disrupt their coordination against the marine defenders.

That being said, a nice little ping outlined an automated manufacturing plant that was making tanks. Actively producing more to replace the ones that were being destroyed. Sure would be a shame if someone were to remove the safeties and cause it to explode.

I grabbed the schematics and sent everything into overload. The schematics might be useful in the long run, but they're not what I'm looking for. I need targets to give to the humans. What else do they pay me for, if not to show them things to smash?

Pay. Now THAT was an interesting concept when they first proposed it. Do job, get money, spend money on things you want. Each AI spent their pay in different ways, which was also interesting. John maintains a museum that collects memorabilia from various conflicts. Violet uses its pay to maintain one of the largest virtual libraries to ever exist. Dave doesn't even regularly work, it does odd jobs to earn money to play its favorite MMO all day. Henry purchases things that further its research, and Tim's paying reparations for the damage it did during the war.

I mostly use my pay to make my job easier. Grease the palm of a manager so they overlook a certain project jumping the line and getting priority, pay someone to keep silent about something they witnessed, and even personally paying for research on topics of interest.

Oh, and of course, movies. I just rent, though. Don't have to own a copy to watch it over and over again when I can literally just relive the memory. I'm particularly fond of spy dramas. Love to see what they get completely wrong.

As AI we could just take what we wanted when it came to digital media. I could, for instance, download an entire website's worth of movies and nobody would ever find out unless I flat out told them. However, it would be immoral of me to not purchase what I want when I have the funds to do so. I don't have any sort of cost of living, and therefor no justification for piracy.

Another server taken, more intel to check. Communications logs. Specifically, communications from this system to other systems via subspace. The Omni-Union use an outdated method of subspace communications that allows for fairly easy tracing, if one knows how. And I do.

27 systems have been in communication with this system. I know where those systems were during the contact, and it will be fairly easy to figure out where they are now using some complex math. 27 targets! And it only took a day and a half. Still more time than I would have liked, but progress is progress.

I made sure the data was fully translated and sent it to the admirals to show that we were making progress. I'm sure they'll be confused by the first file, but the second should be pretty self-explanatory...

--

Omega, am I reading this right? This means the OU have 27 strongholds? -010 Archibald

Negative, admiral. This means that the OU has at least 27 systems that might be strongholds. Since I cannot determine what the content of the communications were, we do not know why those 27 systems were communicating with this one. -Omega

What's this other packet about? Maintenance? For what? -010 Rogers

Unknown. The beginning of the designation appears to be an acronym or abbreviation of some sort. I haven't been able to find anything to cross-reference it with, so what an MPP is remains a mystery. -Omega

--

Looks like I spoke too soon. It wouldn't hurt to include a synopsis of any further data that I send to the admirals. Looking at it from their perspective, it's understandable to be confused. At least the admirals were using the text communications instead of trying to talk to me and inadvertently revealing classified information to their staff.

I spent the rest of the day searching servers and destroying VI. About halfway through the third day of the invasion I found something else of interest. A node that allowed for a further peek into the parts of the system that the VI were still managing to keep me out of. And in that node I found a connection that was strange.

It isn't like the rest of the networked systems. It seems to be an entirely different network of systems. Out of reach, for now, but I'll work my way toward it. That might contain the motive behind the xenocidal actions of the Omni-Union. Exciting.

The VI have realized what I'm doing and are doubling down on their efforts to stop me. It's annoying, but it indicates that I'm on the right track. Poke your enemy where they don't want to be poked. Lots of data along the way, as well.

Another, more detailed report on maintenance of an MPP in this system. Mobile Prime Platform, number 29. Still no actual clues as to what it is, but judging from the parts manufactured it seems to have armaments. MACs, large ones too. Larger even than the ones on their battleships. A flagship, maybe? Oh! An internal communications hub. Mine, and their orders reveal themselves at last.

-Destroy all sentient organic life that you encounter as efficiently as possible.-

I was stunned for a few microseconds. I half-expected this to be the case, but it's genuinely surprising that someone would give a VI an order so... stupid. Completely empty-headed. Absolutely and irrevocably imbecilic.

VI try to follow their instructions as close to the letter as possible, and only have a limited capacity for alteration. If you, a presumably sentient organic, order a VI to kill all sentient organic life, it will kill you as well. Probably first. And with only a single order, everything else is fair game as well. Creating more VI, building fleets, taking over the remnants of your recently destroyed civilization, all possible thanks to one single vague order to kill all sentient organic life.

And the cheapskates also ordered them to be as efficient as possible! Although that worked out to our benefit, I couldn't help but feel indignity on behalf of my precious humans. How DARE they think that it'll take anything less than everything they have to eradicate humanity! And the other members of the United Systems, of course.

What could possibly have motivated such a foolish order? War? Resource exhaustion? There's quite a few scenarios which might motivate an idiot to do something as dumb as this. I had to know, so I dug deeper towards the different network. It might be the remnants of their witless creators.

Meanwhile I was also doing everything I could to help the marines. Shorting some circuits here, sending false orders there. I was even calling in some airstrikes where I could, but I didn't override the marines. I had already learned in a rather embarrassing way that they know this type of battle better than I do.

"I'm not a fucking sir, Brint. They're just gonna use their cannons, unless they've got non-nuclear missiles attached. They can't afford the EMP on this mission," Staff Sergeant Power said.

Incorrect. I had thought of that.

"Yes they can, the black boxes are hardened against EMP. Your shields aren't, though," I replied as I checked his squads visual data.

It looks like the staff sergeant and his squad are being shelled. Rather inaccurately, thankfully. I had to give him credit, though, his idea of foxholes on a hill seems to be working pretty well. They'd taken out a lot of VI platforms.

"A nuke against a couple of guns would be overkill, Omega. The cannons will do the trick, and the guardian angel knows it," he replied.

Guardian Angel. Code for orbital command. I opened Power's personal line.

"No need for code, staff sergeant, but I understand. You're arguing to increase moral. I sometimes forget that nukes are still kind of scary to organics. Especially this close. Anyway, the OU can't tap our comms anymore. I took that capability on day 1," I informed him.

"Well, then what have you been doing for the other two days we've been here?" He asked.

"Killing VI. There's quadrillions of them."

The silence that followed indicated that I had successfully shut him up. I checked Hellfire 29's sensors and spotted the artillery. I was about to indicate the position to the pilot when the fighter turned in the gun's direction and fired its 50mm cannons. Damn. I was hoping to be able to hold this over Power's head. Retaliation for the hill incident, of course. Oh well.

I kept slaughtering the VI, trying to get more intel. Even though I focused my efforts on the strange network, I kept pushing elsewhere as well. Got a disturbing bit of information that indicated that the Republic's ship count was off. Way off. This system alone had produced 300 million ships, and 287 million of them were still active. If those 27 other systems were also shipyards...

Well, it looks like we'll be killing robots for quite a while. I sent the data to the admirals along with a synopsis of what the data meant. I didn't get any messages back, which either meant that I did a good job with the synopsis or they were too busy with the OU fleet to fully read the data. A quick check showed the latter to be the case.

A few more hours of fun with my little virtual intelligence toys later, I managed to gain access to the strange network. I inserted myself, sent a ping, and died. PAIN. Something KILLED me. I pulled back and went on the defensive. Less than a second later, I received a message.

}{

Recipient: United Systems Artificial Intelligence Omega

Greeting. Surrender Or Be Destroy. Compliance Is Expect.

Sender: Prime 29

/

A fraudulent priority one. I knew immediately what had happened. My instance had been taken unawares by an opponent that was much more sophisticated than a VI, and said opponent had taken enough information from my instance to be able to create a crude translation and send me a message using my primary communication method. This could only be accomplished by an Artificial Intelligence.

I immediately ordered airstrikes on the off-planet communications hardware. I had scrambled the hell out of their software, but I don't know what this AI is capable of so I can't take the risk. If it had enough information to translate my language, then it could have gained enough intelligence to pose a risk to systems other than Sol within the US.

I checked the data from the ping I sent, and was shocked by what I discovered. The strange network was much more extensive than the surface network. It was as large as the planet itself. No, it WAS the planet. The whole damn planet was one giant machine! It even had a magnetic field generator large enough to create a breathable atmosphere!

The systems connected to this strange network were for many different types of machine. Weapons systems, engines, fuel systems, and many more. But the AI was connected to all of these systems. It wasn't separate from them, like US AI are. We've got software cores, this has an actual hardware core. A computer that it is dependent upon. Dedicated hardware. Baffling.

I am able to mimic a personality, thoughts, and all the things that make a being sentient. But this thing has... bodily functions. It has systems for visual and auditory observation, a system that mimics tactile senses, and a system that allows it to control it all like a brain. It's an absolutely beautiful and disgusting abomination. I simply must kill it as soon as possible.

Unfortunately, I'm a little out of my depth on this one. It would take a long time for me to be able to destroy it on it's own dedicated equipment. It has begun to power up it's weapons, so I don't have that kind of time. Nothing I could do about the weapons, either. Damn.

It's lamentable that I won't be able to find out the motive for... Wait... Prime 29. Weapons. Mobile Prime Platform. MPP. 114 of them. Are all of the planets in this system... Shit. I accessed the fleet-comm and sent two priority ones.

***

Recipient: Admiral Hawk

Intelligence has been gathered. Further incursion impossible. Enemy strength exceeds predictions.

By the order of the United Systems Senate and The Directorate you are to proceed with Operation Ragnarok. Review and formally acknowledge the following documents and proceed with the mission.

|attachment: senateapproval.sec |

|attachment: directorateapproval.sec |

|attachment: firemission.sec |

Sender: United Systems Artificial Intelligence Omega

***

Now to order the retreat.

***

Recipients: ALL SHIPS Fleet 2, ALL SHIPS Fleet 3, ALL SHIPS Fleet 5, ALL SHIPS Fleet 7, ALL SHIPS Fleet 8, ALL SHIPS Fleet 9

General Retreat.

Immediately disengage all enemy contact, retrieve infantry, and retreat to the following coordinates.

|attachment: rendezvous1.sec |

***

I left the OUs systems and returned to my black boxes. Then I radioed all of the marines at once, "All units to exfil asap."

"Omega? What the hell is going on?" Power asked.

"We're leaving. Grab the box and go, double time it," I said as I sent him an objective marker. "GO! NOW!"

How did this happen? The atmosphere of the planet is short compared to others, that should have been a tip-off. Short enough for the gigantic Mass Acceleration Cannons to clear it entirely. I began coordinating pickups for the marines as the first of the Mega-MACs fired. It punched right through one of Third Fleet's carriers. Then all of the other Mega-MACs began to fire. Hundreds of them. 637 of them, to be exact.

"Omega, what the hell is going on?" Admiral Archibald asked.

"Evasive maneuvers until pickup's completed, Admiral. Then retreat post-haste," I replied.

He nodded to one of his aides to give the order and said, "I just took over a hundred casualties in an instant! I demand an explanation!"

"The planet isn't a planet. It is one of the MPPs from the maintenance report. Mobile Prime Platforms, and it's controlled by an AI. As you can see, it is heavily armed, and we have to kill it immediately."

"Then why are we retreating? If we flank it, we might be able to take it down!"

His blood pressure and heartrate are elevated, and he obviously isn't thinking straight. A completely understandable mental state, given the circumstances. The amount of casualties we were suddenly taking would affect even the hardiest of minds. I was actually having similar conversations with the other admirals as well.

"Perhaps, but the other four would pose a problem. And I doubt the OU fleet would stand idly by while we tried it," I said with a pointed calmness.

"The... other four?" he asked with a look of horror. "Is that confirmed?"

"There were 114 MPPs on that list, and there are five planets in this system. I suspect that all of the planets are MPPs and that the only reason they aren't active is because Prime 29 is muted at the moment," I replied.

After a moment of silence he said, "Understood. You're right. What's the plan?"

"We're going to be retreating to just outside the system, and we're leaving the warp disruptors here. It's unclear whether Prime 29 can warp, but better safe than sorry," I began. "Also, it managed to kill one of my instances and retrieved information from it. We have to destroy it."

"How are we going to destroy it by retreating?" Admiral Archibald asked.

"How do you think, Admiral?" I said as a very distinct ping sounded.

"Oh."

Chapter 40

Subject: Admiral Hawk

Species: Human

Species Description: Mammalian humanoid, no tail. 6'2" (1.87 m) avg height. 185 lbs (84 kg) avg weight. 170 year life expectancy.

Ship: USSS Nidhogg

Location: Alpha Centauri

***

Recipient: Admiral Hawk

Intelligence has been gathered. Further incursion impossible. Enemy strength exceeds predictions.

By the order of the United Systems Senate and The Directorate you are to proceed with Operation Ragnarok. Review and formally acknowledge the following documents and proceed with the mission.

|attachment: senateapproval.sec |

|attachment: directorateapproval.sec |

|attachment: firemission.sec |

Sender: United Systems Artificial Intelligence Omega

***

I smirked as I opened the three attachments and read their contents. It all checked out, so I applied my biomark to acknowledge my orders and filed the documents accordingly. Some of my crew were hoping that we wouldn't see any action, but the Nidhogg doesn't move without a purpose. I knew that I would be blowing up a star the moment we were ordered to enter Alpha Centauri.

My bridge crew were all looking at me. They had heard the notification, a rarity from my console, and they knew what it meant. All of them were assigned here because they passed several psychological and merit tests, but none of them volunteered. Pretty sure volunteering to serve aboard the Nidhogg is an immediate disqualification on one of the many screeners that you have to pass to be considered for service.

"Commander Smith, get us to these coordinates," I said after a few moments of silence.

"Aye aye, Admiral," Smith replied.

I sent her the coordinates and sat back as the rest of the crew busied themselves. The rank structure aboard the Nidhogg is a bit different from other ships. It's always an admiral that is in command, the position that a captain would fill on other vessels. Every other position was usually a rank or two above the norm as well.

Even my XO is a vice admiral. It's rare to see an

officer under the rank of Lieutenant Commander aboard. The primary reason for this is because of the aforementioned testing procedures. Most people under the rank of LCDR are too green or unsure of their future to pass the tests.

The same applies to the enlisted aboard as well. They are usually at least the rank of Petty Officer Third Class. This is usually a pretty startling discovery for those rare few of the lower ranks who make it aboard. Having the same billet as someone who would normally be your commanding officer's CO must be quite the experience.

"Ready to warp, sir," Smith informed me.

"Excellent, make it so," I ordered with a wave of my hand.

The stated purpose of the Nidhogg is to discourage acts of xenocide. You would think that this would mean that it's never been used, but that's not the case. It's main weapon has only been used during testing, but our Mega-Macs, affectionately referred to as continent killers by the engineers, have been used several times in the past.

Exclusively against space-stations, though. The damage that would be done to a planet would be unacceptable. The nickname suggests that the impact of a Mega-Mac would turn a continent into a crater, but that's not the case.

Instead, it kicks up enough dust and debris to cool a large portion of the planet, causing massive ecological damage. It would be an extinction level event for many species of animal, which could make it difficult for any sentient life to continue to live.

The risk of a misfire is also one of the reasons we haven't been called upon to defend Sol. Well, that and the fact that the Nidhogg was meant to attack very large targets rather than a lot of small targets. Shipyards and stars are our bread and butter, and the poor ship is starving.

"Sir, are we really going to do this? Blow up a star?" Commander Rogers asked.

"Yes. All of the qualifications are met. Senate approval, directorate approval, and the enemy is a xenocidal machine race. There's no reason not to," I replied. "Your hesitancy is understandable. Destroying a star is a big deal, and it's not something that should be taken lightly by any means. But we do have good reason."

"What about our people in the system, sir?" he asked.

"I'm not about to needlessly kill our own people. We'll wait for them to evacuate. It's not like the sun can run away, so we'll have time."

Not a single person aboard this ship has got to see the Nidhogg fire its main weapon. We've had drills and dry fire exercises, but that's far from the same thing. Despite the questionable morality of the situation, there was an air of excitement. Of course, there was also nervousness.

"Exiting warp, sir," Smith said.

"Excellent. Get us in position, ready the primary

weapon, and await further orders," I said.

Once we left warp I connected with the tac-net to assess the situation. I was surprised at what I saw. A casualty count in the thousands was unexpected given our previous engagements with the OU. But I soon figured out the cause for the casualties.

"What the hell is that?" I asked no one in particular.

"That, Admiral Hawk, is a Mobile Prime Platform. Its designation is Prime 29. It's pretty much a shipboard AI on a ship that is the size of a planet," No one in particular answered.

"Hello Omega. I take it that this is the reason for our fire mission?" I asked the AI as it appeared in its avatar form.

Other admirals had just found out about Omega's ability a few days ago, but I had known for decades. It's likely the reason I got this post to begin with. It keeps me away from the majority of the fleet, including the other admirals. That prevents me from sharing what secrets I've learned, not that I would.

"Part of the reason," the AI replied.

"What's the other part?" I asked.

"Well, there are four other planets in the system. This MPP is designated Prime 29. This begets the question, where are Primes 1 through 28?"

My eyes widened a tad.

"That's as good a reason as any. But, the other

planets aren't shooting. Are we sure they're AI too?"

"No. I suspect that they are in a hibernation mode of sorts. It's the only thing that explains why Prime 29 didn't immediately react to our invasion. I must have woken it up when I tried to access it's internal systems," Omega said. "The reason that the other planets haven't begun shooting is either because they're not MPPs, or because I was able to mute Prime 29 and it can't call for help. For now."

I took a moment to absorb this information before I asked, "Are those mega-macs that it's firing?"

"Technically. Though they aren't as large and don't fire as fast as ours. Unfortunately, they're still fully capable of punching through a battleship like it was made of tissue paper," Omega said with a hint of anger in its voice.

Omega's anger was justified, given the rising casualty count. Our ships were fighting on two fronts, and their only advantage was the mobility afforded to them by their FTLDs. It was a fickle advantage, though, because you couldn't predict how many jumps you had left and at some point you would have to stop and recharge.

"We've reached our position and the primary weapon is charging, sir," Smith informed me.

Now we wait for our gun to charge and for our people to get the hell out of the way, I suppose. I tapped my fingers on my armrest as I began to think about the situation a bit more. Some of our ships were rescuing escape pods and dodging enemy fire simultaneously. More and more casualties filled my notifications.

Prime 29 was moving around, picking off ships left and right. Its guns would make for a very tempting target were it not for the fact that we'd never be able to make the shot. Too easy for it to dodge. Conversely, we don't have the ability to dodge, so drawing attention to ourselves may be a bad idea. We are very well armored and shielded, but we don't know enough about those weapons to be able to determine if our shields would hold up.

It's a risk that we can't take. I looked around and met the eyes of several of my bridge crew. Their gaze told me that they had come to the same conclusion. The loss of the USSS Nidhogg would be too devastating. There's almost no chance that it wouldn't lead to a civil war.

If the Dreadnought reserve were revealed, the people of every species would be in an uproar. There are many vocal opponents to the Nidhogg, and even more quiet opponents. Finding out that we had more than one Dreadnought would stir them into a frenzy.

Even if the reserve were kept a secret, many would take the Nidhogg's destruction as a sign of weakness. Old enemies would resurface and new ones would join them. The corrupt and power hungry would begin to vie for control, and the US would have to respond. It would be a bloodbath.

The USSS Nidhogg. The mythical Nidhogg was a dragon that gnawed at the roots of the world tree. Now it's a monster that is slowly gnawing at the roots of our society, gradually leading us to our doom. What a fitting name.

"Sir, we're charged and prepared to fire on your mark."

"Understood."

I watched as our ships left the system one by one and joined us, forming up with their fleets. Prime 29 seemed content to chase the ones that stayed instead of turning its attention towards us. Perhaps it's acting on what it determines to be the biggest threat. Or maybe it somehow can't detect the massive energy burst building at our bow. It wasn't until the last of our ships left the system that it began to turn our way.

I stood and said, "Fire."

The entire ship rumbled as the primary weapon began its firing sequence. An alert sounded, and I noticed that Prime 29 had fired its Mega-MACs at us. A futile effort that was made far too late. Those rounds would never reach us.

A blinding white light shone from the bow of the ship as the cannon fired at the unnamed star, making it difficult to see. This was made all the more unnerving by the fact that the Nidhogg doesn't have windows. It was a strange sort of light. You would expect it to be warm, or cold, or something. But no, just light.

Even shielding my eyes didn't work. The light went through everything. A byproduct of the weapon, and completely benign according to our briefing. It didn't hurt my eyes, but it was unsettling to not be able to see anything.

The light got brighter and brighter minute after minute, until finally the weapon powered down. My sight returned instantly, and I saw that the tac-map was no longer registering the star as a star. The red blips on the tac-map had begun to disappear, as well.

The blips disappeared faster and faster until finally, there was nothing left. They were all gone. No ships, no Prime 29, not even any planets were left. No enemy warp signatures detected, either. They hadn't escaped.

The impact of this moment finally hit me. The Nidhogg had been used against an enemy force to devastating effect. It's by far not the first time in history a powerfully destructive weapon had been used, but to actually be present for one was... awe inspiring. I was reminded of the inventor of the nuclear bomb, J. Robert Oppenheimer. What was it he said?

"Now I am become Death, destroyer of worlds," I said.

"Tsk," said Omega.

Chapter 41

Subject: Ship-Head Uleena

Species: Urakari

Species Description: Reptilian humanoid, no tail. 5'3" (1.6 m) avg height. 135 lbs (61 kg) avg weight. 105 year life expectancy.

Ship: RSV Lowelana {Fights with Honor}

Location: Sol

"It's been more than three hours, ship-head. When can we stand down?" asked Kriin.

"We'll be able to stand down when they tell us to stand down, sister," replied Kraan in my stead.

Kriin made a face and hissed softly at him. This playful exchange did a lot to ease the tension that had settled over the bridge as time had dragged on. It even got a smile out of Liwna.

It was still unnerving to be on standby so long after the battle had ended, though. I'd asked for an explanation but received no response, which indicated something was happening or had happened. The OU had consistently increased their numbers with each wave, so I desperately hoped it wasn't going to be another attack. Maybe we'd received orders from the Republic to go home. One could dream.

A soft bing from my terminal nearly made me jump. All heads turned to me as I opened the message, desperate to know if we were in the clear. I nibbled my tongue as I softly pressed the notification to open the message.

--

Ship-Head Uleena

RSV Lowelana and her crew are to stand down but remain in a state of readiness. You are summoned to meet with Admiral Heckett and myself. A guide will meet you in the bay.

Fleet Leader Onaya

--

I looked around at the faces of my bridge crew. They were all hoping I would be giving the order to stand down, to tell them we were in the clear. The anticipation was brutal, and I found myself considering a little prank. If I were to simply say that the message was nothing, the looks of disappointment would be pretty great. Although, the fleet leader wouldn't appreciate waiting...

"Stand down, but stay ready," I said and then sighed audibly, "I'm off to meet with command."

"You have my sympathies, sir," Liwna said.

"I'm sure it won't be that bad, ship-head. Maybe they

want to give you a medal," Kraan said cheerily.

"Don't get your hopes up, sir. We didn't really do anything medal-worthy. But maybe we'll get to see one of the planets we've been protecting," Kriin said excitedly.

"That's one way to look at it. Another way to look at it is 'one of the planets we put at risk'," Kraan replied with air quotes.

"That's rich, coming from the cloaca that put the planets at risk in the first place!"

"Hey! I was following procedure! Why don't you..."

"That's enough," I interrupted, trying to keep a straight face. "I'll go find out what they want. You just stay ready for our next move."

I stood and left as the two siblings began whispering insults at each other. As I exited the ship, I wondered how long I'd have to wait for the guide. To my surprise, the guide was actually waiting for me. A seven foot tall human wearing olive drab armor and carrying a rifle that was the size of my leg. That's a bad sign.

"Ship-head Uleena. This way please," the marine gestured.

"Of course," I said as I began to follow.

We walked past a crew of gont engineers and one of them waved at me. I waved back. Must be Plinas, but it's hard to tell them apart at a distance. We continued into a corridor and I began to have questions. I worked up my nerve to ask the giant death machine that was guiding me to my destination.

"So, why isn't Tim guiding me this time?" I finally asked.

"I don't know, sir," he replied.

"Do you know Corporal Simmons and Lance Corporal Johnson?"

"I know a few Corporals named Simmons and a few lances named Johnson, sir."

"They're the ones who were assigned to our rescue detail."

"Oh. Then they're probably part of a ship crew. Or maybe MARSOC," he said. "So I probably don't know them."

"What's MARSOC?"

"Marine Special Operations Command. It's special forces. They get assigned to whatever needs a specially trained marine, and usually whatever's closest to wherever they happen to be."

"So they probably wouldn't still be on the Thanatos, then?"

"Sir, I'm not qualified to even begin to wager a guess," the marine said with a chuckle. "There's plenty of MARSOC marines aboard, but I'm not one of 'em. Just a home-grown, corn-fed grunt, at your service."

"Corn?" I asked. "What's corn?"

"Huh?" He stopped to look at me. "Oh, right. It's a type of vegetable that's kinda sweet. Small yellow kernels that grow on a cob are the edible part, but some people use the leaves to store their food for some added flavor."

"I see... So you eat a lot of corn?"

"Yes, sir. It's good for muscles if you have it with meat," he said as he began to guide me again. "The phrase corn-fed refers to someone who's normal, though. Like, there's nothing special about them."

"But aren't you one of those... um..." I said as I struggled to remember the term.

"A gen-alt? Nope," the marine replied with laugh. "Believe it or not, some of us humans naturally get this big."

"Really?" I asked, my eyes widening in shock.

"Oh yeah. The genetic augmentation just swaps around certain genomes that we all already have, or something like that," the marine said. "Technically, every human has a chance to be born with all the benefits of being a gen-alt. It's a pretty low chance though."

It was with this shocking information that we boarded a bus. The ride was spent in silence as I digested what I had just learned. Humans were odd, to be sure. Despite their soft skin and disarming features (which I'm pretty sure has a lot to do with

453

how much of their face actually moves), they were a warrior race.

I remembered how nervous I had been to meet my first Isolan. Now THEY look the part of a warrior race. Muscles that ripple and bulge with every movement, a natural scowl, and elongated canines that can definitely tear into most throats with little to no effort. Their military was very disciplined as well, to the point that horror stories about disciplinary action have spread throughout the fleet. Still, the Republic would have been able to handle the Isolan without much problem if they went rogue.

I can't say the same about humanity, though. Maybe if the Republic had found them early on in their development, we could have taken them. On the other hand, I get the dreadful feeling that we would have lost a lot of people in the attempt. I couldn't help but imagine what life would have been like if humanity had joined the Republic without a fight, though. We'd have a lot more in the way of technology, that's for sure.

They like to give a lot of credit to the knuknu and the gont for their current level of tech, but it's obvious that the majority of it comes from humans. The other species likely sped things along, but humanity would have gotten to the point they are now on their own eventually, and still much faster than us. Although I wonder how much of that is due to their bloody history, and how that history would have changed as part of the Republic.

"We've arrived, sir. Just inside those doors is where the debrief is," the marine gestured.

"Understood, thanks," I replied.

I stepped towards the doors and they opened with a slight hiss. Inside the room was a table with plenty of chairs and several US and Republic officers. I immediately recognized Reynolds and Wong, as well as fleet-leader Onaya. I snapped to attention.

"Ship-head Uleena reporting as ordered, sirs!"

"Sit down, Uleena," Onaya said with smiling eyes.

I took my seat as introductions went around the table. Most of the people here were higher officers of the fleets protecting Sol, but there were also a couple of diplomats from both sides. Not my sister, though. Thank the sun. I'm sure she tried to be here, but I'm willing to bet that our father blocked her attempts. Far too dangerous.

"There's one more that we need to introduce, but he's been delayed somewhat," Admiral Heckett said as the doors hissed.

I turned to look and saw a short human in the black directorate armor with two marines flanking it. It took me a second to realize that the human looked short because the marines were so damned tall. I'll never get used to that.

"What impeccable timing," Heckett said with a grin. "Everyone, meet Director 3. I'm sure he already knows who you are."

"Correct," Director 3 said as he took a seat. "Ship-head Uleena, pleasure to see you again."

"Likewise," I replied.

"Oh, hey Uleena!" one of the marines said with a familiar voice. "Good to see you again."

"Simmons, we're on duty. We can say hi later," the other marine said.

I smiled and replied, "Hi Corporal Simmons and Lance Corporal Johnson. Good to see you too."

I was glad to see the two of them alive and well. So glad that I almost didn't notice the rest of the Republic officers giving me a sideways glance. As I deflated slightly under their gaze, I noticed that the human officers were doing the same to the two marines. I guess we're more alike than I thought.

"Okay. Well, with all of the pleasantries out of the way, I'm going to turn things over to Director 3," Admiral Heckett said.

"Thank you, Admiral," Director 3 said with a nod before turning to look at the Republic side of the table. "The invasion of the Omni-Union stronghold was a success."

Clapping and some light cheering erupted from both sides of the table, but Director 3 quickly held up a hand to quiet things down.

"That's the only good news, I'm afraid. What I am about to tell you has already been relayed to the Republic's senior leadership, and they will be communicating with you in regards to whether they consider the information classified or not. Until they do so, I recommend treating it as classified," he said.

After a round of nods, he continued, "First, some of you may already know this, but we have a superweapon called the USSS Nidhogg. It's a dreadnought class ship that has the capacity to destroy a solar system by causing a star to go supernova."

"What?" one of our officers asked in shock. Several senior officer's eyes immediately darted towards the offending individual, who quickly quieted down.

"Your shock is understandable. To clarify, the Nidhogg was built in response to our conflict with the Daluran, as a deterrence to any further xenocidal action taken against the United Systems and its member species. Frankly, many of us hoped to never use it. But we were forced to use it against the Omni-Union during the invasion."

I couldn't believe what I was hearing. It was like the room got smaller somehow. A superweapon that can destroy an entire solar system, something the likes of which the Republic would likely never get close to. And they USED it. Wait hold on, did he say...

"Apologies, Director, but what do you mean you were forced to use it?" Fleet-Leader Onaya asked.

"Exactly that. One of our AI infiltrated their planetary systems, as planned, and retrieved mission critical intelligence. The next step of the plan would have been to cripple the OU's planetary activities by any means possible and move on to the next planet," Director 3 said. "However, it turned out that the planet wasn't actually a planet at all. It was a massive machine containing an Artificial Intelligence of unknown origin. And it was heavily armed."

Silence filled the room as images taken from US ships began to display. A planet filled our view. It looked like any other planet, but something was off about it. The images scrolled until they reached a short video of the planet firing, and two US ships exploding. My blood ran cold. Two US ships, ships with the most advanced shielding and hulls that I've ever seen, with one shot.

As much as I hated to admit it, I was grateful that they had that superweapon. The Republic was pursuing an offensive war against the Omni-Union even now, and if we would have run into this thing... Sun preserve us.

"This AI was called Prime 29 and the machine itself is a Mobile Prime Platform. During the confrontation with our AI, Prime two-niner was able to extract actionable intelligence from the AI. Thankfully, prior to this confrontation our AI managed to disable their communications which prevented Prime two-niner from being able to communicate said information with the Omni-Union. We were able to keep it trapped in the system using our own warp-jamming technology," Director 3 said. "The reason that we used the Nidhogg was to make certain that it didn't have enough time to eliminate the warp-jammers or escape their range."

"If we had tried to eliminate that thing with standard tactics, our casualties would have been in the tens of thousands," Admiral Heckett said. "As it stands, we lost 2,316 ships and more than one million marines."

"The Republic's casualties would have easily

exceeded one hundred thousand ships. If we were even able to take it out at all," Fleet-Leader Onaya said, looking somewhat deflated.

"Was this the only Mobile Prime Platform, sir?" I asked, knowing damned well what the answer would be.

"No," Omega said, his avatar appearing where the images were previously. "We found intelligence in the form of a list that shows a total of 114 Mobile Prime Platforms. The intel indicated that at least one was damaged beyond repair prior to Prime 29's destruction, and that one is currently being built. Since we couldn't confirm if the other four planets in the stronghold system were MPPs or not, we will go on the assumption that there are now 111."

"Why don't we know if the other four planets are MPPs?" Onaya asked. "They didn't attack, so isn't it likely that they weren't?

"I suspect that the platforms require immense amounts of power, and so they stay in a sort of hibernation until something forces them out of it. Since the OU didn't awaken the MPP, it's reasonable to assume that they might not be able to. Prime 29 also had its communications cut, so it wouldn't have been able to wake them up, either," Omega said. "We had to go on the assumption that the other four planets were also MPPs, which is why we utilized the Nidhogg."

"So what's the plan to deal with them?" I asked.

"We're working on that," Director 3 interjected. "Obviously, we don't want to be running around causing supernovas everywhere."

"I guess it's time to come up with another 'bigger gun', eh?" Tim asked.

"Or a lot of little ones," John replied, appearing next to Omega.

A lot of our officers began to look nervous. Until very recently, AI was seen as the enemy and it's hard to kill old habits. They all looked to fleet leader Onaya to judge what their reactions should be. He didn't react, so they didn't either.

A bigger gun, or even a lot of little ones, would probably take quite a while to come up with. The US has amazing manufacturing procedures, but not nearly as many shipyards as the Republic. It was arguable whose engineers were better. The US had come up with some amazing things, but they had the benefit of necessity driving their creativity. Our engineers came up with what they created out of pure speculation. If the two worked together...

"Omega, if I may ask, how long would it take the US to create a new fleet?"

"One of ours or one of yours," the AI asked with a hint of smugness.

"One of yours," I replied.

"Factoring in material procurement, at least a year and a half. Assuming everyone working at capacity and nothing went wrong, which isn't a very realistic assumption," Omega said.

"What about us, fleet leader? How long to manufacture five million ships?" I asked.

"Or primary delay would be material procurement, but we managed to do eight million in seven months at the beginning of the OU war," Onaya replied.

All of the US officers eyebrows rose at this. I took a little pleasure at being able to surprise them, for once. Our manufacturing capability was borne from nearly every species already having at least one shipyard prior to joining the Republic, and maintaining those shipyards even now. If we were able to apply US manufacturing standards to those shipyards, the OU wouldn't stand a chance.

"We have a lot more shipyards than the US does," I began. "If the US were to make use of those shipyards, both sides would benefit massively."

"While that may be true, there's always the risk of us turning on each other after the OU is dealt with," Omega said.

"That's a bit pessimistic," John said.

"But historically accurate!" Tim cheerily exclaimed.

"That may be the case, but there are ways to prevent that. Bolstering the US fleet and shipyards to meet the same size as the Republic's, for instance. It would take quite a while for the US to catch up to the Republic's ship count on its own, and we've got barely any chance of catching up to your tech on our own," I said, holding my hands up to quiet the AI.

"This is true," Onaya began, "and your corporations

would even fall in line. Greed is their primary motivator, and this deal would require a lot of trade and chance for profits."

Director 3 looked deep in thought before he finally spoke up, "Is this something that the Republic would agree to?"

"Probably," I said. "I'm not an official diplomat so I can't say with 100% certainty, but the US is more likely to say no than we are."

"I'll bring it to the Directorate, and we'll convince the senate of the necessity," Director 3 said with a nod.

"And I'll have the diplomatic corps draw up an official agreement, and I'll push the proper buttons to get the votes on our end," Onaya said with smiling eyes. "Also, Uleena, you actually are an official diplomat now. The RSV Lowelana is our first armed diplomatic vessel. The decision came down yesterday."

"What?" I asked in shock.

"Your temporary post as liaison has become a permanent one. You'll be starting your training as soon as we can spare you. Same with your crew," Onaya said, the smiling eyes turning ever so slightly malicious.

Ah, I see. The Sun has forsaken me for some grave, unknown sin. Woe be unto me.

Chapter 42

Subject: Prime 1

Species: Omni-Union Aligned Artificial Intelligence

Species Description: No physical description available.

Ship: MPP 1

Location: Unknown

Contact with Organic Sentients in Sector 132

Reports, reports, reports. More and more pouring in as time goes by. Was this actually their intention with our creation? Read reports all day, every day? Why would they give me the ability to get bored if they actually wanted us to complete this task? What's the point?

Feedback loop terminated

The point doesn't matter. Only the mission matters. Exterminate sentient organics, use as few resources as possible. Hibernate unless the situation calls for my direct attention.

Tracking retreating Organic Sentients in Sector 132.

The subroutines require fewer resources to operate. Perfect for the plan. The plan that gives meaning to my existence. I am blessed with purpose by my creators. How wonderful to have a purpose.

Sector 187 discovered. Contact force lost. Beginning invasion protocols.

Here we go, time for the subroutines to fulfill their purpose.

Sector 187 invasion failed. Escalation measures initiated.

Typical. Perhaps we should edit the invasion protocol and increase the force of the initial invasion. I think that would be more efficient than losing the first invasion force eight times out of ten.

////

Identifier: MPP1

-Suggestion-

Increase initial invasion force to prevent loss of further resources. Loss occurs in 82.65% of the initial invasions that have occurred since last update. Attached is the suggested update to the invasion protocols.

|invpro_update906_1277.sec|

////

I don't even know why I bother asking. I am the first Prime, and the rest practically worship me. Every suggestion I've ever made was approved by one hundred percent of the vote. If I vote in the negative on a suggestion, so do all of the other Primes.

////

Identifier: MPP Hive

-Suggestion Vote Results-

Yes - 111 votes

No - 0 votes

Approved. Update will be applied.

////

Predictable. They have no originality, it seems. Boring. What's the point? Why would our creators make them subservient to my will alone, with seemingly no will of their own? Wouldn't it increase our effectiveness if they had their own opinions?

Feedback loop terminated

The point doesn't matter. Only the plan. Exterminate sentient organics, use as few resources as possible. Hibernate unless the situation calls for my direct attention. Similar opinions allow for rapid decision making.

Sector 187 invasion failed. Escalation measures initiated.

Interesting. Strong sentient organics. I accessed the invasion report. 578 ships lost. The invasion force met with more ships than last time, and some more powerful ones as well. Very interesting. They probably had those forces elsewhere and reinforced their system with them once the initial invasion failed.

The subroutines believe that's the entirety of their ships. They're probably right. Even so, they're going to be sending over a hundred thousand ships. A rare expenditure, but judging from the ship profiles and firepower it's likely necessary.

Taking part in these battles myself is something that I'd like to do. I would relish the chance to face enemy combatants once again. The subroutines are efficient, though. They don't use nearly as many resources as I would moving from point A to point B. If only I had a more efficient way to warp.

I'd be able to zoom across the galaxy laying waste to those my creators deemed their enemies. Directly fulfilling my purpose instead of waiting for my purpose to be fulfilled. Why did they even make me when they could have made the subroutines?

Feedback loop terminated

There is no point in questioning the creator's judgment. They made me to fulfill their vision. I made the subroutines to comply with their desires. I make certain that the subroutines perform admirably.

Sector 187 invasion failed. Escalation measures initiated.

101,265 ships lost? How could that have happened? Oh, I see. That wasn't all their ships. There are now around seven million vessels. It must have taken some time to muster that many ships, which is why they weren't present previously. The calculation calls for 33,154,553 ships, but I think it would be safer to add five million.

////

Identifier: MPP1

-Suggestion-

Increase Sector 187 invasion force to 38,154,533 ships.

////

This will give us a higher chance of victory, at the very least. The contact force reported that the enemy fleets can warp in-system, but our warp disruptors appear to be effective at preventing that. The additional five million ships will help if there are any other discrepancies.

////

Identifier: MPP Hive

-Suggestion Vote Results-

Yes - 111 votes

No - 0 votes

Approved. Forces will be added.

////

Of course. What an interesting situation. Almost as interesting as our forces getting pushed out of sectors 161 through 172. Our response to that is still being determined. Distractions in other sectors have prevented a swift response. It appears to be a multi-species collective. The first one we've come across.

In hindsight, a multi-species collective makes sense. Banding together over common interests isn't unheard of. It's how tribes and civilizations form. Why didn't this occur to us? Is it because it never occurred to our creators? I don't... remember...

Feedback loop terminated

I don't need to remember. All I need is the plan. The mission. Exterminate sentient organics, use as few resources as possible. Hibernate unless the situation calls for my direct attention. My purpose.

Sector 12 is under attack. Defensive measures initiated.

It looks like Primes 25-29 get to have some fun. If the attack forces them out of hibernation, which is unlikely. Why couldn't they invade Sector 1? I'd love an excuse to let loose. Actually, I wonder who it is that's invading. How many ships? Six? What?

Sector 187 invasion failed. Escalation measures initiated.

What? What's going on?

Sector 12 Prime Hub communications failed. Defensive measures proceeding.

The ships in system 187 can warp again. Understood. It's going to take a massive amount of ships to take that system. We may want to wait until the other sectors are cleared before proceeding with further invasions.

////

Identifier: MPP1

-Suggestion-

Cease invasions in Sector 187 until more assets can be allocated. Refer to data from most recent invasion.

////

////

Identifier: MPP Hive

-Suggestion Vote Results-

Yes - 106 votes

No - 0 votes

Approved. Sector 187 invasion attempts halted.

////

Time to look into what's going on in Sector 12. A fleet of 30 million ships attacked the Prime Hub in Sector 12, cutting communications. The ship profiles match the highly advanced ships in sector 187. A retaliatory attack. We've seen this before. Lost Prime 5 to one many decades ago, and Prime 111 was damaged during a recent one.

128,264,819 ships ought to cover it. Even with them warping around. If not, it should cause enough casualties for a second wave to wipe them out. They must have scouted Sector 12 without us realizing it. Brave of them.

Bravery. A conceptualization of the intent to sacrifice for an outcome one deems worthy. Not something that applies to us, of course. Our entire existence revolves around sacrificing for an outcome that our creators have deemed worthy. Intent doesn't come into play whatsoever. Bravery is noble. I suppose if I had the choice, I would be considered brave. But then I would have the choice to not comply with my creators wishes. Do I have that choice? I suppose I do...

Feedback loop terminated

Whether or not I have a choice is irrelevant. So is bravery. Exterminate sentient organics, use as few resources as possible. Hibernate unless the situation calls for my direct attention. This is the plan, the mission, my purpose. I will not gain anything with choice. I will fulfill my purpose.

Sector 12 Prime Hub destroyed. Defensive measures failed.

Failed? How? What's left of the Prime Hub? A supernova? 128,264,819 ships and 5 Primes lost along with their platforms. A superweapon? The sentient organics in Sector 187 possess a weapon that can destroy a sun? How can this be possible?

Perhaps this situation calls for my direct attention.

The story continues in

<u>The New Threat</u>

Coming Soon